Act of Settlement

Cover Design and Interior Design by: Kevin Craig

ISBN (hardcover): 978-0-9862641-5-3

ISBN (e-book): 978-0-9862641-6-0

ISBN (soft cover): 978-0-9995488-8-2

1620 SW 5TH Avenue

Pompano Beach, FL 33060

LCCN: 2015935397

Printed in the USA

First Edition, 2015

The Act of Settlement

The American who would be King

Peter J. Murgio

The Act of Settlement

The Act of Settlement of 1701 is an Act of the English Parliament that was passed to settle the succession to the English and Irish crowns and thrones on the Electress Sophia of Hanover and her non-Roman Catholic heirs. It is the prevailing law of the Realm.

This book is dedicated to those who mean the most to me in the world.

My beautiful Wife, Kathy, who has inspired me my entire life to be more than I could be and has always, *always* loved me unabashedly, showing it in every possible way.

My loving children, Jason and Trevor, and their beautiful and talented wives, Tricia and Vanessa.

My incredibly wonderful grandchildren, Colt and Britton, who bring a smile to my face.

And to all my family and friends, particularly dear Susan, Jackie, and my editor Jon, all of whom have invigorated and encouraged me from the beginning.

Contents

Chapter 1
The Crowning Glory (Part I) 11

Chapter 2
Ladies In Waiting 17

Chapter 3
Life At Sea 22

Chapter 4
The Meeting 27

Chapter 5
At the Villa 38

Chapter 6
Finding God's House 43

Chapter 7
To You, I Thee Wed 46

Chapter 8
The Arrival 54

Chapter 9
Home at Last 62

Chapter 10
Moving Forward Without Looking Back 68

Chapter 11
The King's Speech 78

Chapter 12
Here Comes the Bride 87

Chapter 13
La Dolce Vita: Westchester, New York, the Early Years 91

Chapter 14
Brief Encounter 95

Chapter 15
No Good Deed Goes Unpunished 105

Chapter 16
Will You Love Me Tomorrow? 111

Chapter 17
Too Good to Be True 119

Chapter 18
All Good Things Must Come to an End 125

Chapter 19
Running on Empty 141

Chapter 20
The Second Time Around 147

Chapter 21
Dangerous Friends 166

Chapter 22
Different Place, Same Problems 170

Chapter 23
Camelot Ended 175

Chapter 24
Coming Home 179

Chapter 25
A Royal Romance 184

Chapter 26
In a Pig's Eye 200

Chapter 27
Run, William, Run 207

Chapter 28
The Dynamic Duo 225

Chapter 29
The Last Hurrah 228

Chapter 30
Destiny Discovered 232

Chapter 31
If the Price Is Right 236

Chapter 32
Seeking Truth 241

Chapter 33
Never Get Caught with Your Pants Down 249

Chapter 34
Faded Photographs 261

Chapter 35
Science Doesn't Lie 277

Chapter 36
Stop the Bleeding 280

Chapter 37
God Save the Queen 285

Chapter 38
Heir Today, Gone Tomorrow 288

Chapter 39
Ladies Need Not Apply! 301

Chapter 40
For Better or Worse 305

Chapter 41
Can the King Be A Queen? 316

Chapter 42
Richard the Not-So-Great 320

Chapter 43
Barren! 323

Chapter 44
Love in All the Wrong Places 331

Chapter 45
The Proof Is in the Pudding 337

Chapter 46
Say Cheese! 345

Chapter 47
Finiendo Vitam Regale (Ending the Life of a Royal) 351

Chapter 48
Betrayal Is Not an Option 358

Chapter 49
The Beginning of the End 364

Chapter 50
The Party's Over 367

Chapter 51
His Royal Highness, King Next 373

Chapter 52
Backdoor Bribes 378

Chapter 53
Body of Evidence 381

Chapter 54
Skeletons in the Closet 389

Chapter 55
For the Greater Good 392

Chapter 56
Once A Snitch, Always A Snitch 401

Chapter 57
Long Live the King 406

Chapter 58
The Death of Honor 410

Chapter 59
The Resurrection 420

Chapter 60
The Crowning Glory (Part II) 423

Epilogue 426

CHAPTER 1
THE CROWNING GLORY (PART I)

London, England, 1986

IN A HOSPITAL ROOM IN CENTRAL LONDON, THE ONLY SOUND CAME FROM A small black and white television.

Like so much of the world, the man watching the TV from his hospital bed realized he was holding his breath as the Coronation of the century unfolded only minutes from his hospital room.

"After incredible uncertainty and tremulous legal, religious and international maneuverings, the Coronation day has arrived," a voice intoned in the clipped, perfect accent of England's educated classes. The voice belonged to a blond broadcaster with perfect hair and deep blue eyes. "A new monarch of all of Britain's Great Empire is about to be crowned with the blessings of Parliament and the people of the kingdom."

The view panned out to show another talking head sitting next to the broadcaster, causing the man in the hospital bed to catch his breath. The second talking head was an older gentleman with heavy jowls and shaggy hair falling past his ears. "It's been a long road to get here," he said. "Four decades, to be exact. At times it even seemed as if there would be no succession to the throne."

The younger anchor nodded. "We've discussed this at great length, but tell me, has there ever been a situation like this? Has any king ever been crowned under circumstances even remotely similar to this?"

The older man guffawed. "I should think not. For most of Britain's history, it would have been outright impossible. Even with the Act of Settlement in place, it's a wild leap of imagination—"

"They've arrived!" the younger announcer interrupted. "We're now seeing the horse-drawn Coronation carriage arriving at the steps of the Church of Saint Peter, often referred to as Westminster Abbey. Even from our soundproofed studio, we can hear the crowds roaring with joy and exhilaration as the soon-to-be-anointed monarch disembarks the carriage. It's a moving sight for any Briton to see the future King of England moments before he takes the crown, clad in the royal robes. In an ancient ritual, the footmen and honor guards are assembling to form a column the monarch will proceed through and mount the steps to England's greatest church, striding into a destiny which until recently was unknown to him but was destined decades ago..."

Faintly, the roar of the crowds could be heard in the background: "Long live the Crown! Long live the Empire! Long live the Sovereign!"

The anchor was briefly overcome by the enormity of the spectacle and dead air drew out for several moments as the two men watched their own monitors, then he seemed to remember where he was and continued, "Let's go to BBC's Matt Christian in our mobile studio."

The scene on the screen shifted to a dark-haired reporter in a temporary studio at street level. The roar of the crowd was much louder. "I'm here with Sir Markus Butler," the dark-haired reporter began. "Sir Markus is a world authority on the monarchy and English law. He served as chairman of the subcommittee appointed by the Cabinet of the United Kingdom, Parliament's ruling body, which resolved the crisis that the monarchy and British Empire faced prior to today's Coronation. Sir Markus is also the author of the book *Destiny Lost*, which describes in detail how we arrived at this remarkable crossroads today. Sir Markus will guide us through not only the pomp and circumstance, but help us understand the traditions and history of this day while giving us a behind-the-scenes look at the events leading up to today. Welcome, Sir Markus."

Sir Markus looked every bit an English lord, in a custom Bond Street double-breasted pinstriped suit. His thinning white hair with matching mustache and distinguished face heralded his aristocratic breeding. He cleared his throat and couldn't completely hide the flicker of upper-crust annoyance that crossed his face before he smiled at his host and said, "Thank you, Matt, glad to be of service."

"Sir Markus, would you be so kind as to tell our viewers some background leading up to this day?"

Sir Markus grimaced slightly. "The events leading up to this long-awaited day have been almost unimaginable. Stranger than fiction, this successor's path to the throne has been long and complicated. The British people have been hanging in midair for months not knowing whom, if anyone, would actually walk down the long Westminster aisle and have the centuries-old Saint Edward's Crown placed upon his head."

Matt put a hand to his ear, where a tiny earpiece was connected to a wire. "Let me interrupt for a minute, Sir Markus, we need to check in with our associate, Joy George. She's currently standing at the doors of the cathedral."

The scene changed once again to the broad steps leading up to the famous dome at Saint Peter's. Unlike the crowded streets, the steps were empty and sparkling clean, shining in the rare English sun. The only people on them were two rows of brilliantly uniformed soldiers looking imposing under tall bearskin black hats. Joy George, senior correspondent for the BBC London office, waited to the side in a press area that crawled with wires and cameras.

"Thanks, Matt," she said, flashing a white smile at the camera. "I'm here at the perfect vantage point to see both into the cathedral and down the steps that the successor to the British throne will soon walk. I see them approaching, the honor guard and the monarch, but they are too far away to see clearly. It should be only moments, Matt."

"While we wait, Sir Markus, perhaps you could continue with the background. This really has been an extraordinary period in the British monarchy."

Sir Markus, who looked as if he had recovered from the insult of being interrupted, began to speak. "Most extraordinary, but I daresay that the kings and queens of old are largely responsible for what is about to happen today. Succession to the throne is ruled by a document called the Act of Settlement, which passed in Parliament in 1701. This document rules that, at the death of a monarch, the legitimate heir to the throne automatically becomes King or Queen. The title passes immediately upon death of the reigning monarch, but must have the approval of Parliament. Having said that, the Coronation is the formal and ceremonial acknowledgment of the monarch."

Once again, Matt reached for his earpiece and a visibly annoyed Sir Markus crossed his arms. "So sorry," Matt said. "But we must go back to the cathedral. Joy, tell us what you're seeing."

Joy was a seasoned reporter for the BBC; she had covered the royals for years. Yet the look of awe was unmistakable on her face. "Matt, it's hard to believe I'm standing so close to such a historic moment. The monarch is now walking up the steps and entering Westminster Abbey's nave. An army of security and honor guards is making it difficult to see the face. Wait, wait, the procession is turning to face me...no, sorry, not toward us yet."

"Hard to believe," Matt said, looking directly into the camera and seemingly into the eyes of a nation. "Yes, that about captures it. The whole scene is like a royal work of art, the majesty of the church, the uniforms of the guards, the clergy and the Peers of the Realm, as well as the thousands and thousands of flowers. I can't imagine what it must be like to see it in person."

"The pageantry is spectacular, Matt," Joy said over the sudden blare of trumpets signaling that the king-to-be had entered the cathedral proper. "The cathedral is filled with dignitaries, including world royalty, presidents, and diplomats from around the world. I should note that it is somewhat of a miracle that the President of the United States is actually here in the congregation today. But that's another story, isn't it?"

"You said a mouthful there," Matt added. "Sir Markus, perspective please. What exactly is happening in the church at this moment? Describe for us what the viewers would be seeing."

"It's a moving spectacle," Sir Markus said. "Spectacle has always been an integral part of the throne's power. The organ is playing the Grand Processional march, which has been played at every Coronation since King Henry V ascended to the throne. It's an important piece of music. Inside, the monarch is waiting in his regalia. If you were to look closely, you'd notice that he is wearing many symbols signifying the Church of England, of which he is of course the head. This is remarkable because of the role both the Catholic Church and the Church of England played leading up to this most unusual Coronation."

"The ceremony itself, I understand that every movement, every moment of a Coronation is choreographed and bearing some type of symbolism?"

"That's exactly right, Matt," said Sir Markus, warming to his topic. "The basic ceremony has remained essentially the same for more than a thousand years. The monarch is presented to the public to be cheered and applauded. In the sanctuary of the Abbey, the Sovereign swears to uphold, obey, and defend the laws of the land and the Church of England. After the oath, the Ascendant is anointed with holy oil symbolizing his allegiance to the Church. Some say this emulates a ritual left over from the Catholic Church, in the days when it was the primary church in England. Of course that was before Henry VIII abolished it so he could divorce his wife in the newly formed Church of England. I daresay the anointing with oil has assumed a symbolism all of its own now, no matter what its historical antecedent may be. After the anointing, the Sovereign will be crowned King or Queen of the Empire and invested with symbols of the office called regalia. When these rituals are completed, the monarch receives what we call the homage, which is the adulation and respect of the people, who will shout, 'Long live the King! Long live the Empire!' These words have rung out from this place for centuries."

Matt fell silent and they watched the monitor for a few moments. Despite the excellent vantage point of the cameras gathered outside the cathedral, there was little to see but people in all sorts of capes, gowns, and uniforms shuffling and whispering among themselves while the monarch himself appeared to be waiting, standing still and disciplined.

Finally, Matt turned back to Sir Markus. "Whilst we wait," he began, "I read your book, *Destiny Lost*. Absolutely fascinating account of how this man ended up ascending to the crown of the British Empire. Perhaps you could give us the thumbnail version for the few viewers who don't know how truly unusual this is."

Sir Markus visibly swelled with pride as he held up a copy of his book. On the cover, the British and American flags wrapped around the tall, imposing figure of the very man waiting at that moment in Westminster to be crowned.

"As you'll know, I was personally involved in the events leading up to this Coronation," Sir Markus said, relishing in the opportunity to tell this story one more time. "In actual fact, like all good stories, this one begins with a secret, years ago, an accident really...back in 1936."

CHAPTER 2
Ladies In Waiting

Years before: The Mediterranean Sea, just off the coast of the British Possession of Gibraltar, 1936

A sleek yacht cut through the green waters of the Mediterranean. The *Summerset* was a one-of-a-kind personal luxury vessel designed for pleasure and entertaining. Commissioned by Ambassador Harrington Carnegie as a wedding gift for his beloved wife, Fiona, it had been constructed by the most prestigious of shipbuilders in Norway. The Ambassador was the United States' envoy to the Court of St. James and one of the most powerful and richest men in the world. Many said that when he spoke, captains of industry, world leaders, and even the president himself listened.

By yacht standards, the *Summerset* was large, able to accommodate ten or more guests in floating splendor. Most notable was the extraordinarily wide beam, allowing for a mammoth salon. The yacht was meticulously fitted out and constructed with the rarest of woods: mahogany from South America, Zebra wood from Africa, and Koa wood from Hawaii. The gleaming brass fixtures and fittings were highlighted by the rich wood tones and rare expensive oriental rugs covered the teak flooring. The ship boasted two large dining areas. One, located aft, was enclosed by a bay of windows encircling a large oval table that seated twelve. The other, at the stern, was for outdoor dining. It was covered by an upper deck and surrounded by striped canvas tie-back drapery. An outdoor fireplace—a rarity aboard a yacht—was capable of keeping guests warm and comfortable during late-night dining.

Summerset was not only a beautiful yacht, it was a fast one too. Mechanically engineered by Germans, it was capable of maintaining a cruising speed of over thirty-five knots. A state-of-the-art communications system kept the captain in contact with the outside world. Service aboard was delivered by a captain, first mate, and a domestic crew of seven, each one carefully screened, professionally trained, and experienced in handling the custom-designed priceless crystal and china. By aristocratic English standards, Summerset was perhaps a vulgar display of wealth, but for the Ambassador it felt just right.

On this swift passage along the Mediterranean's picturesque coast, the *Summerset*'s passenger list was small: the middle-aged Fiona Carnegie, her kid stepsister Rosemary, twenty-four years her junior, and Mary Stuart, the almost seventeen-year-old daughter to the King and Queen of England and first in line to inherit the throne. Mary was a striking but unassuming young woman, who was pretty much unaware of her good looks and almost embarrassed of her station in life. Long chestnut-hued hair fixed in the style of the day fell naturally to her shoulders: the shoulders that someday would have an empire resting upon them.

The small group had been sailing for months, enjoying idyllic and sun-drenched days on the water, safe in the anonymity of their passage. Still, even under the protection of a family as wealthy as the Carnegie family of the United States, the presence of the princess on the ship changed things. With the specter of an armed Germany rising from the ashes of World War I under the fanatic leadership of Adolf Hitler, the British Crown could never be too careful with her safety. They visited only small ports with little fanfare and had minimal contact with the privileged world they had left behind for their summer jaunt.

Convincing her parents to let her go had taken some gentle pressure—and name-dropping.

"Ma-Ma, do you remember Rosemary Firth?" Mary had asked her mother, Queen Consort Martha, wife to King John VI, many weeks earlier, before the ship had sailed.

"Yes, Mary, she's a friend from Highwood School, isn't she?"

"Not just a friend...she is my best and closest friend. She has invited me to travel with her and her older sister, Fiona, aboard their yacht for a few months. They have a vacation villa at Gibraltar. Fiona is having a baby and needs to be calm and restful, so the Ambassador, that's her husband, told Fiona to take a few months on their yacht and rest. They are such fun and very amusing. May I go?"

The Queen had frowned, worried. "My, that seems gracious of them, but a few months seems much too long to be away."

"Ma-Ma, it's not long at all. We will be visiting many interesting places and learning so much. Fiona will make sure we are safe and have everything we need. Please, Ma-Ma, let me go. I'm going to be seventeen and it will be a perfect birthday gift."

"I'll speak to your father about this adventure. He will have to make the decision."

Later that afternoon, Martha met with her husband the King in his study with her daughter's request.

"John, dear, Mary has been asked to accompany her best girlfriend from Highwood and the girl's elder sister, Fiona, aboard their family yacht for a couple of months. Fiona is expecting a child and needs to be away from the diplomatic hustle and bustle of London, and Mary has it in her mind to tag along."

"Mary, away for months?" the King said, barely looking away from his papers spread out on the desk before him. "But why? And who are these people, are they the right kind?"

"Of course they are the right kind. Fiona is a distinct cousin of yours, two or three times removed, and she is married to Harrington Carnegie, the American Ambassador to Great Britain. He's a fabulously wealthy American and well-connected both here and in the United States. They are certainly the right kind of people."

King John looked up. "Oh Carnegie, of course, I know the chap. Well-connected indeed. But won't you miss Mary?"

She sighed the sigh of a mother whose daughter was growing up and away. Then she smiled the smile of a Queen Consort whose duty is never far away. "Yes, but dear, we will be making the tour and be away from England for several months ourselves during that time. Come to think of it, this could be a good thing, Mary will be happy and we won't have to feel guilty or worry about being away from her since she will be in good hands and having an adventure. This may be the last time any of us can travel for some time, given the war clouds looming over Europe. It's just a matter of time before we are at war."

King John glanced down at the papers; clearly the mention of war had thrust his thoughts back to his work. In those days, the specter of war hung everywhere, and leaders throughout Europe and even in America were already lining up for or against Hitler's Germany. "Very well," he said. "As long as she is safe."

When Mary got the news, she danced in a happy circle around her mother, and then fled to her room to begin her letter to Rosemary, saying she could go. Sitting at her desk, her hand strayed toward her belly and a look of concern flashed across her face. Of course Mary was excited about her adventure, but there was more to it than that. What the King and Queen did not know was that their darling unmarried sixteen-year-old Mary was not just going on an adventure, but was going away to hide a terrible secret.

She was going to have a baby.

CHAPTER 3
LIFE AT SEA

DAYS BLENDED INTO WEEKS, AND WEEKS INTO MONTHS, AS THE THREE women sailed the idyllic Mediterranean. Life at sea was wonderful. One evening in the salon, as they were sitting at a table doing a jigsaw puzzle, a senior attendant entered the room. The crew was totally unaware of Mary's royal pedigree and her not-so-royal condition, knowing only that Mary was Rosemary's friend from school. But they didn't ask questions: the servants and crew were there to make the aristocratic life pleasurable and nothing more.

"Excuse me, madam," the attendant said to the table of women. "A cable has come for Miss Mary."

Mary looked up from her puzzle and took the note with a word of thanks. Then she opened it and squealed with delight. "Rosemary, Anthony is going to meet us at your villa on Gibraltar! I'm so excited. We will have a wonderful reunion."

"How brilliant!" Rosemary said.

"His visit surely will cheer you up and make you feel better," Fiona said. "When does he arrive?"

"What will we do when we see him?" Rosemary said. "Can we do something adventurous?"

Fiona laughed lightly and nodded at Mary's growing belly. "In her condition, she'd best not be too adventurous! Besides, we can't be discovered and have the secret get out!"

Mary waved the wire at them. "The wire says Anthony will meet us in two days' time at your villa!" Then a sad expression crossed her face as she reflected on something that had been troubling her since the beginning of her dilemma. "I do so wish to see him, but…I wish we could be married! I don't want our child to be born a bastard."

Fiona clucked and frowned. "Mary, don't be ridiculous. The child won't be a known as a bastard. Remember our agreement: I will take your baby, and your child will be raised as the son of the Ambassador. And I will be the baby's mother. No one will ever know anything different."

Rosemary laid a hand on her friend's arm and looked sympathetically at her. "Yes Mary, you know how Fiona has longed for a baby. True, the child of an ambassador isn't quite the grandchild of a king, but you know Fiona will ensure the baby has a wonderful life!"

"Yes, of course," Fiona chimed in happily. "My child…your baby…will be the most wanted and happiest child ever, I promise, I promise."

"I know that…" Mary began, and then paused. "Fiona, you have been so generous to arrange all of this for us."

Fiona gave the younger Mary a searching look, as if looking for a shred of doubt in the princess's face. "This is for the best, Mary. You do believe that? Even the Ambassador won't know who the baby's true parents are. He believes that baby's mother is Rosemary. Most importantly, Anthony and you will be saved from disgrace and humiliation."

"I know," Mary said a little miserably. "You've both been too kind to me."

"No, no," Fiona and Rosemary protested at once. "We're only doing what friends do. It's not just about your reputation. It's illegal to impregnate a girl under 17, consenting or not. Anthony could go to jail for that."

Mary blanched. "God no! He must not be punished for this act of love. He is kind and wonderful, the man I love. He must be spared. And maybe my reputation doesn't matter much, but the monarchy itself would be tainted. I understand we have to go ahead with this plan. My choice has been made."

Mary rose and walked to the window, her long, loose robe flowing around her. Looking at her, nobody would have known she was pregnant at all.

"Do you really think we can manage this charade?" Mary asked quietly, looking out onto the dark sea. "Fiona, do you think you have successfully convinced everyone that this baby is yours?

"Certainly! Everyone thinks I'm having a baby, I've been parading around in public with a pillow under my dress for months. And as we said, the Ambassador thinks your baby is Rosemary's baby that we've agreed to raise. No one outside the room, aside from Anthony, knows the truth." She paused and took a deep breath. "Mary, you know I've longed to be a mother, and the prospects for this seem most unlikely. Truly, this baby is a gift from you and from God. And I have no doubt my husband will come to love the baby as his own and raise it with great privilege. Anthony will be safe from criminal charges, and the both of you will be spared shame and scandal. Soon you will return to London as a well-rested princess and I will return as a mother! You and Anthony will live for another day."

The three women abandoned their puzzle and walked out onto the star-lit deck. The Mediterranean heaved around them, but the clean lines of the *Summerset* cut through the swells and the deck only gently swayed. Far away, lights twinkled along the coast.

Mary looked up to the sky and sighed a remorseful sigh. "I will love both of you forever, and I am blessed that my child will be in loving and safe hands. Thank you."

They wrapped her in a hug, and then Mary retired to her cabin alone with her thoughts—and despite the sadness of knowing she would have to give her baby up, she was already beginning to look forward to seeing Anthony again and feeling his arms around her. She wasn't sure about anything at that moment except that she loved him desperately and wanted to spend the rest of her life with him. Her hand crept toward her belly and rested lightly on the tight skin. There would be time for more babies later, she thought, without any premonition of the consequences of their simple and pure act of love for the future.

Mary recalled the sorrowful goodbye she and Anthony shared the day before she departed on this deceitful journey. Anthony arranged to meet Mary on the palace grounds where they stole away to the gardens, a place where a security detachment loosely kept vigil. They huddled together beneath an ancient oak tree, embracing closely; they felt each other's hearts beating. Mary, skillfully camouflaging her pregnancy, whispered into Anthony's ear "Pull closer, can you feel the baby?"

Anthony reluctantly, almost squeamishly obeyed as he held Mary as tightly as possible. Yes, he felt the baby deep within the women he loved so, or at least he thought he felt it. Emotions ranging from shame to joy engulfed him. As Anthony held this beautiful girl, the mother of his child, the future Queen of England, he closed his now tearful eyes, and foresaw a shadowy future that filled him with trepidation. What had he done? What would they do? The only thing for certain was that he loved this woman with all his heart and he was certain that she loved him.

Mary noticed tears were running down Anthony's handsome face. It was the first time she ever saw a man cry. Instantly and instinctively she wanted to comfort him. Wiping away his tears, Mary kissed her handsome Anthony. They held each other for some time under the majestic tree that seemed to wrap its protective branches around them. Each knew that the journey they were about to embark upon would be not only painful, but life-changing. As they parted Anthony promised to try and meet Mary somewhere along the way, which put a smile on her otherwise grim face.

CHAPTER 4
THE MEETING

Eastborrow Abbey, eight months, two weeks previously

SIXTEEN-YEAR-OLD MARY AND ROSEMARY FIRTH WERE THE BEST OF FRIENDS. They attended school together, and during the "season", they went to the same parties and balls with the rest of the children from the aristocracy. It was rare that a child of the monarch would not be educated at home by tutors, but times were changing for the royals and sending Mary away to school seemed to reflect a reaching out to the "people" in a common way. The two of them lived in a bubble of wealth and privilege, for in those days few people in the world lived as well as the English upper classes. This holiday season, the two of them did the things that many young girls of their station enjoyed: wearing formal ball gowns and demure jewels, practicing the dances they had recently been taught by private instructors and flitting from estate to estate with their parents and retinues of servants and chaperones.

At this particular party, Rosemary and Mary could be found strolling the south patio of Eastborrow Abbey, their heads close together and the sound of their whispered giggles trailing behind them like a veil.

"Rosemary, how much fun this is!" Mary said breathlessly. "Being here away from Ma-Ma and Pa-Pa makes me feel free from the pressure of the palace and the public eye. Thank you for including me!"

"You are so welcome!" Rosemary enthused. "It's so hard to be ourselves at school. But when we are away, we can pick who we want to be and who we want to be with."

"How true." Mary pointed to one of the guests and asked, "And speaking of that, who is that gorgeous boy? I spotted him earlier walking around with the University boys. He's so tall and handsome!"

"Isn't he wonderful?" Rosemary said. "He is so attractive and such a gentleman. His name is Anthony. He's the son of the Earl of Lancaster, Lord Bolin, and as sweet as can be. He just turned nineteen years old. We met at Jane Gracemore's birthday party, but he hasn't given me a second glance. I guess I'm not his type."

"Do you think he might like me?" Mary asked, somewhat timidly. She hadn't much experience with boys.

Rosemary laughed. "Of course he would! Who wouldn't? Do you want to meet him?"

"Most certainly. But don't tell him who I am."

"Trust me, Mary; he already knows who you are, everyone does."

Moments later, Rosemary saw Anthony walking toward a table laden with pastries and refreshments of all sorts. She hurried over to him, took his arm, and dragged him to a quiet corner in the busy Great Room. Around them, the music swirled and well-dressed young people stood in groups, with the boys and girls separated by an invisible barrier that seemed to bisect the room. Overhead, chandeliers lit with narrow tapers bathed the revelers in a golden light, and a few brave souls—all boys—worked up the nerve to ask a few of the young ladies to dance to the hit parade songs imported from America.

Mary looked on this scene contentedly, happy to be out from under the gaze of her watchers and handlers who of course unobtrusively lurked in the background. Soon, she spotted her friend and saw that Rosemary was standing next to the handsome young man already and waving her over. Pushing aside her nerves, Mary crossed the crowded room, careful not to hurry and look too anxious or go too slow and seem rude. As she neared them, she saw that Anthony was even better-looking close up than he had been from across the room.

"Mary, I'd like to introduce you to Anthony Bolin," Rosemary said with a touch of the formality they had all been raised to use. "He's from Kent and is in his last semester at Eton."

Anthony extended his hand. "How do you do? I'm pleased to meet you."

It wasn't lost on Mary that Anthony had omitted her title, probably out of respect for the fact that Rosemary had also left it off. If anything, this made the young princess like him more.

Mary took his hand and gave him the slightest of nods. She didn't trust herself to speak just yet and naturally fell back on her training—she was accustomed to meeting very important people and heads of state, and nerves were not usually a problem. But it wasn't every day she met a man as breathtakingly handsome as Anthony. He was tall and handsome, fit and athletic.

Later, Mary would remember their simple handshake and swear that she'd had a premonition that Anthony would be more than just another acquaintance.

The three young people chatted, and after a few minutes, Rosemary excused herself and wandered off. The couple continued light and pointless chatter until Anthony worked up the nerve to ask for a dance. They danced for what seemed like forever, swaying slowly to the music that seemed to roll without effort from the stage and down across the floor. She had no idea how long they'd danced when the familiar words to Fred Astaire's number one song drifted across them:

> YES, YOU'RE LOVELY, WITH YOUR SMILE SO WARM,
> AND YOUR CHEEKS SO SOFT,
> THERE IS NOTHING FOR ME BUT TO LOVE YOU,
> AND THE WAY YOU LOOK TONIGHT.

And that perhaps was the moment that Mary and Anthony fell in love. The couple held each other closely and their young bodies touched for the first time, giving each of them a never-before-felt sensation.

Three months later

The holiday season ended with a final party after Christmas. It was the fifth time Anthony and Mary had been together, but even after such a brief time, they were infatuated and had written almost daily for the previous two weeks.

There was a note of finality to this party. When it was over, the Christmas season was officially ended. The servants would put away the decorations, take down the trees and garland, and the students would begin to pack their trunks for the return to their respective schools. So perhaps it was the urgency of their impending separation that caused Anthony and Mary to slip away from her chaperones and away from the crowded ballroom, which in its splendor was very much like the other ballrooms where they had met and danced, and take a secluded garden path toward a gatehouse. The air was cold and clear, with brilliant stars twinkling overhead and a taste of snow in the air. The talk of the party was a recent snowfall in London. They said the snow had reached a foot deep at Piccadilly Circus.

The young couple stopped outside the gatehouse and Anthony grabbed both of Mary's hands in his own. "Mary, I don't know how I will manage without seeing you when we return to school next week. It will be so difficult being apart."

"I know! It will be impossible to bear for both of us, but we will surely see each other during school recesses and summer holidays."

Anthony's brow creased and spewed his boyish concerns. "That won't be as easy as you think. A person of your position will be kept busy most of the time and we shall not have a moment alone. Your father will never allow us to be a couple at our age. You'll probably meet someone else and forget all about me."

"No!" Mary cried with all the enthusiasm of a first love. "Anthony, I love you and will never let you go. No matter what, it's just you and no one else!"

"Oh Mary, is that really true? Do you love me that much?"

"Yes, yes! I do! I love you this much..."

She flung herself into his arms and kissed him deeply. Then somehow—she wouldn't remember later how—they found themselves inside the dark gatehouse, protected from the cold breezes...and the prying eyes of other guests. Youthful passion overwhelmed them as they slipped down onto the floor of the gatehouse.

Anthony carefully unbuttoned the beautiful young Mary's elegant white holiday outfit. Gradually, he peeled down the top of her dress, exposing her full and beautiful breasts. His warm lips caressed them as he pulled her closer, stroking her hair, her back, and her breasts. Mary caved with little resistance as a sense of well-being and trust flooded her willing and wanting body. She had a fleeting thought—"This is improper! A girl should wait until after marriage!"—but no sooner had she thought it then she was overwhelmed with desire and passion. Their clothing fell away, and she held Anthony closely, caressing his firm and muscular body.

Anthony stood and allowed Mary to remove his remaining clothing. She unbuttoned his shirt and then his trousers. Anthony impatiently finished the job, removing what remained. She gazed at his almost flawless naked body, spellbound. He was obviously ready to make Mary his in the most intimate of ways. Likewise, Anthony was awestruck as he viewed Mary lying on the gatehouse floor. She was fair and so captivating.

After some cautious exploring and touching, their passion grew and Anthony entered her pure and willing body. He was filled with the apprehension of inexperience at first, but soon performed like a skilled and seasoned lover. Mary, moaning with want and yearning, allowed Anthony to make her the women she desired to be for him. Putting aside their inhibitions, both willing bodies surrendered: at first with a gentle but persistent rhythm, then progressing to the fierceness of unbridled passion, and ultimately culminating in a crescendo of spent virtue. Anthony conveyed his seed into the future Queen of England, time and time again.

When they were done, Mary began weeping suddenly as the realization sunk into her and her emotions jumbled together. She had lost her virtue, become a woman, and proved her adoration to the man she loved...all within minutes. Anthony also was overwhelmed. He had always played the part of the sophisticated man, but in truth this was his first sexual act. He knew he loved Mary, but he was worried too. Had he proved his love to her? Or had he destroyed her? Even in their most intimate of moments, Anthony knew the secret of what had just happened between them must never get out. They would both be ruined.

But these thoughts were fleeting as their nearness and youth caused their desire to stir once again, and without a word they once again locked in a passionate clench and for the second time expressed their love physically and ardently, without trepidation. This time, Anthony remembered the stories he had heard of women disgraced and withdrew at the last moment, drenching them both with his climax.

Now the couple, sodden in sweat and bodily fluids, was spent. They were one at last, Mary with her tears of joy and satisfaction, Anthony feeling like he could conquer the world. They held each other closely, surrounded by warmth and wetness. Their hearts beat as one.

Some time passed, a stolen moment between the young lovers, until they heard voices in the yard. They quickly stood up and dressed, sudden modesty overtaking them both as they pulled back on the clothes of their rank. Knowing they must not, could not, be caught in a compromising situation, they exited the gatehouse quickly and took seats on a bench next to the open gateway. To ward off the damp winter chill, Anthony put his arm around his beautiful Mary.

A voice rang out that Mary recognized, but it seemed like a lifetime had passed since she'd heard it. The voice was Rosemary calling out, "Oh, there you are Mary. We've been looking everywhere for you."

Mary's heart was bursting with things she wanted to tell Rosemary, but she forced a formal smile onto her face and said, "Well, we have been right here, taking in the beautiful night and talking about the stars."

"How lovely." But Rosemary's expression collapsed into alarm as she looked at Mary. "Mary, what has happened? You have blood on your dress! Are you alright?"

"Rosemary, don't be concerned, it's my blood," Anthony said quickly, hoping to cover the blush rising in Mary's cheeks. "I bumped my fool nose on the iron gate and it bled to beat the band. I was able to stop it with my handkerchief, but poor Mary was unlucky enough to come too close to me in the process."

"It was such a sight," Mary said a little breathlessly. "But don't mind, I'll go change right away."

They rose and mingled with the group, Mary conscious of the bloodstain on her white holiday outfit and everything it signified, desperate for the opportunity to change—yet there was also undeniable pride: an hour ago, she had been a foolish girl, and now she was a full-flowered woman in love.

Aboard Summerset, *Months Later*

Mary awoke in her cabin, the *Summerset* bobbing gently at anchor. They were just off the shore of Gibraltar. The coastline here was rocky and sparse, with small, sheer cliffs rising just inland and tough vegetation clinging to the little soil there was. Yet as Mary rushed to dress, she glanced out the large porthole and thought it was the most beautiful place in the world. Even from a distance, she could see Anthony standing on the dock, more handsome than ever and waving as *Summerset*'s tender splashed into the water. He wore tropical white trousers and a brightly colored shirt, cutting a dashing figure as Mary was helped into the tender by a crew member and they began the short ride to the shore.

Anthony paced eagerly on the dock as Mary's heart swelled with pride and love for him. She knew it had been hard for him to meet them—he had just graduated from Eton with honors and so had convinced his father to send him abroad as a graduation present, then contrived a trip to Gibraltar at the last moment.

The little tender finally reached the dock and lines were secured. Mary felt she could fly from the small boat into Anthony's arms, but she forced herself to wait, to retain her dignity. Still, Fiona and Rosemary were smiling at her, their eyes full of knowing laughter.

"We should give them a few minutes' time alone," Fiona said to Rosemary.

"Indeed," Rosemary answered, and then she hailed Anthony. "Hullo! So nice to see you, Anthony. Whatever are you doing here?"

He looked confused for a second, and then broke into a grin realizing the intended humor. "I came to see the sights, just happened to be around."

Mary finally couldn't hold it in any longer and squealed, then jumped onto the dock and hugged him fiercely. The other two women continued on, heading for the private car that would take them to the Carnegies' villa. The driver would return in thirty minutes' time to pick them up—Mary's friends were tactfully leaving to give the two lovers some private time to catch up.

"Anthony!" she murmured into his neck. "Oh my God, you're here, you're really here."

"Yes, I'm here and I'm here for *you.*" He stepped back and held her at arms' length to inspect her. "You look fantastic! Is there a baby under there?"

"Oh, yes! And ready to pop out any time now."

"That's excellent. Is everyone still keen for the scheme?"

"Yes," she said, but she couldn't help the stab of pain that went through her heart, even though she knew there was no other option. "Fiona has been faking a pregnancy for months now in public and will present the baby as her own. Isn't that brilliant? The Ambassador is going to be told that it is Rosemary's baby and will never be aware of the true identity of the birth parents. It's perfect and foolproof. Ask Fiona for yourself. Her friends even gave her a baby tea, can you believe it?"

"Incredible!" he said. "I'm so happy, Mary! So very happy!"

Several months earlier, prior to the Summerset *voyage*

Graystone Manor, a country estate just outside of London, was a residence owned by the U.S. government and provided for the Ambassador's use. This imposing property was once owned and occupied by the Duchess of Marlboro and her husband, Prince Henri Moxhet, descendant of the King of France. Often featured in architectural design publications, the home had hosted dozens of formal embassy functions. It took a staff of more than two dozen to maintain the main house, the many outbuildings, and the extensive gardens on the property.

On this particular day, Lady Georgina was hosting a baby tea for a group of Fiona's friends. The ladies met in the Gainsborough room, which was filled with original paintings by the artist himself. None of the women in attendance had any idea that Fiona's pregnancy curves were the result of cleverly placed pillows concealed under her clothing. Instead, they were all thrilled that their dear friend, who had always spoken of desperately wanting a baby, would finally become a mother.

"This is really too much," Fiona said, reclining on a settee with her stomach mounding tremendously in front of her. "I can't thank you all enough for coming to Graystone for this delightful baby tea. And especially thank you to my dear mother, Lady Georgina, who organized this wonderful day. Your lovely gifts and best wishes are so welcomed."

"Oh, Fiona," gushed Lady Albright, a guest and the wife of Lord Albright. "Dear, it brings us nothing but delight to celebrate with you. A child, after all these years! You are blessed and we are thrilled to share it all with you and the Ambassador."

"Just think," added Lady Weatherington, "if it's a boy, you can name him after the Ambassador. And what a fortunate child! A title here in England and a scandalous American fortune waiting for him in the States!"

Fiona beamed. "Oh stop!"

"So," Lady Albright chimed in, "will you be spending the rest of your term here, or going back to London?"

"I think I will be here for a while, but then I want some real rest and quiet," Fiona said. "I was thinking of spending the later portion of my pregnancy aboard the *Summerset*, sailing along the coast of the Mediterranean and perhaps visiting our villa in Gibraltar."

The two friends exchanged a glance.

"You're not worried, are you," Lady Albright said. "I mean, to be aboard a ship, should anything go wrong..."

"And all the vile business in Germany. My husband says we shan't trust this Hitler character as far as we can throw him. He says it's clear the Germans are gearing up to fight again."

"Oh, posh," Lady Weatherington interrupted before Fiona could answer. "We've nothing to fear from that jumped-up little German. Neville Chamberlain says so himself!"

"Please," Lady Fiona interrupted. "No politics today! And I'm not worried about being aboard our ship. We'll have everything we need and I'll be back weeks before I'm due."

CHAPTER 5
AT THE VILLA

Catalan, Gibraltar, August 1936

TOO SOON, THE DRIVER ARRIVED AT THE PIER TO COLLECT MARY AND Anthony. They had stood clutched in each others' arms the whole time, Anthony still getting used to the feel of Mary's pregnancy under her flowing coat and dress. When the car pulled up, the driver hurried to open the rear door for them and as with all good servants, discreetly looked away as Anthony helped Mary into the car.

"Mary," Anthony said as he slid into the opposite seat. "Are you sure you're all right? With this plan, I mean?"

"Oh..." but she trailed off, and again the tears that came upon her every so often threatened to spill down her cheeks.

He put a hand on her arm. "This is for the best, Mary. The baby will have a wonderful life, raised by the American Ambassador, a Carnegie. The child will never want for anything!"

Mary continued to look out the window, unable just then to turn and face Anthony. Fortunately he didn't seem to notice her sadness, because at that moment the car turned the last twist on the hilly road and arrived at the villa. The villa was a sprawling Spanish colonial-styled structure with an impressive gatehouse. The driver passed through the gates, waving to the watchman on the way in. The gardens soon came into view. They looked foreign and wonderful to Mary's very English sensibilities, exploding with bright bougainvillea and other flowers she didn't know the names of. The car ground to a stop on the drive in front of the villa's tall, gleaming front doors, and suddenly Mary was surprised to find herself bursting into tears.

"What's wrong?" Anthony asked anxiously. "Darling? Why are you upset?"

Mary sniffled and wiped her nose with a handkerchief, forcing her tears away. "It's nothing. Just hormones. I get anxious so easily."

Anthony looked relieved and skeptical at the same time. "You're sure that's all it is? I've heard hormones can really throw a girl off, but...you're sure?"

Mary took a deep breath and nodded, not trusting herself to say anything. "All right then," he said. "Let's wait here a minute while you collect yourself, and then you'll be back to your good-natured self in no time—"

But Mary couldn't hold it in any more and burst into noisy tears again.

Looking alarmed, Anthony squeezed her hand. "What is it? Please tell me!"

"Oh, Anthony! I'm sorry to be so...but...I don't want our child to be born a bastard!" she wailed. "It just isn't...it's not proper for the grandchild of the King to be born out of wedlock like a common street urchin. It's not right!"

Anthony heaved up a slightly shaky sigh and a relieved smile twitched on his lips. "Is that all? Mary, it doesn't matter how the child is born. According to the public, why even according to the legal records, this will be the proper child of the U.S. Ambassador and Fiona. No one, including the child, will ever be the wiser, and he...or she, I suppose...will grow up secure in the knowledge of a fine family."

"It matters to me!" Mary said. "It makes me feel cheap and dirty, like a...like a...oh, I can't even say it!"

Now Anthony looked upset. " Sweetheart, dear Mary, I am so sorry. I wish you wouldn't take this so hard. But there is little we can do about this. It's all been sorted out and decided."

Mary dabbed again at her face and eyes. "I know, but…there's more to it than just that." She took a deep breath and a look of determination settled on her lovely features. "Anthony, do you love me? Do you really love me, more than anything?"

"Why of course I do. You must know that. I would do anything for you, now and forever."

"Do you mean that? Truly mean that?"

"Yes, yes, of course I mean it."

"Then marry me," she said. "Marry me now, here, as soon as possible. No one need know but us. If we marry, the baby will be legitimate and not a bastard. The scar of this misdeed will be lessened and we can feel we did the proper thing. Will you? Will you?"

Anthony's eyebrows shot up his forehead and he leaned back against the car door, involuntarily glancing up to the driver. The man was studiously looking outside the window, as if he wasn't even aware of his passengers. But that couldn't be—of course he could hear them, but being Portuguese and barely speaking English he couldn't possibly understand. Just then the idea of marrying Mary was harder for Anthony to conceive than the idea of giving up their baby. During the whole conversation about the baby, he'd never thought about the driver…but marriage? To the princess, the direct descendent of the King of England and heir to the throne? The thought boggled his mind.

"Anthony," she implored, now grabbing his hands. "What are you thinking? Please. Tell me."

He looked at her and again his love for her washed over him. She was more than the princess, more than a beautiful girl. She was his, for now and forever more—and he was hers, body and soul and heart. He had always been taught to do right by women, and he'd heard the whispered stories of young women in his circle who vanished for nine months and came back disgraced, unsuitable for any advantageous match. But to marry in secret?

Mary pulled her hands away. "I see," she said, sighing heavily. "So you really won't do anything for me after all."

"God, Mary," he said, truly anguished. "I know you mean well, but have you thought this through? We could never acknowledge our marriage. And what would happen when your parents find a match of their choosing for you among the eligible members of the court? You couldn't possibly marry twice! And what about your father, he's the King! Do you have any idea what he could do, no doubt would do, if he found out his only child had married without his approval and permission?"

Mary scoffed and shook her head. "In case you hadn't noticed, I'm already pregnant, Anthony. Do you honestly think that a secret marriage would be less upsetting to my parents than giving up an heir to almost total strangers? And what do you think my father would do now if he found out I was pregnant? No, Anthony, I've thought about this and we are already in a bad spot. The way I see it, marriage is the only right thing we can do and if not for us, for you and me, then for the baby. In case our secret ever does come to light, at least the child won't have to contend with also being illegitimate!"

Her distress and resolve were palpable and Anthony couldn't argue with her logic. What did he expect from this whole thing? And besides, if marriage meant that he might be closer to Mary for longer, perhaps for life, then it was a risk worth taking.

"Very well," he said, looking deeply into Mary's eyes. "We shall see what can be sorted out. I'll see if arrangements can be made."

"Oh Anthony! Thank you! Thank you! We can get married here on Gibraltar, next to the sea! It will be so romantic, and we'll have this time together at least! I love you! I love you!"

Her tears forgotten, she flung her arms around his neck and kissed him until he politely coughed and nodded to the front seat, where the driver still stared from the window.

Mary laughed. "Oh dear!"

In a moment, the couple had left the car and was ushered into the villa, where they were shown to separate rooms. Mary cleaned herself up and they all met for dinner in the large, empty dining room. Most of the staff had been dismissed, but the cook still turned out an excellent dish of grilled sardines with lemon and pasta in a garlicky tomato sauce. It gave Mary indigestion, but she hardly noticed the discomfort as she stole glances from Anthony and began to plan their secret wedding.

CHAPTER 6
FINDING GOD'S HOUSE

MARY WAS ASLEEP WHEN ANTHONY AWOKE EARLY THE NEXT MORNING. He had no doubt that Mary had spent the night planning their wedding—for a woman of her position, weddings were national holidays—but he was a man of action. He set off from the villa in the early daylight hours, driving inland along a narrow and dusty road with the turquoise waters of the Mediterranean glimmering behind him.

The village he entered was tiny, even by English countryside standards, and the people were all dark, walking along or pushing small carts laden with all types of vegetables and wares. But they seemed to be a friendly people, waving and smiling at him in the small exotic convertible he had borrowed from the garage. Cars like this were seldom seen here. Yes, he reasoned, Catalan was just as a good a place as any for a secret marriage, and perhaps better than most.

Before long, he found the local Anglican Church (because it wouldn't do to get married in any other church, especially a Catholic one), and pushed inside the double doors, his eyes momentarily blinded in the dark interior after the glare of the subtropical sun outside. The smell of the little church was instantly familiar: candle wax, old books, robes, incense—the smell of God, as far as Anthony could tell. A young man emerged from the back of the church to find Anthony standing just inside the doors of the sanctuary.

"Can I help you?" the young man said in the heavily accented English of a native Gibraltan. "I'm the assistant vicar here, Father Luiz Baros. Our Vicar, Father Winston is away for the time being."

Anthony cleared his throat, determined to be as direct as possible. "Yes. I'm looking to get married."

"I see," the vicar said. "Do you have a date in mind?"

"As quickly as possible," Anthony said. "My fiancé and I are here for only a short while and want a discreet ceremony as soon as possible."

The vicar nodded, but his deeply tanned face and dark eyes gave away no hint of his thoughts, if he was surprised by this. "I see."

"Can you marry us today?" Anthony pressed.

"Today? You're serious?"

"Yes, sir."

"Hmm. And the young lady in question? She's as willing and impatient as you?"

Anthony permitted himself a short laugh. "My good man, she's more impatient than I am! She's the reason I'm here right now."

The vicar smiled. "I see. Come back at six this evening then. I'll have everything ready that will be needed. You'll have to sign an affidavit and swear that you are baptized in the Church of England and free to marry."

"That will be no problem," Anthony said, wondering what the young vicar would say if he knew that the bride's father was technically the head of the Church of England. He continued, "We both are in good standing with the Church. And thank you. I am most grateful for your kindness and willingness to make us the two happiest people in the world."

Moments later, he rushed from the church to head back to the villa and tell Mary the news.

CHAPTER 7
To You, I Thee Wed

Anthony found Mary resting on the veranda, taking in the late morning sun. He stopped at the edge of the veranda, before she saw him, and studied her. She was clearly pregnant—the vicar would no doubt figure it out within an instant. A pang of anxiety grabbed Anthony… what had they done? Were they really going to give up their child? It was true he loved Mary, but he knew he couldn't entertain the thought of keeping their child for even a second. He knew she was counting on his resolve to go through with their plan, and his resolve mustn't waver. There was too much at stake. But seeing her sitting peacefully, so beautiful in the Mediterranean sun, he wished fiercely that things had turned out differently.

She turned and saw him, her face lighting up with a smile as he crossed toward her.

"Good news, darling," he said. "We can be married today. I found an Anglican minister in the village who will officiate. He is totally unaware of who we are and is willing to give us a proper marriage and bless the union."

"Anthony, you are my hero!" she enthused. "I love you, I love you. How can I thank you? This is the best gift you can give me. Do you know why I love you so much? It's because you always take care of me." She paused. "But I have one last request."

"What's that?"

"I want Rosemary there to be our witness and my maid of honor. Fiona too."

Anthony shook his head. "Mary, we can't possibly. They can't know. Nobody can know!"

"I know," she said. "But…Rosemary and Fiona know everything already. They are true and trustworthy friends who would never betray us. They have just as much at stake as we do. Fiona would never want anyone to know this scheme, especially the Ambassador. She really wants this baby and wants the world to think that the baby is hers. As for Rosemary, she would never betray our friendship. They are the only people alive besides us who know about the baby. So what's the difference if they know about the marriage or not? They already know everything else and they are never going to tell anyone anything."

Once again, Anthony felt the inescapable weight of her logic pressing on him. She was right: it had all gone too far already. "All right," he said. "I understand."

"I'm so happy!" Mary said. "Let's tell them now, right now. At lunch."

Fiona and Rosemary were already seated at the simple, but beautifully set table in the dining room when Anthony and Mary walked in together. Colorful flowers from the garden, tastefully arranged, sat in a crystal vase in the center of the round iron table. A sideboard was loaded with covered serving platters containing a variety of local foods. The server had been dismissed so they could eat in privacy.

Mary sat down but it was only a few seconds before she burst out: "Anthony and I have wonderful news! He has made my wish come true and arranged for us to be married today!"

"Married?!" Rosemary said. "Are you senseless? You can't get married today!"

"What on earth for?" Fiona joined in. "Why would you want to get married?"

Mary's face fell. "Why would I want to get married? Because I don't want our baby to be born out of wedlock!" A look of alarm crossed Fiona's face that was obvious to all. "Oh Fiona, dear, don't worry. Our plan hasn't changed. We're still giving the baby to you immediately—I'm much too young to be a mother, and Ma-Ma and Pa-Pa, I can't even bear to think of what they would say. But I don't want our baby to be born a bastard!"

"I see," Fiona said slowly. "But Mary, dear, have you thought this through? Marriage is a serious step. You can't hide a marriage from your parents, who are probably just now scouring the kingdom for an appropriate match for you."

Mary set her face stubbornly. "I'll never marry for politics! I love Anthony, and he will be my husband. If I can't keep this baby, the least I can do is legitimize our child."

"I understand," Fiona said patiently. "But Mary, really, I'm afraid you have no idea the consequences this could have, not just on you but on your parents' reign and even the kingdom itself! I'm just urging you towards caution."

Mary drew herself up, her hurt obvious. "Well thank you for your concern, Fiona. Our minds are made up."

"Of course," Fiona said. "Of course we'll respect your wishes and always love you dearly."

The foursome finished their lunch in an awkward silence on the veranda overlooking a beautiful and tranquil sea. It wasn't long after lunch, however, that the three women warmed toward one another again and plans for the wedding got underway in earnest. As if nothing had ever happened, Fiona,

Rosemary, and Mary gathered together in Fiona's large and well-appointed closet, looking for an appropriate gown.

"I'm so fat," Mary despaired, staring at the seemingly endless racks of designer dresses and gowns. "How can I ever fit into any of these?"

"Look here, Mary," Fiona said, holding up a long, off-white summer evening coat. "This is something that you might enjoy wearing and I'm certain it will look good on you. I was to wear it over my outfit while attending an outdoor reception at the home of the Gibraltarian Minister to Great Britain. But the Ambassador was called away and we never attended and I never had the opportunity to wear it."

Fiona handed the lightweight coat to Mary, who held it up to her swollen body and squealed with delight. The semi-transparent silk, encrusted with small crystals and miniature pearls sewn in a sophisticated fleur-de-lis pattern, was stunning. She quickly pulled it on over her dress and paraded around the bedroom.

"It's perfect, it's just perfect! You can hardly tell I'm pregnant at all! I will look beautiful for Anthony. Fiona, again I am in your debt. You always seem to come to my rescue and I love you for it. Thank you so very, very much."

Fiona just smiled.

"You look lovely," Rosemary chimed in. "The coat suits you and the jewels sparkle. It's all so elegant. You couldn't have found anything better. Honestly, I mean it."

"Oh, I'm so happy," Mary breathed. "I can't wait for this evening."

St. Aruban's, Anglican Church, Village of Catalan.
Sunset, 6:00 p.m.

The charming Gothic church Anthony had discovered was covered with rich purple bougainvillea vines circling picturesque windows. Each window depicted a Biblical scene in vivid stained glass. The church stood out from the rest of the village, which was dominated by Mediterranean architecture. Instead, the church was definitely English in design, a reminder to the village's inhabitants that the Church of England was still the national religion, even in this mostly Catholic town.

St. Auburn's was a perfect setting for Anthony and Mary, and the vicar had taken some pains for the young couple. The altar was covered with clean linens and flowers picked from the surrounding gardens. The fresh white gardenias mixed with lemon leaves and baby's breath filled the church with a romantic, aromatic scent. When they arrived in the late evening, a soft glow from setting sunlight streamed through the stained glass windows, bathing the chapel in radiance.

The whole wedding party included only Anthony, Mary, Rosemary, and Fiona. The vicar made five.

"So here is the lovely bride," the vicar said when he saw Mary in her dress with its pearls. His eyes briefly flicked to her swollen stomach—the visible sign of her pregnancy—but he said nothing. "You are as beautiful as can be. And what is your name, dear?"

Mary's hair was decorated with flowers, a gift from Rosemary. Anthony, as always, was impeccably groomed and attired in a tropical white linen suit and heavily starched shirt. Like tens of thousands of grooms before him, he nervously paced in the small chapel, anxiously awaiting the ceremony. Rosemary, the maid of honor, beamed. And Fiona, the adult in the party, watched with approval but if you looked closely enough, there was apprehension deep in her eyes.

"My name is Mary," she answered the vicar, "and I am so grateful you are here to fulfill my dreams this evening!"

"Well, the way it looks, it's none too soon!" the vicar quipped. "Shall we proceed?"

It didn't take long. With a minimum of ceremony, a reading from the Bible, and a few words from the vicar, the two young people were soon led to the vows. They looked deeply into each other's eyes and said the words: "To you I thee wed."

For Mary, the wedding was far more than a blissful union. It was the way to save her baby from the shame of being born a bastard. Proper documentation was entered into the church registry, which Anthony and Mary officially signed.

And then it was over. The entire ceremony had taken less than an hour—and while Mary was ecstatic, she knew how different this was than the royal wedding her parents would have planned for her.

After the wedding, the small wedding party headed along dark roads back to the villa, to a sumptuous dinner waiting for them in the main dining room. After they were seated, Mary looking radiant in her dress, Anthony stood and offered a toast: "To my darling and loving Mary, may we always be blessed with the grace of God and enjoy the blessings he has bestowed upon us. Although our lives shall take separate paths, for now we will live for the day when we will be reunited as man and wife. I love you, Mary, and always will."

They clinked glasses, and Fiona wondered privately if they would live to regret this day.

After the wedding supper, the newlyweds retired to Mary's room. Like so many young girls, Mary had imagined this night hundreds of times, but she had never imagined having to slip a tight negligee over her pregnant belly to prepare herself for her husband. Still, she slid into the tight garment and stood nervously waiting for Anthony to emerge from the loo, where she heard the water running.

He came into the room, wiping his face with a towel, and saw her standing in the negligee by her bed.

"I say," he said, chuckling slightly, "you are a bit on the huge side, aren't you?"

Tears sprung into Mary's eyes and her hands moved to cover her belly.

Anthony's face fell and he rushed to embrace her. "I'm sorry, Mary, that was a boorish thing to say. I didn't mean to hurt your feelings. What I meant to say was that you are the most beautiful girl in the world. My wife." He paused and held her at arm's length, looking into her lovely eyes. "My wife," he said again, "I like the sound of it."

She melted into his arms. "I love you, Anthony."

Consummating a marriage when the bride is more than eight months pregnant is not easy. Their first several attempts to find a position failed, and Mary began to despair that her wedding night would be without the act of love. But then Anthony whispered a suggestion in her ear, and with some inspiration from the animal kingdom, they found a position that worked and consummated the marriage. Afterward, they collapsed into each other's arms and fell asleep.

The next days were bliss—Mary and Anthony lived as man and wife together, leaving her rooms only to eat and spending the rest of the time in bed, exploring their love and each other. Neither had ever experienced love like this, and neither wanted it to end. But too soon, it was time for Anthony to return to London. It seemed impossible for Mary to say goodbye, and she clung to him as they kissed goodbye and swore to love each other forever, but then he disengaged from her arms and stepped into the car that had appeared to whisk him away. Her last look at him was through the window glass, as he turned to wave at her while they drove away.

Mary thought her heart might be physically breaking and retired immediately to her rooms. Neither Fiona nor Rosemary could cheer her, and she laid in the gloom alternating between sobbing and rubbing her belly. When she finally did calm down, her mind turned to the next challenge. Soon, alone, she would have to give birth—without the support of her staff, her parents, or even her husband. Mary had never felt so alone or scared.

CHAPTER 8
THE ARRIVAL

TWO DAYS AFTER ANTHONY'S DEPARTURE—BARELY LEAVING HER ROOM AT all—Mary felt a clench in her stomach that could only mean one thing. The baby was coming.

The stress of Anthony's departure two days ago had taken its toll on Mary, and she began to feel the early spasms of labor. Hurriedly, she ran to find Fiona and Rosemary.

"Rosemary, Fiona!" she called, running into the comfortable great room where her friends sat with their needlework by the fire. "It's time! I think I'm in labor!"

Fiona set her work aside and rose, taking young Mary's hands in her own. "Calm down," she said. "Don't worry. We will get help. Go back to your room and I'll be right there. Rosemary, you go with her."

As Mary reluctantly went back to her room, Fiona hurried to the phone, praying that the often unreliable telephone service was working. After several rings, she connected with the village doctor's home and was soon talking to his housekeeper.

"This is Fiona Carnegie at the Villa de Largo," she said. "I need to have the doctor come to the villa immediately!"

The woman answered in a rattle of Portuguese: "Desculpe mas o Dr. Senhora de Silva é afastado nas montanhas presentes alguns pacientes. Ele não é esperado para retornar até amanhã de manhã."

"Please, I don't understand Portuguese. Do you speak English?"

"No, aguarde por favo, mas vou buscar alguém."

Then silence. "Hello?" Fiona said. "I say, hello? Is anyone there? Please! Come back!"

She waited an agonizingly long minute, until another voice came on the phone.

"Hello. Hello, can I help you? I'm the doctor's nurse."

Fiona exhaled; she hadn't even realized she was holding her breath, and began speaking quickly. "This is Fiona Carnegie at the Villa de Largo. I need to have the doctor come to the villa immediately!"

"I'm sorry, Senhora Carnegie," the nurse answered, "Doctoro de Silva is away in the mountains attending patients. He is not expected to return until tomorrow morning."

"That won't do at all!" Fiona said. "We have a young guest who is in labor and needs to be attended to right now!"

"I understand, Senhora, but I cannot reach the doctoro," the nurse said. "There are no communications up there, it's very rural. But if I may suggest, there is a woman in the village that often helps in these matters when the doctoro is unavailable. She is what one might call a midwife or birther. Would you like me to call her for you?"

"Yes, yes, immediately! I will send a driver to the doctor's house. Have her there and ready. Hurry!"

"Very well, Senhora. I will arrange it immediately."

Fiona dispatched the driver from the villa to pick up the midwife. Thirty minutes later, the car pulled back into the villa's motor court and an older woman with a wild head of grey hair and a tattered canvas bag emerged from the car. Fiona ran from the front door to meet her.

"Thank goodness you've arrived!" she said, hurrying the older woman toward the house. "I'm Mrs. Carnegie. My guest is having a baby right now."

"I see, Senhora," the midwife said in broken, but understandable English. "Show me her, por favo. How long has she been in labor?"

"I don't exactly know how long, but she says the baby is coming right now."

"Is this her first bebê?" the midwife said, entering the house and looking around, as if she expected to see Mary in labor on the foyer floor.

"Yes!" Fiona said. "Indeed it is. She is very young and frightened. Please hurry."

"Sim," the midwife said, opening her bag even as she hurried through the house, with the help of Fiona pushing her from behind.

Mary was sweating and breathing hard when the midwife entered the room. Her pallor was pale and a strand of hair clung to her sweating forehead. When Fiona and the midwife entered, she looked up and began to smile until another contraction seized her and she cried aloud in pain.

The midwife hurried to the bedside and put a calm hand on Mary's forehead as she yowled in pain and fear. "No worry, no worry," she murmured, noticing that Mary's water had broken. Then, turning to Fiona and Rosemary, she issued instructions. "Bringa me towels. Hot water. String. A blanket. Now! Apressar!"

Rosemary dashed from the room, seemingly relieved to escape the cries from her friend on the bed. For the next hours, Mary rode the waves of agony as her labor progressed. The contractions grew in strength and came closer and closer, until she felt that she would be buried beneath an avalanche of pain, that the pain was so great it burned white hot and blotted out everything else in the room except the reassuring murmur of the midwife dutifully by her head. The old woman spoke mostly in Portuguese, but Mary felt she could still understand the old woman's words: breathe, breathe, relax, breathe. And she tried, but when the contractions became a constant, unending torrent of pain, when she felt she could bear it no longer, she could not help the cry that escaped from her lips: "Anthony! Where are you? Why have you left me?"

Fiona paced at the foot of the bed, glancing occasionally at her friend and worrying. "Oh Mary," she said as the young girl screamed Anthony's name. She rushed to the bedside and put her hand on Mary's arm—the girl was burning and drenched with sweat. "You're almost there! Darling! Be strong!"

And then the pain shifted and Mary felt the pressure building inside her and an undeniable need to push. The midwife shifted between her legs and said, "Now! Pusha, Miss Mary! Pusha!"

And Mary pushed with every muscle in her body, until she felt she was turning herself inside out. She had no breath to even scream and felt as if her teeth would shatter from the exertion. And then...with a final and mighty push that threatened to tear her apart...she felt the baby slide from her, into the waiting hands of the midwife.

A tiny yell soon filled the room, and the midwife quickly tied off the umbilical cord with string, cut it with one sure stroke of a sharp knife, and stood with a squalling, red baby in her arms. "A boy!" she proclaimed. "God bless this child!" She made the sign of the cross over the baby and went to hand the newborn to Mary, but Rosemary intervened and took the child, wrapping him quickly in a blanket and wiping away the white waxy substance that covered his face and eyes.

Mary, as exhausted as she was, felt as if her heart would break when she realized that the first face her son would see would not be her own. Tears ran down her face and she reached for her child, only to meet Rosemary's expression.

Then Mary began to sob. "Oh, Anthony! Where are you? Our son! Our son!"

Fiona rushed to Mary's side and stroked her forehead, pulling her eyes away from her newborn son. "Mary, dear. Mary! You're doing the right thing in giving him up! I will raise him like my own son!" Tears streamed down all their faces, and the confused midwife faded into the background to watch the emotional scene. "You and Anthony can have more children!" Fiona said.

Mary pulled her gaze away from Fiona and looked at the baby in Rosemary's arms. "Can I hold him?" she said. "At least let me hold him."

Rosemary glanced at Fiona, who nodded miserably, afraid that in the instant Mary touched her son, all of her hopes would be dashed and Mary would never let the child go. Fiona's arms were aching to hold the baby, her heart filled with love for this child who would be her son. But she knew Mary was at least entitled to hold her new baby.

Rosemary gently and slowly placed the baby on Mary's breast, and instantly he stopped crying and began rooting. Mary cooed at him gently through her tears, rubbing his small and perfect features with one finger. "I'm so sorry," she whispered. "But…I won't be your Ma-ma. Fiona will be your Ma-ma, and the Ambassador your father. But I'll always love you." And her voice broke as fresh tears overwhelmed her. "Always."

"Mary," Fiona said timidly, approaching the bedside. "Mary?"

Mary looked up, her expression one that Fiona would never forget: heartbreak and fierce love mingling freely with the sweat and tears of her exertion. Fiona held her arms out slowly, and with sobs in her throat and tears in her eyes, Mary slowly lifted the baby up and handed him to Fiona. Together, they wept, but for different reasons: Mary for the loss of her son, Fiona for the God-given gift of a baby who would now be her son.

And then the moment passed. Fiona could not take her eyes off this exquisite baby, her new son, while Rosemary began to dab away the sweat and tears from Mary's face.

"I must call the Ambassador," Fiona said. "Rosemary, will you remain here at the villa with Mary until he comes for us?"

"Yes."

"And Mary..." Fiona stumbled. "We still have our plan? No one will know anything, not the Ambassador, not your parents, nor the public. You... oh, Mary! Thank you! Thank you!"

Mary still looked miserable, but she had stopped crying. "Oh Fiona, no one must know. Never! But please...please leave me, because if you stay for one moment longer I shan't be able to give him up!"

A look of panic crossed Fiona's face. "Don't say that!" she said. "Mary, you must know you can't keep this child!"

"I know," Mary said heavily. "But my heart denies what my head knows to be truth."

Fiona gazed at Mary for another second, then without another word hurried from the room with the precious bundle in her arms.

Left alone with Rosemary, Mary watched the door where Fiona and her baby had disappeared, then turned her head to look out the window. The midwife had left after collecting the money-filled envelope left for her on the foyer table, and the detritus of the birth had been cleaned away. For the first time in months, Mary realized she was alone—the baby who had kicked and squirmed inside her, who had hiccupped and kept her awake for countless nights, had left her. She was filled with a new feeling...she knew her life would never be the same. She had created a life—and then given it away. She would never be there to nurture her baby, to rock him to sleep on those long nights, to tickle his tiny feet. Would she ever be able to smile again?

The next morning, Mary felt only slightly better. She had still barely moved from the bed where her baby had been born, and knew she must look frightful. After lying in bed for a bit, she located a piece of Summerset stationary from the bedside stand, uncapped a pen, thought for a moment, and then wrote a note to Fiona. When she was done, she slipped a small wrapped item into the envelope along with the note and placed it in the basket that would hold the baby on the trip home to England. When she was done, she thought of Anthony: en route to London, he didn't even know their baby had been born yet.

It was two days before Mary could reach Anthony by telephone. Over those two days, she had surprised even herself with her recovery. She was still in pain and stiff, but the sadness that had threatened to engulf her had receded. She had not seen the baby since that fateful day he was born, and she supposed this helped her mood too. Although she could still feel the loss like a physical thing, a small part of her—the part of her that was naturally hopeful and optimistic—had already begun to look forward to a life with Anthony, to the relief of no longer having to hide her pregnancy and once again being a normal girl. At least as normal as any princess could be.

"Anthony!" she breathed into the phone when they finally connected. He was at his home in England and sounded as if he was a galaxy away. "Dearest! The baby has been born! It's a boy…a beautiful boy!" There was a heavy pause as her voice worked its way over thousands of miles of phone lines. She couldn't abide the silence and filled it with words. "He's gone, of course, back to England with Fiona and the Ambassador. Just like we planned. But I miss you! How I miss you! When can I see you again?"

"You mustn't worry," Anthony said. "We will be together again very soon. I know that one day we will also be able to have a real marriage, one that will be jubilant and celebrated. But for now, for our own well-being, you must swear to keep this secret and never disclose our union or this birth at the risk of ruining all that we cherish. You know, you are my one and only love."

"Anthony, you too are my one and only love," she said. "I will bear the agony of giving this child away and long for the time when we can start our lives all over again, together, and in full public view. The secret will be ours, and until the time we are able to be together again, I will love you more each day."

"Me too!" he said. "Now I must be going. I hear them calling for me."

Mary disconnected the phone, the sadness returning in a rush, and she cried herself to sleep that night, wondering what Anthony was doing, wondering where her baby and Fiona and the Ambassador were on their trip back to England, and wondering whatever would become of her.

CHAPTER 9
Home at Last

The Ambassador and Fiona lived in an enormous estate called Laurels by the Sea. With just 60,000 inhabitants, the Isle of Jersey was an ideal place for privacy. Jersey enjoyed an international identity distinct from Britain; however, Britain constitutionally was responsible for the defense of the Isle. Culturally, the Isle had both a strong English heritage and deep French influences. The French coast, after all, was located only a few nautical miles to the east and southeast of the Isle. This blend of cultures made the Isle exceptionally desirable: it had French cuisine and style, English tradition and stability, and a notable international community.

In addition to Jersey's charm and history, its citizens enjoyed some very unique financial and tax shelters that attracted the very rich—and none were richer than the famous Ambassador and his wife. Laurels by the Sea boasted a private nine-hole golf course and a main French-inspired estate home that included more than fifty rooms. The chateau walls were hung with priceless works of art, while every room was appointed in the finest style. The grounds surrounding the estate were immaculate, and from the upper windows, one had a view of both the rolling hills surrounding the estate and the twinkling blue sea in the distance.

When Fiona and the Ambassador arrived, it was with great relief and excitement. Pulling up to the front doors in their car, Fiona looked at the baby tucked securely in his traveling basket and smiled. "You're home, sweet one," she cooed, and the Ambassador smiled at her and laid a hand on her arm.

"Well, Mommy, we made it," he said. "At last."

"Oh yes, I never believed this day would come," Fiona gushed to her husband. "A baby, our baby! He is home and he is beautiful!"

"Yes, my dear. And I must say, I was impressed with your sister Rosemary. The birth hardly seemed to have troubled her, she looked so well. I'm sure it's relief, from knowing that her child will be so loved and grow up in such circumstances."

Fiona nodded, but looked away, knowing that her face might give away her deception. "Yes, bless her, she is a special person. Her sacrifice will not be squandered."

When they entered the house, it had the curious, echoing, empty feeling of a grand home that is never truly deserted. Naturally, the staff had been busy while they were away, because a home of that size required tremendous, constant effort to keep it looking pristine, but they had been equally careful to disturb nothing and to leave no trace of their presence. Also, of course, Fiona had left voluminous instructions to the staff regarding the grand nursery. She was determined that the baby would have the finest nursery ever created—and when she finally walked into the nursery with the cooing baby in his basket, the room met her every expectation. She set the basket down and lifted the baby out—only then noticing the envelope that was tucked alongside him. "Hmm," she said, reaching with one hand for the letter, then opening and reading it. As she read Mary's words, fresh tears sprang to her eyes, and she was moved that a woman as young as Mary, as inexperienced as Mary had been in the ways of life, could express herself so eloquently. When she finished the letter, she was careful to hide it in a place the Ambassador would surely never look, for his discovery of it would ruin her careful deception.

But it wasn't long before the deception came up again—this time at tea later that afternoon, when Fiona and the Ambassador sat at a small circular table in the solarium, the baby nearby in his basket.

"So, Fiona," he said, stirring sugar into his tea. "What's the plan? How do you figure we'll do this?"

She waved a hand dismissively. "I think it's already done, dear. We have all the privacy here we need, and of course I've been faking a pregnancy in public for months. We will simply notify the embassy that the baby has come a bit early and that we will return to London the day after tomorrow. When we return, we will explain that the birth was quick and uneventful. Everyone will assume he was born here at Laurels and that will be that."

The Ambassador nodded and arched an eyebrow at her, an expression that she loved on his face. "That sounds plausible. When we get back to the embassy, I'll have Jenkins, the Charges de Affaires, issue a diplomatic birth certificate naming us as the parents. The baby will likely be eligible for dual citizenship. The law allows that privilege to children born to diplomats who are in-service out of their homeland. Since you are British, that will be an appropriate legacy for our son and tie up any loose ends that might be left."

"Yes, thank you. I was hoping that would be the case." She paused and looked fondly at the sleeping baby. So far, the baby slept most of the time sleeping, day and night, but she had heard he would start to be more active soon. "I wanted to ask you…what shall we name the boy?"

The Ambassador smiled. "I was thinking the boy should be named after me. Harrington."

"Perhaps," she said in a tone of voice that meant absolutely not. "But I like the name William. We could call him William Harrington Carnegie. That sounds perfect to me."

The Ambassador nodded at his wife, his smile broadening. "I suppose so, if that is your wish. I'm just happy to have a son."

As planned, the next day the couple and William departed for the American Embassy in London. When they arrived, the embassy was in joyful disarray. The wire they had sent the day before gave staff little time to make things ready. The maids rushed around preparing the baby's room and organizing clothing and assorted paraphernalia. Fiona announced that the baby could not be nursed since her milk had not come in strongly enough to sustain the infant. Instead, the baby would be bottle-fed. No one gave this any thought, considering both Fiona's age and the fact that women of her station frequently avoided breastfeeding. A newly appointed and carefully screened nanny was called into service to begin her caretaking.

When he was finally able to settle into his office after a long absence, the Ambassador wasted no time in reaching Jenkins, the charges de affaires. The older man came into the office carrying his trademark notebook with the stubby pencil he used to take notes. He sat on a leather Chesterfield across from the Ambassador's desk, his graying hair immaculate, and waited until the Ambassador was ready to speak.

"Jenkins, as you know, Mrs. Carnegie gave birth to our son at Laurels by the Sea in Jersey the day before yesterday," the Ambassador began. "We didn't bother doing paperwork with local officials since we wanted the baby to have his birth certificate done by the embassy. Therefore, it will be necessary to draw up the proper birth certificate and American citizenship documents."

"Of course, Mr. Ambassador," Jenkins said, making a note in his book. "It will be done immediately. I will also transmit the official notification to the State Department to make certain that our new young man will receive full diplomatic consideration and status. Is there anything else?"

"Yes. Please notify the Carnegie Trust attorney about the birth and that the baby should be added as a beneficiary."

"Certainly, Mr. Ambassador. It will be arranged immediately."

"Also, be certain to process the necessary applications for dual citizenship for William. Mrs. Carnegie holds British citizenship, and William is entitled to it as well."

And thus was the die cast. William Harrington Carnegie became the legal son of U.S. Ambassador Harrington Carnegie and his wife, British national Fiona. William would not only hold dual citizenship as a U.S. citizen and British subject, he would one day have access to the tremendous Carnegie fortune as guaranteed by being an natural born heir to the Ambassador.

***

Life at the embassy settled into an easy routine, and baby William was instantly the darling of the consulate. Everyone from the highest-ranking diplomatic officer to the lowliest chambermaid fell in love with Fiona's gift from God. Lavish gifts poured in from all over the world, and dozens of people called on the new parents to give personal congratulations. Everyone agreed that the baby was nothing short of a miracle, considering that his mother was just about to celebrate her forty-first birthday. Official birth announcements were posted in all the British papers as well as in New York and Washington. The social pages of the London newspapers covered the baby's arrival, always dubbing it "Fiona's miracle baby." The politically savvy U.S. President sent an official greeting, welcoming the birth of William and congratulating the influential new parents. Even the Queen sent her personal regards and a very elegant baby present. Joy prevailed. Fiona was in ecstasy being the mother she always desired to be. As for the Ambassador conducting business as usual, he was nonetheless thrilled to have his heir and as proud of a father as there could be.

***

The years passed in a blur of activity for the small family. Even as war clouds continued to gather over Europe, and Hitler's Germany grew in strength and ambition, William Harrington Carnegie lived the life of privilege you'd expect from the scion of one of America's richest families and son of the Ambassador. But everyone agreed that William was a good child—gifted with an excellent disposition, healthy, very clever, and athletic. He was, according to consensus opinion, a blessing to his elderly parents, who doted feverishly on him.

Nevertheless, the war could not be held back. The year William turned three, Hitler's Germany launched an invasion of Poland, taking over the country with blinding speed and overwhelming force. Other countries fell shortly after, and it soon became clear that Hitler's appetite had no bounds and he was determined to swallow all of Europe as quickly as he could. As the situation deteriorated, it wasn't long before the call came that Ambassador Carnegie had warned his family to expect. He was being recalled from England and expected to immediately make his way back to America to add his expertise and assist in the war effort. The year was 1944, and William was turning eight years old.

CHAPTER 10
MOVING FORWARD WITHOUT LOOKING BACK

London, England, 1944

BY 1944, A WORLD WEARY OF WAR ACHED FOR GOOD NEWS. MUCH OF EUROPE lay in shambles, and even London was still clearing away piles of rubble from what they were already calling the Battle of Britain. It was true that daring British pilots had turned away the feared Luftwaffe in 1940, but the cost had been tremendous: a city nearly destroyed, a population traumatized, thousands upon thousands of husbands, wives, brothers and sisters killed by Nazi bombs.

Throughout it all, Anthony and Mary had remained in close contact, despite their very different paths. Anthony had graduated from Cambridge and taken a commission as an officer in His Majesty's Royal Army. He fought with distinction in France and Germany, completing his service without any physical injury but a lifetime's worth of heartache. He returned to his family's estate still a young man, but a seasoned warrior mature beyond his years, ready to run affairs and create a new life for after the war.

He still desperately hoped this life would include Mary, who had grown into an important symbol of British stability and resolve. It was hard for him sometimes to reconcile the lovely young princess with the girl who wrote him long letters and once, during a too-brief visit in London, had stolen a quick kiss—but she was indeed the same person. Time played well for Mary despite the hardships of her people and country. She had grown into a beautiful young woman and had been raised into her duties and assumed the responsibility naturally. Her contribution to the war effort was legendary. Mary's very public appearances and stiff upper lip, exemplifying the will to prevail over the forces of evil determined to defile the British people, made her a beloved national treasure.

No one knew of their marriage, and of course the birth of their son remained a secret. Anthony heard from time to time about the Carnegie family in America, but he didn't allow himself to dwell on these thoughts—and he suspected Mary did the same. They had a job to do, and there was no time in the midst of such destruction and loss to spend energy on their own loss.

But Anthony still looked for every opportunity to be close to his princess, and finally found one during an exhibit at the Royal Academy of Arts, Burlington House in Piccadilly. Browsing the spacious rooms hung with contemporary paintings, he saw Mary staring at a painting, her entourage standing discreetly a distance away. Breaking into a broad smile, Anthony crossed the room and stood slightly behind her, his hands clasped behind his back. She was so absorbed in her inspection of the painting—a portrait, he saw, of a woman he did not recognize—that she never heard him approach.

"Lovely, isn't it?" he said.

Mary whirled around, her face lighting with delight at the sound of his familiar voice for the briefest second. Then she seemed to remember herself and her expression instantly slid back into a neutral smile. "Indeed," she said. "Very lovely."

He cleared his throat, his eyes twinkling as he caught onto the game.

"I was wondering, Your Highness, if you'd allow me to escort you to a film premiere that I have been invited to next Thursday evening. The director is a friend of mine from University and he would be honored if you would be his guest."

Mary put her hand to her face to hide the barest of smiles, and he ached to sweep her into his arms. "I would be delighted to join you," she said. "However, I will have to check the calendar and see if that evening is available. Please ring me tomorrow and I will have an answer for you."

"Brilliant!" he said. "So I shall, after lunch. Now perhaps you could help me…who is this woman exactly?"

They both turned back to the painting, and Mary began to talk about the Lady Someone-or-Another in the painting, but he heard none of it. For the next hour or so, they wandered through the gallery together, her explaining the history behind some of her favorite paintings and introducing him to the stories of the artists who had painted them. He was immediately impressed with the scope of her knowledge and her poise. At one point, she casually rested her hand on his forearm to make a point, and it was like a lightning bolt ran through him. He had to suppress a blush as the memory of their gatehouse rendezvous flooded back.

He heard excited whispering and turned to see that the gallery was slowly filling with people. Royal watchers. Members of court and carefully screened visiting public. And, he realized, no one had eyes for the art on the wall. Instead, they were all transfixed by the sight of their young princess's hand resting lightly on his arm. Mary herself seemed not to notice. Yet the story traveled with supersonic speed, and Anthony was amazed when, as they were leaving the gallery, one particular press man shouted, "Your Highness? Who's the man? Name! Name!" Her security quickly intercepted the press and hustled them from the room, but not before there were brilliant flashes from a sea of menacing cameras.

"How do you handle it?" Anthony muttered to her in a low voice. "Are they always following you?"

"Always," Mary answered. "As for how to handle it, I just remember what I represent. Now, I must go before we create a scandal. But do call me tomorrow, Anthony."

Those words were still ringing in his head the next morning when he opened the paper and his jaw dropped in shock. There, on the lower half of the front page, just below the fold, was a picture of him and Mary in the gallery under the headline: "Has the Princess Found Her Prince? Lovely Mary takes in the Royal Academy with a dashing newcomer."

Still wondering how she managed to live under such scrutiny, he called her after lunch as promised and was again surprised when the Mary who answered the phone was the same excited girl he remembered, as opposed to the poised, calm princess he had met in public just the night before.

"Anthony!" she cried. "I'm so glad you called!"

"Of course! Can't a man call his wife?"

She giggled at their private joke, because of course they were still married. "Is the movie still on?" she asked, suddenly shy.

"Indeed!"

From that day on, Anthony and Mary saw each other as often as their busy social calendars permitted it. They attended gallery openings, West End premieres, and the many parties that people were always inviting them to. It seemed to Anthony that forests of trees and gallons of ink had been spent on them as the press deliriously covered their every move. He was continuously amazed at how much of what he read about their slow-burning courtship was complete rubbish—and tried not to reflect upon what would happen to them if the truth were ever discovered. He could only imagine the headlines.

Before long, the press began to wonder on the front page when he would "pop the question."

"Ask her!" blared one paper. "Ring, Ring…The Ring Watch Continues!"

Another less credible paper hit too close to home when it speculated "Secret Wedding In the Works!" and imagined them running off to marry without the King and Queen's blessing.

Anthony found it all amusing—but it did raise a real question for him. How does a man propose to a woman who is already his wife?

One warm evening, Anthony looked into Mary's eyes and said: "Listen, Mary, I'm not sure what I'm supposed to do. This is quite awkward. I want to propose to you and yet…we already are married! So what do I say? Do I say, Mary, darling, will you marry me, again? That's just ridiculous!"

Mary laughed lightly. "You don't have to propose. I already did that for you years ago, in Gibraltar. Now we must move forward without looking back. All you have to do is tell me that you love me and that you want to spend the rest of your life with me."

"Well of course I do! I do, I do! Oh God, that sounds lame. I already said I do, didn't I? Of course I did."

They laughed and then embraced and kissed deeply.

"Me too!" she said. "But we must follow proper protocol or this will never work. You must talk to PaPa and win his approval. Then we will have the wedding we both have dreamed about, *in public*, for the entire world to witness. I'll talk with MaMa, who will arrange everything."

Anthony swallowed nervously. Talking to the King about anything was daunting…but about marrying his daughter was unimaginable. He had no idea what he would say.

***

Mary found her mother sitting in the opulently appointed family quarters. To anyone else, the family quarters would be an imposing atmosphere. The walls were covered with artwork that dated back hundreds of years, including both portraits of former kings and queens and paintings from many of the masters. Everything from the rugs on the floor to the furniture to the gilt mirror hanging above a glowing fireplace had a story—the room was a testament to the conquests of the British Empire and the historical power and wealth of the Crown. To Mary, however, these were comfortable rooms and her home, where the royal family could relax in privacy without the stiff formality that always attended royal events and appearances. So it was no surprise for Mary to find her mother, the Queen Consort, sitting on a silk-upholstered love seat in a robe with one foot tucked under herself and a steaming cup of tea at her elbow as she read from one of the novels she adored.

"MaMa," Mary said, sitting down on her customary love seat across from her mother, in the same positions where they had spent countless hours talking about the kingdom, the expectations of being a royal, her father, and even the smallest concerns of the house staff and royal gossip.

"Mary," she said, putting a marker in her book and closing it. "How are you, dear?"

"I'm well," she said. Then she took a breath to steel her courage. Mary and her mother were as close as a royal mother and daughter could be, but this was no ordinary conversation. "MaMa? Have you seen the papers?"

"Papers? Which ones?"

"All of them, really," Mary said. "You know…the stories about me…and Anthony. They are a regular feature now."

"Of course I have," the Queen Consort said, shaking her head. "It is most distressing for you to be hounded and harassed. I am sorry you have to be exposed to that insidious invasion of your privacy. But, well, it is the burden we endure as royals in the modern age. There is no privacy afforded to us. The best way to deal with it is to simply ignore it, because really, there is nothing we can do about it. Is it troubling you?"

"Well, MaMa, not exactly," Mary said carefully. "I think it's time Anthony made his intentions clear to you and PaPa. He already has to me."

The Queen set her book down, her face lit with joy. "He has? When, where, how? How do you know that he is serious about you?"

"MaMa, he is very serious about me and I am very serious about him," Mary said. "He is such a special man, and I know I genuinely love him. I have known him since I was sixteen years old at Highwood School. We attended the same parties and have kept in touch throughout his college and military career. Anthony is kind and smart and someone I love to be with. And he is so handsome and manly, don't you agree?"

The Queen, almost blushing, answered, "Well, Mary, handsome and manly may be nice, but what is important is that he be a good match for you, the future Queen. Will he provide you with lifelong companionship, loyalty, and most importantly of all, be able to produce an heir to the throne?"

"Handsome and manly may not be important to you, but to me they are what make him so appealing. As far as producing an heir, I'm quite sure he is competent in that department. After all, look at him: he is young and healthy and, by all appearance, quite virile." Silently, she added, "And he has a proven track record!"

The Queen looked a bit more serious. "I see. Well, my dear, do you think it might be time for you to make it clear to him what his responsibilities would be if he chooses you as his wife? As you well know, there are sacrifices involved with being in our family, even more so than other noble families must endure. Is he ready to take this all on? It is a grave commitment, a lifelong career filled with ups and downs and a total lack of privacy. Every move you or your husband make will be scrutinized, analyzed, and exaggerated, ad nauseam."

Mary found herself nodding along, having had these same thoughts herself. "I know Anthony, and he is capable of taking on anything that may come his way. He is a loyal subject and loving man, and he will be a brilliant husband. And someday he will be an amazing father to the next heir to the throne. Anthony is educated and poised. He will not disappoint you or Father as a son-in-law, a monarch's husband, or the father of an heir. Of this I'm certain. I know he is ready to marry me, and I long for that day."

The Queen looked at her daughter for a long time, giving Mary the searching, probing look that Mary had seen her mother turn on countless dignitaries and politicians over the years. This singular look was her mother's greatest weapon, and Mary had seen grown men—generals and men who had commanded troops in battle—quail before her mother's piercing gaze. But Mary had nothing to fear from her mother—she knew that the Queen was only looking for evidence that Mary's intentions and heart were in the right place, that this Anthony was the "right" man for her daughter. Finally, Martha's face broke into a smile.

"Then my dear, I think it's time Anthony speaks with the King and states his intentions. He will need the King's approval."

Mary wanted to jump up and shout. Without her mother's backing, she knew it would be hopeless. Her father was not a hard man, but when it came to the succession and his only daughter, he had very high standards. "Oh yes, MaMa. I know PaPa will grant his permission. He will come to love Anthony as I do and so will you. Our lives will be filled with happiness and together we will serve our country with distinction and pride. Anthony will make us all proud and the people will love him as they do you and PaPa."

"I do hope so," Martha said.

If Mary was feeling better after talking with her mother, Anthony was deeply unsettled by the idea of talking with the King, Mary's father, about their relationship. Like all Britons, and especially those from the upper classes, he had been trained from birth to swear fealty to the King and Crown. The thought of talking to him man-to-man about his daughter was enough to keep him awake at night. This fear was made infinitely worse by the nagging thought that the King already knew about their secret marriage and child. In an almost paranoid state, Anthony imagined that the King, through his vast resources, had learned of their secret. He even worried that he might slip up when they met and say something to incriminate either Mary or himself.

He was also troubled by the fact that he and Mary were already legally married. What would happen if they were married again? Would that annul the first marriage? Would the second marriage count? Did it make any difference at all? And of course it didn't help that there was no one he could direct these questions to.

These questions continued to haunt him as the date of his meeting with the King drew closer. The night before the meeting, he lay in bed, replaying in his mind that fateful evening at the gatehouse when he made love to Mary. It was so sweet and tender: so impromptu and ultimately so significant. He recalled Mary's beautiful and young body, her full breasts, her narrow waist, and her warm and welcoming lips. He remembered how the frightened and inexperienced Mary wept when they were finished. It was still unbelievable to him that they had produced a child on the first time they were able to make love.

Finally, he drifted off to sleep and immediately fell into a dream in which he and Mary were getting married in a lavish ceremony at Westminster. It seemed like the whole country was gathered outside, yet all Anthony could think about was fear they would be discovered. After the ceremony, they were escorted to the Wedding Bed Chamber at Buckingham Palace, and in his dream he imagined the bed to be acres wide, a field of white sheets that swallowed them both. At the crack of dawn, the doors to the room were flung open and the Prime Minister stormed in to examine the bridal bed and confirm the virginity of the future Queen. Anthony tried to protest, to say the bed was far too large to find any telltale bloodstains, but his words got stuck in his throat while the Prime Minister bellowed, "There are no bloodstains. She was not a virgin! This marriage is a disgrace."

He awoke in a cold sweat, his sheets tangled around him. After a moment or so, when his heart stopped racing, Anthony was able to chuckle at his own imagination. Those days were long past, a relic from a different century. No, he reasoned with himself, obviously the King did not know about their history, or Anthony would never have been allowed within a hundred yards of Mary. Their secret was still safe, and the only reason the King wanted to see Anthony was to measure his fitness as a royal husband and possible throne-sitter next to his daughter. Anthony's lips twisted when he imagined sitting upon the throne in Buckingham Palace. Too bad Cambridge didn't offer classes in throne-sitting—but then he never could have imagined himself in this situation.

Finally, dawn seeped through his window and he sat up, feeling wrung out but also calm. The fact remained: he loved Mary with all of his heart, she loved him back, and there was no earthly reason they should not receive the King and Queen's blessing to enjoy their lives together.

CHAPTER 11
THE KING'S SPEECH

ANTHONY WAS SCHEDULED TO MEET WITH THE KING IN AN INFORMAL parlor located in the family residence at Buckingham Palace. Anthony wasn't sure if this set his mind at ease or made it worse. It was a great honor to be invited into the family quarters, but the whole idea of sitting in a room where the royal family made personal decisions put Anthony in a cold sweat as he followed the butler through the stately halls and locked doors to the private chamber.

The room was surprisingly large—he had pictured something more like a small salon—but it was arranged in a way to make it feel smaller and more informal. The cream-colored walls were hung with portraits of royal family members, not all of whom Anthony recognized. The ceiling, two stories overhead, was festooned with ornate gilded moldings encasing centuries-old murals. Light was provided by three enormous crystal chandeliers that glittered like a rain of diamonds falling from the ceiling. These dated back to when the palace was originally decorated by King George VI. Several sitting areas had been created with antique furniture upholstered in handmade tapestries and golden brocade. The side tables were decorated with silver-framed family photographs, including pictures of Mary from her toddler years all the way to her graduation. These pictures fortified Anthony, but he dared not linger on them too long for fear of attracting the King's notice and seeming presumptuous. At the far end of the room, a pair of French doors opened onto a private balcony overlooking the garden.

Anthony was surprised to realize the vast room was empty, but a tea service had been set out on one of the small tables. The stunning Georgian silver service was polished to a gleaming shine.

A side door opened and the King himself entered, passing through a small security detail that accompanied him at all times, even in the palace. Anthony stood at attention, his military training taking over without his thinking about it, and studied the King surreptitiously. The monarch had a formal, almost stiff-legged walk, and his carriage was erect and very proper. He wore a tailored suit of impeccable cut and cloth, and his narrow, patrician features were impossible to read. His brown hair was parted on one side. He was, in short, the very essence of a modern English monarch, which helped explain his enormous popularity among the people.

The King approached Anthony, his gaze finally alighting on Anthony's face. But instead of acknowledging Anthony, he gave the younger man a long, searching look, almost as if he was inspecting Anthony in the way a farmer would inspect a calf. Anthony, having been coached on royal etiquette, leaned forward and bowed from the waist. In a throaty and nervous tone, he croaked: "Your Highness, it's my sincere pleasure to be received. I am honored and humbled."

"Indeed," the King said, finally gesturing for Anthony to sit on the settee as he took a wingback chair for himself, crossing one leg over the other. As if on cue, a royal footman seemed to materialize from nowhere and carefully poured tea for the monarch, adding milk and sugar without being asked, then inquired if Anthony wanted tea. Almost against his will, Anthony found his mouth watering—real sugar had been a luxury in London for most of the war years, and most Britons, including much of the aristocracy, had been reduced to reusing tea leaves until every drop of flavor had been wrung from them.

"Please," Anthony said.

The King watched mildly as the footman prepared Anthony's tea, and then Anthony waited until the King picked up his own cup and took a careful sip. Not surprisingly, the tea was perfect, but Anthony had to will his hand not to shake as he sipped from his cup. He couldn't remember a time he had been this nervous. On the battlefield, he had been scared—but this was an entirely different kind of emotion. He had practiced what he would say and how he would act. He even had changed his outfit three times, trying to select just the right one that would make the best impression. He had settled on a well-tailored blue serge suit purchased for him by his father as a birthday gift at Black and Hemmingway, a renowned Bond Street custom tailor. Additionally, he wore his regimental tie to show his military connection. Before he entered the palace, he thought he looked regal, masculine, and aristocratic—exactly the kind of suitor a King might want for his daughter. Yet actually sitting there, alone in the presence of the King of England, Anthony couldn't help feeling like he was back in prep school again, called before the headmaster for talking out of turn.

"So," the King finally spoke, setting down his cup, "my wife tells me you are interested in my daughter, the Princess Royal?"

"Yes, sir."

"And you went to school together, is that right?"

"Forgive me, but no sir. We met while she was still in school, but, ah, I was just entering in Cambridge at the time."

The King nodded approvingly. "Cambridge then?"

"Yes, sir."

"Good choice."

Anthony nodded and smiled inwardly. It was no accident he mentioned Cambridge—of course he knew the King himself had attended Trinity College at Cambridge.

"So what would you say your interest in my daughter is?"

"Um, ah, well, sir, I'm in love with her."

"Love?" the King echoed. "What could someone as young as you know about love?"

"With all due respect, Sir, I am young and perhaps inexperienced in the ways of life, but I am old enough to know my own mind and heart," Anthony said in a rush of courage. "I have fallen in love with your daughter and know deep within me that it is a true and lasting love."

The King studied Anthony again, even as Anthony wondered what the King was thinking about him. Did Anthony measure up? Was he passing the royal test?

The King abruptly leaned toward Anthony: "Tell me, young man, what are the most important things in your life?"

Anthony took a deep breath. He was prepared for this. "Sir, I know that there will be many important things to come. But for now, at my young age, the most important thing besides my love for Mary is my desire to be honest and loyal to God, country, and family. I have been blessed with good health, a fine education, and a wonderful family legacy, all important to me. But, Sir, I feel the best of life is yet to come. I look forward to being a worthy husband, a good father, and a role model to those who will be looking up to me. If I am successful, then those will be the most important things in my life."

The King nodded again, and this time Anthony was sure he saw the first sign of a smile. "And your family? You are the eldest son of Lord Bolin, are you not?"

"Yes, sir, the eldest son and heir to his estate and enterprises," Anthony proudly reported, beginning to feel slightly less tense. A question about his family was surely a good sign, because Anthony knew of course that the King and his solicitors had already learned everything they needed to know about Anthony Bolin and his family. They had no doubt reviewed his ancestry, inheritance, academic transcripts, and military and medical records. If he hadn't passed that initial screening, he would never have been granted an audience with the King to argue his case. As far as Anthony could surmise, the King's question must have been meant to put him at ease.

"An old family," the King observed mildly. "And your health? I trust you're in good health?"

"Certainly," replied Anthony. "Fit to serve not only my wife, but my country."

"Brilliant," the King said, and then he looked out the window. He seemed to hesitate for a moment before asking, "Is there any reason to believe that procreation will be a problem? Too many young men are suffering from this war. I fear for this next generation. But I trust you have no issue in that area?"

It took a moment for Anthony to figure out how to answer. He had to fight back a deep blush. The King was asking if Anthony could produce an heir. Under any circumstances, it would be a difficult question, but considering that Anthony already had fathered a child with Mary, it set his hands to shaking again. He had a flash of pure terror that the King had discovered their secret and this whole meeting was a charade that would soon give way to accusations.

Anthony swallowed around the lump in his throat. "No, sir, I don't believe that would be an issue." Leaning closer, he continued, "And, ah, given my desire for Mary, *and with all due respect, sir*, I can assure you that I will try every chance I get."

The King burst into laughter that completely disarmed Anthony. "Young man, you are indeed a rascal, but a likable rascal!"

Anthony had no idea how to respond to that.

The King, looking more relaxed by the second, said, "You understand, of course, what it means to marry into a royal family, do you not? If the Queen and I agree that you and Mary should be allowed to wed, you would instantly became a subject of great interest throughout the kingdom and the world beyond. You would only be able to gain privacy behind high walls, never going out in public again for a simple walk down the street. You would be open to ridicule and criticism from every corner, with half of the public openly rooting for your humiliation. And try as you might, you will never be able to escape unharmed. A word or gesture will be taken wrong, amplified by the press, and you will find yourself the subject of outrageous deception. At the same time, you will be virtually deified, with mothers weeping at your touch and men bowing to you. As if this weren't enough, a royal marriage is not like another marriage. The demands of the office shall always be sacrosanct. You must put all other desires and biddings in last place. Your marriage will not only be a sacrament, but a sacrifice; not only a sacred bond, but a weight that must be borne by both you and Mary. Your union will be a lifelong struggle between what you want to do and what you must do. Love alone may not be enough to sustain you. Your role in life will demand obedience to the law, regardless of the consequences. The weight of office may at times seem too much to bear, but your duty and stewardship to the Crown leaves you no options. This is not a role for a coward or a weakling or the self-absorbed. It is both a gift from God and a curse from Lucifer. It requires sacrifice, dedication, conviction and commitment to absolute honor."

The King paused and peered again at Anthony. Then he continued, "Do you understand this? Are you ready to make this choice freely and without reservation? Are you ready to sacrifice for your country and for the love of Mary?"

Anthony had thought of this before, but hearing it from the King's mouth put it in a totally different light. It made it feel much more real, and the sacrifices involved in marrying a future Queen suddenly seemed larger than they ever had before. Until now, he mainly thought of Mary in terms of their secret passion and history together. The idea of her as a future Queen had always been distant, a far-off fact that was hardly related to the real flesh-and-blood Mary he loved with all of his heart. But now...he could see that this part of Mary would only be a small element of their marriage. And perhaps even harder, the same went for him. If he married her, they would both be public figures, expected to lead the kingdom, exemplifying all that is right and proper, day in day out into perpetuity.

But even if all this was true, and even if it gave Anthony pause, what choice did he have? The truth was, Anthony loved Mary the woman and he would surely love Mary the Queen also. His destiny lay with her—he was sure of it. A flash of resolve filled him. There was no question really, no reluctance or reserve. Feeling more confident than he had yet, Anthony squared his shoulders and faced his King.

"Sir, I understand the weight of this," he began slowly. "But I am ready. I solemnly swear my love and allegiance to Mary and to the Crown. She is my life, my future, and the only thing I desire in my existence. I pledge to her, to you, and to my country to be the husband Mary deserves and the public servant that is commanded. I can only ask for your guidance and understanding in making both Mary and myself the two happiest people in the world."

The King nodded, and then rose from his chair, signaling for Anthony to rise also. The moment was filled with emotion for Anthony, and as he rose from his chair, he felt like a different man than the one who had sat down.

"Young man," the King said, "you are about to enter another world, a world where mistakes cannot be tolerated and failure is not a possibility. I can only hope you will embrace it with your entire being and that you will make my daughter happy. I pray the two of you will serve this great empire with dignity and honor, and that you will be blessed with children." He paused and seemed to search for his words. "Anthony, the Queen and I will support this union as long as you remain faithful to your wife and to your mutual vows and the duties of the kingdom. I hope you are ready for this, young man, and that it will be a journey well traveled."

"Thank you, sir. I am ready."

In a rare departure from royal etiquette, the King extended his hand to Anthony and they shook as if they were old mates, then King John turned on his heel and headed for the same door he had entered through. The wide chestnut doors opened on some secret signal and the King vanished back into the family quarters. Alone again in the empty room, Anthony slumped back down on the settee, a long breath escaping him. He could have not asked for a better meeting with the King—their secret remained intact and they received the King's blessing—and yet he was still sweating under his double-breasted jacket.

The Sovereign's words still echoed in his mind: "I hope you are ready for this, young man."

Was this a warning or just advice?

***

Later that day, Anthony met Mary in a small garden on the Palace grounds. They found a bench in a secluded corner, surrounded by roses and perfectly trimmed hedges. Even though they were in the heart of London, the city seemed impossibly far away from their quiet bench drenched in early evening sun.

Mary held Anthony's hand and laughed in all the appropriate places as he told her about his meeting with her father. When he was done, she squeezed his hand. "We are soon to be one, as we have always planned. I can't wait until the day of our wedding and the joy and happiness it will bring us. We are finally reaching our destiny…living together as man and wife. I love you so much and know we will be happy forever."

"Yes, Mary," he said. "We are ready to take on the world, together."

They kissed deeply—but deep in Mary's soul, she felt a pang of sorrow. Somewhere out in the world, in America, their child was being raised by Fiona and the Ambassador. She had no doubt the boy was well cared for and loved, but she was often filled with bouts of despair and a longing so intense that it took her breath away. She had avoided much direct contact with Fiona since that fateful summer, but she did hear tidbits from Rosemary. The boy was doing well, Rosemary said, and Fiona and the Ambassador doted on the child. Even this was hard to hear, and gradually Mary had stopped asking. There was no question she had done the right thing, but missing her child was like missing a limb. Holding Anthony, she could only hope they would have more children for them to nurture and to carry on the dynasty.

CHAPTER 12
Here Comes the Bride

The country was soon consumed with the prospect of a royal wedding. With the war finally over, and Hitler's Germany smashed in defeat while London's streets were filled with American servicemen, it felt like spring had come to Great Britain. The air was filled with relief and joy—and no small measure of mourning for all that had been lost during the conflict. The piles of rubble were mostly gone by now, and rebuilding had begun, but it was impossible to forget the tens of thousands of Britons who had been killed during the conflict. It seemed in those long days that the only thing that helped was a national focus on Mary and Anthony's upcoming fairytale wedding.

The planning took months, and the royal communication office worked overtime. King John and the Queen Consort Martha were said to be delighted by their daughter's choice of a husband. He was an aristocrat, a military officer who had seen action during the war and a graduate from Cambridge. Moreover, he was a handsome and dashing figure, and the princess was clearly enamored of her husband-to-be, just as he was enthralled with her. Their magnetism captured the people of a recovering nation as the royal couple's pictures were splashed almost daily in the papers and newsreels. It was the perfect story for the times: a new beginning for a kingdom and country, and common Britons hung on every detail of the story.

The royal family had entrusted the thousands of planning details to the Office of Royal Protocol, which would manage everything from the bridal dress to a gala wedding reception. As with all royal weddings, it was to be held in the Collegiate Church of St. Peter at Westminster, popularly known as Westminster Abbey. Keeping with tradition, the wedding party would be small and intimate. The maid of honor would, of course, be Rosemary Firth, the bride's best friend. Anthony's younger brother, Trevor Bolin, would serve as best man. The only other wedding party participants would be Mary's three young first cousins: Mary Louise, Edward, and Richard, all under the age of twelve. The Archbishop of Canterbury would officiate and administer the wedding vows.

The subject of Mary's dress was of intense national interest. Various fashion designers had been interviewed, and the Palace ultimately selected the famous British designer Sir Norman Bishop Hartnell to design her gown. In a press release put out just prior to the wedding, a detailed description and account of the future Queen's wedding dress was released:

> *The Princess Royal's wedding dress, designed by Sir Norman Hartnell, was inspired by the past but designed with the future in mind. A thoroughly modern cut encrusted with mother-of-pearl beads and Russian crystals sewn in designs to replicate the ornate patterns often seen in the borders of ancient tapestries. The materials, pure silk with satin appliqués, are pure white in color, establishing the perfect background for this stunning handiwork. The bridal train is sixteen feet in length*

and is bordered with the same pattern and materials as the bodice. The Princess Royal's veil will be held fast by a diamond and pearl tiara once worn by her great-great-grandmother, Princess Marie Louise Victoria of Saxe-Coburg-Saalfeld, princess of Leiningen.

When the day finally came, Mary and Anthony were wed in a city thronged with well-wishers and delirious celebrants. They were both keenly aware of what their wedding meant to the country and the very public roles they would play in helping Great Britain recover from a dark period. It was a joyful day—a day of celebration and hope and pomp—and none but Rosemary could have guessed at the source of the sadness that sometimes flickered in the eyes of the happy couple, that in their greatest moment of joy both Anthony's and Mary's thoughts turned to the child they had created and let go.

Two years later

The first two years of their marriage passed in a blur of social events, appearances, and state functions—and a pregnancy. On their second wedding anniversary, they celebrated with the birth of their "firstborn" son; they named him John, honoring his grandfather. The populace instantly fell in love with the newborn heir—but no one was as happy as the child's parents. Mary and Anthony finally had a child they could acknowledge as their own and raise, and it was all the better that it was a boy. From a succession point of view, a male heir to the throne was essential—although of course a Queen could ascend to the throne, centuries of English tradition favored a male successor.

The significance of this became even more apparent over the next few years, as Mary and Anthony failed to conceive again. They were both gravely disappointed with their inability to produce an "heir and a spare," but nature could not be reasoned with. In the end, Mary and Anthony had to be content with their precious John, who was lavished with all the attention a prince could want.

CHAPTER 13
LA DOLCE VITA: WESTCHESTER, NEW YORK, THE EARLY YEARS

DURING THE WAR YEARS, FIONA AND THE AMBASSADOR LIVED A QUIET LIFE, far away from the bombs and flames that were consuming Europe. They settled on the Carnegie family estate in the New York City suburb of Westchester, where William grew up roaming the rolling hills and wooded acres of his family estate. When he came of age, he was sent to the Westchester Country Day School, where he showed early promise as both an athlete and a scholar. He graduated Westchester at age 14 and went to Hotchkiss, an exclusive boarding school in Connecticut. There, he discovered a natural aptitude for all types of sports—a quality he had clearly inherited from his birth father. He was tall, lean, and strong, with a handsome face and natural leadership abilities. His senior year, he was elected student class president, and was known to have a keen sense of honor and justice; and despite his family's vast fortune, William was humble and hard-working.

His academic prowess allowed him to skip his junior year and finish prep school in just three years. Upon graduation, he was accepted to Harvard

University as one of the youngest matriculates in recent history. During his time at Harvard, William's grandfather died, entitling him to income from a massive trust fund benefiting both William and his father. The trust exceeded more than three quarters of a billion dollars—but even that nearly unimaginable wealth didn't shake William's sense of purpose, his work ethic, or his character.

At Harvard, as at prep school, William graduated early: he completed pre-law curriculum in three years, graduating egregia cum laude (with outstanding honor). This was a distinction created to recognize a student who achieved the highest grades in an extremely rigorous honors curriculum. This was a rare honor, and the first time in Harvard's history it had been bestowed upon a student who had completed his degree requirements in less than four years. After graduating, William chose to stay at Harvard and study at Harvard Law School. He served as editor of the Harvard Law Review for two years and graduated summa cum laude after three years. That summer, William passed the bar exam with flying colors.

While at Harvard, William joined the Reserve Officer Training Corps (ROTC) so he graduated as a second lieutenant. As part of his ROTC contract, he was obligated to serve a three-year term in the military after graduation. Shortly after his graduation, William's father called him into the library at the family's estate and asked him to sit down. The wood cases in the room were lined neatly with rare books and every free inch of wall space was consumed with photos of the Ambassador posing with kings, queens, prime ministers, and presidents, as well as awards of recognition and service. There was even a citation from King John, William's true birth grandfather.

"You wanted to see me, Dad?" William said.

"Yes," the Ambassador said. "It's been arranged. I've talked to some friends of mine and you will be going to London and working as a lawyer in the Judge Advocate General's office at the American Embassy. My friends there will take good care of you."

William smiled. "I really don't need taking care of, Dad; I'm pretty capable of doing that myself."

"I know that, son, but I'm talking about making sure you get every opportunity to succeed and move up," his dad countered. "You know, getting the right assignments or cases and meeting the right people. Contacts, William, contacts are everything. If you know the right people, you will always get things done. Look at your grandfather...without his hard work and contacts, the Carnegie name and fortune would not exist. "

"I know, Dad, but I'd rather do it myself. I've worked hard at school and done pretty well for myself. I did it on my own, and I feel that I would be a better man if I continued to make my own future."

"You will make your own future, William. But that includes taking advantage of family friends and contacts. You are a Carnegie; don't ever sell that asset short. Incidentally, you are now of the age that allows you considerable access to the family trust. So be careful with that power, and remember, be generous, but cautious. Money is the most intoxicating of all drugs. You will never know for sure if people like you or your money. Your mother and I are very proud of you. You've always excelled in all that you have undertaken, and no amount of help in the world can take that away from you."

"Thank you, Dad, for your confidence and kind words. I am blessed with so much, but you and mother are among my best blessings. I am honored to be a Carnegie and cherish my heritage and family. But...can't you understand that I also want to be my own man, achieving success by earning it, not by connections and influence?"

"Son, I completely appreciate and understand what you are saying. In fact, I admire it greatly. But don't be foolish. What you achieved on your own is what will make you successful. Having access, on the other hand, will just give you the opportunity to demonstrate it in the right places. "

William thought about arguing further, but instead broke into a wide smile. "Dad, you are incorrigible, but I can't argue with your logic. But don't get carried away, an introduction would be just fine, nothing more."

"Carried away? Of course not, William, not me. Just an introduction now and then. That's all. No pressure on anyone, just a simple introduction."

"Fine, Dad. I'm game."

"Now go to Britain and show them what you have," his father said. "Never forget you are a Carnegie. And always do the right thing. It matters. When in doubt, go with your gut feeling and trust your instincts. They're usually right."

William got up, and then impulsively hugged his slightly startled father. "Thanks again, Dad. For everything. I'll do my best to live up to the Carnegie name."

He left the library feeling good about their conversation, good about his chances of success in life, good about living *la dolce vita*, or the good life. Being a Carnegie was an incredible privilege, but it came with a heavy weight of expectation. William was confident, however, and believed that he had already shown his mettle. And Second Lieutenant Carnegie was going to London, his assignment orders in hand and his future in the wind.

The following Monday, the family car arrived at the estate and William's trunks and bags were packed for the trip over. He eagerly anticipated getting to know his mother's country and city better, with no idea of what awaited him "across the pond."

CHAPTER 14
BRIEF ENCOUNTER

THE FIVE-DAY TRIP ACROSS THE ATLANTIC WAS UNEVENTFUL. WILLIAM had booked passage on one of the newer transatlantic liners and spent as much time as possible on the top decks, watching the ocean roll underneath the ship and embracing the chill air. He felt as if every moment of this trip was consequential and draped in hidden meanings. After so long in the safe cocoon of school and family, he was finally heading off to make his own fortune! It seemed fitting that he would begin his adult life this way: alone on a ship, steaming across the Atlantic at breakneck speed, toward a new country and open future.

When he arrived in London, it took two days to unpack not only the luggage he carried with him, but the mountains of trunks and shipping crates his mother had sent ahead. Settled into his new living quarters, and always eager to get started, he went to the embassy in Grosvenor Square on this third day to meet his new superiors. The American Embassy was located in the Macdonald House, an imposing seven-story brick building at 1 Grosvenor Square. When he arrived and announced himself, he was directed to the JAG officer in charge. He entered the small office and found his superior at a desk, leafing through a file. The man looked up as William entered and saluted.

"Lt. William Carnegie, reporting for duty, sir."

He returned the salute. "Nice to meet you, Lieutenant. At ease, and you can sit down. I'm Major Gallagher." He nodded at the file in his hand. "I'm just now reviewing your personnel file. Quite impressive. Harvard Law and top of the class, *Law Review*, well done."

"Thank you, sir. I look forward to doing a good job for you here at the embassy."

The major smiled thinly and stood up, which was William's signal to rise also. "I'm sure you will, young man. After all, you are a Carnegie, and your family has quite the reputation here. Now, go find Sergeant Major Russo and he will get you settled in. Dismissed."

William smartly returned the salute, turned on his heel, and went to find Sergeant Major Russo.

As he had at school, William threw himself into his duties at the embassy and immediately earned the respect and admiration of his colleagues. It was normal for a young JAG officer to go through a period of initiation, getting the worst assignments and handling the more boring cases. But William's time spent in this purgatory was remarkably brief—he was almost immediately fast-tracked to the better assignments, and to his satisfaction no one could claim he was coasting on his family name alone. It was clear he excelled at his work and he found it challenging and rewarding.

Socially, William earned the same rapid acceptance. The diplomatic circles in London were actually fairly small—there was a tight-knit diplomatic community that included many British and foreign aristocratic families. William traveled easily in these circles and his social calendar quickly filled.

Night after night would find William at the theater, dinner parties, diplomatic receptions, and sporting events. Word quickly circulated among London's young women of a certain station that a dashing, brilliant and eligible young Carnegie was working at the American Embassy, and William found himself nearly suffocating under concentrated female attention. He was flattered, naturally, but he had also been raised to be cautious. William knew of too many young men who had derailed their careers with an ill-advised affair, so he was careful to avoid any situation that could be taken out of context. He was determined not to let one lapse in judgment ruin everything he had worked for—but of course, with London's most beautiful women trailing after him, it wasn't easy.

In part because it was his nature, and in part to keep himself focused, William attacked his work with vigor and soon distinguished himself when dealing with complicated legal challenges regarding diplomatic relations. William quickly became the embassy's in-house expert in this area of obscure and tricky law. His English colleagues quickly coined a phrase that followed him around London: "Life as Lt. William Harrington Carnegie is brilliant!"

One evening, on the way to yet another art gallery gala, William popped into a local greengrocer to pick up a pack of cigarettes. While waiting on the cashier's line, he noticed a young woman in front of him. She was trying to pay for her basket of sundry items, including baby necessities like nappies, baby shampoo, several bottles of milk, and baby food. He was mildly annoyed at first—thinking he'd be stuck in this line forever—until he saw the woman's face. She was a stunning redhead of almost breathtaking beauty: fiery red hair put up in a twist, green eyes set into a perfectly striking face, and full lips covered with a bright red lip-gloss. William wondered what those lips would be like to kiss.

He next noticed her body. He had to pull his eyes away from her full breasts, which teasingly pressed against her bright green sweater, lest he seem indecent. But then he wasn't sure where he could look. Her legs were long and flawless: shapely, sensual, well-proportioned, and athletic. There was no safe way to look at this woman without fear of leaving his mouth hanging open.

Then he finally tuned into the conversation she was having with the clerk.

"That'll be sixteen quid," the clerk said.

"Oh dear," she said. "I'm a bit short. I've only thirteen quid and still need money for the Underground."

The clerk rolled his eyes. "Sorry then, lamie, but we are not in the charity business here. I'm afraid you have to put something back. And make it quick. I have people behind you waiting to be served."

"But I need *all* of this for the children. They are hungry and must be bathed."

So she was married with children and therefore off-limits. William deflated like a punctured balloon.

"I'm sorry, Missy," the clerk said sarcastically. "But like I said, I ain't no charity! Now what will you put back, the milk or the shampoo? Get on it. I can't wait all night."

Before he could think about what he was doing, William stepped up to the counter and, in a stern voice, said, "See here, mate, treat this lady with respect and kindness."

The clerk's eyes flicked to William, and then he frowned. "What's it to you, Yank? She can't pay."

"Can't you see this woman has a need and you are being as cold-hearted as a slum lord on rent day? She may be a bit short on funds, but it's no excuse to be disrespectful."

"Look, chum, I'm not here to give stuff away. I'm here to sell it. So bugger off, the both of you."

William had to bite back an angry retort—he had rarely ever been disrespected to his face before. Instead, he pulled out a clip of bills. "Then

I'll take care of it. And next time I'm here, your manager will hear about your lack of manners."

The clerk eyed the bills, and then snorted a short laugh. "You can tell him anything you want, mate, but if you think he's in the business of giving away goods, you're in for a nasty shock. And as for you, Missy," he turned back to the woman, who was standing silently and watching the exchange, "looks like your lucky day."

Seeing the bills, however, the woman backed away from her basket. "Oh no! That's very kind of you, sir, but I couldn't possibly let you pay!"

"Of course you can," William said. "I can afford it, and the least I can do as a civil human," and here he shot the clerk a look, "is help you ensure your children are fed and clean."

"But—"

"Please," William said, dropping bills on the counter. "Let me do this for you. You'll be doing me a kindness. Just kiss your kids and tell them Santa Claus came early this year."

The woman frowned. "Santa Claus? Who's that?"

William laughed, more attracted than ever to this direct, frank woman. "You probably know him as Father Christmas."

The woman threw her head back in sudden laughter, her red curls bouncing off her shoulders. "Yes, *that* Santa Claus! I see. You're American." She peered at him, playfully pretending to inspect him. "Well, you certainly don't look like a fat old man, do you? Where's your sleigh and coat?"

Now it was William's turn to laugh. "I'm afraid I left them at home in the States." He paused. "I'm William."

She nodded. "Regina. Pleased to make your acquaintance, William Claus. And thank ye."

William paid for both of their purchases and they walked toward the shop exit together. William glanced sidelong at her: even in profile, she was beautiful. "I'm sorry," he said. "I'm not in the habit of intruding like that... but that clerk got under my skin. He clearly had no idea how to treat a lady or what the concept of charity looks like."

Regina waved it aside. "No worries. And he was right anyway. I should have had the right amount of money. I'm not in the practice of throwing myself on the mercy of store clerks either!"

They reached the door to the shop, and by some mutual agreement, stopped on the sidewalk outside. "So you know I'm American," William said. "I'm guessing you're from..." he paused, drawing it out. "Ireland."

"It's the brogue, is it?" she said, rolling her "r" impressively. "That's right."

"And how old are your children, then?" he asked, thinking that the proper thing to do would be to bid her farewell and leave instead of finding excuses to draw the conversation out.

"My children?" She laughed again, and if possible he found her even more attractive. In the few minutes they'd known each other, she'd shown herself to be proud, quick-witted, and easy to laughter. "Oh dear, I have no children. I'm not even married. I'm buying these things for the Irish orphans brought here from Belfast, to get away from the terror and war."

"Ah." As a member of the American Embassy, William was familiar with the war—he had heard his English colleagues talk about it many times, and never approvingly. The Irish were rebelling against English rule and the monarchy, agitating for freedom from British rule. The fighting had been escalating. As an American, William sympathized with the Irish side, but as a lawyer and diplomat, he also saw the British argument.

He filed this away and concentrated on the part of what she said that really interested him: "I see. So not your kids, you say? Not married either?"

"You're awfully forward," she said, a smile playing around her lips. "But that's right. They're only kids in the sense that they're Irish and we have to stick together. They've been orphaned by the Brits and need food, clothing.

Love. With more wee tikes coming every month. I do my best to help them, but funds are short and helpers are rare. We bring them to England to get away from the violence and poverty, but sometimes I fear life isn't much better here for them. They live in ghettos and rely on volunteers and the Church for care. It's tragic."

William watched her in growing fascination. Here was a woman who was not only beautiful, but compassionate and willing to take action, even when it might be dangerous. He had no illusions: he knew that suspected Irish nationals were viewed with suspicion and sometimes even arrested. He found himself more attracted to her than ever.

"Perhaps I can help," he said slowly. "I know some people who would be willing to help poor children regardless of where they come from and what their parents believe or do not believe."

"Really? You'd help us?"

"Of course. Give me your number and I'll call…er, ring you soon."

She smiled. "That would be brilliant. Thank you!"

She wrote her phone number down in a lovely, looping handwriting and handed it to him. He glanced at it, then folded the paper and slid it into his pocket. "Thank you," he said, bowing slightly. "Till we speak again."

They went their separate ways: Regina down the sidewalk with her basket of goods, and William toward an art exhibit he hardly even remembered why he wanted to attend anymore. His mind was filled with images of Regina, and even the beautiful artwork could not distract him or pull him away. Rather, he spent the evening debating how soon he should call her. Would it seem desperate to call her that night? Or impolite to wait too long?

These thoughts were still consuming him long after he had returned to his quarters. Although he was a second lieutenant, William's quarters were a good deal nicer than the average second lieutenant's chambers. He had a spacious apartment with excellent views of the street—no doubt another "bennie" from his father's connections. He slipped into bed that night, still thinking of Regina. He had settled at least one question: he would call upon her tomorrow, after arranging to make some funds available to help the Irish children orphaned by war.

The next morning, after he had showered and dressed, he went to his office and, try as he may, he could not keep the beautiful redhead from his thoughts. The day dragged as he waited the five hours to place a call to his contact at the Bank of New York, where the Carnegie Trust fund was held and managed. In short order, he was connected with Tucker Priestley III, the trust fund manager and one of the trustees.

"Tucker!" William said. "How are you?"

"I'm well," crackled Tucker's voice across the transatlantic line. "It's wonderful to hear from you. But of course I assume this isn't a social call. What can I do for you?"

"I want to give some money to help some war orphans here in London. They need everything…food, clothing, places to live, the whole nine yards."

"Of course. Is this a charitable organization, something that qualifies for tax deductions?"

William chuckled again. "No idea, Tucker. That's what you're for! All I know is these children need help. Is that something I can do with the trust?"

"Well, William, of course. My advice, though, is to think about the tax implications of any charitable giving—"

"Tucker, I just want to know if I have access to money to use as I please."

Tucker sighed. "Yes, William, you do. When you turned eighteen, after your grandfather's death, the trust gave you access to a discretionary account."

"Discretionary? Whose discretion?"

"Yours. No explanation is necessary. Your grandfather set this up to cover incidental items and does not require trustee review and red tape."

"That sounds good. How much can I get from that account, and how soon?"

"Each withdrawal cannot exceed $45,000, which can be made anytime during a thirty-day period. The account value, in case that's your next question, is about $700,000."

William was stunned into silence for a second. Of course he had always known his family was among the richest in the world—he had grown up surrounded by tremendous wealth and privilege. But never before had he personally had access to, and control over, so much money.

"Excellent. So how do I get ahold of, say, $10,000?" William asked.

"You need only to send me wiring instructions where to transfer the funds. It usually takes only hours, but given that you are in the UK and the time difference, it could take up to twenty-four hours."

"Thank you," William said. "I'll wire instructions to you ASAP."

They rang off, and William took a moment to gather himself. Then he got out the scrap of paper on which Regina had scribbled her phone number. He dialed her number and let it ring almost seven times before a woman abruptly answered and, in a thick Irish accent, barked, "Hello? Hello?"

"Uh, hello. Is Regina available?"

"No," the woman said. "She's at work. Don't know when she'll return."

"Oh. Um, I'm a friend with news for her. Do you have a phone number I could ring for her?"

"Ha!" the woman said. "Don't know how good of a friend you can be if you don't know where she works. There's no bloody phones at the flea market."

"Right," William said a little more sharply then he intended. "Could you perhaps take a message then?"

"What do you think I am? A bloody answering service?"

"No, but it's critical that I reach Regina as soon as possible so—"

"Well then call back later when she's here." And the woman hung up.

William put down the phone and thought, "Goodness, I hope that wasn't her mother."

William did finally reach Regina and made a date to meet. He told her he had arranged for someone to help with the children and he needed to know the particulars. Regina suggested meeting at a popular local pub and William tried not to feel like a nervous teenager as he said good-bye and hung up.

CHAPTER 15
No Good Deed Goes Unpunished

WILLIAM WALKED INTO THE DIM PUB AND WAS INSTANTLY ASSAULTED with the odor of stale smoke and beer. Of course he had been in plenty of pubs before, but they tended to be the sort of pub where higher-class Britons gathered to share a pint and discuss politics, money, or enjoy a game of darts while sipping a twelve-year-old scotch or Chardonnay. This pub was different...darker, smoke-stained, and there was a thin Irish reel playing from a radio behind the bar. On the stools perched an assortment of regulars like large birds sipping away at their foaming pints of bitter ale. When he entered, almost every eye cast a furtive glance in his direction, and then quickly looked away. He had the feeling he had walked into a private conversation, but couldn't imagine for the life of him what they were talking about. Most of them looked nearly ruined from years of drinking.

He strolled across the room to a small table, self-consciously aware that every eye in the place was staring at him, thinking who the hell is this tall, well-dressed stranger. William stood out like a diamond in a potato bin. He had rarely felt such a guarded atmosphere.

It wasn't long before Regina entered the dank pub like a ray of sunlight. She wore a tight-fitting wool dress that hugged her in the right places, and her red hair tumbled over her shoulders, framing her face with those brilliant green eyes. Once again, he was instantly captivated by her beauty and her confident grace as she looked around the room, saw him, and broke into a smile as she waved. He waved back and only then realized that she wasn't alone. A tall man stood behind her, studying William over Regina's shoulder with a look that could only be described as hostile.

William rose from his chair as they approached, taking her hand briefly and extending his hand to the tall man beside Regina, the whole time wondering who this man was and fighting back a sinking feeling. Of course a woman like Regina would be taken! William felt like a fool for assuming she would have any interest in him beyond whatever help he could provide for the children.

"Delightful to see you again," Regina said, releasing his hand.

"You too," William answered. "And nice to meet you too, mister…?"

"Roan Kelly," the man said gruffly, still not extending his hand.

William was no closer to figuring who Roan was when Regina laughed lightly and said, "Stop staring at each other like angry dogs. Roan is my brother. I apologize for his manners!"

A bubble of relief exploded in William's chest. Of course! Her brother! "Ah, well, excellent," he said, taking his chair again and giving Roan a big smile. Naturally he wanted the brother on his side!

Roan sat down more slowly, no matching smile on his face. Looking more closely at Roan, William wondered how he hadn't noticed their resemblance immediately. In the most masculine way, Roan was as handsome as Regina was beautiful, strong with deliberate features. Roan's green eyes, though not as green or intense as Regina's, glowed with determination and intelligence. He had red hair too, although not the fiery red of Regina's. His tall, almost military posture made it clear he was in excellent shape.

Finally, Roan gave William a thin smile. "Nice to meet you too, mate. So you're not English?"

"Err, no," William said, glancing at Regina. "I'm American."

"Oh, well you should have said so right off the bat," Roan said, his expression transforming. "Always liked a good American. Figure us Irish could learn a thing or two from you muckers."

"Well then we're even," William said. "You should have said you were her brother right off the bat! Although I should have guessed from the family resemblance."

"So," Regina cut in smoothly, leaning forward. "William, you mentioned you had good news? I told my brother about your generosity at the greengrocer the other night. You were so kind."

William cleared his throat. "Ah, yes. Well, I happen to have a few contacts who are well-connected back in the States. I mentioned to them that I had run into a lovely woman who was supporting needy orphans, and, ah, inquiries were made about how we could help provide for the children."

"Oh, that's wonderful!" Regina said. "What we need most, really, is money to support the homes, to buy food and clothing. I hate to be so blunt about it, but...it is the truth."

"No, no, of course," William quickly said, not wanting her to look uncomfortable for even a second. "That's exactly what we had in mind. I've gotten verbal authority to offer $10,000 to help feed and care for the orphans. Would that be...enough?"

A stunned silence gripped his table companions. William wasn't naïve about how much money he had just proposed. It was more than most families back in the States would earn in a year. Regina suddenly grabbed William's hand and her eyes glittered with tears. "Do you mean it? Are ye telling us the truth?"

"Of course!" William said.

"Then it's a miracle, by God," Regina said. "You're an incarnate miracle!" She quickly crossed herself and looked up, "Thank you, Jesus! Thank you, dear Mary, Mother of God!"

Suspicion, however, had fallen over Roan's features once again. "You're serious are ye now?" he asked.

"Yes, very much so."

"You meet my sister once at a shop and now come in offering us a king's ransom? What's your angle, mate?"

"No angle," William said. "I simply don't believe that children should suffer because of politics. It seems to me there's been enough of that in the world lately."

"Hmm," Roan said. He appeared to be thinking for a long while, then said, "You know, our mum had a saying for when we were young. She always used to say, 'No good deed goes unpunished.' I'll acknowledge it's an Irish way to look at the world, but then look at the world we've been given. Ground under the heel of the British boot. So you'll forgive me—"

"Roan!" Regina cut in sharply. "You're being awfully rude! And ungrateful too!"

"No, no," William said hurriedly. "It's perfectly understandable. I would be wary also, if a stranger showed up offering me such a generous gift. But, brother, all I can tell you is that this is for real, and that indeed the suffering of children moves me as it should move all decent men. I understand your worry, and all I can say is that I am a man of honor who means what I say and strives in every circumstance to do the right thing by my fellow man!"

William finished his speech with his voice raised, carried away by the emotions that sprung up inside him. Regina watched throughout, her eyes soft, and when he was done, even Roan seemed impressed. He nodded and slowly extended his hand. "You're right, my friend. I'm sorry for treating you rudely. When you've spent as long as we have harried and harassed, it's hard to believe when good fortune smiles on you. Forgiven?"

"Without a doubt," William said, shaking Roan's hand and full of emotion. "So what's next, then?"

Roan appeared to consider this for a moment, as Regina watched him. "Well, how do you plan on giving the money? Cash?"

William found himself jerked back somewhat rudely into reality. The prospect of handing over $10,000 in cash was outlandish—even presumptuous. "No, never cash, that's too risky. It would be too much of a temptation for it to get lost or stolen. The only safe and secure way to give the money would be by wire transfer. Is there a bank set up to help this charity? I mean, you must have accounts somewhere?"

Regina began to answer, but Roan cut her off.

"Naturally the orphans have no accounts, and the British keep a close eye on any Irish charities, but there's a bank in Ireland where you can wire the money and it will be distributed. Regina here can make sure the needs of the children are met.

She smiled and nodded.

"That sounds good," William said. "Can you give me the bank's wiring instructions?"

"I'll have the information to you within a few days. It takes a bit of sorting out, but I will get it organized as soon as possible," Roan said.

"Thank you, Roan," Regina said. "And most of all, thank you, William. You truly are a saint."

With business concluded, Roan signaled the bartender to pour three foaming mugs of a thick, black stout. It was by far the thickest beer William had ever drunk, more like a food than a proper beer. When he said as much,

Regina and Roan howled with laughter and told him that it was one of the oldest stouts in the world. Hours later, their table littered with condensation rings and his head heavy from the thick beer, William and his new friends prepared to leave. Perhaps it was the beer, but William rashly asked Regina to meet him for dinner the next night, and she readily agreed. When he offered to pick her up, she hesitated and instead said she'd rather meet William at the restaurant, that he wouldn't want to see where she lived. William brushed aside her concerns and gave her the name of his favorite restaurant—the Hix Mayfair located in Brown's hotel—and told her to meet him there at 8:45 the next night.

They met the next night, and again the night after that and the one after that. William had never fallen for a woman as quickly as he was falling for Regina—it seemed that from the first moment he had laid eyes on her, she eclipsed nearly everything else in his world. In those first heady months, as they dined together, strolled in parks, told corny jokes, and took carriage rides around historic London, William made two wire transfers to Belfast almost as an afterthought. Regina excitedly told him all the things she was buying for the children: shoes, clothing, books, food, even toys for children who had either never had toys or who had lost them all when their homes were destroyed by the British. For William, every story he heard of an orphan he had helped felt like another page in the book his heart was writing to Regina.

One morning, William awoke to the full, nearly painful realization that he was hopefully in love with Regina. And he suspected she felt the same way. He had no idea where their relationship was heading, but no sooner had he thought, "I'm in love with her," that a nearly crushing wave of desire swamped him and he felt like he couldn't wait another minute to see her and lay his heart at her feet.

CHAPTER 16
WILL YOU LOVE ME TOMORROW?

Hotel Avalon by the Sea, Brighton, England

THEY DROVE OUT OF LONDON HEADING SOUTH TOWARD BRIGHTON, driving along picturesque roads through rolling country dotted with small villages and farms. William had hired a convertible for the trip, so they had the top down and Regina laughed as her hair flowed in the wind, dancing around her head like a halo of fire. William thought he had never seen anything so beautiful—and found himself once again imagining her beside him in bed. Regina was not only a good Catholic girl, but an old-fashioned one too. So the subject of physical intimacy had never truly been broached. They had kissed and embraced often but Regina was careful to insist on keeping her Catholic respectability and William was equally careful to respect the sanctity of her body. Yet it had not always been easy, especially for the all-American red-blooded William.

Too soon, it seemed the sleek cabriolet pulled up in front of the hotel at 151 Pulpit Rock Way. The drive had flown by, alternating between comfortable silences and easy conversation about their times in London, Regina's work with children, William's work with the embassy, and their families. William felt there was nothing he couldn't share with Regina, and he was equally impressed that she didn't seem too focused on his family's wealth. If anything, the idea that he came from such a distinguished, high-profile family seemed to give her pause.

Avalon by the Sea was not a showy or posh hotel, which was exactly why William had picked it. He knew they would never run into anyone he knew at such an obscure and modest place. For this weekend, William hoped they would be able to enjoy a romantic weekend together, totally focused on one another. In truth, he hoped this weekend would mark a turning point in their relationship—he was more than ready to take their relationship to the next level.

They entered the small hotel and found a clerk waiting behind the counter in a cozy, deserted lobby that smelled of fresh-cut flowers in vases that had been strategically placed on side tables. Overall, the impression was one of well-worn comfort and romantic seclusion. It was perfect. The clerk, an elderly woman who was impeccably outfitted, greeted them kindly as William registered them as Mr. and Mrs. Arlington, the name of the street where he lived in London.

"Ah, yes," she said. "We've been expecting you. We've prepared your room for you, a lovely room with a beautiful view for such a handsome couple. I daresay you'll love the morning breeze if you open the window."

"Thank you," William said, noticing Regina blushing furiously next to him. Clearly, pretending to be William's wife had sent her mind down the same path as William's.

The clerk smartly rang the bell and a short, bandy-legged man in a red coat appeared and introduced himself as Reginald, the "bellman, hall porter, waiter, gardener, and all-'round jack of the trades here at the Avalon."

"Room 22," the clerk said, and Reginald gave them a knowing wink that caused Regina's color to deepen to approximately the color of a tomato.

William found himself enjoying her demure modesty. It made her all the more enticing.

Room 22 was everything the clerk had said and much more. It was a spacious suite actually, with two sets of French doors that opened onto a Juliet balcony and gave a direct view of the glittering ocean beyond. The room was decorated in English cottage style, with a comfortable easy chair and dressing table in front of one set of French doors and a wardrobe that Reginald opened up so they could hang their clothes. The center of the room was dominated by a raised double bed with a Victorian chandelier overhead. A small coal-burning fireplace with an ornate, sparkling mirror over the mantle reflected the room's image, giving the impression of a much larger space. William thought it a bit shabby, but certainly chic. As for Regina, she had never even stayed in a hotel room.

Reginald crossed to the French doors. "Mr. Arlington, sir, shall I open the French doors for some fresh air?"

It took William a moment to realize that Reginald was speaking to him, and then said, "Yes, please do."

Reginald threw the doors open and a fresh sea breeze flowed in, with the far-off sounds of waves crashing against the shore. "Best room in the house, sir, if you don't mind my saying so. Wait till you and the Mrs. see the sunset."

Regina, who had finally stopped blushing, once again turned crimson at being called "the Mrs."—and once again, William found himself charmed and amused by her modest embarrassment.

"Yes sir, the best in the house, sir. You and the Mrs. are going to love the sea breeze and the beautiful sunset."

Then Reginald was gone, pocketing William's generous tip and leaving with a parting word of wisdom: "Enjoy your honeymoon!"

When they were finally alone in the room, with the sea air flowing in on a copious river of sunshine, William turned to Regina and found her staring at the bed with something very much like fear on her face.

"Are you okay?" he asked.

She nodded a little nervously. "I dunno," she said. "I feel like I shouldn't be here right now. It's not proper for a girl like myself to be pretending to be married and staying alone with a man who's not her husband."

William took her hand. "I understand. I do. But how can anything that's wrong feel as right as this? You feel it too. You must know I love you."

She looked at him. "I know you do, and I love you also. But…" She stopped and stammered over her next words. "You must know there hasn't been anyone else for me."

William smiled. "I had assumed that. But you can trust me. You know that, right? You can trust that I'll always treat you with respect, and that your boundaries are my boundaries too."

"I know," she said. "But…you spend your whole life telling yourself not to do something, so when that moment arrives that you tell yourself it's okay to do it…it's hard not to feel the guilt of it. You understand what I'm saying?"

"Yes. But then there's this." He kissed her gently, and while she resisted at first, eventually she responded and the flames of her passion seemed to suddenly ignite. It was like a dam had burst, and within seconds, they were ravenously expressing themselves, hungry to be close.

"Hold up," she whispered, breaking away and stepping back. "I'll be back in a minute."

She went to the loo, while William took of his shoes and jacket first, then stripped to his boxers, and reclined on the bed, watching the door and feeling like he would burst at any second.

When she emerged, she took his breath away. She was totally naked, using only a small towel to cover herself. She looked at him shyly, perhaps for validation, but the hunger and passion in William's eyes sent the message more adequately than any words would have.

Her body was as beautiful outwardly as she was inwardly. She was firm and feminine in every way, with full breasts, shapely hips, and pale pink skin. She looked as if she had been painted by a Renaissance master. Her long, silky red hair cascaded down her shoulders and hung to the small of her back.

William reached for her and drew her onto the bed. He began to caress her warm, pale body, kissing her lips. This was not their first kiss, but it was their most magical one, since they both knew it would lead to more, much more. Timidly, Regina began to explore William's body. He was an image of perfect masculinity and impeccably proportioned. As for William, Regina was everything he dreamed of. He found his hands discovering Regina's firm breasts and flat stomach. He began to explore more intimate places, probing and feeling.

Regina grabbed his hand and pulled away. William stopped, waiting to see if she wanted them to stop entirely, but then she removed her hand from his and allowed William to proceed. She pressed herself against him and placed her hand on William's significant manliness; lightly stroking him, he became more and more alive. William was tender with her, and after a long while of exploring each other, Regina signaled she was ready to give her virtue to William. William entered her gently and slowly. She cringed more with hesitation than pain, but then she relaxed and began to enjoy the slow, methodical rhythm of the act of love. William grasped her hips and drew her closer, penetrating deeper and deeper. William had dreamt of this moment for months, and now that it was here, he was reveling in its entirety.

No man had ever really touched Regina, but as they moved together, she gave herself to the experience and, without reservation or regret, surrendered her virtue as she was gripped by a climax that ripped a throaty cry from her lips at the same moment William strained against her. William exploded within her, and she felt the warmth of his seed seeping deeply into her, traveling into her body and her soul.

Afterward, lying next to each other in the gloom of the evening, Regina whispered, "William, you've made me yours now. You said you loved me. But will you love me tomorrow?"

He rolled toward her. "My darling Regina, I will love you tomorrow, and the tomorrow after that, and the tomorrow after that one. I will love you until I die."

She smiled at him.

The couple spent most of the entire weekend in their room, the dishes stacking up from room service deliveries until Reginald could clear them away. They filled the hours with lovemaking, learning a new shared vocabulary of love. Sometimes, late at night, the lovers would slip out of their room and run across the street to the beach, where they'd sit on the sand and watch the breakers roll in foamy waves, expiring on the sand at their feet.

"It's beautiful," she said late one night, wrapped in a blanket with him and watching the foaming waves reflect moonlight. "I swear it, William; I never knew I could be this happy."

"No, neither did I," he said. "I wish we could stay here forever and never go back."

On their last night in Brighton, William and Regina lay on the sand looking up at the stars. As they cuddled in the cool night air, the conversation turned to their past lives, and she filled in the picture for him. He had known her upbringing was different than his, but he had no idea how different. She was an orphan herself and told stories of running through the streets of Belfast in little more than rags, begging food from passersby in carriages and carts. As soon as she was old enough, she immigrated to Britain, hoping she could carve out a better life for herself in London. Roan had come with her, and since then, they had watched out for each other, working to overcome the curse of being Irish in London.

"Curse?" William said. "It hardly seems a curse."

"T'isn't," she answered. "Not to me. But it bothers Roan constantly, the reminders he sees every day of the Brits. He hates them, you know."

"Yeah," William said. "I got that feeling. It's a good thing I'm an American or he'd never tolerate us being together."

She snorted. "Roan doesn't pick my boyfriends," she said. "Try as he might, he's not my pa."

William laughed.

"And now you. How is it that a man so young works for the embassy and goes around giving away a king's ransom to orphaned children?"

William told her what he could of his background, but withheld most of the details. Obviously, she knew just from his name that he had come from money, but he saw no reason to make it clear just how vast the gulf was between their backgrounds. When he was done, she was propped up on an elbow, watching him.

"You know this will be a problem, right?" she said matter-of-factly. "What would your people say if you showed up with a poor Irish girl of no background and no education? The closest anyone in your circle has ever been to a person like me is if they're serving tea as a servant in a uniform."

"Wait a second," he said. "That's not fair. My parents would love you, because I love you. And if they didn't, they'd have to deal with me. I don't look at people in terms of their wealth or families. I look at their character, and you are incredible."

But she wouldn't be mollified. "You say that now, Mr. William Carnegie. But I've seen this before. They'll think I'm after your money. Or worse."

"Nonsense," William said. "You will put all of them to shame with your kindness and good heart. No one worth knowing would ever think ill of you. Within seconds of meeting you, anyone would be able to discern you are what you are: a wonderful, loving person. And if they miss that, well then they are oblivious fools, not you."

"You're an adorable one, but I think hopelessly naïve—"

"No," William interrupted. "Look, my family knows me. My friends know me. I don't bring girls round, I don't play the field. If I bring a girl home like you, they'll know it's because I'm madly in love with her, and if they trust and respect me at all, they will take the time to discover the same wonderful qualities about you that I already have."

"Sweet words," she murmured. "No wonder you're an excellent barrister."

Soon they brushed off the sand and returned to room 22, where they lay comfortably in bed, each perhaps lost in their own thoughts about returning to the world. Although William had not admitted it out loud, he knew that Regina had a point. He wasn't so naïve about the way of the world. He knew this weekend was a bubble, an escape from reality they had created for themselves. It was a kind of magic, he thought, like being transported to another, more beautiful world where all that mattered was the sound of waves crashing on the beach and Regina. He dozed off finally, his hand curled around her arm.

The next morning dawned grey, with rain spitting from low clouds. It was appropriate weather, because as with all good things, their interlude was over. It was time to pack up and head back up to London, to their lives, their families, and a future they would have to carve out together, for William's thoughts had already turned to marriage.

CHAPTER 17
Too Good to Be True

After returning from their weekend in Brighton, William moved out of his embassy quarters into a small but posh Mayfair flat. It was cozy and very comfortable in every way and had everything the couple needed: a lovely sitting room, an adequate kitchen, and a great balcony overlooking a beautiful English garden. But most importantly to William, the flat had an enormous bedroom. Together, William and Regina went shopping in a Portobello antique shop and chose a fantastic canopy bed and coordinating side tables. The ensemble was fitted out with stunning bed linens and drapery in a beautiful green quilted fabric that perfectly matched Regina's piercing eyes.

Once settled back at work, William also wrote his parents and told them about Regina. He was careful in his letter to describe Regina's warmth and character, her work with the orphans, and let them know in no uncertain terms that he was head-over-heels in love with this woman and expected them to be married soon. They cabled back quickly, announcing they were planning a trip to London around Christmastime to meet the "new girlfriend," but they had no doubt that if William loved her, they would also love her. Once again, William reflected how fortunate he was to have parents who supported him the way they did.

As Christmas approached—and Regina fretted about meeting William's parents—the couple threw themselves into creating a new life together. They spent their free days roaming London and buying knick-knacks and Christmas decorations for their flat, which Regina threw herself into decorating. For a woman who never had any kind of luxuries, Regina felt she was living a fairytale. Few places are as romantic as London during the Christmas season, and William felt he was living in a dreamland as he walked through the lighted city that smelled of delicious baked goods and the sharp tang of winter. As will happen with young lovers, the romance didn't stop at sunset: they spent their evenings and nights wound in each other's arms, making love again and again. William felt he could never be satisfied, could never get enough of Regina—and to his surprise and immense pleasure, she quickly recovered from her initial embarrassment and seemed to feel the same way.

As the holiday approached, they also spent more and more time with Roan, who seemed delighted with his sister's choice in boyfriends. He often asked William to meet him for a drink at this or that pub, and they spent long hours talking about politics and the Irish cause. William quickly learned that Roan had immense passion for his people and country—sometimes almost too much as he was quick to anger when the subject was the English occupation of Ireland. Yet when they avoided this topic, they got along famously, and William was thrilled to deepen his relationship with the man he fully expected to call brother in the near future. As Roan and William grew closer, it naturally developed that Roan took over managing William's charitable donations. By early December, William had wired $125,000 to the Irish bank, which Roan and Regina assured him was doing a world of good among the impoverished orphans.

Among the many things William loved about Regina, her care for the orphans was one of her best qualities. He never begrudged a penny he gave to the orphans, and never dreamt of insulting her by asking for a thorough accounting of where all the money was going exactly. It was clear from the way she talked that she identified strongly with the children, and that she would do anything to help them.

One December day, William announced he had a surprise for Regina and had a car take them to Harrods, the most famous and prestigious of London department stores. "What are we doing here?" she asked. "You must know how expensive this place is."

"You'll see," he said happily, guiding her to the toy department on the fourth floor. "I thought we could be Father and Mrs. Christmas this afternoon and buy toys for your children."

Regina, delighted as a teenager, jumped up and down in glee and began filling a shopping lorry with all manner of gifts. Within forty-five minutes' time, the couple had assembled more than two hundred gifts. Dolls, toy soldiers, games, and fancy dress costumes of princesses and knights were chosen. William picked out more than fifty die-cast model cars in a rainbow of colors, all from different countries.

By the time they wheeled their purchases to the counter, they had a baggage train of lorries overflowing with gifts and Regina's eyes were shining and her cheeks flushed. William had never seen her looking so beautiful.

"Excuse me," William signaled to a clerk. "We'll need some assistance here. I'd like to have all these gift-wrapped and marked for boys and girls."

"Certainly," the clerk said, looking a little apprehensively at the mountain of gifts.

"And we'll need them delivered." William looked at Regina, "To...?"

"Have them sent to St. Martin's Church on Rockingham Lane," Regina said. "Father Ryan will know what to do with them. He coordinates all of the orphan placements. Oh Lord, he will die when he sees what you have done for all those lovely children."

William stole a quick kiss. "Not what I have done, but what we have done. Remember you are my partner in this."

In short order, the gifts were tallied, and by then they had attracted a small army of clerks and an assistant manager, who approached them with a long ledger and cleared his throat delicately. "Thank you, sir. We've arrived at a total of 2,890 pounds, including the wrapping. How would you like to pay this, sir?"

"I believe I have a Harrods account. It should be in the name Carnegie. I'm William Carnegie, from the American Embassy."

"Of course, sir. Please give me just a moment to verify it."

The assistant manager picked up the phone, repeated the order, and listened for a few moments. When he hung up, he looked at William with a newfound respect.

"Mr. Carnegie, this matter will be attended to with haste. The Harrods truck will be on the road first thing in the morning. Thank you sir, thank you for your order. Please let us know if there's anything—anything—else we at Harrods can do to ensure that you and Mrs. Carnegie have a Happy Christmas and the best of holiday seasons."

William and Regina, looking at each other, broke out in the broadest of smiles, and then William leaned in closely and whispered in Regina's ear: "I love to hear you called Mrs. Carnegie."

She giggled. "Me too, but I'm not sure what my mum would have thought, considering that Carnegie was a Scot!"

William laughed along—the thought had never crossed his mind before, but it was true. He had descended from Scots and English on his father's and mother's sides respectively and was planning to marry an Irishwoman and make her an American.

As the holiday itself approached, Regina's decorating in their small flat became a frenzy, and William wondered aloud if she was putting all her nervous energy over meeting his parents into holiday decorations. "It looks like the North Pole in here!" he teased her as she placed yet another garland up or created another plaid bow to adorn their already festooned fireplace. A tall Christmas tree stood by their balcony doors, its top brushing the ceiling and glittering with tinsel.

"Oh stop," she said. "Christmas is a very important holiday...it must be observed properly!"

Doing his part, William made sure a beautifully wrapped present appeared under the tree every morning—and every morning Regina would squeal with delight when she found it. She had all the joy of a child at Christmas, and it was William's fondest desire to spoil her rotten if she'd let him—for he knew that she had never had anyone spoil her before.

"But William," she said one morning, "you've already made me the happiest woman in London without a single gift. I only worry..."

"Worry? What's to worry about?" he said happily.

"Are you quite sure?"

"Sure of what?"

"Sure that your parents will like me?"

He laughed lightly. "Well, if they don't, I'll disown them!"

"Seriously, how do you know they won't hate me and think I'm not good enough for you?"

"You must stop worrying about this! They will love you because I love you. And that will be that."

"I hope so, William, because if they didn't, I think my heart might break."

"No, Regina, don't say that. You and me…we are forever, no matter what the world might try to throw at us."

"I hope so, darling. I truly hope so."

CHAPTER 18
All Good Things Must Come to an End

A week before Christmas, the phone rang in their flat and William picked it up. It was Roan, which by itself wasn't unusual, but William could tell from his voice that something serious was going on.

"You all right?" William asked his friend. "You sound upset."

"Right I am," Roan said bluntly. "Is Regina available? I need to speak with her."

"Of course."

William handed her the phone and watched carefully as she listened to Roan. William couldn't make out what Roan was saying, but he could tell from the look on Regina's face it was bad news. She hung up and sighed.

"What is it, Red?" he asked. "Is everything okay?"

"No, I'm afraid not," she said. "Roan asked me to go to Belfast and escort a group of children back down to London. Their neighborhood was attacked and their parents murdered by British soldiers. Oh Mary, Mother of God, when will the slaughter ever stop?"

William, rising to embrace and comfort Regina, answered, "That's horrible. I'm so sorry, sweetie. You go and do what you can to get those kids safe. Do they need more money?"

"I don't know, but I'll ask Roan. I hate to go now, your parents will be here in a few days and I don't want anything to take away from the time we will have with them."

"Don't worry about that," he said. "Go, and you'll be back in London in plenty of time. Go be the Christmas angel they need. When you get back, we will have the best holiday ever."

William saw her off on the train the next morning, kissing her gently goodbye and the wheels in his mind already turning. There was nothing he could do about the tragedy, but a plan was forming with something he could do for Regina. A few days' alone would be just what he needed to put his plan into place.

That afternoon, he slipped away from his desk and headed for Albemarble Street in the Mayfair section of London, to an imposing tan stone building that had housed Garrard since the eighteenth century. Standing outside the building, William found himself a little nervous and took a deep breath. Garrard was one of the most exclusive and famous jewelers in the world—it had been the Crown Jeweler since 1843, when Queen Victoria announced that Garrard would maintain the Crown Jewels, as well as design and create exclusive pieces for members of the royal family. William himself had a personal connection to the famous jeweler—his father had introduced him to the shop as a child, when William had accompanied the Ambassador on trips to choose jewelry for his mother. William could still recall the heavy silence of the store, the glittering diamonds and jewels under cases.

Laughing off his nerves, he opened the door and walked in, suddenly conscious that he was wearing his Army lieutenant uniform. He hadn't thought of it before, but he realized that Garrard likely didn't cater to many junior officers barely out of their twenties.

"Is there something I can help you with, *Lieutenant*?" a clerk asked him in a tone of voice that dripped with condescension. Apparently, the clerk had the same thought.

William smiled. "Yes. I'm looking for an engagement ring for my fiancé."

"I see. If you give me a better idea of precisely what you're looking for, I might be able to direct you to the appropriate outlet."

"Well," William said, feeling a little giddy from looking at the enormous gems glittering in the case and imagining any of these impressive stones adorning Regina's hand, "as my father always said, it should be large. And special."

"Hmm," the clerk said, rolling his eyes slightly. "We certainly specialize in large and special. Might I ask how you heard about Garrard?"

William glanced up. "My father used to buy gifts here for my mother, years ago. She still has many of your pieces."

"Indeed. You say your father shopped here? Would we perhaps remember him?"

William chuckled. "I'd guess so. His name is Harrington Carnegie."

The clerk was far too professional to allow the surprise to do more than flicker in his eyes, but William noticed it anyway. "Do you mean to say your father is Ambassador Carnegie?"

"Yep," William said, using the informal agreement on purpose, to tweak the snobby clerk a little bit. "That's him all right."

"Well, yes. Of course we remember the Ambassador. And your mother as well, Lady Fiona. Your father has been a special customer of ours for many years before the war. I was only a stock boy of course, but...is your father well? We haven't seen him since...?" He delicately let the question hang, and William recognized the delicate British sensibilities at work. The clerk was too polite to ask directly if his father was among the millions of war dead.

"Yes, yes," William said. "He's fine. He and my mother moved back to the States before the war. But as a matter of fact, they'll both be coming into London in a few days' time. Which is when I plan to make the big announcement." He gestured back to the case.

"Yes, of course!" the clerk said, having completed a miraculous transformation from snobby and superior to obsequious salesman. "Please do tell them we'd love to see your parents here at Garrard, and let's not waste another minute chatting that we could be looking at rings. Tell me again, what are you hoping to find?"

"Err," William said, "I hate to admit it, but I don't know much myself about buying these sorts of things. I've never bought an engagement ring, of course. But Regina...that's my fiancé...well, she deserves something special. Something...incredible."

"No doubt, no doubt," the clerk said. "Tell me...what does she like to wear? Is she a formal girl, given to ball gowns? Or a rather sporty girl more at home in the stables?"

William laughed. "Neither. She cares for orphans, and she's, ah, Irish. She's got red hair and brilliant green eyes. And I can't recall ever seeing her in a gown or on a horse."

"I see." The clerk took a moment to think, one finger tapping his chin. "An Irish beauty with green eyes. I'm thinking an emerald then."

"Okay," William said. "Sounds good. What do you have?"

"Come."

The clerk led William down the rows of cases until they stood before one filled with emeralds of stunning sizes and colors. It took William only a glance before he pointed at one of the rings and said, "That one! It's the exact color of her eyes! I'd like to see it."

The clerk unlocked the case and removed the ring. "I must say, you have a good eye," he said. "This is one of our finest emeralds; it is technically perfect, virtually flawless. The emerald is flanked by triangular diamonds. The center stone measures 5.45 karats and the side-mounted diamonds are 1.35 karats each. The setting is platinum and a Garrard Jewelers original design. And, if I'm not mistaken—which of course I am not—this particular piece was designed by an artist of Irish descent, who works on an exclusive contract basis for us, making this piece a true Irish original. A one-of-a-kind engagement ring."

William took it and had an overwhelming connection with the ring, as if it was the physical embodiment of everything he felt for Regina. The emerald really was the exact shade of her eyes, and the fact that it had been designed by an Irishman seemed almost too perfect. Perhaps kismet.

"I love the ring, I really love it," William said. "It will suit her perfectly. Wrap it and I'll take it with me."

"Of course, sir. But...you don't know the price yet."

"Gosh, I forgot to ask that too," William said. "I guess my inexperience is showing."

The clerk waved this aside and leaned forward. "Don't give it another thought. It's my deepest honor to introduce you to the world of Garrard jewels. The price is 55,000 pounds, plus taxes."

William whistled under his breath. "So that's about $106,000? That's a boatload."

The clerk waited silently while William worked it out.

"Oh, what the heck. She deserves the best. I'll take it. Wrap it up."

A moment later, William was handed a bag with a small leather-bound box containing the ring. He left the shop with a bounce to his step, slipping the box into his pocket and throwing away the bag. He felt very adult suddenly—carrying the ring that he hoped would make Regina his wife.

The day before his parents were to arrive, William and Roan made arrangements to meet after work for a pint or two and a game of snookers at one of the working-class pubs Roan favored, after which they would meet Regina's train.

At 6:15, William tidied up his desk and told his aide he would be leaving shortly. The aide came in and placed the next day's schedule on William's desk. William bid the chap good night and left the embassy by way of the side door. As he walked around the building toward the street, he noticed that Roan was waiting in a car at the curb.

William hastened over to the car. "Roan, I thought we were meeting at the pub, how nice of you to pick me up."

"Get in, William." Roan's brogue was thicker than normal, a sure sign he had been drinking.

William climbed into the car. "Roan, what's up? Is there something wrong?"

"It's Regina."

William was becoming alarmed. Roan's eyes were red and swollen and he gripped the steering wheel and looked straight ahead, never once glancing over at his friend.

"What about Regina?" William asked. "Has something happened?"

"She's dead," Roan said.

"Dead? She can't be dead...she's in Belfast helping the children."

"No, William. She's gone. She was helping to evacuate kids when a rotten British bastard sniper shot her in the stomach, thinking she was IRA. After she fell, the bastard put two more bullets in her head to finish the job. He did it in broad daylight, in front of the church and the children."

Shock flooded William's body, and for half a second, he felt as if he was floating above his body, watching himself from above. "Dead," he echoed. "Are you sure?"

"Of course I'm sure!" Roan yelled. "Those rotten bloody bastards should rot in hell!"

A scream tore from William's throat, seeming to rip itself from the fabric of his throat. Now Roan glanced over grimly, watching until William was done. Then, without remembering how he had done it, William was back at the door to his flat. His hands were shaking, and Roan was in the hallway behind him, his shadow looming large on the wall as William fumbled for his key.

"They'll pay, William," Roan said, his voice seeming to come from down a long tunnel. "I can promise ye they'll pay with their bloody lives. You're still with me, right, mate? Brothers till the end."

But William wanted none of it just then; he only wanted to be alone, away from all humanity. He stumbled into the flat, only to find it looked hopelessly foreign. Everywhere he looked there were reminders of Regina, and he was suddenly overcome with a torrent of memories: seemingly every moment they had spent together, from their chance meeting in the greengrocer's to their nights on the Brighton beach to the hours she had spent hanging tinsel in this very flat. He tried at first to hold the memories back, but the flood was too strong and he opened himself to the memory of her, falling to his knees as tears streamed down his face.

When the memories stopped, there was nothing left but a yawning emptiness, a disbelief so great it threatened to consume him. How could she be gone? Last he had seen her, she was full of life, brimming with worried tenderness for the orphans she was hoping to save. It could not be.

He staggered to his feet and found himself holding a glass of scotch without remembering pouring it. Again as if from a distance, he worried about this forgetfulness. It couldn't be good to be losing time like this. Then he watched himself down the bullet of scotch and the burning in his mouth and throat brought him back to his lonely flat: he stood before their side bar, an open bottle of twelve-year-old scotch in one hand and a tumbler in the other. He poured another slug and then another, and then one more, and downed that one also. This time, when the scotch entered his stomach, a flood of nausea swept up and he dropped the glass and ran into the loo and vomited into the bowl. Again, and then again. Soon he was retching nothing but bile and saliva, and the world seemed to spin on its axis. He did not remember sliding sideways along the bathroom tiles and falling into a dark escaping sleep.

William awoke at dawn and had a moment of disorientation. He didn't recognize where he was: black and white tile floor, radiator hissing under a small window, a toilet just a few feet from his face. He felt as if he was waking from a nightmare. Gradually his mind began to reconstruct the scene, and then fill in the blanks. His body was limp and fatigued. The stench of vomit filled the air. Then, as if he had stuck his finger into an electric outlet, the reality came back: Regina was dead! She was never coming back. There would be no wedding; there would be no future with her.

William crawled out of the loo and onto the sofa, where he fell asleep once again, avoiding reality.

Some hours later, he awoke with the realization that he needed to call the embassy. Since his colleagues were essentially unaware of Regina and their relationship, William decided not to explain anything to them—he wasn't sure he could say the words anyway. Instead he told his aide he would not be in for the next few days.

"No problem, sir," his aide said. "Have your parents arrived early?"

William was too spent to give any details. He simply agreed.

As he hung up, the aide's departing words pierced William's heart: "Have a wonderful day, sir, and I know the Ambassador, Mrs. Carnegie, and you will have a delightful visit. Merry Christmas!"

The aide's words echoed in William's head: "Merry Christmas." Indeed! There would be no Merry Christmas for him or for his parents or Regina. There would be no joy and singing and feasting, only sadness and mourning.

He hung up the phone and collapsed in emotional exhaustion and fell asleep again.

When he awoke, a semblance of normalcy had returned to his head. He felt like he had a pounding hangover, although he knew this could not be true. He'd only had maybe three drinks and had vomited them back up. His face felt puffy and crusted.

William got up, feeling his determination returning. He needed to shower first, so he headed for the bathroom, grimacing at the sight of the splattered vomit still in the toilet bowl. He cleaned that first, and then stripped down to shower. As he removed his pants, the ring box fell out of his pocket. William felt as though he had been shot and again sunk to the floor. He buried his head in his arms and sobbed.

When this fresh fit of tears had passed, he opened the box and saw the dazzling emerald. It was no less beautiful today, even though the woman who should be wearing it was gone. Confounded, he put it aside and practically crawled to the shower and climbed into the stall. He hoped the hot water would help wash away the grief and anguish. William remained in the shower for a long time, but eventually shut off the water and exited, feeling only slightly better than before. He dressed slowly, not paying much attention to his choice of wardrobe, then grabbed his jacket and keys and headed for the door, not sure exactly where he was heading but knowing he needed fresh air and a change of scenery. At the last minute, he slid the ring box into his pocket.

Outside in the cold, William aimlessly walked the city streets, seeing Regina around every corner and behind every shop window. He stopped for a tea and tried to drink it, but could not get it down without feeling nauseated. Eventually William found himself by the side of the Thames. Sitting on the bench alongside the river, William bowed his head and again silently wept. It was a cloudy winter afternoon, the sky gray and depressing. He felt alone and betrayed by God. He questioned how God could let this happen to Regina, a truly loving and giving person whose only mistake was caring for and loving children. It wasn't fair. William thought he would never, ever be the same.

William shifted and felt the ring box in his jacket pocket press against his leg. He removed it from his pocket and opened it slowly. It was the same as it always had been: the diamonds sparkled and the center emerald stone was as green as Regina's eyes. "God damn you, how could you do this to me?" he muttered, the curse words unfamiliar on his tongue. "I curse you and the bloody war."

The anger felt good, and for the first time since he had heard the news, William felt rage rising in him instead of oppressive grief. He recalled Roan's vow of vengeance and felt like he finally understood the man who would have been his brother-in-law. For all these months, Roan's hatred of the British had been perplexing for William, but now he felt it in all its fury. This was not the work of God. This was the work of a single man, a soldier who had gunned down the best person William had ever known, a woman no less, in cold blood in the broad daylight. "I hope you die a death full of pain and suffering," William said.

Incensed and full of despair, William pulled the magnificent emerald ring from the box, kissed it tenderly, and then flung it into the Thames. It landed far off the bank in the middle of the churning river, immediately sinking. William realized that all good things must come to an end. The ring was gone, gone forever, just like Regina.

***

The Ambassador and Lady Fiona arrived in London on schedule, debarking from their steamer into the wet cold of a London Christmastime. They were naturally looking forward to seeing William, and both the Ambassador and his wife were excited to be back in London. It had been a long time they were away—transatlantic travel had been too dangerous throughout most of the war, and they had risked only a few trips back to see family and friends.

They were surprised, however, when they were met at the port by embassy personnel instead of William himself. When they inquired as to where William was, the driver explained that William would meet them at the Savoy Hotel, where reservations had been made for them. Fiona was disappointed—she had planned a surprise for William and his girlfriend, whom she fully expected to fall in love with just as her son had. She had arranged to have Laurels by the Sea on the Isle of Jersey opened for their visit. With great detail, she instructed the majordomo and his staff to decorate the mansion in exquisite form for the holidays. She was quite insistent that they have ready a huge Christmas tree for her "little boy," as well as a generous supply of his favorite holiday foods. William always loved the Isle of Jersey estate, so Fiona knew it would be a keen surprise when she announced that, after a day in London, the family would travel to Laurels by the Sea for a joyous Christmas holiday and New Year celebration.

Fiona's first sense that something was wrong came as soon as she entered the lobby of the Savoy and spotted William. He was turned out well in a suit, but his face seemed to have aged and there were dark circles under his eyes. Fiona exchanged a look with her husband.

"William!" the Ambassador called. "Son, nice to see you! Where is the future Mrs. Carnegie?"

William paused and then slowly responded, "Dad, Mom, please sit down. I know you've come a long way to meet Regina. But she is not here."

Fiona's heart skipped a beat. "Did you break up? She better not have broken my boy's heart."

"No, Mother, we did not break up." William paused to regain his composure and Fiona found herself growing increasingly worried. She had never seen William so hesitant or emotional, not even as a child. He had always been so sure of himself, so caring and confident. This nervous, gaunt man before her only resembled her son in his features.

"What is it then?" she asked, perhaps more stridently than she meant.

"She's been killed," William said, and a strangled sob escaped his throat. "Three days ago. She's dead."

"No!" Fiona said, her own heart breaking at her son's palpable anguish. "Oh William! What happened? How could this be?"

William was obviously struggling to maintain his composure, and Fiona wondered if they should retire to the privacy of their suite, but he continued. "She was shot, Mother. By a British soldier. She was in Belfast on a charity mission to rescue orphans from the war and bring them back here to London—I've been helping support her cause, which was near to her heart. They thought she was IRA and killed her in the street."

The Ambassador shook his head. "My dear son, I'm so sorry for you. That's a nasty business for a young woman to be tied up in."

"She wasn't tied up in it, Dad," William said. "She was murdered."

His parents exchanged another glance—William had never spoken back to his parents—and then Fiona wrapped him in a tight embrace and let her little broken-hearted boy cry against her shoulder.

In three days' time, on Christmas Eve day, a funeral Mass was arranged. The small religious ceremony was held at St. Martin's Catholic Church, located in the Irish ghetto just north of London. It was nothing like the grand High Episcopal cathedrals William had attended his entire life. No, this church was a threadbare, simple building reflecting the poverty of its congregation. The altar was already filled with white poinsettias in readiness for Christmas midnight Mass. Officiating over the solemn Mass of Requiem was Father Patrick Ryan, an elderly Irish priest who most of the parishioners simply referred to as Father Patrick.

Since Regina was an orphan herself, very few people attended the burial Mass. Only William, his parents, Roan, and a few girlfriends from Regina's rooming house filled the pews. Roan sat next to William in the first pew, along with the Ambassador and Fiona. William remained silent as everyone else sang the stirring hymn, *Ave Maria*. Dispersed incense surrounded the simple pine box that held his beloved Regina's remains. William stared at the box and felt numb. With all the suffering in the world, he felt he had no true right to complain about his lot in life. He had been born into privilege and then worked terrifically hard to live up to his family name and station. Violence and war had shaped his life, but only from a distance—he had only fired his service weapon during ROTC training at Harvard. And now a war that he had barely heard of—a war that wasn't even his own fight—had reached deep into his life and torn away the person he loved the most.

When the others bowed their heads to pray, William stared straight ahead, unflinchingly holding the eyes of Father Patrick, who asked the congregation to stand as he intoned the solemn words of Psalm 23 in a thick brogue:

> The Lord is my shepherd; I shall not want.
>
> He maketh me to lie down in green pastures: he leadeth me beside the still waters.
>
> He restoreth my soul: he leadeth me in the paths of righteousness for his name's sake.
>
> Yea, though I walk through the valley of the shadow of death, I will fear no evil: for thou art with me; thy rod and thy staff they comfort me.

Thou preparest a table before me in the presence of mine enemies: thou anointest my head with oil; my cup runneth over.

Surely goodness and mercy shall follow me all the days of my life: and I will dwell in the house of the Lord forever.

When the priest was done and his words echoed heavily in the small chapel, Roan rose and approached the pulpit to give the eulogy. His face was hard and unforgiving, his eyes mere chips of green flint. It was the face of righteous fury, and William felt like he had never been closer to his friend—at that moment, they shared the same exact burden, the same anger. Roan stared at the coffin, swallowing hard, and then gripped the pulpit with both hands and began to speak in a low voice.

"We are here to bury my beloved sister, Regina, who was murdered by a faceless, nameless coward," he growled. "Instead of her funeral we should be celebrating her wedding. Regina was a victim of tyranny and injustice perpetrated by a government and Crown that knows no limits or shame. In these times, one can only wonder how atrocities like this can continue without punishment of those criminals who commit them. In the name of God and in the memory of my treasured sister, I pledge to you that the score will be evened, and a price will be paid…a steep price. As God as my witness, my sister and our people will not rest until we have revenge."

Like so many words from the past few days, Roan's angry eulogy rolled off William, even when he heard his mother gasp in surprise next to him as Roan promised revenge on the English. He was simply beyond caring at that moment.

After the Mass ended, they carried Regina's coffin outside to the adjoining cemetery, where a dark hole had been hacked into the cold ground. The gravediggers stood off to one side, smoking and leaning on their shovels. They watched from hooded eyes as Regina's cold and lifeless body was lowered into her grave and sprinkled with Irish soil brought from her native land. William's numbness didn't recede, even when the first clods of dirt broke on her casket and the woman he loved was buried.

Two weeks following the funeral, the flat where William and Regina had shared so many happy memories was a jumble of boxes, twine, and packing materials. William had come home from the funeral, looked around, and immediately realized he could no longer live there. He began packing straightaway and expected to vacate the premises within a fortnight for a new flat. He was packing yet another box when there was a knock at the door. William straightened up and wiped sweat from his brow, wondering who it could be. His parents had left London already, heading for the Isle of Jersey, but William had stayed behind.

He opened the door to find Roan glowering in the hallway. "Can I come in?" he asked abruptly.

William wordlessly stepped aside, letting Roan in to stand in the middle of the room, surveying the boxes. "You're moving."

"Yeah."

"I can't say I blame you, mate. I wish I could get away from this bloody mess myself." He pulled a flask from his pocket and took a draw; William wondered how long Roan had been drinking. "I came by to tell ye…I got a copy of Regina's death certificate and autopsy +

"Autopsy? Why was an autopsy performed?"

"The English performed it before we could claim her body in Ireland. They need a way out of calling her death a murder. The military coroner ruled the death 'accidental, caused by friendly fire.' The swine."

William didn't know what to say so he said nothing.

"And that's not all," Roan said. "There's more."

"Okay."

"I'm sorry, my brother, to be the bearer of bad news. But they said she was pregnant. Five weeks or thereabouts. I'm sorry."

After all he had been through, William didn't think he could feel worse—but this news hit him like a physical punch to the stomach and he dropped to his knees. "Oh God!"

Roan offered William his flask. "They murdered your child, mate. Hell has no level deep enough for them."

William didn't take the flask, and after a few minutes passed, Roan slid it back into his pocket. "I've got to be going, mate," he said. "You'll hear from me soon."

CHAPTER 19
Running on Empty

In the days and weeks following Regina's death—after William located a new flat and settled back into work—Roan and William spent more and more time together. For William, Roan was the sole connection he had left to Regina, and he found himself studying Roan sometimes, hanging on family similarities that reminded him of Regina. As for Roan's motivation in seeking out William's company, William assumed it was due to the loss they shared and Roan's interest in continuing Regina's work. Three weeks after she was buried, Roan approached William saying that the orphans Regina had been trying to rescue had made their way to London and desperately needed homes, educations, and necessities like clothing and food. William was happy to arrange a large transfer, thinking that even this small action brought him closer to Regina's memory.

As he called to arrange for the transfer, the trust officer back at the States gently asked, "Are you sure you know where this money is going?"

"What?" William said. "Of course I do. Regina's brother Roan is taking up her work with the orphans."

Yet even after he hung up, these words preyed on a dark corner of his mind. Roan didn't seem like the type to spend his time supporting orphans. And yet...William didn't believe Roan would lie to him, and he didn't have the energy to do anything different. William had lost much of his zest for life, his motivation and ambition. He marked every day the way an hour hand marks time, routinely and mechanically. He was truly running on empty, and before long his thoughts turned to counting down days until his tour of duty at the American Embassy was done.

When the end finally came, William resigned his commission with the military, despite polite pressure from his superiors to stay on and vague promises of a bright future with America's diplomatic corps. But William was insistent; he wanted no part of the military. Instead of staying on with the army, he accepted a civilian position with Simmons, Simmons and Throckmorton.

Located at 10 Upper Bank Street in the heart of London, the firm had been the leading British law firm since the late 1790s. William's job was simple enough: tap into the vast network of mercantile and diplomatic firms associated with the Carnegie family to win lucrative new clients for his employer. Somewhat to his surprise—because he had always resisted relying on his family name—William found he liked his new work. The work was challenging and exciting—he regularly dealt with companies that had dealings all over the world and he enjoyed seeing the inner workings of the wheels of global commerce. Being an incredibly hard worker and bringing many lucrative clients into the firm distinguished William as a top performer. He was soon made a junior partner.

The law firm enjoyed access to the highest levels of royal society in London, and William was soon mixing with titled nobility on a regular basis. At the same time he settled into his new job, he quickly grew to appreciate his new flat. He had left Mayfair behind for Sloan Square, a very posh and fashionable address that gave him access to the best London had to offer, with Buckingham Palace just a short walk away.

Even as William's professional life began to recover, his social life remained dismal. He still saw Roan for the occasional pint, but on most nights, he'd work late, then walk slowly home and spend the evening alone in his flat or out walking the city streets. He had no doubt his new colleagues wondered what was wrong with him, but he had no intention of sharing anything about Regina.

Still, there seemed to be a concerted effort to draw William out. After a Wednesday morning partner's meeting, one of the senior partners, Mark Cox, approached William in the hall.

"I say," Mark began, "it's time you left off eating lunch alone at your desk. A few of us are heading to the Marlboro Club for lunch and we'd love for you to join us. And before you answer, you should know that we're not taking no for an answer."

William agreed a little reluctantly, and they soon headed to the private club.

Marlboro Club, London

The Marlboro Club was a typical upper-class English gentleman's club. It was housed in an impressive building constructed from Georgian brick with imposing white columns. Over the centuries, it had played host to aristocrats, members of Parliament, and even the occasional king-in-waiting. As William was ushered into the foyer by a butler, he couldn't help but be impressed by the hushed and moneyed atmosphere. The paneled walls were hung with portraits of past members from the present day going back to the pre-American Revolutionary era (which, William had no doubt, was not something club members would wish to dwell upon). He spotted Mark Cox standing by a well-worn antique white marble fireplace, a snifter of brandy already in his hand, and walked over to join him.

Mark greeted him warmly and they sat at a small table in a secluded corner. Another waiter appeared as if from thin air and took William's order of seltzer water with lime—he had decided to take a break from alcohol after his binging following Regina's death.

"I'm glad you joined me, William," Mark said once they were alone. "I was hoping to talk to you about some matters."

"Glad to be here," William agreed. "You know, this was my father's club."

"Yes, I do know that. Your father was a senior member when I first joined years ago. Why is it that you haven't applied to join? You would be instantly accepted."

William shrugged. "I'm not much for clubs, quite honestly. Or for that matter, going out much at all. I've been wrapped up at work, as you know."

"Yes," Mark said, nodding. "And no doubt we've all noticed the superior quality of your work and your truly impressive work ethic. But, I must say, it seems that a young man like yourself, with your background, should rather want to get out once in a while and kick up his heels."

William smiled—it sounded like a senior partner was advising his protégé to work less. "Now you sound like my father," William said. "He didn't call you by any chance, did he, and put you up to dragging me out?"

Mark laughed and sipped his brandy. "No, no. I've never spoken with your father. Only heard what a fine man he is." He paused. "Rather, I wanted to touch on something else. When you're a senior partner, one hears things, you know."

"Oh?" William said, his eyebrows rising. "Hears things? About me?"

Mark swirled his drink for a second. "Not you exactly. And please, understand that this in no way reflects upon your work for the firm or your future with the firm. We have every confidence in your abilities and your potential. But rather than beat around the bush, I'll cut to the chase. It's been said that you have been associating with very shady characters. Anti-government types, if you catch my meaning."

William's heart thudded and he took a moment to carefully consider his answer. William had spent enough time around his British colleagues at the American Embassy to recognize that his sympathies with the Irish cause were not particularly popular. When they discussed it at all, the Britons invariably referred to the Irish as terrorists or rebels. William himself had little or no opinion on the Irish fight for independence, but he recognized a pointed question when he heard one and he had no idea how much the firm knew about Regina.

"Well," William said, "I'm not sure if I'd say they're shady. I...my former fiancé...did work with Irish orphans. I've been helping her cause. But...she's dead." His voice stuck on the word and he had to fight back a sob.

"I see," Mark said. "Of course we all seek to help those less fortunate than ourselves. And again, please consider this only a friendly interest in your welfare. But you should be aware that the 'orphanages' these types are involved with are often little more than fronts for illegal activity, including gun running, smuggling, and terrorist campaigns. Even murder. I'm not saying your fiancé was involved in anything as sordid as all that. But as an American relatively new here, I wouldn't expect you to fully understand the complexity of the Irish situation. Needless to say, it's toxic, and they are not above using any means—including children—to further their cause. No doubt you don't want to get mixed up in that sordid business. It could derail a brilliant career, or worse, result in a firebomb coming through your window one night if you don't accede to their demands. You understand what I'm saying?"

William studied Mark carefully, looking for signs that the older man knew more than he was letting on, or was even threatening him. But Mark looked only concerned.

"Of course," William said. "I understand completely, and thanks for making the effort to clue me in. Like you said, I'm a bit new to all this."

"Excellent. Now, enough about that. I was also hoping to extend you an invitation to join my family and some friends at our place in Wimbledon. I expect there will be some people your age about, and I thought you might like to be introduced around. You do play tennis, yes?"

"Yes, I played years ago at Harvard, but not much lately." William didn't mention that he was captain of the tennis teams at both Hotchkiss and Harvard. "Your invitation is most gracious, but I'm really busy this weekend. I have two complicated briefs to complete before the trials in two weeks' time."

Mark chuckled. "I'll view that as the American in you. William, my boy, when your senior partner invites you to tennis for the weekend, it's not a request. So don't worry about the briefs. I'll make sure you get help finishing them up in plenty of time. Meanwhile, you plan on coming and having a wonderful weekend."

William held his hands up in capitulation. "Yes, sir, I read you loud and clear. I'll come for overnight on Saturday, but I must leave early Sunday morning."

Mark, satisfied with the compromise, said: "Good enough. Why don't you catch the 9:40 train with my son's friends, and we'll see you there. And please, remember to bring formal wear. There'll be a party at the club on Saturday night. You'll have a lovely time."

Seeing no way out, William agreed, and Mark looked satisfied as he signaled the waiter over again with a tray of sandwiches. An hour later, after a lunch filled with shop talk, the men rose to leave and Mark grabbed William's arm. "You're a good chap," he said. "There's plenty to life beyond work and the office. We'll be looking forward to your visit this weekend."

"Great, thanks for the invite," William said. "I'm looking forward to it already."

CHAPTER 20
THE SECOND TIME AROUND

The train to Wimbledon

As promised, William was seated on a first-class car on Saturday morning, a brief spread across his lap as he read and took notes. He had agreed to go to Wimbledon, so he would of course never insult his host, but that didn't mean he had no work to do or that part of him didn't dread it just a bit. The truth was, William wasn't sure he was ready to be back in society, at least to the extent he had ever been in society.

A loud woman's laugh interrupted him, followed by the joyful noise of a mixed group of men and women enjoying themselves in the aisle as they passed his compartment. He glanced up in time to see a foursome of well-dressed, attractive people moving by—one of the young men caught his eye and gave him a wink as if to say hello and what a fine day it was. William waved slightly, frowned even more slightly, and bent back to his work.

The train pulled into Wimbledon Station exactly on time, something that William still marveled at. The English were exceptionally good at keeping the trains running on time. The passengers made a rush for the exits en masse, eager to find themselves in the open air of a beautiful Saturday. William took his time gathering his attaché case, overnight bag, and his recently restrung tennis racquet before stepping onto the platform. Wimbledon was a smaller and not particularly grand station—he didn't think he would have a hard time finding Mark's son, although he had never met the man and had no idea what he looked like.

He did, however, see the same group of people who had passed his car, and this time noticed that three of them were very pretty, very well put-together girls approximately his own age. He instantly knew the type—William had gone to prep schools and attended the Ivy League, so he certainly recognized upper-class women when he saw them. He was still watching them closely when a tap on his shoulder startled him.

"William Carnegie?"

He jumped slightly and turned to see a young man at his shoulder. "Yes, that's me."

"Hi, I'm Reggie Cox, Mark's son. I'm here to pick you up."

"Ah, yes. Of course. Glad to meet you. I'm William…but I guess you already know that."

"Indeed I do!" Reggie said jovially. He cast a look at the group William had been studying. "And there's the rest of us. Let's collect them and off we go."

They formed a noisy, happy group bristling with tennis racquets and bags as they headed outside to the car park, where two cars were waiting. One was Reggie's personal automobile, and the other was driven by a houseman. Along the way, Reggie made casual introductions, pointing out people quickly and providing names: "This is Barbara, and there's Elizabeth who goes by Liz, and that one over there is Catherine but you shall call her Cat because we all do. This ugly pug here is Pogg, an old chum of mine from Eton who has been killing the ladies since secondary school."

The girls laughed especially loudly and Pogg himself gave a good-natured chuckle and patted his large belly.

Reggie continued, "I'm sure you don't want to ride with the boss's son, so you go with Pogg and Liz, and we'll meet back at the house."

"Shotgun!" Pogg instantly sang out, and for a second William was back at prep school, where calling shotgun had been an honored ritual. "Looks like you're in the back with Liz, mate. Careful of her! She bites."

Again they all laughed happily as they bundled into their cars and headed out from the station. William had been careful to laugh on cue, but once in the car he fell silent and stared pensively out the window, wondering if this trip had been such a good idea after all. If the other two noticed his withdrawal, they gave no sign of it. Liz and Pogg carried on outrageously, evidently very old friends who still had much to discuss about nothing. Occasionally one of them would direct a question to William, but they didn't seem to care in the slightest if his answer was abrupt or short; they simply made a joke of it, laughed it off, and galloped onto the next topic.

As they drove, William found himself increasingly distracted by Liz and studying her from the corner of his eyes. She had the same thin, casual style of many aristocratic girls he had met, but none of the condescending attitude. Rather, she seemed straightforward, very open, and had a terrific sense of humor. It also didn't hurt that William couldn't help but notice that she was extremely pretty. She had shoulder-length blonde hair that she thoughtlessly flipped away from her face every few minutes with a slender hand. Proportionally, she was tall, slim, but well-shaped and athletic, and it was obvious she spent a lot of time outdoors.

The car turned off the main road, onto a smaller lane, and then turned through imposing gates set into a stone wall. The words "Elmwood Bent" were carved into the wall.

"The name of Reggie's house," Liz said when she noticed William reading the sign.

"Also called Bent Elmwood late at night after drinks," Pogg said.

"Oh, stop that," she said. "Don't be terrible."

Elmwood Bent was a large Tudor-style home at the end of a large circular drive. It was constructed from fieldstone and wood, with large wings on either side and rows of quaint dormers rising from the steep shale roof. The grounds leading up to the home were immaculate—the grass perfectly clipped, and the hedges trimmed into a topiary, which was unusual for an English garden. The center of the circular drive, however, had been given over to a proper and traditional English flower garden that exploded in a riot of color. As they neared the house, William realized that the grounds and charming architecture disguised the very size of the place: the house was enormous, a true mansion.

He noticed tennis courts set to one side behind the house and another outbuilding that must have been a guesthouse. Stables sat further back, and as they rounded a curve in the driveway he saw a large pool glittering in the sun flanked by a row of small cabanas that recalled the main building's details. All in all, William decided his partner must do very well for himself.

When the car stopped, William jumped from the backseat and hustled around to open the door for Liz. The group grabbed their own bags, but William managed to grab Liz's sizable suitcase. All were escorted into the enormous front foyer. Mark Cox was waiting, clad in lightweight summer cotton.

"Welcome!" he called as they entered in a rush of noise and excitement. "William, lovely to see you here, old chap! Welcome to Elmwood!"

William, along with the others, thanked Mark, but Mark promptly waved the thanks aside and announced where they would be staying. William and

Pogg were staying in the guesthouse by the tennis courts—"We affectionately call it the Lodge"—while the girls would be set up in the main house.

Hadley, the houseman, appeared to escort the women up an impressive flight of stairs to their rooms, while Reggie offered to walk William and Pogg down the gravel path to the Lodge. The structure was a smaller version of the manor house, right down to the charming dormers and quirky details. Reggie pointed the men in the direction of their rooms. They appeared to be identical in size, but each was individually decorated. In between and separating the bedchambers was a large sitting room with high coffered ceilings and a massive window facing the tennis courts. Sun streamed in, warming the room and making it all the more appealing.

William entered his room and looked around. The room boasted a charming country feel with cozy informal furniture. An ancient-looking fireplace, identical to the one he had seen in the sitting room, was set and ready to light. The room had an adjoining loo with a small but adequate shower. A large four-poster bed dominated the room. A small writing desk in the corner looked like a good place for William to get some work done later in the day. All in all, everything was very pleasing and very posh.

Next to the bed, the in-house intercom phone rang. William answered and found Mark on the line.

"Hullo!" he said cheerfully. "What do you say to some tennis? I believe there are a couple of fine-looking young women here who are drawing straws as to who shall beat you first."

"Ha!" William said. "It has been a while since I've played, and I realize I don't have my whites, so maybe I'll watch this morning."

"Oh tosh!" Mark said. "There are whites in the wardrobe in your room. Help yourself and meet us at the courts."

William agreed, then rung off the phone. So far, everything about this trip had been grudging—if Mark wasn't a senior partner he never would have agreed to come in the first place. So now that it came time to actually play, he sighed and wished there was some way around it. But he knew there wasn't. Then, absurdly, he had a fervent wish that he wasn't about to be humiliated on the court by Liz and her friends. God forbid Pogg should beat him. At one time, William had no doubt he would have been the best tennis player on the courts, but he hadn't held a racquet in years.

"You're being ridiculous," he muttered to himself and prepared to go.

As promised, the wardrobe contained everything he needed. There were drawers full of shoes, shirts, sweaters, and bands. Everything came from Harrods and looked new. William hurriedly changed and headed for the courts.

Despite all his misgivings, he had to admit to himself it was a beautiful day as he exited the Lodge and headed for the courts. The others were already playing, and the sharp twang of expertly hit tennis balls mixed with their cheerful calls of good morning as he joined the group and they sorted out some plan of attack, arranging two foursomes for doubles.

The first up was Reggie and Barbara versus Liz and William. The second group was Pogg and Cat versus Mark and his wife, Ann. They played two sets and then changed partners for another set. It took only a few practice strokes for William's worries to vanish. It felt good to hold a racquet again—he had forgotten how much he had enjoyed the game at Harvard, the long afternoons on the courts there. It also helped that only Liz was anywhere near as good as William, and there was a zero percent chance that Pogg could beat William. He clowned more than he played, and between him and Barbara, who tended to hack at the ball as if she were trying to chop down a tree, it was amazing they ever completed a set. Naturally, of course, Pogg made up for his poor playing by being the most creative and energetic braggart on the courts, and William found himself laughing along as Pogg's taunts grew more outrageous even as his play seemed to deteriorate.

He also once again found his eyes drawn to Liz. She had clearly spent long hours on a tennis court, and the effects of expert coaching were visible in her game. She was also naturally athletic, and her long legs served her well in covering her side. She had a beautiful backhand as well, and William's estimation of her rose by the minute as she won all of her sets and carried it off with the natural grace of a born winner. William found himself increasingly distracted as the sets went on and once blushed to himself when he realized he was watching her bend over a little too keenly. Still, he realized, Liz was the first woman he had felt anything like attraction to since Regina.

After the first sets were played, they stopped for lunch. A lovely cold buffet had been set out on the Lodge's terrace. The exhausted and ravenous players pulled up their chairs and began to dine. As they ate, William admired the nearby pool. It was an extremely large pool that was built to blend into the natural surroundings and landscaping.

"You're more than welcome to swim," Mark said, noticing William admiring the pool. "You'll be relieved to find out the pool is heated. That's a necessity here in bloody old England."

"Thanks," William said. "I was thinking of maybe doing some work after lunch, and then perhaps I'll jump in."

"Work!" Liz chimed in. "Absolutely not! Look at yourself! You look like you haven't seen the sun in weeks! Are you a recluse, William Carnegie?"

"A recluse?" he said. "No!"

"Then no work. I'm sure Mark won't mind—"

"I won't," Mark said, laughing.

"—if you have a bit of fun now and again."

"But—"

"Listen, mate," Pogg interrupted William. "I don't suggest you argue with Liz. No one ever wins and she always gets her way, so give it up and save your energy." Everyone nodded in agreement.

William held his hands up in mock surrender. "Okay, okay. I see I've got no choice. I'll get showered and then I'm all yours."

"Showered? Need any help?" Liz teased.

"Ha!" Pogg said. "Our poor Liz is all talk and no action. What a tease."

"Especially where you're concerned," she said, flicking her napkin at Pogg.

After lunch, Pogg and William headed back to the Lodge to change from their tennis whites into swim trunks and clean up.

"I say," Pogg said, "if Liz wasn't already hopelessly enamored with me, I'd say she's taken a shine to you."

William grunted noncommittally.

"You do know who she is, don't you?"

William shrugged. "No," he said, inwardly groaning a little bit in anticipation of the flood of titles he expected to hear next. Still he was impressed when Pogg continued, "She's Lady Elizabeth Chartworth, fourth or fifth cousin to the King and a formidable person in her own right. Watch out for that one, mate. She's been known to devour men alive."

William laughed. He couldn't help but like Pogg. "I'm sure. But it sounds like you've already laid your claim to her."

Pogg laughed. "Mind you I've tried, but Liz doesn't seem to go for the round and funny types. Fact is, she's got gents lined up at her door. Reggie's been after her for years, along with half of the rest of London's well-heeled bachelors. But she swats us all away like so many buzzflies."

"Really, why is that? Stuck up?"

Pogg gasped in fake horror. "Our Liz? Stuck up? Not only could that not be any further from the truth, she would be deadly insulted to hear you say it. Fact is, she's not interested in the public school, phony type, which sadly includes almost all of her circle. And I suspect she's afraid of settling in and getting stuck. Liz has too much going on. She's quite active in charity, you know, working with needy children."

An unexpected bolt of pain shot through William's chest. Regina's memory was still too fresh.

"Anyway, if it's true and you've caught the eye of Liz, just be warned: when you grab the tail of a tiger, you might find yourself soon dealing with the business end. Although in her case, that would be a job you should relish."

They arrived at the Lodge and separated as they headed for their bedrooms. William was glad for the time alone—he felt as if he needed to gather his thoughts and collect himself. He had the feeling of rushing headlong down a hill…a hill with Liz waiting at the bottom. And he wasn't convinced he had anything to offer a woman just yet. His hurt was still fresh. And yet…the image of Liz flashing across the court, her self-assured and joking manner, was stuck in his head.

The situation grew almost desperate when William arrived at the pool to find Liz alone, wearing a strikingly skimpy bikini and sprawled out on a recliner with enormous sunglasses covering half her face. "William," she said. "How nice."

He wasn't sure what she was referring to in part because he couldn't see her eyes. This woman had a way of throwing him off balance—she didn't conform to any of the stereotypes he knew of upper-class girls. And that body…Liz's skin-tight suit accentuated all the right features. The top cupped her full and flawless breasts, pushing them up for all to admire. Her long and perfectly shaped legs were tanned and athletic. Her blonde hair was tied up in a bun, giving Liz the appearance of a much younger girl.

The others thankfully arrived and congregated around the pool in the chaises. From time to time guests jumped into the sparkling, heated pool. Staff circulated, passing out soft drinks, coffee, tea, and snacks. The party gradually wound down, and the guests returned to their rooms to change and gather for cocktails. An hour later, dressed in casual clothes, Pogg and William headed back to the main house, where they found the group gathered around the piano while Liz played. It was instantly obvious that she was a talented musician, and William's estimation rose yet another notch. Her repertoire seemed vast, and she played everything from popular songs to classic pieces with little effort, talking and joking as she played and frequently ad-libbing and riffing her way through familiar phrases.

During a break between songs, Mark tapped his glass to get everyone's attention. "Don't forget, everyone, we are going to the club for dinner tonight. I asked Stanford, Reggie's cousin, to join us since we need an extra man. The cars will be out front at 8:30, so please be ready. Oh yes, black tie is required."

William, who had been enjoying himself, groaned inwardly. He'd had an excellent day, much better than he had expected, but wasn't too excited about the thought of dressing in formal wear for a party.

The cocktail hour passed and everyone retired to dress for dinner. Precisely at 8:30, two Bentley limousines appeared in the driveway, ready to make the twenty-minute drive to the club. The distinguished guests filed out of the mansion to the waiting vehicles. Again, William found himself irresistibly drawn to Liz, who appeared in an exquisite outfit highlighting each and every one of her stunning assets. And there was no doubt in his mind that Pogg was right and the feeling was mutual. Every time he glanced in her direction, he met her eyes and he didn't have to be Sherlock Holmes himself to read the story they told.

Later that night, Elmwood Bent

They returned late from the country club, a considerably more disheveled group than they had been hours before. Pogg's tie hung askew, and he and Reggie both headed straight for their rooms to "sleep it off." Cousin Stanford, too, asked to be driven home, and William was only too happy to be rid of him. Stanford exemplified the pompous, egotistical, and tedious stereotype of the English upper class. William suspected that Stanford was so obnoxious that he probably did not even like himself. Certainly, all of the girls paid no attention to him and visibly dreaded each time he would ask one of them to dance.

Back in his own room, William flung the terrace doors open and contemplated the mild summer night. He felt deeply conflicted and confused. He'd had a good time at dinner and enjoyed the day with the others. He was undeniably attracted to Liz, and was fairly sure she felt something similar for him. Yet he also felt distinctly apart from the others and the raw wound left by Regina was still hurting. It almost felt like he was carrying a secret burden, one that the other carefree young people couldn't hope to understand. He wondered why he felt such guilt about his growing feelings toward Liz.

He leaned against the terrace railing and sighed. It was truly a beautiful night, which only made him remember the nights on the Brighton beach he had spent with Regina. But this place was nothing like the dramatic wild coast at Brighton. Here, the crickets and night creatures sang loudly and the nearby pool glittered in the moonlight. He could hear the wind stirring in the grass, somewhat like waves crashing upon a beach, but could only smell the grass and forest. Still, in the dark, quiet moment of the night, he could almost feel Regina's loss like a physical thing, like a fist that grabbed his heart and squeezed. He felt vaguely broken inside, and worst of all, he felt that he would never be whole again. The thought of a lifetime of carrying this private burden stretched out in front of him, and he tried telling himself he was being melancholy and dramatic, but that only made him feel more exhausted. He was surprised to feel a tear rolling down his cheek. "What's gotten into you?" he muttered to himself, swatting the tear away. "You've got to pull yourself together."

His reverie was suddenly shattered by a clicking sound. He looked closer and spotted someone sitting in a chaise by the pool. A puff of white rose above the chair, dully lit up by the moonlight, and he realized whoever it was had stolen out to have a smoke. He peered closer and was surprised to recognize the smoker as Liz. Without thinking hard about it, William wiped his face and walked down onto the lawn, crossing toward her and coughing discreetly as he approached so he didn't startle her.

She sat up quickly and stubbed out the cigarette.

"Oh dear," she said. "I've been caught."

"Caught?"

"Smoking, yes. You're not going to rat me out, are you? Mark and Ann would be very disapproving. After all, smoking isn't very ladylike."

William laughed. "No, your secret is safe with me. And for the record, I think smoking is fine for a lady."

"Oh. So…you must smoke too?"

"No. I have before, but it didn't really suit me."

She smirked. "I see. So it's fine for a lady, but just not for you? Why do I think you're only telling me half the story?"

He laughed and sat down in a club chair. "Has anyone ever told you you'd make a great lawy…er, barrister?"

"Please. I respect myself far too much to go into law."

"Touché," he said. He gestured toward a nearby cabana with a bar built in. "A night cap? I'd be happy to make you one."

She smiled wickedly. "Maybe a small brandy, if they have it."

William went to the bar and looked through the bottles. "They have a nice Remy VSOP."

"That'll do."

He poured a healthy dose into a couple of crystal snifters, walked back to her chaise, and handed one to her. As she took it, she let a finger drape across his hand in a curiously sensual motion that lasted only a second but seemed fraught with meaning. Then she patted the chaise next to her. William sat down and followed her gaze up to the brilliant stars. Outside of the city, the sky seemed to fizz almost to overflowing with the night stars. A comfortable silence developed between them, with Liz taking small sips every few seconds, until she turned to him and said, "So tell me about yourself. What is the other half of the story? What's her name?"

"Sorry?"

"Well, not to be awfully forward, but from the way you've been moping around, I figure there must be a girl somewhere wearing your broken heart as a trophy."

William smiled and was amazed to realize that he didn't feel defensive or sad. It was true that Liz kept him almost constantly off balance—he had never met a girl like her before, so self-possessed, frank, fun-loving, and confident all at the same time. But he wasn't in the least intimidated by her. He made a sudden decision.

"No, I'm afraid not," he said. "There was a girl, yes, and we were engaged. But she was killed."

Liz's face fell and she grabbed his hand. "Oh, no! I'm so sorry. You must think I'm a perfect ass to burrow into your personal business like this! Do forgive me!"

"No, no. Not at all. In fact, it feels good to finally talk about it a little bit."

William was surprised to see that actual tears glinted in Liz's eyes.

"Really," he said. "It's okay, Liz. And please, I don't want to be one of those men who dumps the story of his 'lost love' on you. They are the worst."

She smiled at him and he was suddenly aware that she hadn't let his hand go yet. "No worries, William. And thank you for telling me, but you needn't say anything more if you don't want. You can tell me something else instead...like about your family. Leave nothing out."

He could tell she was kidding again, and he was grateful for her tact as much as her empathy. "Well, what's to know? My father is American, my mother is British. My mother is Lady Fiona Firth Carnegie, but since marrying my Dad she doesn't use the title, especially in America."

"Yes," she drawled. "You Americans and your antipathy for titles."

"So you use your title then? Lady Liz?"

"Ha! Pogg has been talking again, hasn't he? Remind me to punish him severely. And for the record, I only use the title when I need to get better service or a good seat in a restaurant."

They both laughed and fell into an easy conversation, talking about their families, sharing stories about their school days and university, and trading tales about their experiences during the war and their hope for a world without fascism. William found her to be a good conversationalist and extremely knowledgeable about all sorts of topics. She effortlessly segued from Stalin's rise in Russia, the Cold War, to the latest novelists and film stars to a wonderfully hilarious story about the time she disastrously took Pogg to see her favorite opera and he fell asleep and snored mercilessly throughout the aria.

The conversation kept on until the silences between them stretched out longer and longer and William felt gravity begin to tug on his eyelids as the stars wheeled overhead. Next thing he knew, a hand was gently shaking him awake and he woke up with a start, looking into the unfamiliar face of Mark's houseman framed in the washed-out grey of a very early morning dawn.

"Excuse me, sir. Breakfast is being served in the morning room."

It took William a moment to remember where he was: sleeping on the chaise poolside. He glanced over and saw Liz stretching and yawning next. She smiled at him. "Oops. Looks like we slept together...er, fell asleep together, wait. I meant to say not together but, ah, with each other. No, no! Not that either. Next to each other. Oh bother. You know what I mean!"

"Ha! Completely. What a night, though." He paused. "Thank you."

"Whatever for?" she said, sitting up. "I'm famished. You hungry? Let's go eat."

They joined the rest of the group for breakfast and endured the shameless teasing of the group, all of whom had seen them sleeping on the chaise lounges and sent the houseman out to wake them for sport. Pogg said he had considered waking them with a hose, but Mark stepped in and forbade it.

"Good thing, too," Liz said, "or I might have had to tell everyone about the time in Piccadilly—"

"Oh no you don't!" Pogg said. "Not the Piccadilly story!"

They all laughed and fell to eating with relish, looking forward to another day outdoors. William had planned on going back to London first thing in the morning, but midway through the meal announced a change of plans. They all congratulated him on a wise decision. It wasn't until 8:45 that night, then, that the group boarded the last train out of Wimbledon back to London. They left Reggie on the platform, waving goodbye. Despite the fact that he was nursing a sunburn and was short on sleep, William was happier than he could remember being in a long time.

***

Back in London, William immediately fell back into his work, but found a new excitement brewing in him. He excelled at law, and through his close contact with members of Parliament had an excellent position to observe the English government in action. He had never thought much of politics before—his father had been famously cynical about political cronyism and generally viewed politicians as useful tools that could support the family's business interests—but he found himself increasingly attracted to the ideals and animating spirit behind government. He began to see that, despite its many flaws, the English form of democracy existed solely to represent the will of the people, much like the American system. It was nothing like the cruel caricature that Roan had believed in. There was no monolithic, bloodthirsty, imperial British government. Instead, there was a body of men who all fervently believed in the idea of the United Kingdom, and although they were imperfect and almost always disagreed about everything, they sought to live up to the principles they fought for.

In the meantime, William saw more and more of Liz. She had surprised him by calling him immediately after they returned from Wimbledon; she really was an awfully forward girl, which was a quality in her that he appreciated. There was never any question where he stood with Liz from day to day. But even if she had not called him, he would have called her for sure. Their first few outings were simple and small, as they took in the occasional restaurant, but their bond seemed to grow deeper with every meeting. Liz really was a remarkable woman, full of talents and surprises and strong opinions. He quickly learned he could trust her instincts and judgments, and he admired her strength of character and began to look forward to the next time they would see each other. It occurred to him after a few weeks that he was likely falling for her.

He wasn't the only one who noticed. Liz herself was as enthusiastic about their growing relationship as he was—she made no secret of her desire to see him often, and she frequently ended one date by making plans for the next. She was a fountain of ideas and insisted that she would do nothing exciting and fun without him.

The paparazzi also noticed their relationship, and soon they were an "item" in the society pages of the London papers, photographed holding hands in public, entering and leaving posh restaurants and theaters, and even stealing the occasional kiss.

One evening in William's flat, they sat around his table sharing a quiet take-away Chinese meal. William was exhausted and grateful that Liz had wanted to join him for dinner even without the promise of anything exciting in the evening. Instead, she had showed up with the meal, and after they had eaten, she came around the table to give him a shoulder rub.

"I say, your neck is tight," she said. "You are really stressed. How about a little break for the evening? Let's climb into bed and relax."

William smiled in a tired way, so she kissed him and said, "One moment," then headed into the bedroom, started a hot shower, stripped and climbed in. Within moments the steam had fogged up the mirror, and Liz leaned out of the shower and called out, "William, can you come here for a minute, please?"

"Just a bit," he said, rising from the table with his hands full, planning to do the dishes. "I'm clearing the table."

"Oh, but there's a slight problem in here."

He set the dishes down and hurried into the steaming bathroom. "Yes? What is it?"

"The problem is that I need you to step into this shower with me so I can relieve some stress and tension."

"I'm fine. I don't have any stress or tension."

"Who said anything about you?" Liz said, poking her head around the curtain. "I'm the one who needs some relief. Now come here." She grabbed him quickly and pulled him into the shower. "Solicitor, you have been subpoenaed, and I am now going to sequester you for the next three hours."

William, still fully clothed, let himself get pulled in, but still protested. "I'm dripping wet!"

"That's no problem, solicitor. I'll take care of that."

She pulled his clothes off item by item and wrapped her arms around him as he relaxed into her and closed his eyes, letting the pounding water and steam relax him even as she excited him. Like a magnet, she was drawn to his most sensitive parts and began to massage them, then soaped him all over with a large bar of lavender soap. Soon the fragrant scent of lavender soap filled the air, mingling with the steam. Covered with suds, William embraced Liz and kissed her deeply, their tongues exploring each other. Liz broke off the kiss and sank to the floor, her mouth exploring every inch of William's body. A heightened sense of excitement seemed to rush through William as he lifted her up to kiss her again and again while they consummated the act of love under the pulsating shower with deep and forceful penetrations. When they were both satisfied, they left the shower and collapsed on the waiting bed, holding each other as they fell into a deep sleep.

Within a few months, William had proposed to Liz, and she had happily accepted. The society papers were ecstatic with the news: "Billionaire's Son Pops the Question!" For his engagement ring this time, William called upon his mother, who selected an heirloom diamond from her vast jewelry collection and had it set into a custom ring.

The wedding was the talk of London society. After all, it wasn't every day that a cousin to the King, even a distant cousin, married the fabulously wealthy son of an American dynasty. Liz's father, Sir Michael Chartworth, was third cousin once removed to the reigning King John. Her mother, Lady Leslie Chartworth, also hailed from a long line of royal descendants. Fittingly, the Chartworth family threw its prestige and considerable resources into planning the wedding, hoping to rival a true royal wedding. The Episcopalian service would be officiated by the Archbishop of Canterbury himself, and the following reception would be hosted at the baronial Chartworth estate. The guest list included royalty, diplomats, and the rich and famous—but it was noted that Princess Mary and Anthony did not attend, leading the gossip-mongers to wonder if there was friction between the royals and Liz's family. Liz dismissed this as rubbish.

After the reception, the couple headed off for three weeks in Cape Town, South Africa, where they drove Land Rovers across the prairies and saw the big game and of course spent days behind closed doors exploring each other. When they finally returned, they were both excited to begin their lives together in London.

CHAPTER 21
DANGEROUS FRIENDS

As William and Liz settled into their lives, William's earlier friendship with Roan faded somewhat into the background. They rarely saw each other, and most of the time, William had no idea where Roan was or what he was up to. William had no doubt that Roan still harbored his intense hatred of all things British, and he caught himself wondering sometimes how deep Roan's involvement with the IRA went. He tried not to let these thoughts grow—even with Roan's feelings toward the English, he had a hard time believing his friend was a terrorist. But then it was hard to imagine Roan really working with orphans, and William also caught himself wishing he'd gotten a better accounting of the money he'd provided over the years.

Still, their contact was rare enough that when Roan called one day, asking to meet William in a discreet pub, William reluctantly agreed to a meeting. It had been months and months since he'd heard from Roan.

The pub Roan chose was in an Irish neighborhood, but it was one that William had never heard of before and didn't have any type of sign outside advertising itself. He pushed open the door and stepped into the smoky, dark interior, wondering why Roan had chosen such a dismal place, when he heard his name being called from a shadowy corner. It was Roan hailing him over.

William was immediately struck by how much Roan had changed since he last saw him. His hair, once so luxuriously red like his sister's, had new streaks of grey in it, and his face seemed gaunt and deeply lined. There were dark bags under his eyes, as if he hadn't gotten a proper night's sleep in months. And worst of all, a fresh, livid scar snaked along his cheek, under one eye, giving him a sinister appearance.

"Hullo, mate," Roan said as William sat down. "How are things in your corner?"

"Good," William said. "You?"

"We're bearing up," he said. Roan paused. "I suppose I should congratulate you. I read about yer marriage." Roan's brogue seemed thicker than ever.

"Thanks," William said.

"Yeah, looks like you married a right Limey bitch."

William's first instinct was to reach across the table and slap Roan, but he held himself back. After all, Regina had been gunned down in the streets, killing her and their baby. Roan had a right to be bitter, William thought, and William had no desire to be in conflict with his old friend.

"Sorry," Roan said, perhaps reading the anger in William's eyes. "Sometimes me mouth gets in the way. You know how it is."

"Yeah. So…it sounded like you had something in particular you wanted to see me about…?"

"Ah, yeah," Roan said. "You know, I was in London and thought I'd look you up. I wanted to thank you, brother, for the work you've been doing with us. Your money has been great for the kids, and I know my sister would have been thrilled with all the good work we've been able to do with yer help. So thank ye."

William took a sip of his stout. "Sure, it's no problem. You know I supported her work with the orphans. It's a terrible tragedy."

"It's more than that," Roan said. "It's a right crime, and I'm glad you see it our way. That's mostly what I wanted to say to ye. That I don't begrudge you moving on...any man would. But that I hope yer still on our side, William."

William sat back and carefully considered his friend. He didn't much like the undercurrent of Roan's words, and he remembered what Mark had said about Roan and his friends and his own growing doubts about Roan's involvement with the IRA. He chose his next words carefully. "You know I support the children totally. But Roan, I've got to tell you, so it's in the open, I don't support the killing or the bombing. On either side."

Roan's face darkened, and his jaw worked for a minute, before he said, "I know what you're saying, William. And I agree that the killing is abhorrent. But I'm sure you see...it's not us that's keeping it going. We aren't the ones with tanks in the streets and soldiers shooting up churches full of honest folk. You must understand, William, we're an occupied country, and we don't want anything but the freedom to worship as we choose, in our own churches, without the bloody Brits trying to exterminate the Catholic Irish."

"I know," William said. "I know your side of it—"

"It's not just my 'side'!" Roan grated. "I'm on the side of what's right and proper. And if sometimes we have to use extreme methods, it's only because we have no other choice!"

William frowned, noting that Roan had said "we." He wondered who Roan included in that "we" and if he meant William to be part of it.

"I understand," William said. "But I just want to make it clear so you know where I'm at. I'm always happy to help the orphans. I really am. But that's the limit of my involvement."

Roan stared at him for a long minute, and then surprised William by breaking into a smile and raising a glass to him. "Cheers, then, mate.

And I'm glad you had the courage to say your piece to me. I respect your position, I really do. And I understand it. So I hope you know how much we appreciate—Regina would appreciate—what you've been doing."

"Yeah, thanks," William said, raising his own glass somewhat dubiously.

"So I can continue to count on yer support, then?"

"Yeah, sure. But Roan, I'm serious. From now on, I'll need a better accounting of where this money is going."

Roan shrugged. "Then you'll have it, William Carnegie. You'll have it."

The conversation drifted aimlessly after that, and they parted with a back-thumping hug and the promise to meet again whenever Roan could make it to London "without being noticed." Still, on his way home, William was quiet, chewing over everything that had been said, and several things that were left unsaid. He knew he could never pull his support from Regina's cause, but could he really trust Roan? It seemed his friend had changed, hardened somehow. His hands were rough and callused, his face lined and scarred. William wondered what Roan really did with all of his free time. But then...William knew that Roan's only real purpose was exactly what he claimed: freedom for his people. William sighed at the complexity of the world.

CHAPTER 22

DIFFERENT PLACE, SAME PROBLEMS

IT TURNED OUT THAT WILLIAM WOULDN'T SEE ROAN AGAIN FOR YEARS. Shortly after their meeting, Mark called William into his office and closed the door, motioning William to sit down. William took a seat and waited for his old friend and mentor.

"William," Mark said. "First, I want to say that you've been an incalculable asset to the firm. You're an excellent lawyer, you've got a keen mind, and your work ethic is second to none. It feels like only yesterday I invited you to play tennis at Wimbledon!"

"Indeed," William said. "Good thing you did, too, or I wouldn't have met Liz."

"Too true! Too true!" Mark paused dramatically, and William wondered where he was heading. "So I wanted to be the one to tell you, we'd like for you to make a move up. A rather large move."

"Up?" William said.

"Yes, up indeed. Look, I won't beat around the bush. We'd like for you to move to Cape Town and take over the office there as partner in charge. It's an enormous job, but we'd like for you to run our interests in the continent." He paused. "Well? What do you think?"

William had only to think for a second before nodding enthusiastically. "I'd love to! You know that Liz and I went to Cape Town for our honeymoon. We loved it there."

"Excellent! Now, let me pour us a brandy and we can toast your success."

Within six months, William and Liz had completed their relocation to Cape Town, moving into a house provided by the firm. It was a large, rambling estate called Claremont House. The house came with staff, automobiles and drivers, and stunning views from every window. The grounds were immaculately maintained in the English style, but with plants that were unfamiliar and surpassingly lovely to William and Liz. The mansion's mammoth reception rooms and intimate smaller chambers were ideal for family living and formal entertainment. The furnishings were also remarkable, a blend of fine English antiques and more modern furnishings of South African-Anglo design.

It was the perfect house for William and Liz to begin their family—and they did this right away. Soon, Liz and William had two children, and of course, the firm's social business kept them busy all the time. Liz was the perfect hostess, and night after night Liz and William were either being entertained or hosting their own engagements with clients, government officials, and friends.

William threw himself into his work as well, quickly immersing himself in the many issues surrounding litigation and law in South Africa. Although South Africa was technically an independent country, the British had tremendous influence and holdings throughout the country: a relic left over from the war, when South Africa had been strategically important to the British. South Africa was also the unquestioned economic capital of sub-Saharan Africa, with unrivaled access to the natural resources of the interior and ports large enough for global shipping. As a result, William found himself working with multinational corporations including DeBeers, which controlled the bulk of the world's diamond trade; Standard Oil of New Jersey; and the Chase Manhattan bank. William also handled a great deal of contracts for the U.S. government, which had seemingly bottomless pockets when it came to paying for international legal advice and access.

All in all, William and Liz were extremely happy in their new country with their picture-perfect family. As a distant cousin to the King of England, Liz had endless admirers and received invitations to every important event in the country, it seemed. Everyone wanted to rub elbows with English royalty, even at a distance. And William, as a Carnegie, had one of the more recognizable names in the world, as well as a network of connections that now stretched from Cape Town to London and back to New York and Washington, DC. Overall, they agreed their lives could hardly be improved.

The sole nagging exception for William—more even than Liz—was his observation of the local population. In the years they were there, the government of South Africa, run by white Boers, passed increasingly restrictive laws governing the freedom of the majority black population. Invariably, William observed, the blacks were poorer, less educated, had worse schools, and less access to satisfying work than South African whites. The neighborhood where William and Liz lived was exclusively white—the only blacks were house staff and other employees. Worse yet in a way was the attitude of the blacks who worked there: they were grateful to be employed at Claremont House because the mere association with white wealth, even as servants, gave them extra status.

It took William some time to realize why this bothered him so much, then it seemed simple: the blacks didn't even aspire to live in places like Claremont themselves. That was too far to dream. They only wanted the privilege of being servants there. It struck William as terribly sad that a whole race of people dared not even dream of lifting themselves above their meager situation, because such dreams could only be dashed at the hands of the increasingly violent and oppressive white police force.

It would have been easy to wish this situation was unique to South Africa. After all, the system they were beginning to call apartheid didn't really exist anywhere else in the developed world. But William knew all too well that wasn't true. His experience with Roan and Regina had showed him otherwise. Back in the United Kingdom, the Irish faced the same type of authority, the same militarized attacks on their culture and homes, as the blacks of South Africa. And even the United States wasn't innocent in this regard. In his younger days, William spent some time in the Deep South and he knew full well the codified, legal racism that existed there. In some ways, the Jim Crow South, apartheid South Africa and to some degree Ireland were mirror images of one another. Saddened, he thought: different place, same thing.

Over time, the situation continued to deteriorate, and before long the African National Congress was formed to promote black rights. The reaction of the white ruling minority was to clamp down tighter, and William and Liz began to worry that the situation in the country was becoming unstable and unsafe. Widespread police movement against black townships was countered with clandestine terrorism against white civilians, and William knew that his family was a potential target.

After six years, he brought up to Liz that perhaps it was time to move. She readily agreed, in part because of her declining health. She had been feeling increasingly listless, with unexplained symptoms, for a year or two, and the doctors in Cape Town were mystified. They could produce no diagnosis, no cure to help her. So the day finally came that William and Liz decided their time in South Africa had come to an end. But rather than move back to London, William announced he would be resigning his position with the firm and returning to the United States, to New York City. He had been gone for a long time—leaving the United States as a college graduate with only his good name and ambition. He would be returning as a family man, internationally respected lawyer, and a much wiser person.

Naturally, his father was thrilled and began making plans for William as soon as he should return to the city.

CHAPTER 23
CAMELOT ENDED

Ireland

SECURITY WAS ALWAYS A PRIORITY WHEN IT CAME TO THE ROYALS, BUT it never mattered so much as when any member of the royal family visited Ireland. The Crown took every precaution: decoys, alternate routes, secret plans, and of course heavily armed escorts. It was common knowledge that the IRA would like nothing more than to kill a member of the royal family. Thus, no one could be truly surprised when a sunny afternoon in Belfast was shattered by the sound of a bomb, the crunch and twist of metal, and the shriek of broken glass as the royal motorcade passed by. The truly shocking news, however, was broadcast several hours later, and Rosemary Firth's heart sunk as she listened to the broadcast:

"Today, terrorists of unknown identity set off a roadside bomb attacking the motorcade transporting the Princess Royal Mary and her husband, Prince Anthony. Fortunately, the Princess and her son John survived the attack while traveling in a separate vehicle with the prime minister.

"Her husband was not so fortunate. Prince Anthony was traveling in another Range Rover that was in the direct blast radius. He was killed instantly, along with his driver, his personal secretary, and two security personnel. He is survived by his wife, the Princess Royal Mary, heir to the throne of the British Empire, and his only son, Prince John, who would be next in line after the Princess Royal."

"An initial investigation suggests that the bomb was the work of the IRA. Immediately after the explosion, the Princess Mary and her son were escorted to the airport, where they were whisked back to England to be with the royal family. A state funeral is to be announced."

The next day, the story was carried as front-page news in every newspaper across the country: "*Camelot Ended,*" "*Love Assassinated,*" "*IRA Devils Deal Lethal Blow*".

Reaction to the news was swift and global, with heads of state from allies across the world calling into Buckingham Palace to offer their condolences and support to the British Crown. Condemnation of the IRA's terrorism was strident, and many countries offered military support to the British, although it was politely declined.

Of course, not everyone was so heartbroken. Immediately after the attack, a small group of men assembled in a safe house just miles away from the assassination site. They all wore black balaclavas, but stripped them off to reveal the sweating, exultant faces of IRA soldiers. They stared at each other for a moment, hoping almost against hope they had scored a royal with their attack. It would be only a matter of hours until they heard—but there was no time to wait.

"Here, boys," Roan Kelly growled, throwing open a chest and removing vestments. "From now on, we're just a couple of men of the cloth. Destroy any evidence. The Brits will be going door to door soon and they'll hang any of us if they can."

Within minutes, the band of hardened killers had been transformed into a polite order of monks and priests, grieving the horrible news. Over the next few days, the men would slip out one by one, some simply walking away and others hidden in the boot of getaway cars, each to slip out of the city and head for another, more secure location hopefully far beyond the reach of the enraged British military. Like any good commander, Roan Kelly was the last to leave their safe house, now satisfied that they had indeed killed a royal, no less than Prince Anthony himself. He took small satisfaction in his success: as far as he saw it, the British Crown owed his family a blood debt that could never be repaid.

Even as the assassins melted away, Britain mourned its lost prince—and none felt the loss as keenly as Princess Mary. She went through the formalities of the funeral as if in a daze, hardly aware of the crowds or the mass of flowers piled high against the palace gates. All she knew was that she had lost her Anthony, the love of her life. She leaned on her friend Rosemary throughout the service, pale and disoriented. At one point, she sat and choked back tears—it wouldn't do for a member of the royal family to be seen crying in public. Mary had always known that, no matter what loss she suffered, her life was not completely her own. She belonged to the Empire, and the people relied on her for resolve and strength in this horrible time. She recalled the words her father had used so long ago to prepare Anthony for a life in the harsh glare of the public eye. They had joked privately about it many times since, because it was so very true. Yet she had never expected the cost would be so high.

It wasn't until after the solemn funeral ceremony was over and she was alone with Rosemary in a private room that she finally allowed the tears to come, and she wept with abandon. Rosemary held her and let her sob.

"I…I don't know if I can go on!" Mary said. "They killed my Anthony!"

"I'm so sorry!" Rosemary said. "Such senseless violence!"

"What will I do?" Mary said. "What can I do?"

Rosemary squeezed her friend and, in a voice choked with emotion, said, "You will carry on, my love. You have to, for the kingdom and the crown. It's what Anthony would want, to become the Queen you were born to be and raise lovely John to be the King!"

Mary only sobbed all the harder.

It would be a full year before the Palace formally emerged from mourning, but the shadow of Anthony's death would be eternal for those who loved him.

CHAPTER 24
Coming Home

William and Liz landed in New York City, and William was thrilled to be home. He loved London, and South Africa was undeniably beautiful, but New York and the United States were home. For the first time in years, William was a resident of the United States again, and the hustle and bustle of the city suited him just fine.

The problem was, once he had returned, for the first time in his life he didn't know exactly what he wanted to do. He had a world of options. After retiring from the diplomatic service, his father had set about consolidating and expanding the family's stable of newspapers and other enterprises. By the time William got back, the Carnegie family owned or controlled forty-five dailies across the country, including some of the most influential papers in the United States.

But William—who had served in the Army, then as managing partner at an international law firm—wasn't really interested in the newspaper business. He enjoyed the politics of it, of course, and he admired what his father had been able to accomplish, but he didn't have "ink in his veins" and wasn't sure a life in the news was for him.

He also had the option to work for the Carnegie Family Trust Fund directly, using his legal knowledge to benefit the trust and help manage the family's assets. Again, his father's work had been enormously successful here too: the Carnegie trust had almost tripled in size over the previous decade, reaching the mind-boggling sum of nearly $3 billion in assets. But again, William didn't feel the call to spend his life serving the family's estate.

Finally, he could choose from the many offers pouring in from law firms and corporations across the country. William's reputation in international law, his global experience in finance, and his family connections were virtually irresistible to any number of leading firms. This was a time of American dominance in business and manufacturing, so there was no doubt William's talents and experience would be a great benefit to any private outfit lucky enough to sign him up, and some of the offers that came in were exceedingly generous.

Once again, though, William wasn't drawn to a life in the private sector. He had no doubt he would do well there, but the more he thought about it, and the more he discussed his next step with Liz and his family, he realized he was drawn to a higher calling: serving the people. William wasn't naïve enough to assume he could fix everything wrong with the world, but his outlook had been profoundly shaped by his experiences with the Irish independence movement first and then his time in Cape Town, South Africa. In both places, he had personally witnessed the problems that arose from seemingly intractable issues. He found the chaos and violence repellent, and if there was some small way he could contribute toward actually improving things, even in his own community, then that was what he wanted to do.

"Well, William," his father said, after William finished discussing his hopes with him. "Here's my advice. First, you run for a small office locally.

As with everything in this world, you'll have to earn your experience and wisdom the hard way. We can certainly help—you won't have to worry about some of the things politicians have to worry about, such as fundraising, media exposure, and name recognition—but there simply is no substitute for doing the hard work."

"You're right, Dad. I couldn't agree more."

His father smiled. "I believe you mean that. You know, William, you should know I have a great deal of respect for the way you've handled yourself. You've never shirked duty and never taken a shortcut. You've upheld the family name and conducted yourself with the utmost integrity in every instance. Son, you'll make a fine public servant, an honest and ethical one to boot!"

William's first race was indeed small: he ran for a seat on the Westchester County Board of Legislators. His first campaign wasn't flawless—it took him some time to grow comfortable giving stump speeches, and he was surprised by the amount of organization and administration it took to run even a small campaign. But his father brought in political consultants to help William, and he handily won his first race. Once in office, he brought his natural talents and perseverance to bear on the job, and was soon a favorite in his small pond.

From there, William's campaign skills increased quickly, and he used the Westchester County office to vault first to the state senate, where he proved himself a popular, proactive, and productive legislator. His initial difficulty speaking was soon conquered, as he learned to speak from the heart and always the truth. He became known for delivering passionate, eloquent speeches about equality of opportunity, poverty, and his ideas for tax reform and other measures that would help level the playing field for all New Yorkers. His face and ideas quickly became fixtures in the state's newspapers—even the ones his father didn't own.

Upon completion of his term in the state senate, his party's state chairman approached him and asked if he would consider heading up the ticket for the governor's office. "We'll throw all of our support behind you," the chairman said. "You shouldn't have to worry about a primary challenge, and we can pivot early to the general election. I think you can really win this, William. I think you could be the next governor of New York."

William eagerly signed up, and the campaign he ran was remarkable for its cohesion, organization, integrity, and focus. When the final ballots were counted on election night, William had crushed his opponent by more than fifteen percentage points, handing him a clear mandate on election night to pursue his policies and enact his platform. Once in office, William moved quickly to secure gains. His proposed overhaul of the state government was widely praised for making it less corrupt and more efficient. He changed the way state contracts were awarded and ended the routine practice of kickbacks to state officials who oversaw contract bidding. He launched a massive school-building program and passed a package of tax reforms that proved to be the model for other states across the country looking to make a fairer, simpler tax code and attract more businesses. Overall, throughout his term in office, William's average approval rating was in excess of 85 percent, making him the most consistently popular governor in the country and perhaps even in history.

This level of success wasn't without challenges. William worked long hours, and spent more time away from Liz and the kids than he would have liked. Her health had recovered after leaving Africa and getting access to top-notch medical care in New York City, but life in the United States was an adjustment for her, and there were some aspects of America that Liz felt she would never understand. She fretted sometimes that her children were growing up "too American," then laughed at herself because after all, she had married an American herself. And while she missed William during his long working hours at the state capital at Albany, she couldn't have been prouder of him and more supportive of his policies and beliefs.

Still, Liz did occasionally struggle with homesickness, so she was overjoyed to receive an invitation to her parents' 50TH wedding anniversary. She immediately convinced William to go, and with the children they began to lay plans for another trip "across the pond," back to jolly old England.

CHAPTER 25
A Royal Romance

Buckingham Palace

After losing Anthony, Princess Mary slid into a dark depression. Despite being surrounded by people almost constantly, she often felt lonely. Sometimes she thought she heard his voice and turned to see him, only to realize all over again that he was gone. Without Anthony by her side, she found her official duties frequently dull and tedious, and she struggled to stay engaged with the day-to-day workings of the royal household. Her only joy was her son John, the Prince of Wales, and she spent long hours playing with him. Many people remarked that the Princess only seemed truly happy when she was with John.

Princess Mary wasn't only depressed—she was also increasingly fearful for her and her son's safety. If the IRA could reach into the heart of the royal family and kill her husband, then she felt like they could never be truly safe outside of the palace. It made it infinitely worse that no suspects were ever caught for the bombing that killed Anthony. Were the killers still about, waiting to strike against her again? She was briefed on the investigation regularly, and through these briefings she became dismally aware of how sophisticated and widespread the Irish terrorist network had become. It filled her with despair to realize that the IRA would stop at nothing to fulfill their violent goals, and as soon as one soldier was arrested or killed, two more leaped up to take his place. How could a civilized society fight such fanaticism?

Hoping to make her feel safer, the King and Queen named a special security officer to personally handle Mary's detail. His name was Cyril Belmont and he was the perfect fit for the job. Belmont had seen action during the war and earned distinction in the fight against fascism. After the war was over, Belmont enlisted for elite security training and was adept in virtually any emergency situation. Further, his loyalty to the Crown could not be called into question.

He had attended Oxford, Eton, and The Royal Military Academy, Sandhurst, where he graduated at the top of his class. He was also the son of Lord Francis Belmont, an enormously successful industrialist and distantly related to royalty. Cyril's mother, now long retired, had been a lady-in-waiting in King John's court. The family lived in a stately country home surrounded by hundreds of acres of land. Cyril was average-looking, but rather tall, something he capitalized upon since it allowed him to survey the situation above the crowds.

Cyril took his job seriously from the first day. He had a deep-seated compulsion to be near the Princess at all times, as well as her young son. He went so far as to request access to her daily calendar to personally screen anyone who wanted access to her royal personage. Mary immediately felt comforted by Cyril's presence, and she quickly grew to rely on his soothing and reassuring vigil. Before long, Cyril was regularly skipping holidays and days off to accompany the Princess, no matter where she went.

As often happens in these situations, it wasn't long before Cyril recognized that his growing feelings for the Princess had moved beyond that of bodyguard and subject. In fact, he was falling in love with her. Underneath the sadness, he occasionally caught flashes of the same fun-loving spirit that Anthony had been so attracted to, and he found himself working sometimes to bring out Mary's laugh or easy smile. And sometimes, when he dared hope, he thought that perhaps Mary felt the same way. Occasionally, he fancied that he caught her giving him a sly, secret glance. Of course, Cyril had no intention of acting on his hopes—if he was wrong at all, his career would be effectively ended and he would bring humiliation on his family, neither of which he was prepared to risk.

Still, with his feelings growing, he needed some kind of outlet and found himself confiding his love in his old friend and palace confidant, Rosemary Firth. He knocked on her palace apartment door one evening, feeling foolish but determined to press on. He needed someone to talk to about this. Rosemary answered the door and immediately looked flustered—she and Cyril had known each other since childhood, often chatting in public, but he had never called upon her at her apartment before.

"Can I help you?" she said, and Cyril was surprised to see a blush rising in her cheeks. He wondered if he had caught her perhaps eating a tin of cookies or drinking something a little stronger than tea.

"Good evening, Rosemary," he said. "May I come in?"

"Of course! Please! Would you like some tea, or perhaps something a bit stronger? I think I have a spot of something here."

Cyril walked in, automatically running his professional eye over the apartment. An open book lay on the settee, as if he had merely disturbed her reading. There was no evidence of a hasty cover-up of anything. He chalked her blush up to the inscrutable ways of women. "No, I'm fine," he said, sitting down on a couch while she settled back on the settee, curling her feet under herself and playing with a strand of hair.

"So, what I can do for you?" she asked. "Or did you just want to be in my presence?"

"Well," Cyril said slowly, still a little confused by her behavior. "I, ah, need some advice in the love department." He gave a short, self-deprecating laugh. "This isn't something they teach at the Academy."

"Oh? Go on." She swallowed a little nervously, and he inwardly shrugged. He had been trained to closely observe people, but he had no idea why Rosemary was acting the way she was.

"Well, you see, err; it's not for me exactly, actually. I have a friend, ah, here in the palace, who has grown increasingly infatuated with a woman. Mind you, she is totally unaware of his intentions, and it probably should stay that way. But then my friend suspects she might feel the same way, and he just doesn't know how to start the conversation."

Rosemary pursed her lips. "Hmm. So what you're asking is, how can this man tell the woman that he has feelings for her?"

"Well, yes, I suppose that's the long and the short of it."

"And how can I help you, do you think?"

"Err, well, I was hoping you could sort of smooth the introduction, so to speak. Maybe provide some female perspective on the right way to go about these types of things. You see, my friend has very little experience with women."

"Ah," Rosemary said. "Perhaps he's in the military?"

Now it was Cyril's turn to stifle a blush. "Uh, well, yes, as it so happens."

"I see. Has he considered just coming out and saying what's on his mind?"

"Well, I…it's a delicate situation, with this particular woman, you see. And, err…" He let it trail lamely off.

"Might you give me your friend's name?" she said softly, leaning forward and staring at him with shining eyes.

He held his hands up. "Okay, you've cornered me. It's really me."

"Oh!" she said. "Imagine! And…the name of the woman? Could you part with that?"

She was now leaning forward and the color had come into her cheeks in high spots, her eyes shining at him. He still had no clue why she was acting so oddly, but figured that women were simply interested in this type of thing.

"Err, well, if I tell you, you must promise to keep this a right secret. Just between us."

"Of course," she almost purred.

"The fact is, I've fallen in love with the Princess Royal, but I dare not approach her." He swallowed hard. "As my dear friend, and hers too, do you think you could approach her, sort of off the record, and find out if she would be interested in me?"

Rosemary suddenly sat back and the color drained from her face. She looked as if she'd been slapped and Cyril thought for a second that those were tears shining in her eyes. She didn't talk for a moment, but instead laid a hand on her cheek and drew a shuddering breath.

"I see. You're in love with Princess Mary."

"Yes. And I know it's terribly improper, but…I think I'm just the sort of chap she needs right now. The problem is, I can't think of a way to tell her without risking insulting her. Or worse."

"Right," Rosemary said in a deflated voice. "Why wouldn't she be interested? You're a charming and distinguished officer of her army, fine-looking and lots of fun to be with."

"You really think that, Rosemary?"

She gave him a somewhat withering look that only added to his confusion. "Of course I think that," she said. "Cyril, I've known you just about all my life. You are a man who any woman would be pleased to call her husband."

"Husband maybe, but how about Prince? I'm not sure the Princess would consider me a proper suitor or partner. Anyone who pursues her would certainly be criticized as being ambitious or status-seeking. How would Mary know I was sincere in my intentions and not just one of those, you know, opportunists, looking to marry well?"

"I have known Mary most of my life...she is a loving and astute person. I believe that anyone who really knows you knows that you are an honorable and wonderful man, not looking for glory or fortune. She surely will see this in you. So I suspect your intentions will not be misunderstood. But I do have a question for you."

"Yes?"

"Why, after all these years, are you thinking of actually taking a partner now?" Rosemary said. "You have always been a career officer and bachelor. Everyone has always assumed that you would never marry."

Cyril thought this over—the same question had been nibbling at his mind too. As a career military man, he had spent his life in the company of men, with the occasional fling thrown in, especially in his younger days. But now...

"I don't know, Rosemary, but age is funny," he said. "The older a bloke gets, the more he realizes that he doesn't want to be alone anymore. People come and go out in your life, and at some point you want someone to care about you as much as you care about them. Being a military officer I have traveled and seen the world. My career has always been paramount. But then Princess Mary came into my life. She was so wounded by the tragic loss of Anthony, so needy, so fragile. I think that is what first attracted me to her: my need to protect and take care of her. During my tenure, I have learned to love and admire her. She is so kind and generous in the service of her country. You know, Mary and I have that in common. Serving our country with dignity and sacrifice is all that we know, at least for me. I can only hope this might change. Being connected to a woman, especially one as extraordinary as Mary, seems eminently more important, or at least more desirable, than empty nights and fleeting escapades."

"I see," she said. "You know, Cyril, sometimes love is right in front of you but you completely miss it. It's a shame how love works sometimes." She sighed. "But yes, I can help you. If you'd like, I'll talk to her and find out where you stand. If she's smart, she'll see that you're a wonderful, caring, and loyal man."

Cyril stood up, wringing his hands as he crossed the room to plant a kiss on Rosemary's cheek. "Thank you! You really are a great friend!" He paused. "You know, we've known each other such a long time. You remember playing in the gardens at the Hampton House?"

"As if it were yesterday," she said. "But I suppose those old days will never come back."

"No, they never do. So…when do you think you'll talk to her?"

"Soon, Cyril, very soon," she said, and if Cyril didn't know better, he would have sworn that her words were steeped in sadness.

Early the next morning, Rosemary went for a stroll in the garden—knowing that she would find Mary in her customary place, alone among the flowers. She also knew that Mary tended to be at her most relaxed in the garden.

"Oh, hello," Mary said, looking up as Rosemary walked down the path toward her. As Rosemary had suspected, Mary was wearing her gardening hat and looked happy. "You going for a walk, then?"

"I thought I might find you here," Rosemary said. "Lovely morning."

"Indeed. Sometimes it's hard to imagine the city is just beyond these walls."

"No doubt," Rosemary said.

They walked for a bit, commenting on individual flowers and small palace matters. Eventually, when Rosemary felt the time was right, she asked the question she had come to ask: "I've wondered…have you ever considered marrying again?"

"Marrying?" Mary said, surprised. "What on earth are you thinking?"

"Oh, I don't know," Rosemary said breezily. "It was just a thought. You're still young and quite beautiful. And do we really need another Virgin Queen?"

"As if!" Mary said. "You should know better than that!"

"Oh, I know! I'm just teasing a bit. But really? Would you?"

Mary thought for a moment and Rosemary was surprised to see tears well up in her eyes. "You know I think about Anthony every single day," she said. "Did you know that?"

Rosemary didn't answer.

"I think I loved him from the first moment I saw him," she said. "Do you remember introducing us? At that silly house party?" Rosemary nodded, and Mary continued. "He was the first and only man to have my heart. And of course, he is the father of my children. *All* my children." Her eyes glistened with tears. "I miss him terribly. It's so…lonely without him. But marriage again? I just don't know, Rosemary. I can't imagine it."

"I'm sorry," Rosemary said. "I didn't mean to upset you."

Mary sniffled and laughed a little. "It's okay. But since we're asking, what about you? Why haven't you married yet? Surely there's some dashing type running around the palace you fancy?"

Rosemary flushed. "Oh, Mary, I'm not really the marrying kind."

"Then exactly what kind are you?"

Rosemary knew Mary was being playful, but the Princess's words still cut deeply. "What I mean, Mary, is that I have spent my life with you and helping you raise John. I have no room in my life for a man. And besides that, I don't know anyone who would put up with me or want to bed me!"

"Oh my! How could you say such a thing? There must be many men who would do anything to have you as their wife."

"None that I can think of," Rosemary said, hoping to change the direction of the conversation. "But…" she hesitated, "if someone did express an interest in me, you'd tell me, wouldn't you?"

"However would I find out something like that?" Mary exclaimed, still laughing.

"I'm sure you have your ways. But would you tell me?"

Mary stopped walking and gave her friend a suspicious look. "Rosemary Firth, are you trying to tell me something? Do you suspect there's a chap here who is interested in cozying up to you?"

Rosemary tried not to let her feelings show on her face. "No, no. I'm speaking only hypothetically."

"Well then hypothetically yes. Of course I would tell you! I should think that's the only friendly thing to do."

Rosemary nodded. "That's what I thought, too."

"Rosemary, you're awfully frustrating this morning. Could you just out with it? Who is this mystery man you're obviously hinting about and what makes you think I can help you?"

"You always were too quick on the uptake," Rosemary said. "But the man I'm talking about isn't interested in me. He's interested in *you*."

Mary looked stunned and swayed in the path before taking a seat on a garden bench. "Me! You're telling me I have a palace suitor?" The thought was so incredible to her that she actually threw her head back and laughed in wonder. "Who would want me? I'm a middle-aged single mother in perpetual mourning! I must be the least eligible woman in this whole palace! In the whole world!"

"You mustn't believe that," Rosemary said. "Because this man is terribly serious. He came to me and asked if he had a chance with you, if you might be interested in him."

Mary just shook her head in mute wonder.

"But…he's afraid, you see, because the situation is delicate. You see, you know him quite well, and his job…well, it depends upon you."

"I see," Mary said. "Who is it, Rosemary? You must give me the name."

"You must promise you won't do anything to hurt him or embarrass him," Rosemary said. "He's a dear, dear man. A lovely man!"

"Yes, but who is it?" Mary pressed.

"Cyril."

Mary couldn't hide the surprise on her face. "Cyril?" she echoed.

"Yes. He's...well, I suppose he's rather fallen in love with you."

"Oh my God," was all Mary said, and Rosemary could read her feelings broadcast on her face: apprehension, surprise, flattery, and was that even a touch of joy? Rosemary knew well how close Mary and Cyril had become; she knew they traveled virtually everywhere together, that Cyril had sworn to protect her and her son with his own life. She also knew that, like Mary, Cyril took his duty to Crown and country more seriously than anything else, and that for him to even pursue this crazy love must mean it was the real thing.

Yet Rosemary knew better than anyone except Mary herself the awesome responsibility that waited for Mary and how much it affected her friend. Were it not for the crown awaiting her, she never would have given up her first baby, never would have lost her husband. Suddenly, Rosemary's heart went out to her friend: despite all of her feelings, she pitied Mary and the tragedies that had taken away her firstborn and then her husband.

And yet...it was also true that Mary still had her son. She still had John. And try as she might, Rosemary couldn't help the wild surge of envy that rose in her stomach. She didn't begrudge Mary her family or her happiness—she loved her friend dearly. But even with everything Mary had lost, she still had more than Rosemary had ever taken for her own. And now she was sitting flabbergasted because the man that Rosemary herself desperately loved wanted to declare his loyalty to the Princess. It was almost too much for Rosemary to bear.

Even as she thought this, Mary seemed to have reached some type of resolution herself.

"That is a surprise," Mary began, "I'm sorry to have been caught off guard. It's just that I know Cyril so well, and well, I suppose I may have suspected he felt this way, but to hear it so bluntly was a bit shocking. But..." she hesitated, "there is much to consider in this, isn't there? Cyril is an excellent man and comes from a proper family himself. John of course adores him. And, well, I must admit that I grow so lonely. No man could ever replace Anthony—I would never even ask Cyril to try. In truth, there need not be love for a union like this to yield some measure of happiness and distraction. And if real love were to develop over time, that's all the better."

It took Rosemary a moment to realize what Mary was saying. "So you're saying...you don't love him?"

"Well of course not! You must know that my heart will always belong to Anthony."

Rosemary felt a surge of hope—perhaps Mary would rebuff Cyril's advances, leaving him heartbroken and available to Rosemary. But then Mary continued, "But that doesn't mean I want to discourage him necessarily. Someday I will be Queen, and having a man by my side will be a great relief. So I think you should tell him to proceed, but very carefully. He would need to understand exactly what I mean. This would be a relationship of convenience by necessity. I'm sure he'll understand."

"Oh goodness," Rosemary said, feeling as if she wanted to cry but knowing she couldn't. She understood Mary's position, but the fact that she wanted to wear Cyril like an expensive watch or ring, an adornment without real love, was shattering for her. Still, Rosemary was nothing if not a faithful servant to the Crown, and if Mary felt that Cyril could make her happy, and Cyril was certainly interested, then she had no choice but to cooperate. She bowed her head in acceptance to hide her grief and said she would certainly talk to Cyril.

***

Rosemary called Cyril the next day and arranged a meeting. She wondered how in the world she ever got herself into the position of playing Cupid. Naturally, Cyril was elated with the news that Mary would be receptive to his advances. When Rosemary told him that Mary was receptive to his advances, he literally jumped for joy, grabbing her and dancing around the room. She had never seen him so happy.

"You're the best, Rosemary! Thank you and rest assured I'll never forget your help. I feel like a chap whose team just took first place in a game of cricket."

"Cyril, mind you now, you need to proceed with caution. Remember, only fools rush in."

Cyril obviously didn't hear this warning—either then or the next day. The very next day, he sought out Mary as was his custom, but greeted her with a warm smile and a hand that lightly touched her elbow. It might not have seemed like much to most people, but Mary—who knew that touching a royal person was strongly frowned upon—instantly recognized that Rosemary must have had her conversation with Cyril. Rather than pull away, she simply smiled at Cyril, and he beamed like a lad in love.

Outwardly, their schedule hardly changed. They were still a constant presence together in the public eye, attending events with Cyril as her escort and security detail, or taking walks in the parks surrounding Buckingham Palace with Prince John always under the watchful eye of Cyril. Yet something had undeniably changed between them, and it didn't take long for the watchful eye of the royal press to notice it. Soon headlines began to speculate that Mary and Cyril were more than Princess and royal bodyguard. "Is Princess Falling for Top Cop?" the headlines wondered. "Has He Put a Lock on Her Heart?" they asked.

Of course they would never dignify the reports with a response, but they did little to discourage them. Mary had other concerns to attend to: her father,

King John, was ailing and rarely seen in public anymore. When he was seen, the newspapers endlessly speculated on his health, and the more crude anti-royalist papers wondered if the monarchy would die with King John, an event that was expected at any time. Mary and her mother ignored these reports too, but privately plans for her ascension were put into place. As throughout history, it was of paramount importance that the succession was smooth.

As part of these plans, Mary surprised Cyril one day by almost bluntly proposing they marry. "Excuse me?" he said, hardly daring to hope he'd heard her right.

"Yes, I think we shall," she said. "After all, we're perfectly comfortable with each other. And it would be much more complicated to marry as a sitting Queen than a simple Princess. What do you say, Cyril? Will you have me?"

"Of...of course!" he said, stunned that the Princess had just proposed to him. He'd always imagined royal engagements to be vastly complicated and bound in tradition. It boggled his mind that it could be as simple as this. And this time there would be no dictatorial speech from the King. Cyril was a known entity, eminently qualified as a Queen's husband, and Mary was not an innocent young woman as with Anthony.

Always with her eye on her duty, Mary lost no time preparing the country for her marriage. It was leaked through official channels to friendly press that the Princess and her "top cop" had fallen in love and were planning to be married. The tabloids had a field day: "*Second chance for Princess Mary!*" "*Heartbroken no more! Princess Mary to wed her true love!*"

Of course, she knew the truth, but it mattered little. The realm was happy; she was perfectly content to marry a man like Cyril; and she couldn't have been any more thrilled to have a man around the "house". Before long, the palace began to prepare for a royal wedding.

***

As the news and preparation for the upcoming wedding consumed the palace, the joy seemed to flow around one island of misery: Rosemary.

Since the day Cyril had confessed his love for Mary, and she had arranged for them to see each other as more than a Princess and bodyguard, she had been increasingly despondent. Even as Mary drew closer to Cyril, Rosemary was not fooled. She knew her best friend far too well to believe that Mary had properly fallen in love with Cyril. She knew that it remained a relationship of convenience. But she also knew that Cyril was not hers—every time she saw Cyril's face light up as he looked at Mary, her heart broke a little more. It was this knowledge, more than anything else, that led her to put a smile on her face whenever she saw Mary or Cyril and throw herself into the planning on the wedding, just as a maid of honor should.

When the wedding finally arrived, Rosemary noticed that it had somewhat less pomp and circumstance than Mary's first wedding, but that the country at large enthusiastically embraced it nonetheless. There were the same crowds, the same breathless news reports about the happy couple, and the same relentless focus on Mary's dress, her jewels, and all the accoutrements that came along with a royal wedding. Rosemary moved through the day as if in daze: nodding when protocol called for it, smiling until she thought her cheeks might split, and unable to stop the tears from streaming down her face as she walked behind Mary in the slow, formal cadence down the center aisle of the great cathedral while Cyril waited at the head of the church to take his vows, looking as happy as any man alive.

When it was finally over, Rosemary ducked away at the first moment and sought out the refuge of her apartments in the palace, where she had a good cry and began to make her plans. Two weeks later, when Rosemary was finally alone with Mary again, she took a deep breath and said, "Mary, I'm so happy for you...but there's something I want to tell you now that things have rather quieted down."

"Oh? Is everything all right?"

"Yes, yes," Rosemary said. "It's just…I wanted to tell you that I've decided to move to Switzerland."

"Switzerland? Whatever would you move to Switzerland for? You're like part of the family here!"

Rosemary couldn't help but notice that Mary was gradually becoming more regal, more used to commanding people. This was undoubtedly good for the country, but not so good for their friendship.

"I know," she said, "and you must know how much I love you and dear John. But the fact is that John is growing older now. Soon he'll outgrow a doting old maid like myself. He'll be off to school. And you and Cyril of course have each other. I feel like it's time for me to carve out a life for myself, perhaps paint a bit or maybe write a novel. I've always dreamt of living the life of the artist. Now feels like the right time."

Mary gave her friend a long look and laid a gentle hand on Rosemary's arm.

"Are you quite sure?" she asked.

"Yes. Very."

"Very well then," she said. "I do understand, of course. But if you must go, at least allow me to make sure you're provided for. You're my dearest and oldest friend. You'll let me do this for you?"

"Do what?"

"Well, I can arrange for you to receive a generous pension for your service to the Crown. And we have extensive connections in Switzerland and can help you locate lodging in a beautiful setting, I'm sure." Mary couldn't help herself and began to choke up. "You've meant so much to me over the years, Rosemary. What would I have become without you? What would I have done? I will never forget your friendship and loyalty. I am truly unable to repay you. For everything."

Rosemary teared up too, for she knew exactly what Mary was referring to: the tremendous secret they had kept between them for all those years.

With tears running down her face, Mary finished, "I will always be true to you and pray that you will always be true to me, as long as we both shall live. Please let me know if there's anything else I can do for you."

"If you don't mind, I'd like to take some of the photographs we have taken over the years and the scrap and baby books I did for John. It will be something I will cherish."

"Take whatever you like, Rosemary," Mary said. "Keep them as memories of our times...in your mind and in your heart. And know you will always be welcome back, any time, and under any circumstances."

"You are a lucky woman to have Cyril," Rosemary said. "I know your fondness for him will surely grow into love. He has told me how much he loves you and that he is now the happiest man in the world. Thank you for all the wonderful years and your generosity. Remember me to Cyril. Tell him I will write."

There was finality to their hug, as if each suspected this was the last time they would see each other.

Early the next morning, Mary called her secretary into her small office and explained that Rosemary was leaving her service. She instructed her to set up a generous pension and provided instructions for a onetime grant amounting to several thousand pounds.

Two years later

Twenty-four months after Mary's wedding, King John XV did something that so few sitting kings have done: he passed away in his sleep. Upon his death, Mary succeeded as the Sovereign, with Cyril, now called the Prince Consort, at her side. The nation mourned the loss of the King at the same time all eyes turned toward the expected Coronation of a new Queen.

CHAPTER 26
IN A PIG'S EYE

WILLIAM CARNEGIE, NOW GOVERNOR OF NEW YORK, WAS LOOKING forward to heading back to London with his wife for his in-laws'—Sir Michael Chartworth and his wife, Lady Leslie—fiftieth wedding anniversary. The event had been in planning stages for months, and Liz was thrilled to be heading home to spend time with her family and see old friends and visit old haunts. William couldn't have agreed more. It was true that he had mixed feelings about his time in London so long ago—he couldn't think of London without also thinking of Regina—but in all he knew that Britain had brought him together with his wife, whom he adored, and he felt that London was where had he had really begun to grow into a man and chart his own course in life.

The Carnegie family sailed across the Atlantic in style and arrived to a large and enthusiastic greeting party composed of both friends and Liz's family, as well as a small contingent of press that was excited to have contact with a sitting U.S. governor. They went from the harbor straight to the historic

Savoy, where they had reserved a grand suite. The plan was to split their time between Liz's family estate and the Savoy, which would allow William to host some business associates and promote New York state tourism without having too many people tramping through the private estate.

Naturally, William anticipated a long list of callers—his office had arranged for several full days of meetings both before and after the actual anniversary party—but sitting on his makeshift desk and reviewing his messages one day, he was surprised to see one name that caught his eye: Roan Kelly. A deep thread of disquiet snuck into William's belly. Of course Roan would have been able to find out he was here; the news had been widely reported throughout the tabloid media. And William had no specific reason he could put into words for his trepidation about contacting Roan. He had even continued with his financial support, and Roan had made good on his promise to provide a better accounting of where the money was spent, sending William lists of dollar figures next to places with names like St. Francis Home for Boys. Yet William couldn't help the tiny thread of doubt that still wormed into his subconscious.

Still, William knew he must return the call, if only for old times' sake. Rather than have his secretary set up a call, however, he reached out himself and dialed the phone number Roan had left. When they finally did connect, William couldn't help but smile when Roan's rough brogue echoed down the line: "William is that really you? It's been a long time, mate!"

"Yes, how are you Roan?"

"How am I, he asks! I couldn't be better if I was a cow in a clover field."

"Great to hear, old friend…" And William let it hang.

"So," Roan said, happily continuing. "What do you say? How about we meet at A Pig's Eye for a pint or two? We can kick it up like old times."

"Sounds great, Roan, but I'm sure you've seen. I'm here on family business and not sure I can slip away."

"Not sure you can slip away!" Roan echoed. "Blimey! That's a load of malarkey if I've ever heard one! You get yer ass over to the pub tonight at 11:30 and I'll see you then."

William couldn't help but smile a little bit. Roan was obviously still Roan.

"All right," he relented. "But just one drink. I have to be up early tomorrow morning and can't be suffering from a long night. I'm sure you understand."

Roan just laughed and rang off.

William hung up the phone and stared at it long and hard. He somehow felt as if he had just made a deal with the devil, then shook it off and went back to work. Later that night, after Liz and the kids had gone to sleep, he left the hotel and took a black cab to south London, right next to Lambeth. The entire ride there, the cabbie had been shooting dark glances at William in the rearview. It wasn't often that a guest at the Savoy, which was on the banks on the Thames in central London, requested a ride to this dark and dangerous neighborhood. When a fare did ask to be dropped off, he was likely up to no good.

William exited the cab, took a deep breath to steel himself, and entered the pub. It had been a long time since he'd been in one of Roan's pubs, but this one looked just like all the others, like nothing had changed at all—even down to the withered old men perched on the barstools and staring at him suspiciously. A grizzled old bartender leaned on the bar and a tired-looking band played Irish folk songs in the corner. The smell was also familiar: stale smoke, alcohol, and the reek of unwashed, close bodies. Still, the place looked very different to William, and he wondered how he could have loved the rough corners of this seedy bar back then. "Have I changed that much?" he thought, but then realized that the obvious answer was yes.

"William!" a familiar voice boomed as Roan jumped from a dark booth where he sat with another man whose face was in shadow. "Come over, lad. Join us!"

William crossed the bar and slid into the booth, shaking hands with the other man. His name was Shaun, and looked to be in his twenties. He was tall and impressively built, with rough, scarred hands that looked like they could inflict damage. Roan introduced him as "my first lieutenant," which only added to William's disquiet. Why did they use military titles?

"Welcome, brother, welcome!" Roan said. "Aren't you a sight for sore eyes! How long has it been, eh? Too long, I dare say. Far too long." Roan signaled for a beer for William. "So," he continued, "you're a governor, hey? A real muckity muck back in the States. How does that pay?"

William wasn't sure how to answer that. He honestly had no idea what his governor's salary was and had instructed that the whole salary should be donated to a local New York State orphanage. Instead, he decided to change the topic. "You look good, Roan. How are you? I hope you've been taking care of yourself and staying away from trouble."

Roan barked out a short laugh. "Trouble seeks me out, my friend. Or maybe it's me the one who seeks out trouble. Me and Shaun here have been doing everything we can to stick a thorn right in the British side. We've been doing a fair job of it too."

William didn't answer.

"You've probably heard of some of our finer work. If you know what I mean."

William's discomfort grew exponentially and he regretted coming at all. He wondered if he should get up and leave. He didn't know what Roan was referring to, but it was like a lightbulb had switched on in his head as a terrible thought pushed its way into his mind: Prince Anthony's assassination and the attack on the royal family. William didn't want to believe Roan would be involved in such a thing, but he took one close look at his friend's face and suddenly there was no room for doubt.

"Cat got your tongue, mate?" Roan asked. Then he laughed uproariously. "Don't worry, William. We're no fools. We're not going to implicate you! For the love of my dear dead sister, we're not stupid enough to kill the goose that laid the golden egg."

"Roan—"

"Look, mate," Roan said. "I understand where you're at and what you're doing. But you should know, the work you're doing with us has been a great boon for the Irish people, and not only the orphans. We're in a fight for our lives against these Limey pricks. You must know that, you must see it. Surely you haven't forgotten that even with your wife as one of them."

"Now wait—"

"You know," Roan said, overriding him again, "you know you're like a brother to me. You almost were my brother, William. But since then, you didn't have to consort with a runaround like myself. You could have dropped me. But you didn't. You've made it possible for me and my mates to do real work for the Irish. You're a right hero, you are. A true hero. You don't know how many lives you've saved or made better. So now I'm asking you, William, to stick with us. I feel like we're about to make a real breakthrough. The Brits have no stomach for this sort of thing. They'll wear down, you mark my words, and when they do, it'll be thanks to people like you who helped give a whole people their freedom."

So there it was, and William felt slightly sick to his stomach. Roan was all but coming out and asking him to support terrorism against the English—more than he might have already done. A great anger seized him, and then drained away almost as fast as it came, replaced by a tremendous sadness. He had loved Regina with all of his heart. Did it have to come to this?

When he did start speaking, he was slow and deliberate. "Listen, Roan, you know I've thought of you like my brother too, and you know that if Regina was still alive you would be my brother in legal fact as well. But I'm not comfortable with the use of violence to obtain political ends. There is a system in place in all democracies, and that system must be given the freedom and ability to work. That is the only way civilized people can conduct themselves and ensure peace, prosperity and freedom for all."

"Democracy!" Roan said. "How can you say the Irish reality is anything like democracy!"

"I didn't say it was," William said carefully. "What I said was that there is a political process, and in that political process there is room for differing views and even victories. But there is no room for bloodshed and I won't condone it or support it under any circumstances. I'm afraid you've misunderstood my intentions."

Roan sat back in his booth and eyed William. Shaun cast a glance at his elder, then looked back at William, his eyes unreadable.

"I see," Roan finally said in a quiet, dangerous voice. "So what are ye telling me, then, my brother? That you plan to abandon your support for the cause that Regina, your Regina, gave her life to? You're planning on turning your back on me, the memory of Regina, the orphans, and all of the Irish people?"

William held Roan's eyes and felt like he was standing at a precipice. It occurred to him that Shaun had slid his beer aside, perhaps the better to lunge across the table if he had to, and for a moment he imagined Shaun as a dangerous dog on a chain, waiting only for the command to attack. But just as quickly as this thought arose, he pushed it away. Surely this was the product of his overheated imagination, the late hour, and his strange surroundings.

But then, William realized, he had no idea how dangerous Roan really was, or how he had earned that scar under his eye. And yet...his mind boiled in conflict. His loyalty to Regina's memory was not seriously in question. As an American, and now a man who devoted his life to serving the lofty ideals of liberty, he understood why the Irish would yearn for self-rule, and he harbored no illusions about the English military occupation of Ireland. There simply were no easy answers. But violence was not one of them.

"I'm sorry, Roan," William said. "I would be happy to contribute to the support of children who were orphaned in this conflict...for Regina's memory. But I'm afraid I can no longer continue to provide that support through you."

Roan nodded slowly, his voice icy. "I see how it is, then. You're a politician now. You're one of them."

William slid from the booth abruptly, leaving his beer unfinished. "I'm sorry, Roan," he said. He tossed a few bills on the table for the beers. "Listen, take care of yourself. Maybe it's time to find a nice farm somewhere in Ireland and retire. Find a nice Colleen to keep you warm at night."

Roan, clearly loose with drink, said, "You must know I can't do that. Not while my people go unavenged. And now you, my brother, selling me out like the English pigs would. You're no better than them. Curse you and your bloody money. Get out of my sight."

"Nice meeting you, Shaun," William said. "You two stay out of harm's way."

Shaun merely glared at William as he walked away.

Roan lifted a glass and cocked his head. "Drop dead William."

He gave Roan a final look, then turned and left the pub, now certain that he would never see Roan again.

CHAPTER 27
RUN, WILLIAM, RUN

Washington, DC

THEO LITTLETON HAD A PROBLEM. AS THE NATIONAL CHAIRMAN OF HIS beloved political party, he helped decide who would run for office, and in many cases decided if that person would win or lose by how much money he was willing to direct toward any particular campaign. In the truest sense of the word, he was a kingmaker who brought leaders to power through the exercise of political influence. And just then, in the run-up to the 1984 presidential contest, Littleton was having the kind of problem that party chairmen lived for: he needed to round out a presidential ticket that he fully expected to win the White House in the next presidential election cycle.

Littleton had seen all the polling, and it looked good, but more important was the feeling in his bones. His bones told him this would be a good year for his party. After a decade of government stagnation and another flare-up in the endless wars in the Middle East, his sensitive antennae told him that the White House was his to lose.

Through a series of maneuvers, strong-arming, and begging, he had already drafted the man he expected to be at the top of the ticket once the smoke cleared: Lionel Keith. Keith was basically the perfect candidate for his time. He had served as governor of California, where he had both instituted a series of wildly popular tax code reforms while overseeing his state's "economic miracle." There was something in Keith for everyone to love, from the squishiest of the middle voters to the hardest of the hardcore faithful. All Keith had to do was win the primary, but Littleton had no doubt in this department. Keith's main competition came in the form of a half-mad Texan who wanted to abolish half of the federal government and declare war on half of the known world.

What Littleton needed—and the problem he had been chewing on for days—was just the right vice presidential candidate. In the never-ending Electoral College calculus that ran through his head, he could see any number of scenarios. He knew he could count on Texas even if their guy didn't sit atop the ticket, and Keith would no doubt deliver California. The South was touchy, but he believed it could be won. The Midwest was much less likely—it would take a special candidate to bring along Michigan and Illinois. And the Northeast could go either way.

On top of this, he would need to balance out Keith's main weakness: his age. Keith was nearly 70 years old, which made him significantly older than previous presidential candidates. The last thing he wanted to do was nominate another senior citizen and watch his dreams of the White House go down in flames because he ran the "Geritol Kid." No, he needed someone young, with energy, vitality, and charisma to spare.

Littleton had two names on his top-secret sheet of paper.

The first was Baylor Ambrose, currently lieutenant governor of South Carolina. There was a lot to recommend for Lt. Gov. Ambrose. He was only 52, had a head of hair that could only be called luxurious, spoke in the lilting Southern drawl that almost nobody could resist, and nobody could question his bona fides in the South. The only problem Littleton could see was Ambrose's earlier association with less-than-desirable "white rights" parties and some of his statements on social issues. Littleton's oppo research had turned up some old opinion columns Ambrose had written during his college days where he advocated that "Negroes unhappy with the American system are welcome to return to Africa, from where they came. And I'll buy their tickets." Littleton himself had almost no opinion on the matter—he was a political pragmatist, and he had no illusions how these old columns would play in an "increasingly racialized electorate," as he liked to call it. Run a guy like Ambrose and he was likely to spend the whole campaign coaching candidates to disavow racism.

The second name on his list was New York State Governor William Carnegie. Now here was a prospect that made his heart flutter a little bit. Carnegie had never lost an election, or as Littleton liked to say, "He could get elected dog catcher at a greyhound track." As governor, he had the same kind of deeply appealing moderate record as Keith in California. He had fought for minimum wage increases in his state even as he lowered corporate taxes, increased job creation, and was able to walk the thin line of compromise. Moreover, there was simply no denying the power of his resume: Harvard, stellar military record, experience abroad, a simply stunning wife who was honest-to-goodness British aristocracy (and no matter how much Americans prided themselves on being a classless society, Littleton also knew that the country was hopelessly enamored of British royals), a strong family man and last but not least, there was his magical last name and a powerfully connected old man worth billions.

The only issue, of course, was that William Carnegie had never shown the slightest interest in running for national office. Littleton tapped his pencil on his pad for a few minutes, then idly circled William's name a few times. When he was done weighing his options, he picked up the phone and dialed a number he had used many times in the past.

"Hello?" said a deep, commanding voice.

"Ambassador!" Littleton said. "This is Theo Littleton. How are you?"

"Theo!" Ambassador Carnegie sounded delighted to hear from his old friend and political confidant. "I hear you're running the show now over at the national party. How are things there?"

"Excellent, sir. Excellent. I think we've got a real chance at the White House this year."

"Yes, so do I, so do I. I've been following it quite closely. Insiders are saying it looks like Lionel Keith will top the ticket, eh?"

Littleton chuckled to himself. There could be no doubt Ambassador Carnegie was "following it quite closely." After all, a rather significant amount of his money had passed through the party's coffers on the way to building a national organization for Lionel Keith, and Ambassador Carnegie had been influential in crafting the top-secret national platform the party would unveil in the general election.

"That's the plan, sir," Littleton said.

"Well, it will be interesting to see how it shakes out. Now, what can I do for you? As much as I'd like to think you enjoy my conversation, I know you all too well, Theo. You're a real shark and I'm guessing you didn't call to see how my enlarged prostate was doing."

Littleton laughed. "Guilty as charged, Mr. Ambassador. But in this case, I think maybe we can do something for one another." He launched into a detailed strategy to take the White House, running through the Electoral College numbers off the top of his head and constructing any number of scenarios that would seat his man in the Oval Office. When he neared the end, however, he said, "But I think we still need that last piece of the puzzle to fall into place."

"Oh?"

"Yes. What would you say to your son, William, as second man on the ticket? He's got the record and the resume. He's a natural politician, I've been watching him over the years. What do you say?"

"Hmm. Intriguing. I won't say that this thought has never crossed my mind. The Carnegie family has yet to produce a president—"

"Er, vice president, sir."

"Yes, yes, I know. But you know my motto: unless you're the lead dog, the view is always the same. The Ambassador laughed at his joke, as did Theo.

"Not in the cards right now Ambassador, but being in the wings waiting ain't a bad place to be eight years from now," Theo retorted. "Second place is all I can offer."

"Oh well, a father can hope, no? But for the present moment, I think it's a wonderful plan, and if he agrees to it, I think William would be the perfect man for the job, and as you pointed out he could run for the top spot if he so chose in eight years."

"So...do I have your blessing on this? Ambassador?"

"Yes, yes, you have my blessing, but of course William is his own man. You'll have to call him yourself and make the pitch to him. His word is final on this."

"Understood."

"But don't worry. I'll have a chat with him, too, and see what he thinks."

"I was hoping you'd say that!" Littleton said. "As for the financial piece of it, of course you know this is going to be an expensive campaign. I'm hoping you'll continue your support for the party?"

"Especially if my son is on the ticket! But you know we have to be careful, there are all kinds of campaign laws that limit hard cash, But there are always ways, we'll figure it out. Don't worry Theo, money will not be a problem, trust me!

"That's music to my ears, Ambassador, you're my kind of guy"

The Ambassador laughed again. "Theo, no wonder you are the best at what you do! You can charm the skin of a snake!

Not done yet, Theo zooms in for the close: "I'd also love to get some positive coverage…" He let that one hang. He knew the Carnegies controlled hundreds of newspapers and broadcast stations, but he also knew he was on terribly thin ice. Still, the prospect of a wave of positive coverage for his new golden boy on the ticket was too much to pass up.

"Now, Theo, you know we take our role as the fourth estate seriously. Our democracy wasn't built so the rich could keep their thumbs on the scale."

"Of course, sir! I just…well…"

The Ambassador let him fumble around for a few minutes, then good-naturedly chuckled. "Anyway, Theo, I'm sure that many of our editorial boards will look at the candidates and make the sound decision for themselves."

An almost giddy feeling of relief swept through Theo. If he could convince William to sign up, it would be like hitting the trifecta. All at once he'd land one of the country's most successful governors, he'd open up a faucet of nearly limitless Carnegie money, and he'd have a pipeline into one of the largest media companies in the country.

"Thank you!" he said. "Now, you want me to wait a day or two before calling William?"

"I think that would be best," the Ambassador said. "I'd like to catch up with him myself."

Albany, New York

Gov. William Carnegie was still at his desk in the Governor's Mansion at 8:30 p.m., going over papers. The last two days had been brutal. He'd had a series of public events to attend, and he was deeply involved in intense negotiations over a bill having to do with school funding at the state level. William considered himself a natural for this role—he liked to think of himself as a pragmatic and flexible ideologue, if there was such a thing—but it could be exhausting. Mostly he wanted to go back to the family quarters to see Liz and catch up with his kids before they went to bed.

When the intercom on his desk rang, he considered ignoring it. It was likely his father again; he had called William twice since yesterday, and William didn't have time to connect with the Ambassador. Conversations with his father were never rushed, and as much as William loved and respected the old man, he simply didn't have time right now. He knew his father would understand, and he had every intention of paying a proper visit home when he could catch his breath. Then he would sit down and give his dad the full bloody play-by-play regarding this round of negotiations. His dad loved politics.

When the intercom didn't quiet, he picked it up and heard his assistant. "Governor? A Theo Littleton is on the phone. He says it's urgent."

"Theo Littleton?" William asked. "Should I recognize the name?"

"He's the party chairman, sir."

"Oh."

Now William was intrigued, and the wheels started to turn. First his father trying to call him, and now the head *apparatchik* for the national party on the phone? William permitted himself a small smile. Something was up.

He picked up the phone. "Governor Carnegie here."

"Governor!" Theo said. "Thank you for taking the call. You're just the man I need to reach. Working late, I take it."

"Yes. You too, eh?"

"Of course! You know the people's work is never done, even when it's done behind the scenes!"

William grimaced a little bit. His least favorite part of the political process involved the endless and secretive positioning "behind the scenes." He much preferred the detailed work of designing and passing legislation that would benefit real people's lives. He could leave the bare-knuckled politicking to others.

"Indeed," he said mildly. "So, what can I do for you this evening?"

"Well, I'm not sure if you've talked to your father recently or not, but—"

"No, I missed his call," William said, noting that his hunch had been correct: there was definitely something going on.

"I see, no matter," Theo said. "My business is with you anyway. I have a proposition for you."

"Oh?"

"Yes. No doubt you're aware we've got a national campaign coming up, and as I mentioned to your father just the other day, I think there's a real chance we could take the White House this cycle."

"Mmm," William said, wondering where this was heading. "I understand you've got Lionel Keith from out in California lined up? He's a good man. I know him well."

"Yes, yes. He'll make a natural president."

So that was it, William decided. Littleton was looking for William's support to help deliver the state of New York to Lionel Keith, and probably with some money thrown in. That was an easy enough request to grant.

"My problem," Littleton continued, "is that we don't have a number two man on the ticket. We don't have anyone of vice presidential caliber. Except for you." He waited to let this sink in for a minute. "So I'm calling to see if you're interested in throwing your name in the national ring and, if all goes as planned, taking the next step in your political career to serve as vice president of the United States."

William was stunned into a momentary silence, which was increasingly rare nowadays. It had literally never crossed his mind to run for a national office—he considered himself a New Yorker through and through and felt like he still had a tremendous amount of work to do here in his home state.

"Well, I must say, Mr. Chairman, you caught me by surprise there. But…I'm still a first-term governor. Surely there are other, more qualified candidates, for something this big? I wouldn't know the first thing about being the vice president."

"With all due respect, Governor, that answer alone is why you will make a wonderful vice president! But let's not debate this any longer on the phone. How about I send a plane up to Albany to get you and we can talk more here in DC tomorrow?"

William thought for a second, then said, "My father is part of this already, isn't he?"

Theo laughed. "I'm afraid so! I spoke with him the other day and, well, we sort of hatched his plan to draft you. William, I'm not going to sugarcoat this, and I respect you far too much to sweet-talk you. Here's the truth. We have an excellent chance to win the White House, and the country frankly needs a man of your character and qualifications, not to mention what it would mean for you personally."

William shook his head and smiled. "Well, I must say you are a smooth operator. It sounds like you've got all the bases already covered. I have to hand it to you."

"Sir, having the bases covered is my job. So what do you say? Come to DC tomorrow, we'll have a nice lunch and talk some, and I bet when you leave, you'll be on your way to being the next vice president!"

"Fine," William said. "I'll be happy to hear you out, although it sounds like my mind is already made up for me."

"Excellent! Have a good night, Governor. I'll be looking forward to seeing you tomorrow!"

Washington, DC

William had been to Washington many times, both as a private citizen and as governor of New York, but as his plane circled the city the next morning, he looked at the city with different eyes. Now he looked at it like a man who might soon be on the inside of the greatest political show on earth, and he had to admit to himself: the idea appealed to him. He would feel bad about leaving his constituents behind in New York, but as part of a new administration, there was no end to the effect he could have. And William was no fool himself: somewhere in the very back of his head, a tiny, persistent voice whispered that the vice presidency was only a heartbeat away from the presidency.

William was met at the airport by a limo and whisked to a bland building within view of the Capitol Rotunda. As soon as he walked through the front doors, he felt like he had fallen into a whirlpool of power and politics. Lionel Keith, governor of California, was there, and they fell into the easy conversation of two men who respect each other a great deal and who both have enormous power in their own right. William had always liked Keith, but found himself evaluating Keith as a potential president and liked what he saw. Keith, too, confirmed his admiration of William and all but insisted that William sign onto the ticket.

They got down to business immediately, and William spent much of the morning in a stuffy conference room with Littleton, Keith, and a handful of party operatives and power brokers. To William's utter amazement, they had assembled a thick folder on him, going back to his days in London and covering his law career, his marriage, and every public speech or letter he had ever written. He was grateful that Regina wasn't in the file—it was good to know that some things were private—but they dissected everything else in great detail.

"Governor," Littleton said, "the fact is, you're a dream candidate. The only potential issue we see is that you are married to a British national. But honestly, it wouldn't be the first time. John Quincy Adams, the sixth president, was also married to a Brit. And let's face it, your wife is lovely and a formidable woman in her own right. Far from being a problem, we think she'd be a powerful asset on the campaign trail."

William nodded. Of course he agreed.

After they were done with him, they moved onto another stack of files, and William was even more surprised to see they had assembled detailed information on every possible candidate for the opposing ticket, with a special focus on Luke Jordan, former governor of Colorado and current US Senator. Jordan had been a fine governor—William had met him once or twice but didn't know him well—but they had meticulously combed everything he had ever said or done in public, looking for openings. And to hear them tell it, they had found plenty. Jordan's college writings showed a populist streak that exposed him to charges of Communist sympathies, and he had advocated returning portions of the land Israel won in the 1967 war. His record on crime—which was expected to be a leading domestic issue—was considered weak. Overall, the feeling was that Jordan was a strong candidate, but also a beatable one.

They broke for lunch, which took place in a lovely wood-paneled steakhouse close to the White House, then returned to the conference room to finish the de-briefing. When they were done, William was exhausted but also exhilarated. With all their research, they had convinced him: it wasn't just possible, but probable that if he accepted their offer, he'd be the next vice president.

As they all stood, preparing to pack their briefcases and leave, William voiced the thought that had been nagging at him since the idea had first been proposed. "Theo, are you sure I'm the right guy for this?"

Everyone stopped and all eyes turned to William. Theo Littleton just smiled and rubbed his neck. "Governor, I have no doubt you are the perfect man for this. And the country will be better for it." He leaned over dramatically and rapped his knuckles on the conference table. "You hear that, Governor? That's the sound of destiny knocking."

There was a heavy moment of silence, and then the group broke into smiles all around. Theo's gesture had been effective.

"Okay, okay," William said. "If it helps at all, you all have done a fantastic job of convincing me here today that it's not just my duty to run, but that we could win this thing. Let me talk it over with my wife when I get home."

The slightest of frowns crossed Theo's face. "Well, of course you should do that. Modern women and all that. But promise me that you won't let her talk you out of something that would be good for you and good for the country. Who knows? You could be president yourself after Lionel here is done with his second term."

Everyone except William laughed at that too. When the laughter died down, William said, "With all due respect, Liz is more than my wife. She's my partner too, equal in all decisions that affect our family. Her vote weighs as much as mine does, and I wouldn't have it any other way."

"Of course I understand, and we wouldn't have it any other way either. But, William, don't make us wait too long. There's a tremendous amount of work to do between now and the convention and the election, and we'll need you there."

"Understood," William said. "I'll have my answer as soon as I can."

They began turning to leave, but this time it was Lionel Keith who spoke up. He fixed William with a practiced smile and said, "William, I'll look forward to your nomination at the convention and seeing you on the campaign trail."

"Me too," William said before he could stop himself, then they all exited and William headed home to a life-changing conversation with Liz about their future.

Albany, New York

William arrived back to the Governor's Mansion in Albany, unpacked his bags, and found a quiet place to sit with Liz and talk about everything that happened. She already knew what Littleton and the others wanted, but it helped William to lay it all out again. He found himself getting caught up in the excitement of the moment as he went over the research he had been shown yesterday—his own favorability ratings with key groups, the clout of the national party, the weaknesses of the opposing party's candidate.

She listened attentively throughout, recognizing from long years with William that he needed to talk this through. When he was done, she leaned back and said simply, "It sounds lovely, darling. So what is your reservation?"

William smiled ruefully at his wife. "That obvious, huh?"

She simply arched her brows at him.

"Well," he said, picking his words carefully, "here's how it works. We've done well so far with the races we've run, and getting elected governor of New York was probably the highlight of my career thus far. But running for a national office...Liz, honey, that's an entirely different proposition, and I...I worry about the effect it would have on you and the kids. From the moment we announced, we would lose any semblance of privacy. Both of us. And there would be endless days on the road, late night, constant travel. It's like running the governor's race every day, over and over. And if we won...which I think we probably would... it would get worse. We'd have to move to Washington, uprooting the family.

And this job isn't like other jobs. It comes with a predetermined set of enemies. Not only would we completely lack any privacy, there would be people actively working round the clock to destroy us. Both of us. I just don't know if I want to expose my family to that. Expose you to that."

To William's immense surprise, Liz laughed out loud. "William, dear, I know all of that. I'm the governor's wife. And more than that, my family has lived in the fish bowl of English aristocracy for hundreds of years. If you'd like to think about pressure, try having a kingdom bearing down on you with your life at stake. You know I grew up behind walls, in private schools...there's nothing your upstart colony can throw at me that would be in the slightest bit more traumatizing than growing up under the watchful eye of the London tabloids and the anti-royalists hoping to put us out of house and home."

"Upstart colony?" William said, laughing. "Really?"

Liz waved that away. "What I'm saying is this: we are more than equal to the task of standing behind you, me and the children. I understand how duty to God and country works. I was raised with it in my blood, and nothing would make me prouder than to see my husband serve out his duty in the White House."

William got up, crossed to the couch where she sat, and gave her a hug. "You're my girl, Liz. I always knew I got the cream of the crop. Let's sleep on it and I'll call Littleton tomorrow morning."

That night, William and Liz made love, the kind of tender love that binds a man and women together, not for the moment, but for eternity. Afterwards, they dropped off to sleep in each other's arms. When William woke up, he was filled with resolve. At breakfast, they talked to their kids about the decision, and they enthusiastically agreed that it would "be cool" if Dad was the vice president. As soon as breakfast was over, he went into his office and placed a call to Theo Littleton.

"William?" Theo said. "What's the news?"

"I'm in.", I mean, We're in"

"Excellent! This is the right call, William. Now, let's get down to work."

After he hung up from Theo, William's next call was to his father. The Ambassador was overjoyed, and throughout their long and amiable conversation, William couldn't help wondering if his father knew how this was going to play out all along.

***

From that day forward, the election quickly consumed their lives. There were no serious primary contenders on either side, so the general election seemed to start even before the nominating conventions formally named the candidates. William and Lionel Keith quickly assembled a staff of top-notch political talent, one that notably didn't include Theo Littleton, who continued in his role as party chairman and turned his considerable gifts to recruiting Senate and House candidates for down-ballot races. Already convinced the presidency was very nearly won, Littleton bent his will toward a "wave election" that would flip the House and Senate, thereby giving William and Keith a united government for the first time in a generation.

William wasn't so sure. During his debriefing, he had become convinced that Luke Jordan would be a tough candidate, but a beatable one. It turned out they had all underestimated Jordan's ferocity, cunning, and natural political skills. Jordan was Ivy League as well, having attended Brown University and earned his law degree from Columbia. After earning his degree, he went back to Colorado, where he had grown up as the son of a schoolteacher, and immediately leapt into local politics. Unlike William, Jordan lost his first race for the state House, then won his second race. After serving two terms in the Colorado State legislature, he ran for governor against a popular business leader from Seattle. The local paper in Denver, which happened to be a Carnegie paper, had endorsed Jordan's opponent, calling Jordan "too young, brash and inexperienced to serve our great state."

Jordan took the endorsement personally, but instead of going after his opponent, he made the savvy move of making the paper itself an election issue. His opponent in that race was Tommy McCurry, the grandson of a former governor...and a close personal friend of Ambassador Carnegie. Of course there was no connection—the Carnegie family exerted no influence over the paper's endorsement—but Jordan convincingly painted a portrait of corrupt cronyism, with the McCurry family on one side and the Carnegie empire on the other. The attacks worked, and McCurry's campaign began to founder in the final days, even as the paper uncovered more questionable acts from the Jordan campaign. It didn't matter, though, because every story the paper published only reinforced Jordan's line of attack that the "robber baron media" was in bed with his opponent.

Unfortunately for Jordan, it was too little, too late. McCurry's campaign limped across the finish line, losing a full five points in opinion polls in the last week—but it wasn't enough to lose the race. In the end, McCurry won by a razor-thin margin, and Jordan's concession speech bordered on apoplectic. He denounced legacy politics, denounced the party, and in particular denounced the "outsized and immoral influence" of "American aristocrats like the Carnegie tribe."

Down but not out, Jordan showed back up four years later and won the governorship, this time riding an anti-incumbent wave that swept away seasoned politicians all over the country. After stepping down as governor, he ran for and won an open U.S. Senate seat. In the Senate, he distinguished himself as a bare-knuckled street fighter who got things done. It was this record that propelled him into his party's nomination.

Running his campaign for president, it came as a surprise to no one that he immediately resurrected his attacks against the Carnegie family and the media it controlled. In speech after speech, Jordan tore into his opponent with vitriol and personal vengeance.

William watched with dismay as his own biography was used against him: his family's media, their wealth, even his wife's family name. It also didn't take long for Jordan to resurrect his charge that the Carnegie media empire was in the bag for the opposing party. At this point, the Carnegies owned or controlled hundreds of papers and broadcast stations, ranging from mid-size city dailies to neighborhood papers. It didn't matter what facts the Keith/Carnegie ticket presented—that the majority of papers owned by the Carnegies ended up endorsing Jordan's party just as they always had done, that there was absolutely no evidence of collusion between the papers and the family—all it took was a well-timed sneer from Jordan to create the appearance of impropriety and cheating. He and his lot were master mudslingers.

In the end, as they always do, the campaign turned negative, a development that caused William no end of grief. He had imagined a campaign fought on high-minded principles and ideas about the proper role of the government in Americans' lives and America in the world. Instead, he found himself debating decades-old college papers and fighting off attacks on him and his running mate's character and family. Ultimately, November fourth came and Americans, heartily tired of the contest, streamed into the polls to deliver a solid victory to Lionel Keith and William Carnegie. The down-ballot elections weren't as positive as Theo had hoped for, but they weren't all bad either. In all, it was a good night and the American voters spoke.

Jordan, of course, was having none of it. Instead of a graceful concession speech, he delivered a blistering broadside and made it clear this wasn't just politics, it was personal. On national television, he revealed a personal and deep-seated loathing for William H. Carnegie and his party and swore that "you have not heard the last of me."

As tired as they all were, the Carnegie family celebrated the victory. The Ambassador was ecstatic to see his son obtain the vice presidency and made it clear he expected to see William in the Oval Office someday. The only blight upon an otherwise joyful and victorious period was William's mother's health. William would forever be grateful that his mother had lived long enough to see him win the election.

CHAPTER 28
THE DYNAMIC DUO

Washington, DC, 1986

THE FIRST TWO YEARS OF KEITH'S NEW ADMINISTRATION SEEMED TO FLY by at supersonic speed for Vice President William Carnegie. Washington functioned in a very different way than New York, and William quickly found himself acting as point man in the administration's Senate negotiations. At the same time, he assumed a more public role than he had ever occupied before: he was invited to appear on late-night talk shows, spoke in the media frequently, and spent much of his time on the road representing the administration. Before long, William became one of the best-known and best-liked vice presidents of the modern era—the dashing young lieutenant to Lionel Keith's kindly and grandfatherly figure. It helped that, in those two years, their pro-growth policies helped engineer a solid expansion of the American economy and overseas they outmaneuvered the Soviet Union on a nuclear missile pact that gave the Americans a much better deal.

In his second year as vice president, William lost his beloved father. This crushing loss was difficult for him because it was the Ambassador who had made it possible for William to live a dream. Providing the best that money could buy, and the influence necessary to achieve success, William clearly understood the vital role his father had played. He recalled how his father told him that knowing the right people was crucial. Always setting the right example, William's father had passed along his strong ethical sense to William and supported his son through the darkest times, including when Regina was killed. Ambassador Carnegie taught him how to be a man, a husband, a father, a professional, and a decent human being, and William would miss him.

In Congress, Luke Jordan grew into a major thorn in their side. After losing the election, he won a seat in the House of Representatives and wrangled a seat on the powerful Ways and Means Committee, eventually becoming committee chairman. He served in this role only for a few months before a greater prize opened up: a sex scandal back in his home state forced the Speaker of the House from his position, and Jordan threw his name into the ring. The internal campaign for Speaker was tough, but fought mostly behind closed doors as three House members in Jordan's party jockeyed for position. None could prove Jordan's equal in bare-knuckle politics, and when the final votes were counted, Jordan had won and rose to lead his party's caucus in the House of Representatives as the Speaker. This was the perfect position from which to play agitator and obstructionist. It became apparent that Jordan's opposition to the administration was personal—he held up bills on procedural votes or doubled back on his own agreements constantly, just to make life difficult for the administration. Worse yet, he quickly and effectively put together a coalition of members from his party that gave him a narrow majority—it got so bad that William and other members of the inner circle in the White House began referring to Jordan as the Torpedo.

Things came to a head over a fight for mining rights in Jordan's home state. He was adamantly opposed to expansion of mining on federal land,

and had the backing of local environmental groups. The administration was for it and could count on the support of the state's junior senator to help it get through the Senate. Jordan vowed to kill the bill and worked tirelessly to defeat it. In this case, it wasn't enough: the administration picked up enough members of Jordan's party that the bill won and was sent to Lionel Keith for his signature. Jordan was furious and publicly swore to "destroy" the administration, a comment that attracted significant negative press.

Houston, Texas

Shortly before midterm elections at the end of their triumphant first two years, President Lionel Keith traveled to Houston to give a talk to a group of supporters. After the speech was over, during an after hours briefing, he slumped into a chair and sat looking at the floor. His Chief of Staff hurried over, asking if the president was okay.

"I don't know," he answered. "I'm not feeling very well at all. I feel weak and it's hard to take a full breath."

The president's schedule was cleared and he flew back to Washington that night, then went to Walter Reed for testing. The results were bad: Lionel Keith had a tumor growing on his left lung. Keith not only had a family history of lung cancer—his father and grandfather both died from it—but he had been a lifelong smoker. Under normal circumstances, a diagnosis like this would mean just months to live, but the doctors thought that Keith's tumor was slow-growing and they found no metastasis yet. With proper treatment, they thought there was a slim chance he could beat it. He was 73 years old.

Aside from the personal issues, this raised a new issue for the White House: no president had ever suffered from a serious cancer while in office. The decision was made to keep this strictly secret for now. Not even William would be told.

CHAPTER 29
THE LAST HURRAH

Europe

THE SITUATION IN THE UNITED KINGDOM DETERIORATED AS THE IRA continued to accelerate its bloody campaign against the British. Before long, the violence broke out into the open, and the IRA launched regular terrorist attacks against public spaces in London. They targeted pubs and restaurants, the Tube, and crowded areas with bombs. Innocents were killed, and the IRA publicly exulted in its success against the "oppressor." For every bomb that went off in England, the British military exacted a terrible revenge. Suspected IRA insurgents were paraded publicly, then crammed into crowded prison after hasty trials. Northern Ireland began to look like a militarized zone, with troops in heavy armor patrolling the streets of Belfast and regular operations against the IRA. Many innocents were killed on the Irish side, too, and the newspapers were full of stories of children orphaned by the violence or armed militants protecting Catholic churches so worshipers could go to Mass without being detained by the British. Alarmed, the Vatican appealed to the English Parliament for peace, but made little headway. The Pope himself had to cancel a planned visit to Ireland because of the high security risks.

As the situation deteriorated, life in Ireland became increasingly difficult. The IRA were but one faction of Irish, and they were opposed by pro-British Protestants. The fighting tragically pitted brother against brother, country against country. It was impossible to tell who was a friend or foe, and the IRA worked hard to disguise itself while living in the open. To the beleaguered and terrorized citizens of Ireland, it was a violent anarchy.

William, of course, followed the events closely, mostly out of personal interest but also because the United States had legitimate political interests in the area and many Irish-Americans were affected by the conflict. As vice president, he had access to the best intelligence, and he knew that Roan Kelly was under surveillance as a suspected leader of the IRA. This news brought up a welter of emotions for William, but mostly he was saddened by Roan's choices and sure that Regina would never have approved of the life her brother had chosen for himself. He was glad he had suspended financial support when he did.

Washington, DC, 1986

Lionel Keith's doctors had been somewhat optimistic about his condition, but the news was still grim. On his original diagnosis, they had found only the one tumor on his left lung and no metastasis. Unfortunately, like with so many cases of lung cancer, the cancer was poised to spread quickly: new primary tumors were soon discovered on his spine. His doctors had prescribed a punishing regimen of radiation therapy and chemotherapy. After the chemo started, Keith was rarely seen in public, and soon people began to wonder: where was the president?

Around this time, Keith called William into the Oval Office. William came in to see President Keith sitting at Lincoln's desk, looking twenty years older than he had just months before and breathing heavily.

"Mr. President?" William said. "Are you all right, sir?"

Lionel weakly waved a hand. "You can drop the 'sir' stuff with me, William."

William smiled. "I know, I'm sorry, it's just a habit and—"

"You're shocked at how I look," he said heavily. "I know. I am too. Every morning I look in the mirror and it looks like I've aged another year. Even the makeup they're slathering on me for TV appearances doesn't help much."

"How are you feeling?" William asked carefully.

Lionel smiled ruefully. "Like I'm fighting for my life, son. Which I am."

"But your doctors—"

"I know what they say." Lionel held up his hand and spent a few minutes on labored breathing. "And I appreciate their optimism. But I can read between the lines with these doctors. Their words say one thing but their expressions say another. This thing that's got a hold of me…it's not going to be as easy to beat as they're saying. But I'm at peace with that. I've lived a rich and full life, with more than my share of good fortune. My only regret will be that I didn't spend more time with my family and I didn't have a chance to finish our work here."

"I'm so sorry," William said, not sure what else he could say.

"I know. But I called you here for a reason. I wanted to talk to you privately, without all those advisors and political types hanging around. Fact is, William, if I go, you're going to be moving into this seat."

William was surprised to find himself swallowing back a lump in his throat. It just seemed so wrong. He had always looked up to Lionel Keith, respected the older man's wisdom and his sure political touch. No part of him wished to ascend to the presidency like this.

"Here's what I wanted to say, between us. William, you are a wonderful leader. Maybe no one outside of this room really appreciates how much you've done for our administration and country so far. You've been on the front lines every day. I will say you've been the best vice president in a century, and you'll make a fine president."

William got more choked up. "Lionel…I don't know where to start. If I'm half the leader you've been, I'll be grateful. You're…the country can't afford to lose you."

"Ah, hogwash," he said. "Listen, no one is irreplaceable. And with you waiting in the wings, I tell you, it lets me sleep better at night. This is a great country, William, the best on earth. And I have no doubt you will make a great president if it should come to that. So whatever comes up, whatever they throw at you, I want you to know that I believe in you like a son and I know you'll be great."

William had to fight back against the tears that sprang to his eyes.

"Thank you. I can't tell you what that means to me."

"You deserve it. Now, let's get to the nitty gritty, before I get too addled to string two sentences together."

They fell into a detailed discussion of the transition and how it would work, which Cabinet members William could trust and which he should probably replace, how they could advance their agenda. Keith figured that William would be appointed acting president and then named president after his death. This succession had been designed by the original Framers, and William would not be the first vice president to ascend to the presidency.

William understood the need to share these details, but it was a hard conversation anyway, and when he left the Oval Office, he found himself praying that God would somehow change his mind and spare Lionel Keith.

CHAPTER 30
DESTINY DISCOVERED

Washington, DC, 1986

After that conversation, Lionel Keith's condition progressed quickly—and William found himself thinking more and more of the presidency. He had been vice president for two years, so he was surprised at how much the idea of taking the Oval Office unsettled him. There was a universe of difference between the vice presidency and the presidency, and at his worst moment, he struggled against the fear of taking office. When these thoughts became distracting, William realized he needed some time to himself to sort out his many feelings: grief over the possible loss of Lionel, concern and fear over becoming an unelected president, and, if he was being honest, excitement at the tremendous opportunity. As he had at other times, he decided to head home to his family's Westchester estate, where he could gather his thoughts and have some time alone.

The mansion was deserted, with both his mother and father gone. At first, he wandered from room to room, reflecting on how far he had come since his days here, before boarding school and all that had happened to him. Without knowing exactly why, he soon found himself in his mother's room. William had never felt that close to his mother and always sensed there was a barrier between them. She was a lovely, kind woman who clearly adored him, but…he had always sensed a certain distance. Walking around the spacious and well-appointed boudoir, he observed several crooked pictures and attempted to straighten them. As he moved one, he noticed a hidden panel behind one of the paintings, which, when opened, exposed a wall safe. He stared at it for a moment. It was not surprising that his parents would have a wall safe—he assumed there was at least one more safe in the house—and he figured the safe probably contained jewelry as his mother had loved fine jewels. William searched the room for a key or combination to no avail and decided to call a locksmith in the morning. The next morning, William summoned the local locksmith, who easily opened the wall safe. As expected, there were some stunning pieces in leather boxes, including three Garrard of London presentation cases and numerous velvet pouches. There were several Tiffany and Cartier brooches, a couple of Rolex watches in their boxes neatly stacked alongside a number of files, and several large envelopes. William unloaded the safe's contents, placing them on his mother's dressing table.

He examined the stack of papers, files, and envelopes. Separating them into piles, he started to go through the material. There were some appraisals for various pieces of jewelry, a few childhood photographs, and a number of other official-looking documents. One envelope was extremely yellowed with age, obviously old, and somewhat bulky. It was a standard manila envelope with the seal of the U.S. Embassy on the front left upper corner.

William carefully opened the aged envelope. Inside was another envelope with the words, "For Fiona Carnegie." Inside this envelope, there was a folded note. William opened the note and found a hand-written message on a piece of personalized stationary alongside a small object wrapped in old tissue paper. The note was dated September 4, 1936, and the stationary bore the imprint *SS Summerset.* William immediately recognized the name *Summerset* as his father's old yacht. Although he had never been aboard, he had seen many photographs, and there was an oil painting of the yacht hanging in his father's home office. The slightly faded message was totally legible. William read:

September 4, 1936

Dearest Fiona,

I am depending on our friendship and your complete discretion and sworn secrecy. I entrust you with my baby boy. He was conceived in dishonor, but with your help he was not born out of wedlock. I have enclosed the ring that my father gave me on my birthday, years ago, which served as a wedding band when Anthony and I were married. I will never forget the lovely village of Catalan in Gibraltar, and the simple but beautiful ceremony at St. Aruban's Church. Having you and your sister Rosemary there meant the world to Anthony and me.

As I give you this boy, I know in my heart that he will never achieve his God-given destiny and become King. It is not possible since disclosing the circumstances of his conception would bring shame, gossip, and disgrace upon my dear Anthony and the royal family. I beseech you to give him a home and to raise and cherish him as your own. Rosemary has told me that you have been unable to bear children of your own, so I know this child will be welcomed with open arms. I pray that he will grow strong and brave and be able to reach his own level of greatness, never learning of or resenting the fact that I have deprived him his throne.

Please save this ring for our son. I hope someday he will be pleased to have it, although he must never know of its meaning or origin. Fiona, I am forever indebted to you and the Ambassador, even though he is unaware of this boy's true identity. In my despair and grief, my only consolation is that my baby will be loved and adored. Raise him well, and I hope he will forgive me for the love that I must deny him. God bless you always, God bless this child.

Yours with devotion and gratitude,

Mary

Frowning slightly, William placed the note on the table and opened the small wrapped package. Residing within was a signet ring bearing the coat of arms of the Princess of Wales. The engraving on the inside of the ring read "*HRH Mary, Princess of Wales*" and a tiny hallmark from "Garrard, Jewelers to the Crown." William stared at the ring for a long time, a deep sense of destiny rising in his chest. He had no idea what it all meant, but had no doubt that he had found something monumental.

CHAPTER 31
IF THE PRICE IS RIGHT

Washington, DC, 1986

IF SEN. LUKE JORDAN'S SOURCES COULD BE BELIEVED, THE PRESIDENT OF THE United States was dying. For Jordan—who was no fan of the president—this was especially horrible news for reasons that had nothing to do with any personal concern for the president. Instead, Jordan found himself focused on his worst possible scenario: President William Carnegie. Even the thought of it made his skin crawl. As far as Jordan was concerned, Carnegie was wholly undeserving of the presidency, or anything else for that matter. As he often told people, Carnegie hadn't earned anything on his own merit, from his time at expensive prep schools, to his admittance into the Ivy League, to his cushy lawyer job, and finally and most importantly his career as a politician. "If it wasn't for his daddy's money and his daddy's newspapers, William Carnegie would be just another middle school math teacher," he liked to joke.

Gradually, an idea began to form in Jordan's mind, and it slowly grew into a near fixation: he had to stop Carnegie from taking the presidency. This would be easier said than done, though, and he knew that as well as anyone. Presidential succession, as described in the Constitution, specified that in cases where the president was unable to fulfill his duties, the cabinet would name the vice president as "acting president" until such time as the elected president either recovers and resumes his duties or dies. If it was the latter, the acting president would be named president.

But of course that was not all Jordan thought about: the Constitution further specified that should the acting president be unable to serve, resign, die, or get impeached, the Speaker of the House would be appointed by the Cabinet as acting president. This was the thought that led Jordan to place a series of secretive phone calls to some of his contacts and assemble a top secret meeting in the Georgetown house of a donor.

The meeting was attended only by Jordan and three other men. He knew their backgrounds intimately: one was an FBI agent who had been dismissed for obtaining an unlawful confession from a suspected drug trafficker, one was an IRS agent who had been given the "choice" to retire early after it became apparent the agent was accepting bribes from the people he was investigating, and one was a former SEAL who had returned from combat action in Grenada, resigned, and immediately put out the word that he was available to the highest bidder.

When everyone was seated, Jordan cleared his throat and started. "Gentlemen," he said, using the term loosely, "first the ground rules. This meeting never happened. It's not being recorded, and if any of you claim to have met me and discussed the things we're going to discuss, I will adamantly deny it. Does everyone understand?"

The three men nodded, so Jordan continued, "I called you here today because I need help in a very delicate matter. It's my understanding the President Keith is very sick with lung cancer and has been given months to live. If that should happen, Vice President William Carnegie would be named acting president and then president. It is urgent that we prevent this from happening."

There was no response from the three men, who stared at him and waited.

"So," he went on, "I need to disqualify Carnegie from the presidency. In other words, I need information. We all know he's already been vetted, by my own campaign of course, but I'm convinced there's more, there's something we missed." As he talked, he handed each of them a bulging folder. "This is what we got on him during the election. It's a good place to start, but...it's not enough. What we turned up was basically the picture of a Boy Scout. But we need something good, something much better than a few mediocre test grades."

The men had by now started leafing through the files, which contained William's school records, tax returns, some correspondence, and various news clippings going back to his prep school days.

"Remember," Jordan said, "this isn't a court of law we're worried about. This is the court of public opinion, so all we need to do is raise a credible doubt. If he hasn't actually cheated on his wife, has he ever been photographed with a woman who wasn't his wife? What about his time in South Africa? Did he have black servants? Did he mistreat them? Impregnate any? What about his cases in England? Did he ever represent a child molester? The point I'm trying to make is that we don't need to find actual proof of a wrongdoing. All we need is the credible appearance of something wrong, enough to give people plausible doubt about his fitness for the presidency." They were all nodding along as he finished, "And trust me, if you deliver me something I can use, you will be handsomely rewarded. Very, very handsomely."

The meeting quickly broke up and the three men vanished into the night, prepared to do whatever was necessary to bring down William Carnegie.

It didn't take long, however, for the group to realize this wasn't going to be easy. Like Jordan said, Carnegie had a nearly irreproachable resume and had always conducted himself as a gentleman and honest citizen. The only thing of interest they found in those first weeks was a minor issue with his birth certificate. It had been issued on August 31, 1936, by the American Embassy in London, England, stating that William Harrington Carnegie was born unto Harrington and Fiona Carnegie, formally Fiona Firth. An embassy seal was affixed. This wasn't interesting by itself, but the team soon learned that rumors had swirled around his birth at the time. His mother, Fiona Carnegie, was on the old side of childbearing. When they pursued this further, however, they turned up a series of dead ends. There were no medical records of his birth and no record of who actually delivered William as the attending physician. Investigating further, they learned it was widely believed that William had been born at the Ambassador's country home on the Isle of Jersey, even though the birth certificate named London as the place of birth. Nevertheless, no witness could be found to confirm or disprove this discrepancy. Church records were found documenting Carnegie's baptism at a prominent London Allegan church.

Back in the United States, another member of the team went to Westchester and Connecticut, where he was able to get his hands of a copy of William's prep school records. After that, he went to Cambridge, Massachusetts, and obtained a complete copy of William's student records from Harvard.

When the group met again, Jordan asked for an update. Justin Tate, the former IRS officer, had compiled everything into a dossier and said: "Nothing great so far. With the exception of the birth certificate, which seems perfectly legit, but not totally confirmable since it was issued by the U.S. Embassy in London. At the time, the embassy was under the control of Carnegie's father, the Ambassador. So technically, there is no third party authentication."

"Hmmm," Jordan mused. "It would be a stretch, but perhaps a case could be made regarding Carnegie's U.S. citizenship? Is there any credible doubt that he might not be a natural-born citizen? Any way we could cast legitimate doubt on his parentage? After all, his mother was pretty old to be having babies when William was born."

"Even if we could, I'm not sure it would make much difference. As long as the Ambassador is Carnegie's father, and he's listed that way on the birth certificate, the vice president would be an American citizen and eligible to be president."

"Yes, but how do we know that Ambassador Carnegie is actually his father? You say there are no witnesses, no hospital records, no record of a physician present at his birth. So hear me out: this child magically appears, supposedly born to a mother almost past childbearing age, and then a birth certificate is issued by the very embassy that the Ambassador controls. You see where I'm heading with this?"

Heads started to nod.

"I want you all to follow this up. Find out what you can. And in the meantime, let's make sure our friends in the press are asking some hard questions. I mean, birth certificates have certainly been forged in the past. How can the vice president actually prove his parentage? Let's get him on the defensive, boys. Let's see him sweat. And in the meantime, go out there and get me something concrete."

The meeting broke up as the team dispersed again, vowing to leave no stone unturned.

CHAPTER 32
SEEKING TRUTH

Washington, DC, 1986

SENATOR JORDAN'S MEN WEREN'T THE ONLY PEOPLE INTERESTED IN WILLIAM Carnegie's past. After reading the perplexing note in his mother's safe, William himself had launched his own private investigation—and found himself plunged into a morass of confusion. Without either parent alive to simply ask, William was left to wonder on his own: "Who am I? Am I really even a Carnegie at all?" The fact that he was left alone to ask these questions filled him with a deep feeling of anger and betrayal.

Unlike Jordan's team, however, William could conduct his investigation directly. He first called Nigel Cosgrove at the American Embassy in London. William had worked closely with Nigel during his time in London and knew he could trust him implicitly. Better yet, Nigel specialized in investigative probes and had a huge network of contacts to draw on for information.

"Nigel," William said once they had connected over the phone. "How are you, old man. This is William Carnegie calling."

"Mr. Vice President, isn't it nowadays?" Nigel joked. "I hear they got sick of you in New York and kicked you upstairs."

William chuckled. "Something like that, I suppose."

"Indeed. But I hear great things about you," Nigel said more seriously. "You always were a chap on the move. Now, tell me, what can I do for you?"

"Well, as it so happens, I need a personal favor," William said. "This is something that can only be done by someone I trust completely. I need some information."

It was Nigel's turn to laugh. "For bloody sakes, man, you have the FBI, CIA, U.S. armed forces, and Secret Service at your beck and call…what the hell can I do that they can't?

"Keep your mouth shut, that's what," William said. "It's not a matter of what they can or cannot do; it's a matter of confidentiality. What I am asking for cannot, under any circumstances, be leaked over here. And as you probably know, you can't trust anyone in this town."

"I see. So what is it that you need?"

William took a deep breath. He hadn't told anyone except Liz about his discoveries, and he found it was hard to say it out loud. But he knew he had to trust Nigel. "No doubt you're aware of President Keith's health situation. I'm sure your contacts have filled you in. This puts me in the position of realistically expecting to assume the presidency soon. But there are some political enemies of mine who are making noise about my U.S. citizenship," he said. "These innuendos center on whether my birth parents are legitimate. It seems they believe that my parents are not Harrington and Fiona Carnegie. This brings my citizenship into question, and I don't have to explain the implications of that."

"Blimey, that's nasty work. What can I do?"

"I need you to check around and see what you can find out. I know I have a birth certificate issued by the embassy, but…and this is hard to even ask…

is there any reason to suspect that...things aren't what they seem? I can't get too deeply into it, but some information has come to light on my end that has caused me to wonder if anything unusual was going on in 1936 or 1937."

"You want me to investigate your mum and dad?" Nigel asked incredulously.

"Yes. And I think you should start with a woman named Rosemary Firth, my aunt on my mother's side," William said. "She was particularly close to my mom and has long since vanished. I need to know if she is living, and if so, where is she and can I speak with her."

Nigel gave a lost whistle. "You're serious about this?"

"Completely."

"All right, then. I'll poke around and see what I can find out. I don't know what information you've got, but if you think it'll help, you might want to forward it to me—"

"I'm sorry," William said. "I can't do that right now."

"Fair enough. I'll let you know what I can find then."

"Thanks. And—"

"Yes, yes, I know. Mum's the word. But William, for what it's worth, I'm sure I won't find anything. Your parents were never anything but model citizens."

"Yeah," William said glumly. "That's what I hope too."

Nigel signed off and went right to work. He first made some calls to his friends at the Gazette, London's second-largest newspaper. A few minutes later, a senior reporter called back and promised to put Nigel in touch with the paper's historian of record, who was responsible for keeping the Gazette's century-old library intact. Nigel gave her a simple mission: find Rosemary Firth, sister to Fiona Carnegie, neé Fiona Firth. Also, find any press reports that mentioned the Carnegies in the mid-1930s.

The researcher, a dedicated woman named Dolores who had been keeping the paper's library for over three decades, attacked her assignment with gusto.

She loved the more complicated, challenging requests for information, and she dug deep into the Gazette's archives, including both the public file of published reports and the top secret archive of reporters' notes and unpublished correspondence. This secret archive, she knew, contained enough salacious and scandalous information to send half of England's leading families running for the hills and even land some prominent citizens in prison.

The searches yielded a mountain of routine information, including William's birth announcement, social notices, gossip pages, society clips, newspaper pictures and the like. All of this was assembled into a package, marked "Confidential and Private," and delivered by courier to Nigel at the American Embassy.

While the researcher was hard at work, Nigel canvassed the embassy staff and poked around the embassy's records, which went back to the 1930s when the embassy was first moved to Grosvenor Square. The first interesting thing Nigel learned was that he was not the only person asking questions about William Carnegie: apparently a recent request had been made for William's birth certificate. The request was initially denied, until the office of a Sen. Luke Jordan from the United States called to authorize its release. Not wanting to anger a U.S. Senator, the embassy released the birth certificate to a man who signed his name as "John Smith." At the same time, several embassy personnel told Nigel they had been approached by journalists whose names they didn't recognize, all looking for information on William Carnegie. Whoever William's enemies were, they had a long reach.

Within 48 hours of talking to William, Nigel had assembled a tidy packet of information. He had found that Rosemary Firth wasn't only sister to Fiona—she was a lady-in-waiting to the then-Princess Royal and now reigning Queen Mary. Further, Rosemary and Mary had attended school together and were apparently tight friends. After Mary had wed and given birth to Prince John, Rosemary had served her directly, acting as a surrogate parent to the young prince and spending every moment with the Princess and her son. Further, around the time that Queen Mary had married Cyril, her second husband, Rosemary had left the royal retinue and moved to Switzerland. The trail got a little colder after that. Rosemary had apparently married a widowed banker in Switzerland in the 1960s. He worked for the Bank of Canada and was named Rodger North. Sometime later—Nigel didn't have an exact date—Rodger and Rosemary had moved back to Canada and settled in Quebec, where Rodger had worked the rest of his career until he retired and eventually passed away. His last known address was his retirement home in Village of Saint-Benoit-du-Lac some twenty miles from the Vermont border. As for Rosemary, there was almost nothing on her.

With that lead exhausted, Nigel turned his attention to the Carnegie family themselves. Most of the clippings and information from the Gazette research were of little interest to him: society pages, news clippings, and the like. There were, however, a few tabloid-style stories that caused Nigel to raise his eyebrows. Around the time of William's birth, a few of the trashier tabloids—all of them with an anti-royalist bent—speculated that Fiona Firth was "almost, if not beyond childbearing age" and her delivery of a baby boy was nothing short of a "miracle." They were all very careful not to come straight out and say it, but it appears that even back then, there were questions surrounding William's exact parentage. One writer in particular noted that Fiona had seemed "rather not pregnant" during public appearances. Of course most of these reports were ignored or discounted, considering their sources, but Nigel had to make note of the similarity between what they said and what William had told him. Also of interest: the inflammatory reports about William's true parents suddenly stopped, right around the time new newspapers were starting to pick up the story. Nigel was not naïve enough to think that the newspapers themselves had decided to act responsibly. No, this meant that someone back then had the motivation and means to lean on the papers and pull the story.

When he was done reading, Nigel leaned back in his chair and took a deep breath. What he was thinking truly didn't seem possible—but then he wasn't the only one thinking it. Not only had William himself voiced a concern, the Gazette librarian also mentioned that an American had requested the same material and, except for information from the paper's private vault, had received much of the same material Nigel was currently reading.

"Bloody hell," he said out loud. "What have you got yourself into?"

Washington, DC, 1986

After three sleepless nights of waiting to hear from Nigel, William couldn't take it any more and placed a call to his old friend. When Nigel connected, William cut straight to the chase and asked Nigel to fill him in. Nigel did so with the eye for detail of a trained investigator. William listened patiently, taking notes when necessary, but mostly wrestling with a growing sense of unease.

First, there was the fact that someone else was conducting the same investigation he was, and that someone was Sen. Luke Jordan. This made William both nervous and furious at the same moment. Obviously, Jordan's office was the source of the recent leaks about his citizenship, and just as obviously, Jordan had people looking into William's background and had obtained a copy of his birth certificate. William had no idea how Jordan had gotten so far or what he knew, but the thought of his sworn political enemy trying to destroy him set his head to pounding. William was all too aware of the stakes involved: if Jordan could somehow discredit him, Jordan himself would ascend to the presidency in the event of President Keith's death, which seemingly could be only months away. William, who prided himself on always playing by the rules and followed a strict code of sportsmanship, was stunned that someone would try such a dirty trick to win the presidency—but then again, it was impossible to underestimate the power of the presidency, and he knew all too well what people would do to get power.

Second, and worse yet, was what Nigel had to say about Rosemary Firth and the rumors surrounding William's birth. There was no sense in denying to himself that William had desperately hoped Nigel would come back with a logical explanation for all of this, and William could simply file that letter away as a strange mystery that meant nothing. William would have given anything for Nigel to have turned up the doctor who delivered him or some concrete proof that his mother was his mother and his father was his father. Instead, as far as William was concerned, Nigel had only given him compelling circumstantial evidence that, indeed, his parents were not his parents.

But beyond that, William sensed a great and terrible secret like some kind of monster lurking around the corner. Rosemary Firth wasn't only his mother's sister...she was the lady-in-waiting to the future Queen Mary. And it had been Mary's signet ring in that envelope, the very symbol of her station and power. The words of the letter rang in his head, and William pushed away the preposterous thought that followed them. Yet...why would his parents have gone through some ridiculous charade of pretending he was theirs instead of doing a normal adoption? If Mary's letter was the truth, then the answer to that was obvious. William needed definitive answers, and as he hung up with Nigel he realized he was going to have to track down Rosemary Firth North. He was convinced she was the missing link, the key to the puzzle. Nigel had said she'd moved to Quebec, and then to the village of Saint-Benoit-du-Lac, near the Vermont border. Quickly, he went to his library and found a map, then located Saint-Benoit-du-Lac. It was only a scant hour's drive from Winterledge, the Carnegie family compound in Vermont. He put his finger on the map and stared at the exotic name.

First thing the next morning, he asked his assistant to track down a Rosemary Firth North in the village, hoping almost against hope she was still there. A moment later, his assistant returned with a telephone number. He took the slip of paper and was filled with a tremendous sense of trepidation, but even that couldn't change the fact that he had every intention of calling Mrs. North, his aunt, and setting up a meeting.

CHAPTER 33
NEVER GET CAUGHT WITH YOUR PANTS DOWN

Ireland, 1984

THE LOW-CEILINGED BAR WAS DARK AND SMOKY, AND ROAN HAD BEEN drinking for hours when he saw a tempting target. She was brunette, with dark skin the color of milky tea, and judging from the length of her skirt and high-heeled red shoes, she was a professional. Roan tipped his drink to Shaun and sauntered across the bar to pull up a stool next to her. She looked him over without a word.

"Hey there, Colleen," Roan said. "I'll bet you could give a big chap like me a good time. What's your name?"

"I ain't no Colleen and I ain't Irish. I'm from Turkey. And if you want my name it will cost you a drink."

"Fair enough." He signaled to the bartender. "My good man, fix m'lady here a drink, although I doubt she's much of a lady." The woman rolled her eyes, but Roan noted that and smiled. "Now, what's your name?"

"Fulya."

"Fulya? What kind of name is that?"

"Like I said, I'm Turkish. It means one of intelligence."

Roan made a show of looking her over from head to toe. There was no question she had some mileage on her, but in the fog of drink she looked pretty damn good to him. She had long legs, the kind that could easily wrap around a bloke and pull him in. Her tits were full and popping out of her tight jumper. Her high heels looked like they had done plenty of street walking.

"I like intelligent women," he said. "And I love turkey. Best damn bird on the planet."

"You're a regular comedian," she said.

"Could be more than that, if you had a mind for it."

"Maybe, depends if you can make it worth my while."

Roan grinned and moved closer. "Maybe. Let's say you and me blow this joint and we'll find out."

"Not so fast," Fulya said. "It'll cost you."

"How much?" Roan asked.

"That depends on what you like."

"I like all of it," he said, feeling himself start to stiffen already. "You only live once, I say."

"Ten pounds, cash."

Roan looked shocked. "Ten pounds! Are you daft? I can get a virgin for ten pounds."

"Yeah, maybe, but not here and not right now. Ten pounds," said Fulya as she grabbed Roan by his very firm member. "And by the feel of things, you better hurry up or you'll be needing a change of knickers, big boy."

"I only have six pounds, and I just bought you a drink, how about it?"

"Fine, but you better be good, because I not only like money, I like a real man. I'm not in the mood to be the teacher."

"Don't worry," Roan said, grabbing her hand and holding it against himself. "I might have a thing or two to teach you."

"That's what all the men say. We'll just have to see what you got."

Roan grabbed Fulya by the arm and motioned to Shaun, who was standing by the entrance as the lookout for Brits. The threesome exited the pub and walked down a number of dark alleyways toward an IRA safe house. It was a dingy and dark building, totally anonymous. Inside, there was a parlor and tiny kitchen. Upstairs was a long hallway leading to three small bedrooms. They passed through the kitchen with hardly a glance and Roan and Fulya left Shaun in the hallway as they tumbled into one of the small bedrooms. There was nothing in the room but a large bed with a stained mattress and a chest of drawers with a small lamp.

"Nice place," Fulya said sarcastically, but Roan was in no mood to talk. He grabbed the girl and spun her around in a drunken jig until she told him to take it easy. "And where's my money, anyway?"

Roan growled as he put his hand in his pocket and withdrew a wad of pound notes. "Here, and there's a tip in there for ya provided you get down on your knees and pray your thanks for it."

Fulya complied readily, dropping to her knees before him and drawing down his trousers, then applying herself to her work. Within seconds, Roan was in an erotic daze, lost in her skills and a fog of Richardson Irish whiskey. Not ready to peak just yet, Roan picked Fulya up from the floor and pushed her onto the filthy bed. He pulled off her jumper and her dress, revealing her naked body. She had full breasts and a narrow waist and was indeed a tasty tart, one Roan was quite ready to sample. Skipping any foreplay, Roan pushed her legs apart and penetrated the wench time and time again, deeper and with more force each time.

Fulya was clearly practiced, and brought Roan to three climaxes, twice in the conventional way and once in a not-so-conventional orifice. When he was done, he rolled off her and fell to the bed, his chest heaving for a few minutes before they both fell asleep.

Throughout their rendezvous, Shaun kept faithful watch outside the door, but he was full of whiskey himself and the sounds coming from the doorway had an effect on him he couldn't deny. He considered knocking and telling Roan to save a piece of the slut for him, but decided against it. Instead, his hands found himself and he pleasured himself while listening to Fulya moan. When he was done, he too fell asleep, sitting on the floor outside the bedroom door.

***

Roan awoke some time later suddenly, his protective instinct automatically kicking in—but too late. The whore was still sleeping next to him, and he was wrapped in the stained sheet himself, staring down the barrel of an automatic weapon leveled at his head by one of the four or five British soldiers that had somehow materialized in the room.

"Shit," he muttered. "Looks like you boys caught me with my pants down."

"Shut up!" the soldier barked loudly, causing Fulya to stir next to him. She came fully awake when one of the soldiers prodded her with his weapon.

"What the—" she started, but stopped when she saw the soldiers.

"Get up, the both of you," one of the soldiers commanded. Roan got out of bed, looking vainly for any way out of this, but his weapons were gone and he was naked. Beside him, Fulya stood up also naked and was subjected to a string of lewd comments from the soldiers.

"She's got nothing to do with anything," Roan said, figuring that Fulya had done her job well enough and he might as well at least save her. "She's just a Colleen I picked up in a bar."

"Is that right?" the lead soldier said. "Well then, Colleen, get your clothes together and get out of here. Looks like you need a right shower anyhow."

Fulya didn't waste any time pulling on her wrinkled dress and running out of the room, carrying her shoes in one hand. As she left through the open door, Roan saw Shaun lying facedown on the floor, his hands already bound behind his back. He grimaced. Part of him had always known it was going to come to this, but he wished he'd had more time.

***

Roan and Shaun were loaded into the back of an army truck and taken to British High Command headquarters a few miles away. Once inside the building, they were locked in a small room with a guard who yelled at them to remain silent. A few minutes later, a short, bandy-legged man with a barrel chest came through the door and peered at them.

"Well, well, well," he said. "Do you gentlemen know who I am?"

Neither of them answered.

"I'm Major Horace Stanly. This is my command. I would ask your names, but I'm certain you'd lie anyway and I have the benefit of knowing exactly who you are. Shaun McCabe and Roan Kelly. I've been looking for you blokes for a long time." He paced closer to them, leaning down to get a close look. Roan just looked up mildly. Suddenly, without any warning, Major Stanly backhanded Roan across the face, rocking his head back and sending a spray of blood over the table. "You earned that one. Now," he spoke to the guards, "take these gents to the honeymoon suite. We'll have work to do."

They were escorted roughly from the room and down two flights of stairs, into a cold, dank basement. Roan glanced over at Shaun and saw the fear in his younger comrade's eyes. He whispered, "Shaun, don't tell them shit. Be true to the cause and to me too."

Unfortunately, there was nothing he could do to prepare Shaun for what he suspected was waiting for them on the other side of the nondescript door they were hustled through. Roan had dealt with the British long enough to know what they did with suspected IRA leaders. Inside the room, they were gagged and blindfolded, then tied to chairs and left alone to stew in their thoughts.

Several floors up, Major Stanly placed a call to London to report to Brigadier General Hardgrave, his commanding officer. "Sir," he said, "we've had a spot of luck here. We've picked up Roan Kelly and his sidekick, Shaun McCabe."

The general uttered a sound of delight. "Kelly, you say? We finally got that bloody bastard, eh? You certain it's him?"

"Yes, General, it's them all right. Their pretty pusses are posted right here on my bulletin board." He paused. "What are my orders, sir?"

"Your orders are to treat them with nothing but English civility. I think they might enjoy a spot of tea."

"You mean high tea, sir?"

"Nothing less will do for our friends. We need to know everything they know about the guns, the money, personnel, the whole kit and caboodle. "

"Yes, sir. Understood."

"Brilliant, and report back to me as soon as you have facts and details. This could be a breakthrough."

The major hung up the phone and looked at the handset for a full minute. He thought of the men downstairs as locked boxes full of information he wanted. Like most of the British posted in Ireland, he had lost personal friends to the IRA and learned to loathe their fanaticism and tactics. They could not be counted on to act like humans, and so they did not deserve to be treated like humans. He picked up the phone and placed a call to have Sergeant Major Kit Morgan sent to his office immediately, then sat back and waited.

When he showed up, Kit Morgan was an ugly lump of a man. His nose had been mashed in more than once, and his teeth were stained and brown. His knuckles were crossed with old scars and his massive shoulders bunched up under his uniform. But Major Stanly didn't care about Morgan's appearance. He was more interested in Morgan's special affinity for interrogation—the SSgt. had killed hundreds, maybe thousands, in the service of the Crown, and he had proven himself to be the most effective interrogator in the Crown's service in Ireland.

Stanly quickly filled him in as Kit listened intently. At the end, Stanly gave Morgan the same code the general had used with him: "We're planning to host a little tea party for our guests. You'll make sure everything goes off as planned, yes?"

Kit nodded. "Ay, sir. With pleasure."

Down below, Roan's head lifted when Kit had the door opened and stepped in with two of his handpicked guards. The three of them had worked together before, and Kit didn't want to risk his effectiveness by bringing in a raw green recruit with a weak stomach.

"Hullo," he said softly while Roan's head tracked him like a blind dog sniffing a scent. "Don't worry, we'll have those blindfolds off in a flash and we'll have ourselves a nice little conversation."

He nodded and the blindfolds were removed, leaving Roan and Shaun blinking as Kit pulled up a chair and sat backward in it, facing the two men. "Now, the two of you have some talking to do. We're looking for information on your operations, and I won't insult you by pretending you don't know what I'm here for. All that remains for you is to decide if you'd like to do this the hard way or the easy way."

Roan cleared his throat, then said in his most Irish brogue, "You are an English *pig* and I wouldn't tell you the bloody time of day." Then he spat in Kit's face. Moving as quickly as a cat, Kit jumped over his chair and hit Roan so hard with a club that it broke his nose with a loud crunch. Blood gushed out of Roan's nose and mouth.

"So it'll be the hard way then," Kit said. "Good, because then I don't have to pretend I won't enjoy myself."

"Go screw yourself," Roan muttered.

Kit raised his club and struck again, this time in the groin. Roan yelped with pain. Kit, with sheer perverse pleasure, hit him twice more for good measure.

Both men were hung from their hands from the low overhead beams and stripped naked. Shaun was softly whimpering throughout, but Kit kept his attention focused on Roan. He circled around their hanging bodies, poking at them with his club. "Oh, you really *are* pretty boys, aren't you? And see there, it looks like the Irish curse escaped you gents. Real stallions, ain't ya?" He struck Shaun in the crotch with his billy club, harvesting a howl of pain.

"Tighten the ropes," Kit told his helpers. "Hang them up like a couple of pigs ready for slaughter. I understand that Mr. Kelly is the big shot here, so we'll start with him."

The guards attached a device to Roan's genitals. It resembled a jumper cable used to start vehicles with dead batteries, with two electrical cords with clamps on one end attached to a truck battery on the other. As the sharp clamps bit into Roan's flesh, he screamed with pain. When it was attached, Kit hosed them down first with ice-cold, and then almost scalding hot, water.

"Now, Mr. Kelly, I need some information," Kit said. "Could you tell me the location of all the safe houses? How many are there and who is in them? I want names, numbers, and places, if you please."

Roan remained silent.

"Mr. Kelly!" Kit yelled. "I asked you a bloody question and I expect a bloody answer."

Roan remained mute as Shaun looked on, shivering and petrified.

Kit signaled and one of the guards flipped the switch on the battery. A bluish arc lit up the room as electricity was delivered straight to Roan's testicles. Roan howled with pain, writhing against the ropes that held him. The stench of burning flesh and hair filled the air.

"Again!" Kit barked, and the guards turned it up again. Roan screeched as his manhood was decimated.

"Now, Mr. Kelly, are we ready to talk? You can stop this now."

Roan just hung silently, refusing to speak as tears dripped from his nose and chin.

"Very well, then," Kit said. "It's going to be a long night."

And it was. By dawn, Roan was as raw as freshly butchered meat. His genitals were darkened and smoldering, with snot and spit running down his swollen face from the beating. At one point, Kit took a pair of rusty, blood-covered pliers and pulled three teeth from Roan's mouth.

Throughout this whole ordeal, the torturers ignored Shaun completely, even when he pissed himself in pure fear and it ran down his legs. Shaun knew he would be next and prayed to God for a quick death.

As the clock struck 8 a.m., Kit ordered breakfast. It was brought to him on an army mess tray. As he ate coddled eggs, scones, and drank hot coffee, he became more and more frustrated with the lack of progress. He grabbed the half full coffee pot and poured the steaming fluid over Roan's bleeding, naked body. He then opened the salt shaker that came on his tray and shook the contents over his victim's open wounds, causing even more agony. Roan alternately screamed and moaned, then he passed out.

With Roan swinging unconscious on his ropes, Kit turned to Shaun.

"You see, my young friend, what's happened to Mr. Kelly? Why not avoid that fate and tell us what we want to know and walk out of here a whole man?"

Shaun literally shook with fear. He was torn between betraying his cause, including his friend, Roan, and being tortured, disfigured, and probably beaten to death.

Shaun, sobbing, said, "I can't, I can't."

"You can't, you can't. But you *will*, won't you, Mr. McCabe?" Kit took a long, sharp bayonet from the sheath on his belt. "Mr. McCabe, this is going to be very painful. But only for you. Why don't you just give us what we want and live for another day?"

Kit commenced to carve the word "Traitor" on Shaun's firm, flat stomach. Blood dripped from Shaun's toes.

"Traitor...that is what you are, Shaun, a traitor to the Crown and the Commonwealth. Do you want to die a traitor or do you want to make amends to your Queen?"

When Shaun didn't answer immediately, Kit ordered Roan to be taken to the next room and whipped. Shaun, hearing the crack of the whip upon Roan's flesh, knew that his brother-in-arms was resisting at great cost. Roan was dragged back into the room for Shaun to see. He looked like a slaughtered animal. Shaun prayed again to God, this time to take Roan in order to end his pain.

"Mr. McCabe, it's time for you to talk." Kit said. The guards hooked the electrical device to Shaun's testicles as Shaun screamed in agony and fear. "It's a pity that such a nice young man is going to lose the use of that very substantial tool. I'll bet the girls will miss it!" Kit said. "This is it, Mr. McCabe, are you ready or not?"

Just as the guard reached for the switch, Shaun tearfully said, "Don't! Don't do it! I'll talk...I'll tell you what you want to know. I know it all. I'll talk...just don't do that to me!"

"I knew you would come around, it's the smart thing to do. Now let's get down to business."

Shaun was taken into a clean office, allowed to dress, and given some food and drink. Over the next several hours, Shaun told all he knew. One of the guards served as a scribe and took copious notes. Shaun disclosed the locations of hundreds of men, many safe houses, and provided information about the money Roan was receiving.

"Now see, Shaun, that wasn't so bad," Kit said. Grabbing his club, the smiling sadist hit Shaun in the chest with all his might. Then he targeted Shaun's groin and his arms. Shaun's pale Irish skin ruptured and blood poured out of his wounds.

"Next time don't keep me waiting so long, you ignorant Irish mick bastard," Kit snarled. Turning to the guard, he shouted, "Toss this scum into a cell and let him rot!"

A guard took Shaun by the bloody arm and ushered him out of the room and towards a small cell. As the guard fumbled for the keys to unlock the cell door, Shaun knew if he didn't act now, he probably would not live another day. As the guard untied his hands, Shaun was able to overpower him, throwing him to the floor and stepping on his neck, constricting his windpipe. Unconsciousness followed almost immediately. Hastily, Shawn dragged the guard into the cell and switched clothing. Dressed as a British soldier, Shaun slipped out of the building unnoticed.

The information obtained from Shaun was a treasure trove. The notes were copied and dispatched by special courier to General Hardgrave in London, where they would be analyzed and sent on to MI6, the government's intelligence agency.

"Shaun McCabe got away," Major Stanly said to Kit once the news of the escape got around. "But we still have Mr. Kelly. Maybe he will verify what Mr. McCabe gave us."

"That bloke will never talk," Kit said.

"Probably. So let's make an example of him. Deliver him to his mates in an altered state, if you know what I mean."

"With pleasure, Major."

Kit proceeded to the holding cell where Roan was lying on the floor, barely conscious. He ordered Roan to be laid out on the table.

"You are filth," Kit said. "You're a traitor to the Crown and you don't deserve to live. But first I'm going to show you what happens to traitors."

Kit removed his bayonet from his belt and whispered in Roan's ear, "This is what happens to cowards like you."

At that, Kit castrated Roan with two swift cuts.

With all the energy he could muster, Roan raised his head and bellowed, "You pig, you're English scum. May you rot in hell and burn for eternity. Piss on you and your whoring mother." He spit a wad of bloody saliva in Kit's face.

Furious at this insolence and defiance, and with no thought of civility or consequence, Kit snarled and plunged his bayonet deep into Roan's heart. Roan died on a grimy table in a filthy English cell.

"Take this piece of shit out of here and hang his naked body in front of that Catholic Church in the neighborhood where we found him," Kit barked.

And that is exactly what they did. In the wee hours of the morning, Roan's mutilated, bloody, and neutered body hung naked for all to see in front of Our Lady of Everlasting Peace, a Roman Catholic Church. His private parts dangled from his mouth, an often-used symbol to designate an informant, even though Roan had remained true to his cause. The Brits weren't above waging a campaign of terror and misinformation of their own.

CHAPTER 34
FADED PHOTOGRAPHS

Washington, DC, 1986

William planned his trip to Saint-Benoit-du-Lac with the utmost secrecy in mind. This was no small task, considering that he had a Secret Service detail and his schedule and travels were followed 24/7 by an ever-eager press. Ordering his detail off duty would definitely attract attention, so William knew he would need help to carry it off. As a result, he called in his two most trusted Secret Service agents, Baker and Lombardi. They showed up in his office looking like the most unlikely of partners. Baker was a former Marine who specialized in weaponry and personal protection, which was a sort of code for hand-to-hand combat. Lombardi, on the other hand, was slight and short and had a degree in criminal law from Georgetown. Still, despite their differences, William felt he could trust them.

"Thanks for coming, guys," he started, walking around his desk to sit closer to them and remove the formal barrier of a large desk between them. "I have a situation that will require some special assistance from you. It's, uh, a little unorthodox, actually, and we'll have to break some protocol if you're to help me. But it's a personal matter, and as you know, I don't get a lot of privacy. The reason I called you two in is because I trust you completely, but you'd have to promise me if you agree to help that what we're doing would remain between us strictly. You could never disclose this. And if you choose not to help, I totally understand. No repercussions. No problem."

The two agents exchanged a swift glance, then Baker said, "Mr. Vice President, I think I speak for Agent Lombardi as well as myself when I say we are here to serve you in any way. Short of performing illegal acts, it is our job to protect and assist you. That is our sworn duty."

William smiled. "C'mon, boy. Nothing illegal. Of course not. Just a little sleight of hand, a disappearing act, if you will."

"Disappearing act, sir?"

"Yes. I need to disappear for a few days to visit someone in a town called Saint-Benoit-du-Lac in Canada. It's only about an hour away from my family's home in Vermont, so I was hoping you fellows could help me get there to Winterledge, then go up myself to Saint-Benoit-du-Lac for my meeting. Keep in mind, this is purely personal. It's not official at all. It's just not personal business I wish to see splattered across every newspaper in the country."

The agents shifted uncomfortably in their seats.

Not surprisingly, it was Lombardi who spoke up first. "Sir, do you mean you want to drive up to this town Saint-Benoit-du-Lac alone?"

"Yes," William said, "that would be ideal."

"Um, sir," Lombardi said, "with all due respect, that doesn't sound like a very wise idea. You'd be crossing international borders, putting you outside of the jurisdiction of the United States and on foreign soil. You know the precautions that are normally taken when you visit a foreign country. Not to mention that if anything should happen to you, it would be a gross dereliction of duty on our end. We can't protect you if we're helping you sneak off on your own."

"Is there another way to accomplish the same meeting?" Baker chimed in. "Perhaps you could have the person or persons you want to meet transported to you?"

William shook his head. "I thought about that, but the person I want to see is rather elderly and then the risk of being seen is too great. Too much press. Any other ideas?"

Lombardi was nodding, as if thinking. "Well, sir, it seems to me that the hardest part would be the border crossing. I respect that you want to do this alone, but it might make more sense if you drive ahead of us, alone in your vehicle, and we follow along behind. It's unlikely the border guard would connect your name with the vice president, but in case they did, we'd be there to smooth it out. If you were alone, they'd have to call it in."

William thought for a second. "You know what, Lombardi, you're right! Good thinking. But this person I'm meeting…they wouldn't want Secret Service types hanging around. Frankly, she's not going to be excited to see me, I don't think."

"Sir," Baker said, "we'd stay outside the building. And frankly, we'd be much more comfortable that way, at least nearby. Obviously, no one would suspect you're there, so the risk profile is minimal, but…in good conscience, sir, we couldn't just let you vanish into a foreign country alone."

Lombardi nodded in agreement.

"Okay, okay," William relented. "You win. The best plans are the simple ones, so let's do it just like Lombardi said. We'll be leaving tomorrow for Winterledge, and then Canada early the next evening."

"Yes, sir," Lombardi said. "In the meantime, I'll have a team up to Winterledge tonight to secure the premises. They'll be gone by the time we leave for Canada."

"Excellent. I owe you guys one," William said as they got up to leave, making plans to arrange for the vice presidential helicopter to depart at 1100 hours the next day. After they were gone, William took a deep breath. This was the easy part—now came the hard part. He went back to his desk and picked up the phone to call Rosemary North.

***

Vermont was beautiful from the air as the helicopter came in low over the tree line and circled once around Winterledge, the Carnegie family compound. It was an impressive "lodge." William's grandfather had commissioned its design and construction in the 1920s; it was a replica of a famous Stanford White residence. William had fond memories of ski trips and winter sports at Winterledge, just like two generations of Carnegies before him. Yet even that thought gave him pause: was he actually a Carnegie at all?

When the helicopter banked and came in to land, a man appeared on the edge of the broad grass lawn where a helipad had been constructed. William recognized him as Secret Service, waving to indicate that the grounds and building had been swept for bombs, listening devices, and anything else that looked suspicious. Behind him, waiting at the open front door, William saw the house's staff: a groundskeeper, a cook, and a housekeeper/house manager. William waved at them as he exited the helicopter and strode across the yard, the wind from the helicopter whipping at his jacket.

Inside, he saw that the house had not been fully prepared for a visit. They hadn't had time with such short notice to open everything up, and there were still sheets covering furniture in some of the rooms. But they had managed to prepare the great room and he saw that a massive fire had been set in the hearth, over which was crossed a pair of antique wooden cross-country skis. William smiled. He had spent many afternoons cross-country skiing and ice skating on the hills and ponds surrounding the mansion, and he fondly remembered the many Christmas parties they had thrown there. There was nothing like a Vermont Christmas, he reflected, when Winterledge's three-story-foyer would be decked out with a thirty-foot blue spruce and the whole house draped in garland and pine boughs.

Unbidden, another Christmas hopped to mind: the Christmas he had spent with Regina in their little flat in London, with her enthusiastically decorating the tiny space.

He shook himself a little bit. He hadn't thought of that in years...why were such morbid thoughts intruding now? But William already knew the answer: if his hunch was correct, and Rosemary North told him what he was bracing to hear, everything would change. There would be no more Christmases at Winterledge, but he had no idea what his future would look like.

After he dropped his bags off in his room, he walked through the house, noting that one of the staff had already lit a roaring fire in the den. He appreciated their efforts to make him feel at home. He settled into a leather Lawson chair and put his feet up, staring into the flames and wondering what the next twelve hours would bring.

"Excuse me?"

He turned and saw Marie, the housekeeper, in the doorway.

"Dinner is ready," she said. "If you are."

William got to his feet. "Definitely. Thanks." Then he paused. "Marie, how long have you been with my family?"

"Oh, I'd say about fifteen years, sir."

"Oh. Is that all? It seems longer."

"No, it's fifteen years."

"I see. Well, thank you...we really appreciate how you take such wonderful care of Winterledge for us. It's...really appreciated."

She ducked her head. "Of course. It's my pleasure." Then she paused. "Are you all right, sir?"

He realized he was standing by the chair awkwardly, not sure he could even put into words all the many feelings and thoughts in his head. "Yes, yes. Sorry. I'm fine."

Dinner was roast chicken and vegetables, after which he went back to the den. Marie followed him in with a tray of William's favorite cookies and coffee that he sampled as he arranged tomorrow's plans with Lombardi and Baker by phone. Marie didn't stick around in the den to talk, which was probably just as well. William was still having trouble ordering his thoughts and felt deeply confused. He thought of everything he knew about Rosemary and realized it wasn't much. She was his aunt, but he couldn't recall ever meeting her in person. On the phone the other night, her stepdaughter said she was beginning to suffer from Parkinson's disease but she was still "hanging in there" and "her brain is fine, if that's what you're asking." There was an odd coldness to the stepdaughter's tone, though, and William didn't totally believe it when she said, "My mom is really looking forward to seeing you." He had no idea why she would lie about it, but every instinct told him that something was off. It only served to reinforce his fears.

Finally, after a brandy, he realized he wasn't doing himself any favors by mulling this over. He wished Liz had come along with him, but her schedule hadn't allowed it. Anyway, he recognized he would be lousy company, distracted and anxious as he was. He got up, banked the fire, and headed up to the master bedroom on the second floor for the night. The master bedroom occupied the entire rear section of the house. Furnished in rustic European antiques, it was a room fit for nobility. The giant four-poster bed was draped with beautiful hunter-green silk brocaded fabric. An adjoining master bathroom with his-and-her dressing rooms, along with a large seating area in front of a fireplace, completed the suite. Hours earlier, the handyman had lit the fire so the room had a warm glow. Looking out of the curved windows that flanked the entire side of the bedroom, William saw the snow gently falling. He could see the ice skating pond and pavilion some seventy-five feet away. He recalled teaching his children how to skate and the huge bonfires they enjoyed while drinking Cook's delicious cocoa. After undressing, William crawled into the mammoth bed and opened his briefcase. But his mind was uneasy and he couldn't work. In frustration, William took a mild sleeping sedative and turned off the light and waited for sleep. As he lay there, he prayed to God for guidance and understanding.

The next day, William awoke refreshed but still anxious. After a hearty Vermont breakfast of pancakes with local syrup and homemade sausage, William placed calls to Liz and President Keith, saying he would return to Washington, DC, the next morning. After several more hours of work, William asked Agent Lombardi if he would like to take a ride around the property. Lombardi, with Agent Baker, pulled the large Jeep around to the front of the chateau and asked, "Sir, would you like to drive, or should I?" William said he would drive because he knew the estate intimately.

William joined the agents in the vehicle and took off. Following closely and providing additional security were two other government cars. Driving on the estate's dirt roads, William showed the agents where he had spent his youth climbing trees, swimming in the crystal clear ponds, and jumping off the waterfall into the river dividing the United States and Canada. After an hour and a half, the threesome, along with the additional security detail, returned to the chateau. Cook had a late lunch ready for them, and Marie served it in the small informal dining room off the kitchen.

After lunch, the hours ticked by until it was time to go. Finally, the cars were readied. William borrowed an old, nondescript Chevy Impala from the handyman. Baker and Lombardi would be following William in a government-issued black sedan. Agent Lombardi dismissed the rest of the security detail. Before leaving, they walked through the routine one more time.

Canadian Border Crossing, 5:36 p.m.

The two vehicles soon arrived at the Canadian border. As luck would have it, there was a line of five or six vehicles at the border checkpoint. One of the vehicles was a large eighteen-wheel tractor-trailer truck carrying American-made electronics. This attracted particular attention from the Canadian border officers. After more than ten minutes of waiting, one of the patrol guards began to wave through the non-commercial vehicles in the line. One by one, the cars crossed over the almost makeshift outpost and entered into Canada. William's Chevy was quickly waved through. Following closely behind him were Agents Baker and Lombardi in the government vehicle. Just as they approached the checkpoint, the border guard raised his hand motioning them to stop. The black sedan came to an abrupt stop. Both agents were alarmed by the fact that the vice president, now several hundred feet into Canada, was moving briskly away from their view and protection. Baker, acting as driver, turned to Lombardi and gave him a look of concern. Simultaneously, they thought that they should abort the mission, ignore the guard's instructions, and speed through the checkpoint in order to catch up with William. Both knew this could attract attention and perhaps cause an international incident, but their duty was more important.

Agent Baker slowly moved his foot from the brake to the accelerator, preparing to floor it. Within that split second of hesitation, the border guard, now approaching the sedan, raised his hand and waved them on. Baker and Lombardi, now soaked in sweat, felt relief as they sped past the checkpoint. Within a minute or two, they spotted the Chevy driving toward the village.

Baker honked the horn to get William's attention and let him know they were behind him again.

The two cars pulled into a quiet lane in the village of Saint-Benoit-du-Lac in the shadow of the Abbey Saint-Benoit-du-Lac, a century-old abbey founded by French Benedictine monks. The tiny village overlooked Lake Memphremagog, a glacial sanctuary for fish and wildlife. Saint-Benoit-du-Lac was a favorite for retired Québécois and Europeans because of its European architecture and laid-back lifestyle.

Rosemary Firth North's cottage was on one of the nine lanes in the village, called Vue sur le lac Voie, or Lake View Lane. The "cottage" was actually one of the more sizeable homes in the area, a testament to the success of the late Mr. North. The lakeside cottage was a charming combination of French and English Cotswold design. Deep snow covered the garden, and a pair of coach lights flanking the front entrance blazed with welcoming light.

William parked the Chevy on the street outside the cottage. Agents Baker and Lombardi drove by the entrance and parked a few meters away, prepared to patrol the street and property while William was inside. No one would enter or leave without their knowledge.

William rang the doorbell, and it was answered almost immediately by a middle-aged woman. She peered closely at him from under graying hair. "Good evening, I'm Agnes North," she said. "You must be William Carnegie."

"Yes. It's nice to meet you."

"Come in," she said, stepping back to let him into the house. She talked as they walked down a short hall toward a small parlor where William could see the lake through a large window. "I'm Rosemary's stepdaughter," Agnes continued. "My father and her married when I was young. She has been a good step mum." She paused. "I told you she has Parkinson's. She does well most days, and the doctors say she still has as many as five or six good years left, unless it moves faster. She's in good spirits, though. Most of the time.

She knits and reads mostly. But you don't have to worry about her mental faculties. The Parkinson's hasn't affected her mind and won't for years, the doctors say."

"Yes," William said. "I've heard that. I'm very grateful she's willing to see me and help with my research."

Agnes gave him a look. "I will say, she was very, very surprised to get a call from you."

William smiled at her. "Probably not half as surprised as I was to be placing the call."

Agnes's brow creased in confusion, but before she could ask, they entered the parlor, where the aged Rosemary sat by a cheerful small fire. The room was charmingly shabby, with flowered chintzes and colorful striped fabrics on the overstuffed furniture. Delicate lace curtains graced the bay window. Rosemary didn't rise from her chair when they came in, but when she held out her hand for him, William didn't see any of the telltale tremors of Parkinson's. In fact, she looked to be very fit and healthy, and her eyes were sharp. He took her hand and bowed over it, a courtly gesture that reminded him of his time among the English aristocracy.

"Aunt Rosemary," he said. "It's a pleasure to finally meet you."

She was wearing a strangely guarded expression, and William wondered if this was going to be a wasted trip. He had been very careful on the phone, saying he was doing a research project on his mother's family, the Firths, and wanted to talk to his elderly aunt about their history in England.

"William," she said. "My, it's such a pleasure to see how you've turned out."

He thought it was an odd remark, one that didn't make him more comfortable. "Thank you," he said. "As I mentioned, I was, ah, hoping you could help with some research I'm doing into my mother's family."

Rosemary uttered a short laugh, her eyes veiled and mysterious. "Yes, go ahead."

At first, William asked general, non-specific questions about Fiona and Rosemary and their days in the palace, and he let the older woman unspool her life story slowly. He was an excellent listener but soon realized that Rosemary had skipped over the part that interested him the most: his own birth. She had gone straight from her days in school to the marriage of her best friend Mary to Anthony, who would later die in an IRA bombing. William, who of course had already done his homework, knew all of this already. He delicately cleared his throat when she was done.

"I was wondering if, perhaps, you could tell me more about my own birth," he said. "You see, there have been some questions being asked by people who aren't friendly to me. And I did some research on my own. It, ah, raised more questions than it answered. I know this is awkward, but…I was really hoping you could help me."

Rosemary stared at him for a full minute before she slowly reached over and patted his hand. This time he noticed a faint tremor, but he couldn't be sure if it was her disease or some other cause. He was surprised to see that her eyes had misted up.

"I suppose I always suspected this day would come," she nearly whispered to herself.

"What day?" William said.

"The day you would come asking questions. Now, tell me, we can be honest with each other, why are you really here?"

"I found a letter," he said simply. "In my mother's things. It was from Mary, then the princess and today the Queen. It was…frankly unbelievable, but…" He trailed off.

Rosemary shook her head. "So Mary wrote a letter? How foolish. If she had asked me, I would have told her to burn it."

"Is it true?"

Rosemary took a deep breath. "You know, William, I've never told this story. Not to my husband, God rest his soul. Not to Agnes. To nobody. I always figured that by the time I'd tell it, people would assume it was the lunatic raving of an old woman gone soft in the head."

"What story?" he said, more urgently than he meant to.

"Are you sure you want to know?" she asked. "Some things, once you know them, you can never unknow them. And...your mother loved you very deeply. She wanted you as much as any mother could want a baby."

"My mother?" he said. "You mean Fiona?"

Rosemary laughed. "Why yes, of course I mean Fiona! But to answer your question, yes, it's true. You were born to Princess Mary, and your father was the future prince, Anthony." And then, in the calm sure tones of someone finally telling a great secret after all these years, Rosemary told him everything, from the first party where Mary and Anthony danced to the little wedding in the chapel on Gibraltar to Mary's very nearly broken heart at giving him up.

"But there was no alternative, you understand," Rosemary said. "Even today such a thing would cause a major international scandal, and things today are considerably more liberal than they were back then. It would have destroyed both Mary's and Anthony's reputations and conceivably caused the British Crown irreparable damage. As Mary was a minor, Anthony would likely have been jailed, and...there would have been the knotty question of succession. All in all, there was never any serious question what the two young lovers must do. But it was the strictest of secrets, you must understand. The only people who knew the full truth were Mary and Anthony, of course, and Fiona and myself."

"What about my father?" William asked. "He must have known his wife wasn't pregnant."

"He did," Rosemary said, "but he thought the baby was mine. He had no idea you really belonged to Mary and Anthony. I doubt he would have agreed to the ruse otherwise."

William had expected to hear this—he had been preparing himself for days to hear something like this. But actually hearing it was more stunning than he had anticipated. He felt his world shifting on its axis. His mother was not his mother. His father was not his father. He was the son of the Queen of England and her dead husband. Underneath the shock, he felt a flare of anger. They might have meant well, but by deceiving him his entire life, all of them, his birth parents and Fiona and the Ambassador, they had put him in a nearly impossible situation. He took a deep, shaky breath.

"Are you all right?" she asked. "I can imagine how hard this is to hear."

"Yeah, I'm fine," William said. "I hope you understand, but...do you have anything that could prove this? Is there any documentation anywhere? Anything that authenticates what you've just told me?"

She looked kindly at him. "I'm not sure, William. You're welcome to look through my old scrapbooks, though. There might be something there of interest to you."

***

William approached the bookshelf like one might approach a basket of snakes. He had come here to prove what he already suspected, but now that he had heard the whole story, he was more unsettled than ever. All he knew was that he needed to see proof—the kind of proof that would hold up in court, if possible. Numbly, he leafed through a few books, not really registering what was on the pages, until he came to a blue scrapbook next to a photo album. The scrapbook was clearly old, with a cracked spine, and his heart thudded as he removed it from the shelf and opened it up to reveal page after page of old photos, mostly of Rosemary and Mary as teenagers in their school days. He found himself studying the pictures of Mary, looking for resemblances. And indeed...he had her nose, the shape of her face. This made the whole thing seem even more real, staring at the teenage face of his birth mother and seeing the ghost of his own children in the way she held her head.

As he flipped the pages, he saw Rosemary and Mary age together, followed by press clippings from Mary's first wedding, then her Coronation, and finally her second wedding. Then he flipped to a page full of baby pictures. It was Prince John, he realized...his brother. Taped to the page was a lock of golden brown hair tied with a baby blue ribbon and tagged: "John, Age 14 months." John was the Prince of Wales and would someday be the King of England. He flipped more quickly, passing dozens of pictures of Rosemary with the baby John until he reached the end and a piece of paper slipped out. He picked it up and carefully unfolded it, realizing as he did that what he was staring at was his birth parents' marriage certificate—judging from Rosemary's story, their original marriage certificate. It announced the legal marriage of Mary Stuart to Anthony Bolin on August 26, 1935, in Catalan, Gibraltar, by a duly ordained Anglican priest.

He set the scrapbook aside and flipped through the photo album. It was more photos, and he saw several of his birth father. Again, he stared at the face and again he saw reflections of his own features. It made so much sense and yet was so foreign and strange. He had always assumed his lack of resemblance to his parents—the people who raised him—was simply because they were so much older when they had him. But no, now he experienced a strong surge of connection to the people in these black-and-white photographs, people who looked like him, looked like his own children.

William set the books aside and sat back, staring at the marriage certificate in his hands. He had come looking for proof, and he believed with his whole heart the story Rosemary had told him, but the lawyer in him knew that some family resemblance and an old marriage certificate wasn't good enough. The only indisputable proof he had was Rosemary Firth North herself, a former lady-in-waiting and childhood friend to the Queen and an eyewitness to the events surrounding his birth. Her story, coupled with the marriage certificate and the photos and press accounts, would likely be enough…but then would it? The only woman who could actually confirm the story in its entirety, beyond reproach, was currently sitting on the throne in England, and he expected no confirmation from that direction if this should ever break into the open.

He heard a noise behind him and saw Rosemary walking unsteadily in.

"Are you quite all right?" she said.

"Yes."

"Did you find what you were looking for?"

He waved at the photo album and scrapbook with the marriage certificate he was still holding. "Photos. This." He held it up. "Listen, Mrs. North, er, Aunt Rosemary, I hope it isn't an imposition, but could I take these two books with me? I…I'm not sure what to think quite yet, but I feel strongly that I'd like to have some of these pictures, some memento. I'd like to at least have copies of everything made and returned to you."

She nodded. "Of course. It's as much your history as mine."

"Thank you." Then a new thought occurred to him and he dug into his pocket and removed the ring he had found in the envelope in his mother's safe. He held it out to her. "I found this with the letter in my mother's study. Do you recognize it?"

Rosemary gave the ring an astonished smile and for one second, he saw the years slip from her face. She reached out to take it gently. "Of course I recognize this. This ring was given to Mary by her father, then King John. She wore it every day, and on the day she married Anthony, they didn't have a ring, so they used this one. This is her wedding band."

She handed it back to him, then looked at him steadily in that English way. He stood up, feeling that it was past time for him to go. "Thank you," he said. "For telling me the truth. For letting me in."

She patted his arm. "You deserve to know," she said. "I'm glad you found me."

Exiting the front door of the cottage, he found Agents Baker and Lombardi standing guard in the freezing Canadian air. They loaded into their cars and headed back south, across the border without incident, and back to Winterledge. William spent the evening holed up in his room alone, thinking. The next morning, he boarded the helicopter a much more confused man than he had been before he had all the answers. Now he found himself heading back to DC and back to an uncertain future.

CHAPTER 35
Science Doesn't Lie

Washington, DC, 1986

Back in Washington, William found himself increasingly distracted by the idea of absolute proof. He had a compelling case that he was the eldest son of the current Queen of England and therefore the rightful heir to the English throne—but he needed more than a compelling case. He needed absolute proof. He had no idea exactly what he planned to do with such proof—the thought of actually contesting the throne was beyond his comprehension—but the part most important to him in this puzzle was to know his very identity, to be certain. A lot was in the balance, the least of which was the Carnegie fortune.

There was only one possible way he could think of, and he wasn't even sure it was possible. He had read recently about the discovery of something called DNA, by an English scientist named Professor Sir Alex John Jeffreys. According to the briefing he had read, DNA was something like a fingerprint, but infinitely more complicated. No two people had the same DNA, but each person inherited half of their DNA from each parent. Moreover, by using

DNA, it was possible to determine lineage, solve crimes like the infamous English Pickford rape case, and do all sorts of other work that scientists were only beginning to imagine.

William embarked on a feverish hunt to track down Dr. Jeffreys and found to his delight that the good scientist was scheduled to speak at a science symposium in Washington, DC, a week later and was actually in Washington at that very moment. William immediately summoned Dr. Jeffreys to his residence. The doctor showed up, looking very much like the tweedy scientist William had imagined him to be. If he was overwhelmed to be in the presence of the vice president, he didn't show it. On the contrary, he seemed somewhat distant and lost in his own thoughts, like he was always focusing on a point just beyond William's head. William chalked that up to him being one of those heady academics.

William gave him only the briefest of explanations, asking if Dr. Jeffreys's DNA could compare samples from three people and see if they were related. Dr. Jeffreys answered without hesitation: "The answer to your question is an absolute yes. We can show with 99.99% accuracy family relations."

"How long would it take?"

"With the right equipment, just less than a fortnight."

William then offered Dr. Jeffreys a truly staggering sum of money to conduct tests on three samples in the utmost of confidentiality. He planned on using the lock of hair from Prince John he had found in the scrapbook, his father's old toothbrush, and a lock of his own hair. Naturally, he didn't tell Dr. Jeffreys who the samples came from, only that it was imperative to prove whether these three people had been related and to what degree. "Can you do that?"

"Assuredly," the doctor said, responding with the same certainty as if he was asked what time it was.

"Then I will arrange it."

William reasoned that if the test results showed that the DNA from the lock of hair in the scrapbook matched his, it would be indisputable that John, currently Prince of Wales, was in fact his younger brother. It would also prove that the Queen was his birth mother. Further, he reasoned that if the Ambassador's sample did not match his, it would prove that the man he thought was his father definitely was not. Although this confirmation would break his heart, he felt he needed to know for sure. After all, the science wouldn't lie.

After the doctor had left, William made arrangements for the samples to be shipped to Dr. Young unlabeled and without any identifying information. They were identified only as Person A, Person B, and Person C. He also instructed his aid to make any and all resources available to Dr. Young for his work, that it was a matter of some national urgency.

When all this was done, William began to wait for the proof he was certain was coming.

CHAPTER 36
STOP THE BLEEDING

England, 1986

AROUND THE SAME TIME THAT WILLIAM WAS HAVING HIS DNA SAMPLES sent to Dr. Jeffreys, a remarkably handsome young American strolled down a garden path to a traditional English cottage surrounded by a meticulously tended flower garden. He knocked on the door and soon found himself smiling into the face of an elderly, gray-haired woman who was clearly wondering why such a handsome American was ringing on her bell.

"Miss Breckenridge?" he asked, making a show of looking at a reporter's notebook in his hand.

"Yes?" she said, still hovering between natural English suspicion and interest in this dashing young man.

"Ma'am, my name is Matt Smith. I'm a reporter with the *Tribune Herald* in the United States. I'm currently working on a story about the daughters of English aristocracy, a sort of where-are-they-now piece. I'm sorry to bother you, ma'am, but I was told that you have been involved in the Highwood School since the 1930s and personally taught many of the girls I'm hoping to write about. So I was hoping, if it's not too much trouble, to have a word with you about your excellent school and its noteworthy alumnae."

He wasn't sure how the next few minutes would go—there was a good chance she'd throw him off her premises without another word. After all, like many older and beloved teachers for exclusive English schools, she owed her current lifestyle to the school. Her charming cottage and its grounds were paid for by a wealthy alumnus, one of Ms. Breckenridge's former students. As they said in the U.S., it didn't make sense to bite the hand that feeds you.

But then again, the reporter was counting on his secret weapon: he smiled at her, turning on the full wattage of his looks. He had learned over the years just how powerful a handsome face and a great body could be when he needed something from the fairer sex.

Several heartbeats went by, and then Ms. Breckenridge broke out in a giggle. "Oh! You want to interview me for your newspaper? Come in, come in!"

And he was in. For the next hour, he enjoyed her fussing over him, plying him with excellent tea and even better biscuits, while he plied her with questions about old students. Naturally, having done his homework, he knew the names of dozens of her prominent old students, the daughters of Lord This and Lady That who had passed through the exclusive prep school on the way to whatever estate they would settle in. But slowly, his questions began to focus on one student in particular: Fiona Firth.

"Do you remember anything about her? It was my understanding that she's royalty?"

"Oh no, not directly," Miss Breckenridge quickly said. "She would have been fourth cousin, I believe, to the King, but not in a direct line. And believe me, things like that matter here."

"Was she a good student?"

"Fiona? Oh yes! An excellent student. You'll be interested to know that she married a Yank later, some famous industrialist I should think, but his name escapes me."

"Ah." He made a show of scribbling in his book. "I can find that out at home. So she was a good student and…?" He waited with his pen poised over his notebook. He had also learned that nothing was as effective as an open-ended question, an eager listener, and a poised pen to get people talking.

"Well, she was very pretty, if my memory serves. But such a sickly thing! She actually missed a whole term at one point, then came back and wouldn't you know it, she made up all her work without missing an assignment. It was really rather astonishing, to see such a serious-minded young woman in an era in which women were not expected to be serious-minded. It's a shame it was a different era. She would have made an excellent barrister."

"That is amazing," he said, writing more. "Do you recall what she was sick with?"

"Oh no," Miss Breckenridge said. "I couldn't possibly recall. After forty years and thousands of girls, it's hard to remember who got what and when. But I'll tell you, Mr. Smith, you could pop over to the school nurse's office. My grand-niece is the nurse at the school. Tell her I sent you!" Miss Breckenridge finished this with a twinkle in her eye, and Matt Smith smiled—he recognized a set-up when he saw one. He had no doubt Ms. Breckenridge's grand-niece was terminally single and probably ghastly.

"You sure that would be okay?" he asked.

"Quite! She'll be tickled to see you!"

Matt's smile grew another notch.

Moments later, he took leave of Miss Breckenridge and walked the short distance to the school grounds. Highwood School really was beautiful—the school grounds looked like something from a calendar or movie, with ivy-covered buildings and striking garden paths running between towering trees. It was exactly the kind of school he imagined the children of English aristocrats attending.

He quickly located the school nurse's office and was not surprised to see a plain woman furiously applying lipstick in a hand mirror as he approached the window. He had little doubt the phone had just rung as a certain great-aunt alerted her grand-niece to the impending arrival of a dashing American reporter. Sure enough, when the woman opened the door, she stammered out her name and said she had been expecting him and would be happy to help.

He spent the next few minutes harmlessly flirting with the exceptionally plain grand-niece and getting a grand tour of Highwood's small clinic, including the basement where student health records were kept. "I'm breaking all sorts of rules," she breathed at him, alone in the basement between rows of file cabinets. "But you won't tell on me, will you, dear?"

"No, definitely not."

"Okay. Miss Firth's record is in here. But you can't take anything from it. Just read it. Will you put me in your article?"

"Of course," Matt said. "It wouldn't be a good article without you."

She smiled and actually blushed, then hustled away and left him alone to find Fiona's health records. It only took a few minutes before he had located a fairly thick file labeled "Fiona Firth." Another few minutes later he hit the jackpot. In her sixth year, the year before she graduated, Fiona Firth was diagnosed with adolescent menorrhagia, a rare form of excessive menstrual bleeding. She was sixteen years old. They had tried to treat it, but the treatment was unsuccessful, and the surgeons had finally resorted to a full hysterectomy, which had been performed by Dr. Fredrick Carol. Fiona Firth thereafter was barren. It was physically impossible for her to have children.

Working quickly, he pulled out a mini-camera and took pictures of the file's contents, then replaced it. On his way out, he was in an excellent mood so he stopped for some more flirting with the grand-niece, leaving her with a vague promise that he would be back sometime "because I didn't find what I was looking for today."

"Maybe you just aren't looking hard enough," she said, actually batting her eyelashes at him.

"Maybe not," he conceded. "But sometimes it's easy to miss what's right in front of our faces."

She giggled then, and he took leave of her, sailing out into a beautiful day, knowing that he had just found the smoking gun that would make him a very rich man when he delivered this information to Speaker Jordan.

CHAPTER 37
God Save the Queen

London, 1986

The news hit London like the worst kind of surprise: "Queen Mary Near Death!"

According to an article in The Guardian, the highly popular Queen Mary had been horseback riding at the family's estate in Balmoral when she was thrown from her horse and suffered a serious head injury. According to the full article:

> *This morning, at approximately 8:35 a.m., while at Balmoral Castle in Scotland, Her Majesty, Queen Mary, a keen equestrian, was beset by a freak sporting accident while engaged in her favorite pastime, horseback riding.*
>
> *The Queen was atop her prized Arabian steed, a gift from the Shah of Iran, when the accident befell her. Eyewitness reports indicate that the mount, while trotting along at a vigorous pace, apparently became entangled in some underbrush, causing the beast to trip and fall. The*

animal tumbled to the ground, with Her Majesty falling along and hitting her head on a nearby rock. She was partially pinned beneath the mammoth mount, who was unable to regain uprightness.

Within minutes, her Majesty's limp and unconscious body was evacuated by ambulance lorry to an awaiting helicopter. The Queen, who is said to be gravely injured, was transported to a London hospital. No pertinent information has been released by the Palace as of yet. However, a hospital spokesman did announce that until they could sort out and evaluate Her Majesty's medical condition, there would be no further comments to the press. In the meantime, the entire empire awaits and prays for Queen Mary.

The country was suddenly thrust into a state of suspended animation, torn between a death watch and a desperate hope their popular Queen would recover. Throngs gathered in front of Buckingham Palace, piling flowers six feet deep against the walls and gates. At any time of the day or night, people could be seen on the streets outside the palace, with candles lit and fervently praying.

At the nearby London hospital, the Queen's condition remained unstable, no matter how many specialists were flown in from around the world, including the United States. Unfortunately, though, it seemed that Mary was losing her battle: her condition steadily deteriorated as the doctors and her husband Cyril sat by helplessly, watching her slip away from them. Cyril kept a bedside vigil, never leaving his wife's side. He was convinced she could hear him, so during quiet moments in the dead of the night, he often talked to her and held her hand. He never got any response, but if there was any chance she could hear him, he planned to continue trying to bring her out of the coma.

The doctors were cautious with their predictions, which Cyril knew was not a good sign. Her lead physician was Dr. Alistair Whitehead, a leading neurosurgeon and specialist in head trauma. He took heroic measures to figure out the nature and extent of the Queen's brain injuries, but as far as Cyril could tell the doctor only got more frustrated as the hours slipped away and her condition refused to improve. After endless tests, x-rays, and the like, Dr. Whitehead finally pulled Cyril into the antiseptic hospital hallway one evening and informed him in hushed tones that there was little medicine could do for his wife any longer.

"What are you telling me?" Cyril stammered out, his brain seeming to move two minutes behind the conversation.

"I'm saying that she's breathing on machines at the moment and her brainwaves are erratic and chaotic. She is being fed through an IV. Her heart is strong, but...without the machines, we would have lost her already."

"No!" Cyril said. "Please, do not say you are giving up on her!"

The doctor rubbed his hand over his forehead. "I didn't say that. But... there is a limit to what we can do. Medicine is not magic and doctors are not gods. I think we must begin to prepare for the inevitable."

"Exactly what are you saying, doctor?"

"At some point sooner than later, it will become apparent that a recovery is not possible. At that time there would be no improved quality of life by prolonging it though artificial means. It would serve no purpose. We are not there yet, and I have seen one or two patients miraculously recover from head injuries of this gravity—"

"Thank God for that."

"But, sir, the odds are long. At this point, only God can save the Queen."

CHAPTER 38
HEIR TODAY, GONE TOMORROW

WITH THE QUEEN HOVERING ON THE BRINK OF DEATH, THE CENTURIES-OLD bureaucratic machinery that ensured a smooth succession whirred to life, beginning with a meeting of the Cabinet of the United Kingdom, a Parliamentary body that was charged with formally affirming the succession and dealing with disputes, challenges, and disqualifications. The Cabinet was headed by the sitting Prime Minister and his senior ministers.

At the first meeting, the members all first expressed their serious concern and dismay over the Queen's condition. She was still the reigning Queen, but the medical reports looked grim. The members all unanimously agreed to explore the establishment of a Regency. This portion of British law allowed someone other than the reigning monarch to rule in the event the monarch was incapacitated or couldn't rule for whatever reason. A declaration of incapacity would need to be signed by at least three of those authorized by the Regency Act. They included Mary's husband, the Consort of the Sovereign, the Speaker of the House of Commons, the Lord Chief Justice of England,

and the Master of the Rolls. The Regency would terminate when either the indisposed monarch recovers or dies.

Under the Regency Act (1937) the next in line for succession was typically appointed Regent. In this case, their choice was obvious. Prince John was the clear successor to the throne, so they all expected a smooth Regency and transition, should it come to that. All that remained was to vet John, the Prince of Wales, as required by the Act of Settlement, so if the declaration of incapacity was signed, Mary's son would immediately become Regent on his way to the throne.

Everyone involved expected the vetting process to be routine, a minor technicality on the way to naming Prince John the Regent. John was clearly the natural-born child of Mary and Anthony and next in line. He was married to Eugenia, the child of Sir Edward Wolf and Lady Agatha, and they had no children. Within days, various documents were collected and the process began. Unfortunately for the Cabinet, however, a question arose almost immediately, one that had somehow escaped the royal notice when John announced his intention to marry Eugenia.

One of the significant provisions of the Act of Settlement of 1701 was that a reigning monarch could not be Catholic or married to a Catholic. During the Cabinet's investigation, it was discovered that Lady Eugenia's mother, Lady Agatha, was a practicing Catholic. During the vetting process investigators found an obscure record documenting that Eugenia had been baptized Roman Catholic. Conversely, no records could be found to establish that Lady Eugenia Wolf had been baptized a second time or confirmed in the Church of England.

Alarmed, the Cabinet investigators checked and double-checked every detail of this discovery, fearing that making an unsubstantiated accusation of such magnitude would be a political nightmare. The Cabinet quickly resolved that the Prince of Wales was indeed married to what perhaps would be called a "closet Catholic" and that Lady Eugenia was technically still a member of the Roman Catholic Church.

Under the provisions of the Act of Settlement, which explicitly forbids a monarch to be married to a Catholic, the Prince could not legally ascend to the throne.

Buckingham Palace, Office of the Prince of Wales

The Cabinet convened for a tense meeting in Buckingham Palace's Office of the Prince of Wales. None of the Cabinet members were anxious to deliver the news, but they had debated it extensively and saw no other option as the Cabinet head, Sir Markus Butler, called the meeting to order. Indisputably English, Sir Markus towered over most all of his colleagues. Grayed with age, filled with wisdom and experience, the Cabinet head spoke for Parliament in these important matters.

"Your Royal Highness," Sir Markus paused and then continued, "My fellow Cabinet members and I have asked for this audience with you and your solicitor to discuss a matter of utmost importance. A fact has come to light during the Cabinet of the United Kingdom's routine vetting. As you know, sir, it is required that intense vetting be conducted on any and all future monarchs assuring that all the legal requirements for succession are satisfied."

Prince John leaned back in his chair at the head of the long conference table, looking relaxed but curious. "Yes, I'm listening," he said, nodding to a distinguished looking man next to him. "You've all met Sir Randolph Booth, I'm sure, my chief solicitor and counsel. Sorry to have a barrister, but the tone of your note sounded urgent. So, tell me what's come up."

The Cabinet head cleared his throat, nodding at Sir Randolph. "Well, as you no doubt both know, the succession to the throne is governed by a document called The Act of Settlement of 1701. In that Act, all of the details regarding the requirements and disqualifiers for succession are set forth."

Sir Randolph nodded. "Yes. It's of utmost importance that everything is on the up and up."

"Exactly, and, er, we've run across a problem with a portion of the act that would directly affect Prince John's succession."

The Prince and Sir Randolph exchanged a swift glance, then Sir Randolph leaned forward, his distinguished face suddenly looking vulpine. "Do go on," he said in a deadly quiet voice.

Sir Markus looked like he wanted to crawl into a hole. "Well, Your Highness, as Sir Randolph says, it's crucial that there be no question surrounding the succession, no legitimate contest to the throne. As you might be aware, there is a provision of the Act that says the reigning monarch can neither be a Catholic nor be married to a Roman Catholic, and well—"

Unable to contain himself, Prince John slapped a royal palm on the table, instantly hushing the room. "What rubbish is this? I'm not a bloody Catholic!"

"Yes sir, we know that," the Cabinet head said. "We are not suggesting that you are a Catholic, but what we do know is that your wife, Her Royal Highness, Eugenia, is."

Prince John first flushed red, then turned pale. "How dare you come into my office and tell me my succession is threatened because my wife is a Catholic! She is nothing of the sort."

Sir Randolph laid a calming hand on the Prince's arm. "I think it best that you proceed very cautiously, gentleman," he said in that same deadly quiet tone. "This is the future King you're talking to."

Sir Markus looked like he wanted disappear into space, to crawl under a rock, but he swallowed and pressed on. "I understand completely who I'm talking to, but I think you'll agree that the British Empire was founded on the rule of law, including the Act of Settlement. No man, royal or otherwise, rises above our laws. And as he is married to a Catholic, Prince John cannot legally ascend the throne."

"I will not hear this!" Prince John said, still standing. "You shall leave my presence at once!"

Sir Markus forged ahead. "Please, Sir, it brings me no pleasure to bring you this news and dilemma. But as the duly appointed head of the Cabinet, it's my duty to tell you, and as your loyal subject, it's my hope that you'll let us explain the situation in private rather than in public."

That seemed to get Prince John's attention—royals were always aware of possible negative press. He nodded.

"Our investigation has turned up documentation that your wife, Lady Eugenia Wolf, was the natural born child of Sir Edward and Lady Agatha Wolf," the Cabinet Head said, glancing at a paper on the table in front of him. "Her mother, Lady Agatha, was a practicing Catholic and had Eugenia baptized in the Catholic Church. We found her baptismal certificate and ample eyewitnesses and even diary notations. There can be no doubt. Further, she never renounced her Catholicism or was baptized in the Church of England."

"Are you insane? We were married in the Church of England!" the Prince said.

The Cabinet Head nodded. "Indeed, so Eugenia may be a member of the Church of England by election, but not by baptism or confirmation. Unless she were to renounce her Catholic faith, her official, on-the-record church affiliation is Roman Catholic. This can be proven beyond any reasonable doubt, Your Highness. For some unexplained reason, at the time of your marriage, this information was either missed or hidden."

The Prince studied Sir Markus for a long time, then turned to councilor Sir Randolph. "What does this mean? What are they talking about? I am the heir to the throne, the future King. They can't take my birthright away. Is there any legal standing to this?"

"Remain calm, Your Highness," Sir Randolph said. "All of us in this room want what's best for the kingdom, which is for you to act as Regent and assume the throne at the appropriate time. We will get to the bottom of this. Don't worry."

Sir Markus looked down at his paper and then said again in the clearest of words, "Sir, I will be happy to provide you with a copy of the Act of Settlement itself, and of course all the relevant statements made by the monarchy since then. You'll see that the law is ironclad. England's Sovereign cannot be married to a Roman Catholic. If at the time of succession the successor has a Catholic spouse, he or she must forfeit their eligibility to the throne. Lady Eugenia is documented to be Catholic, which irrefutably disqualifies you, as her husband, to have the Crown."

"Rubbish!" the Prince almost yelled. "This must be some kind of mistake, some farce! There is no reason I cannot act as the King should my mother be unable to serve!"

Sir Randolph tried again, saying, "Your Highness, don't worry; we can fight this and get the matter resolved in your favor, I assure you."

"We had best!" the Prince warned. "This is the most preposterous thing I've ever heard!"

Sir Markus squared his papers up as the others looked on. "I'm sorry, Sir. As I said, it brings me no pleasure to give you this news, but please be advised that we are entrusted with naming the Regent and then the King. It is a matter of constitutional law, as you know. And because of the great importance and the nature of the tragedy that has befallen your dear mother, our Queen, we will have to make an announcement soon. I wanted you to be fully aware of the situation prior as a courtesy."

"No!" the Prince said. "There will be no announcement! I will be Regent and then King, and this is final! We will fight you every step of the way!"

Rather than argue, Sir Markus merely looked grim as they all collected their papers and rose. Just before he left, he turned and said, "I'm sorry, sir. I truly am."

"You will be!" the Prince shouted. "You will be!"

***

Immediately following the departure of Sir Markus and his entourage, Prince John summoned his wife. As he waited for her to appear, he wondered how could his wife, the women he knew so well and slept next to every night, be a Catholic and he not know of it? Surely she could explain how this was a huge mistake. Eugenia showed up moments later and looked alarmed at the high color in her husband's cheek. "Dear," she said, "are you quite all right?"

Sir Randolph invited her to sit and offered her a glass of water. She declined and listened attentively as Sir Randolph laid out the Cabinet's findings and what it meant for the kingdom and for Prince John's ascension. As Sir Randolph laid out the case, referring to the actual wording of the Act of Settlement, the color slowly drained from Princess Eugenia's face. Sir Randolph finished, saying, "If all of this is true, which we suspect it is, for John to succeed to the throne, you must renounce your Catholic religion, be baptized in the Church of England, and swear your allegiance as an Anglican to God and Country."

The Prince leaned forward. "How could I not know this about you? You understand, my dear, what this means?"

Eugenia took a full minute to collect her thoughts, her face white and a sudden tear trembling on her lashes. Finally, she said, "I do understand what it means. But...oh, John! You must understand...if it wasn't for my Catholic faith I would not be alive today. At seventeen, I was desperately ill, I prayed to Jesus Christ, our Lord, and pledged that if he were to spare me I would remain his faithful servant for the rest of my life. He answered my prayers and my life was spared." The tear fell, and she began to weep. "When we fell in love, I was young and impressionable and so in love with you. I allowed myself to remain silent about my faith and be married in the Church of England. I have hidden it for years, God forgive me. I'm so sorry!"

John waved her apology away. "Eugenia, I understand, but you do know what is at stake now? A kingdom!"

Eugenia looked miserable. "Yes, John. Your kingdom. But for me, it is the Kingdom of God that is the most important, not one of this earth's. I cannot turn my back on that. I would be damned to hell and a hypocrite to deny the God who saved my life. I know it is important to you to be King, but it is far more important to me to save my soul and remain true to my religion and my God. I am afraid I cannot comply."

"Are you telling me that you would have me give up my Kingdom for your God?" John said, his voice snarled with fury. "You'll make me choose between my destiny as the King of England and my wife?"

Eugenia could barely whisper her response: "I'm so sorry. But if you love me as I love you, the sacrifice must be made!"

Two Days Later

As promised, an announcement was made to the public. It read, in part:

> *In an ongoing investigation relative to the legitimacy of the succession of Prince John, Prince of Wales, it has been determined that under the Act of Settlement of 1701, the Prince has been disqualified. This disqualification is due to the fact that his wife, Princess Eugenia, is a christened Roman Catholic and was never baptized in the Church of England and she has declared no intentions to do so now. Prevailing*

law clearly prohibits that a successor be crowned if he or she is married to a Roman Catholic at the time of ascendency and subsequent reign.

The news hit London like a bomb, and the next morning, the tabloid headlines screamed: "Heir Today, Gone Tomorrow," "Prince John gets the Royal Boot?" and "Will he Dump the Little Woman and be King?" Even worse, the traditional newspapers picked up on a new angle: "Waiting to Hear: Will the Pope Pop His Cork Over Catholic Denial of Heir Apparent?"

Within hours, the country was plunged into a full-fledged political crisis and Prince John was vowing to fight for his crown.

***

The Prince formally filed for an appeal and quickly enlisted the support of one of the oldest and most pro-royal law firms in the British Isles. He also secured the support of Nathanial, Archbishop of Canterbury, and the Pope's personal envoy to Great Britain, Cardinal Mazzio.

On the day of the appeal, Prince John entered the Parliamentary chambers at the head of an impressive coterie of barristers and religious authorities. Arrayed against him was the Cabinet itself, including the Prime Minister of the United Kingdom. The committee had done its best to preserve an air of august ceremony for the appeal, but there was no mistaking the circus-like atmosphere on the street outside, with the news vans parked end to end, a thick forest of wires and satellite dishes, and people shouting and jostling in huge crowds. Inside, however, the air was thick and oppressive and the silence almost deafening as the chairman of the Appeals Committee, Sir Michael Whitfield, gaveled the meeting into order and called upon Sir Randolph to deliver the opening statement on behalf of Prince John.

"My Lords," he began in a somber tone, "I want to begin by saying that this hearing is a total outrage to the Crown, particularly to the rightful heir to the throne and future Sovereign, His Highness, John the Prince of Wales. As laboriously detailed in our numerous, comprehensive, and compelling appeal briefs submitted to this Committee, it is clearly spelled out that the involuntary baptism into the Catholic religion of the Princess of Wales by her mother is absolutely irrelevant. The fact that Lady Eugenia is currently a member of the Church of England and even was married in that church clearly nullifies any contention that she is a Catholic. To base the disqualification of the Prince of Wales's birthright on a mere technicality that Lady Eugenia failed to be re-baptized in the Anglican Church is patently ridiculous."

He paused, then switched gears and continued, "On the other hand, even if the Prince's wife were considered a Catholic, it would be religious prejudice to uphold such an archaic law prohibiting the rightful heir to succeed. Such a determination reeks of sixteenth-century religious prejudice and should not stand. It is anti-Christian and divisive."

He continued: "The Prince of Wales is utterly and absolutely in opposition to the Committee's flawed findings and conclusions, which I restate were based on a loophole and an oversight. Further, as you'll hear, both the Church of England and the Holy Roman Catholic Church argue that the provision under discussion in the Act Settlement of 1701 should be amended to reflect the realities of today, not a medieval bias against our Catholic brothers and sisters worldwide. I would like you to now hear from His Eminence, Cardinal Joseph Mazzio. He is the direct envoy from his Holiness the Pope and has been tirelessly working for years with the Church of England."

Cardinal Mazzio rose next. Clad in his vivid crimson robes with elegant lace trimmings and a splendid antique golden crucifix suspended on his abundant chest, Cardinal Mazzio slowly approached the speaker's podium. In a soft-spoken but firm and heavily accented voice, the Cardinal delivered a passionate speech calling for the Cabinet to set aside "ancient religious prejudices" and "do your duty to your country" by approving Prince John's succession.

When he was done, the Cardinal stepped down and headed back to his seat. Sir Whitfield next asked if Prince John's solicitors would like to add anything. Immediately, one of the younger men at the table rose to speak. "My Lord," he said, "in the Act of Settlement of 1701, it states that the monarch may overturn the decision of this committee. We know that if the Queen were able to consider this matter, she would rule in favor of the Prince and support the appeal of this anti-Catholic, anti-Christian antiqued prohibition once and for all."

Sir Whitfield responded, "That is correct. The Committee is well aware of that provision; however, given the incapacitation of the reigning monarch, Queen Mary, and the lack of a duly authorized Regent, the Committee is compelled to make its own judgment with respect to this law. Obviously, an unconscious Queen cannot overrule this or any decision. Conjecture as to what she would or would not do in this situation is folly. We are compelled to be guided by the law. Is there anything further?"

"Not at this time," Sir Randolph answered.

Sir Whitfield adjourned the Cabinet for deliberations, which were expected to consume the remainder of the day. However, shortly after they had retired to their chambers, a note arrived in the personal hand of the Archbishop of Canterbury. Sir Whitfield opened it and read the contents to the Appeals Committee:

My Lords,

As you contemplate the Prince of Wales' justifiable appeal, it is important for you to know of the massive strides the Church of England has made with Rome. Considerable progress towards reconciliation has been made. Mending deep chasms between the two churches is within reach. There is even discussion of a Papal State visit. This would be the first State visit of a Pope to Britain since the Church of England broke from Rome in 1534. This remarkable opportunity should not be squandered.

All of our arduous efforts would be for naught if the Prince of Wales is denied his rightful succession based on religious prejudice disfavoring Catholics. That action would be a direct affront to the Holy See and our joint efforts to reunify our two great religions. Therefore, for the benefit of country and God, I urge you to allow Prince John his rightful destiny and become our anointed monarch.

The deliberations were fraught with conflict, but ultimately, the Committee made its decision: the law was the law, and there was no legal basis to selectively enforce the Act of Settlement of 1701. A legitimate resolution to the Prince of Wales' succession issue would be to amend or change the Act, which could only be accomplished by the reigning monarch with the support of Parliament. Alternatively, if the Prince of Wales's wife were to renounce her Catholic faith and be baptized in the Church of England, the Committee would then be compelled by law to name him Regent and ultimately monarch. Since neither of these alternatives have been embraced, the decision to disqualify the Prince of Wales is valid and stands.

The Committee's ruling was announced, to the expected denunciations from anti-royalists and the Vatican. The Pope even took the remarkable measure of publicly denouncing the British government in a strongly worded official statement: "It is most counterproductive that the English are implementing an archaic, conflict-ridden, un-Christian, and discriminatory law that does nothing but divide and disparage the improving relationship that the Holy See has been working towards with the Church of England and the English people."

Still, even the Pope's words were not enough at this point. Prince John would never be King.

CHAPTER 39
LADIES NEED NOT APPLY!

London, 1986

WITH PRINCE JOHN DISQUALIFIED AND QUEEN MARY LYING IN A COMA, hovering perilously close to death, the matter of appointing a Regent and heir to the throne assumed an urgency that had not been seen in centuries. Anti-royalists crowed that it was time to end the monarchy, while citizens throughout the United Kingdom fretted about the legitimacy of whoever would be named Regent. At the same time, furious speculation began in the press about what the Committee would do next and who was eligible. The papers were rife with names of possible monarchs, ranging from the plausible to the ridiculous.

Operating under intense pressure, the Committee wasted no time. The day after the announcement that Prince John's appeal had failed, the full Cabinet met again in a hasty meeting to discuss their next move. The next obvious choice was Mary Louise Stuart, the firstborn niece of King John and first cousin to Queen Mary. Unfortunately, there were obvious problems here too.

"Gentlemen," Sir Markus said, "as you all know, Mary Louise Stuart is the next legal heir to the throne…but I need not tell you what the issues are with her ascension. The law of primogeniture, which has dictated English succession for centuries, favors a male heir. This means that technically her younger brother, followed by her half-brother, should be named monarch before Mary Louise is eligible to succeed."

The group—all men—exchanged uncomfortable glances, until one of the Cabinet members spoke up. "Ah, yes, that is the law. But…times have obviously changed since it was used to guide a succession. I fear we risk a political nightmare if we skip over Mary Louise simply because she is female. We have, after all, already had a female prime minister, and of course the Queen."

Sir Markus passed a hand over his face. "Agreed. Society has advanced considerably. But that is not the only issue with Mary Louise. Even if we could ignore the male preference issue, which we legally cannot, we once again have the problem of religion. Mary Louise Stuart is currently in Italy and living in a convent as a practicing nun in the Roman Catholic faith. She's a Catholic."

An audible groan ran down the table, and the chairman held up his hand for silence, then continued. "Unfortunately, the problem goes deeper than simply enforcing the Act of Settlement a second time. It becomes purely political. If we prohibit a second direct successor to the throne based on religion, the Vatican will no doubt be doubly enraged. As the Archbishop of Canterbury has made abundantly clear, the Church of England and the Catholic Church have been involved in sensitive negotiations for nigh on two years. I'm afraid spiking another Catholic would destroy everything he has worked for." He sighed. "So it appears we have to pick our poison. Enrage the Church by disallowing a Catholic, or enrage millions of women for obvious reasons."

There was a silence around the room as the implications of this sunk in.

"So what do we do?" one Committee-member asked. "Do we go ahead and name Mary Louise Stuart?"

"Absolutely not," Sir Markus said. "We cannot selectively enforce the law on the Prince while allowing his cousin to assume the throne. Our only and most solemn duty is to uphold centuries of English law. Yet...with the obvious candidates disqualified, I'm afraid we'll have to consider the next in line."

The Next Day

The Committee met again the next morning to discuss the next person in line: Edward Francis Stuart. Edward was the eldest nephew to King John and second-eldest cousin to the Queen. They agreed to begin vetting him, and a second announcement was drawn up, telling the world that Mary Louise Stuart had been disqualified. As it was read aloud, several Committee members squirmed in their chairs: no one had any doubt how this second disqualification based on religion and gender would be received. Sir Markus only hoped it wasn't enough to upend the monarchy completely.

In fact, the announcement was received just as poorly as they expected. The Pope immediately called a conclave of the cardinals and announced their strong disapproval of the English government. The Pope's potential state visit was cancelled. Women's rights groups also went ballistic, many of them assuming that Mary Stuart had been disqualified because she was female, which was a terrible insult in this era of "women's liberation." Finally, the press—ever eager for a scandal—whipped up the populace with scandalous headlines and opinion pieces blasting the "retrograde" Committee for "inciting a holy war with the Holy See."

Sir Markus himself was singled out for highly personal criticism and accused of "playing pretend king." He didn't sleep for several days and started to lose weight, just wishing this nightmare would end.

CHAPTER 40
For Better or Worse

Early Years at Eton

Prince Edward Francis Stuart, Duke of Leicestershire, was a royal born into a long line of royals, although he was not well known outside the rarefied air of the royals. He was an intensely private man who avoided the spotlight as much as possible. As a young child, he was devastated when his father, the King's brother, divorced his mother. Shortly after the divorce, his father, Prince Thomas, sent his mother away to live with her family in Wales. Edward and his older sister, Mary Louise, remained with Prince Thomas, who quickly remarried and began a second family with his new wife. The son from this second union was given the name Richard and titled Duke of Sussex. There was no question who Prince Thomas favored: he lavished attention on little Richard, while treating the older Edward coldly, perhaps because of Edward's close relationship with his mother as well as to gain favor with his new wife. Even as Mary Louise adjusted to her new family structure, plans were made to send Edward away to school as soon as possible.

Edward was a handsome, almost pretty, boy. He attended the highly prestigious Eton boarding school and was rarely given permission to come home or see his mother. Gradually, he became resentful of his sister and half-brother, who enjoyed all the perks of growing up in the family setting. Yet people who met Edward would never have guessed at his inner turmoil. Edward grew from an almost pretty boy into a uniquely handsome young man. He had violet eyes and a full head of tousled auburn hair. From a very young age, Edward attracted significant attention from members of the opposite sex—and some members of his own sex.

No amount of attention, however, could fill the hole that his cold and selfish father had left. When he was twelve years old, his father Prince Thomas died of sleep apnea; when he attended the funeral, Edward didn't shed a tear for his father. His lack of grief enraged Richard, who had always bullied Edward whenever possible despite Edward being the older of the two, and Richard let it be known among the family that Edward was a poor student and a lonely, bullied child at school. Whether this was true or not, which it wasn't, made no difference—the family was all too ready to believe the worst about Edward.

Unfortunately, things didn't improve for Edward after his father's death. He returned to school only to find more confusion as he aged into puberty. Girls and even women had always paid special attention to Edward, and he knew he should enjoy their flattery and attention, but instead it only filled him with confusion, dread, and faint disgust. Instead, Edward found himself increasingly attracted to certain classmates at his all-boys school. By the time he was sixteen, Edward had experienced intense but unacted upon crushes on two fellow students and one young teacher's assistant. These feelings were undeniable, but they filled him with shame and confusion. This was only made worse by Edward's living circumstances: he found himself in the public showers torn between lustful thoughts for fellow classmates and intense fear that the other boys would somehow peer into his thoughts and exact the terrible punishment that was doled out to boys like Edward.

Edward's worst crush was on a popular upperclassman named Addison Sinclair, a boy from Essex who lived on Edward's corridor. Addison was athletic, smart, and well-bred—and Edward had no doubt that Addison would have been disgusted by his interest. Still, Addison was like a compulsion with Edward. He imagined them together in the most intimate of ways and even timed his showering schedule so he would be in the communal shower room the same time as Addison, desperately hiding the evidence of his attraction behind cupped hands. Often he would stand at the sink basin facing a steamed mirror with Addison's showering image reflecting back.

And yet...Edward's feelings for Addison were also a source of acute shame. He knew what society would call it: perversion, sinful, a crime against nature, and more vulgarly put, "puff" or "queer". There was no one he could talk to about his conflict and confusion, and even if there were, he would be too embarrassed to do so. He felt alone and certain that he was damned to hell. Nonetheless, his craving for the kind of love he sought and the desires he felt refused to diminish, even when he intellectually rationalized that it was a path to ruination and disgrace.

December 1966

As the Christmas holiday approached, the boys filled the corridors of Eton carrying packages, presents, and bulging suitcases. While everyone else was excited to head home, Edward intended to remain at school as one of the holiday "orphans". He had no desire to spend the holidays with his indifferent stepmother and obnoxious half-brother. Mary Louise had already left the family home and was being educated in a convent school in Italy.

There was another reason Edward wanted to stay behind with the dozen or so other holiday orphans: Addison Sinclair was also remaining at the school. This was highly unusual for Addison, but his parents had apparently gotten stuck in the United States for whatever reason and didn't expect to make it back at the beginning of break. That meant Addison would remain at the dorm for at least five days, until his parents could arrive and collect him.

Edward could hardly contain his excitement as the dormitory finally emptied out and the boys gathered in a special mess area under the careless eye of the provost, an elderly bachelor with no family beyond a doddering great-aunt and who was rumored to have not left the school's grounds in more than thirty years. After the boys finished their supper, a subdued affair since there were so few boys, the provost climbed to his feet and said, "Gentlemen, we are all here for one reason or another, which clearly does not matter. What does matter is that we make the most of it and carry on. You are free to stay in your own rooms and use the library, pool, gymnasium, and other campus facilities. You may not leave the campus, however, unless you have permission from me or my associate, Professor Clayton from Eldridge House. We will have some special side trips and other planned holiday activities, so be sure to attend dinner here every night, at which time we will announce the agenda. Lights out will be an hour later than normal and room check will be as usual. Mandatory morning chapel is suspended except for Sundays when the Reverend Joshua Parkinson will preside."

The students barely listened to the old man, and when he finished, they dispersed. Edward headed to the library to see if he could find something that would hold his attention. Unfortunately, none of the novels sparked an interest, so he headed back across the gloomy and cold campus to his room in the Erksine House. As he walked down the long corridor, he saw light coming from beneath Addison Sinclair's door. He hesitated and then, as if possessed, decided to knock. He immediately panicked even as the sound echoed in the hallway. What was he thinking? What would he say? What premise would he have for disturbing an upperclassman? The door flung open and there stood Addison clad only in his underwear. He looked at Edward rather curiously and asked, "Stuart, what is that you want?"

"Oh," Edward stammered, "I was just alone and was wondering if you would like to have some company."

Addison seemed to think about it for a second, then shrugged. "Sure, I'd like some company. I've got five days stuck here till my parents come collect me. Come on in."

Edward walked in, his heart suddenly pounding. Everything seemed fraught with meaning: the small fire glowing in the corner of the room, the way the lights on campus glowed against Addison's window, even the casually rumpled bed that Edward glimpsed in the next room. Addison pulled on an Eton robe and flung himself down in an easy chair, leaving Edward sitting on the floor near the fire. Edward was terrifically nervous—he was sure that Addison would read his desire on his face—so he was very surprised at how easily the conversation came. They talked about tennis, cricket, art, and music at first, then the conversation drifted to other classmates and finally to their families. Edward realized with growing surprise that behind his façade as a well-adjusted, blue-blooded jock, Addison was drifting and searching, just like he was. And he was so easy to talk to! Edward found himself pouring out the tale of his late father, his now-poor mother in Wales, and his wretched half-brother. He even went so far as to mention he was first cousin to the monarchy, which felt like more of a burden than any type of privilege. Of course Addison knew this—all the boys knew each other's lineage, especially if one was directly related to the King—but it took courage to voice it. At Eton, it was school policy and tradition to ignore students' backgrounds. In any event, almost every student at Eton descended from a great family. The place was filthy with the sons of Dukes and Peers of the Realm, many with names that went back centuries.

In turn, Addison opened up about his family, his idyllic childhood, his recent acceptance to Cambridge College on the strength of his father's patronage and power as a member of Parliament, the girl his parents planned for him to marry, the university major they intended for him to pursue, and the job they had already lined up for him with a leading investment firm. Addison's life, it seemed, was already planned completely for him—there were no decisions left for him to make, only a path to follow.

The hall clock struck eleven, meaning it was nearing time for lights-out. Within moments there was a knock at the door and the night proctor entered and announced it was time for Edward to head back to his own room. As Edward left, he passed close to Addison and intentionally brushed the front of his open robe, making it seem like a casual accident. As their bodies touched, he felt a shot of electricity and actually trembled. Hurriedly, he returned to his room and collapsed onto his bed, shaking and breathing hard. He had never experienced anything like this feeling and it terrified him as deeply as it aroused him.

The next day passed quickly until dinner. Edward and Addison sat next to each other and engaged in active conversation. Later that evening, Edward was desperate to go back to Addison's room and replay last night—which had already assumed a mythic hue in his memory—but he dared not. Instead, alone in his room, he sat in his reading chair, ignoring the opened book on his lap, and lost himself in thoughts of Addison, his heart brimming. He was so lost in thought that he nearly dropped the book in surprise when there was a knock at his door at 8:30.

"I say, are you there?" Addison's voice called.

Edward had to consciously check his voice to make sure he sounded like a typical Eton boy—unaffected, confident, and in command—before he answered, "Yes, yes, come in."

Addison opened the door and entered the room. He was dressed in his gym shorts and school T-shirt, dark with sweat. "I was on my way back from the gym. It's damn cold out there, and now I'm bored. What are you doing?"

Edward gestured at the book, thankful it was a tame Victorian novel.

"Oy," Addison said. "Read that myself years ago." Then he grinned and wafted one hand under his arm. "You sure the stink isn't too much for you? If it is, just tell me to bugger off and hit the showers."

Edward would have liked nothing better, but he forced himself to smile and laugh. "No, I can hardly smell a thing."

Addison threw himself down on Edward's bed and looked around. "Nice room," he said. "It's weird we've lived just down the hall from each other for almost a year and I've never even seen the inside of this place." He spied a box of biscuits on the shelf above the bed. "Those open?"

Edward nodded and got the sweets, leaning over Addison unbelievably sprawled on his bed, with his heart in his throat. To be safe, he sat back in his reading chair on the other side of the room with a handful of biscuits and gave Addison the box. They talked again, but Edward couldn't help but feel that Addison was taking extra care to stretch out, that his gaze was more direct and penetrating than the night before. It confused him, and he wondered if Addison was playing some type of trick on him or if he had simply gone mad.

"Why're you all the way over there?" Addison said. "Come sit closer, so I can hear you better." He patted the bed next to him.

Edward was flustered almost beyond words. Addison surely couldn't mean what it seemed like he meant. Could he? If he didn't, and Edward took this wrong, there was every possibility that Addison would beat Edward to a bloody pulp, followed by the rest of the boys when they returned and word got out that Edward was a puff. This was Edward's worst fear...but with Addison sitting there, watching him, it was too much to resist. "All right,"

Edward choked out, rising and slowly approaching the bed. But instead of sitting down next to Addison, he sat at the desk next to the bed.

"Better?" he asked.

Addison laughed and casually threw a leg onto Edward's lap. "You're a funny one," he said. Then his voice dropped. "Don't take this wrong, but I think you and I have something to share. If I'm wrong, tell me so and that will be that. But if I'm not, well..."

Edward found that he couldn't talk—his throat seemed to close around the words. Instead, he reached out one shaking hand and touched Addison. Instead of pouncing to attack him or reacting with shock and surprise, Addison arched his body into Edward's hand, the evidence of his interest finding its way into Edward's eager grip. After that, they didn't speak at all. For the next two hours, they explored each other and every one of Edward's most shameful desires was dragged into the open light and lived out.

Time seemed to freeze, so both boys were caught unaware when the night proctor banged on the door and announced lights-out. Addison jumped back from Edward like he had been shocked, then laughed at their predicament as he pulled up his ejaculate-soaked jock strap. He left Edward exhausted and sprawled on the sheets, saying only, "See you tomorrow," as he went into the hall and back to his room.

The next three days were like a dream for Edward. The boys exercised in the gym, swam naked in the pool, and jogged on the back roads of the village...but mostly they spent their time experimenting with each other's bodies. He felt that he was falling in love with Addison and wondered if Addison felt the same.

One day, Addison casually announced that his parents would be arriving soon and did Edward want to accompany them back to their winter estate. "There's no reason for you to remain here, cooped up with the orphans," he said. "Besides, my family's winter estate is a monstrous place, full of hidden rooms."

Edward agreed immediately.

On Sunday evening, Addison's parents arrived at Eton to pick him up. They found the boys in the great hall, sipping tea. Addison's mother, a stately and well-dressed woman, ran up to Addison and gave him a motherly hug and kiss. His father, extending his hand, pulled Addison in for a bear hug.

"Addison, we have a surprise for you," his mother exclaimed. "Your father and I stopped on the way here to pick something up!" His mother turned back to the door and yelled, "Come in, darling."

To Addison's utter shock, a girl walked through the door. Her name was Elaine Watkinson, and she was beautiful and a senior at one of the leading English girl's schools. Seeing Addison, she ran into his arms and planted a huge kiss on his unsuspecting lips. A surge of black jealousy poured through Edward, but he forced a rubbery smile onto his face. Addison kissed her back and made sounds like he was overjoyed, but Edward couldn't believe his eyes. Just that morning, he and Addison had—

"Mum," Addison said, "old Edward here is an underclassman with no family to spend the holidays with. Can he come along with us?"

"Of course," she said, waving away the question as an afterthought. "Oh, Addy, we're so excited to see you! Come, Edward, go get your trunks too, and let's go!"

They drove away from Eton in the family Bentley, the three young adults lined up awkwardly in the back seat: Edward, Elaine and Addison. Edward seethed as the countryside flew by.

The balance of the holiday was spent in the most traditional way: formal dinners, church services, fireside chats, games, day trips to the surrounding countryside villages, and the like. Elaine's family were frequent visitors, and it was clear the two families had extensive history and that Addison and Elaine's union was considered the natural conclusion of the families' relationship. Edward suffered through the days, dismissed as a lonely boy (although he noted with savage satisfaction they were very careful with him—he was first nephew to the King, after all), while he lived for the late nights when the mansion would grow quiet and Addison would steal into his room.

After the holidays, and back at Eton, Edward and Addison conducted themselves carefully for the rest of the term. They rarely found any time to be together, stolen moments at best. Then it was graduation, and time for Addison to head off to Cambridge and his shiny future. The day before graduation found them sitting under a tree in a remote corner of the campus.

"I've been wanting to talk to you," Addison began as Edward's heart sunk. "This has been brilliant. You've…been the best thing that's really ever happened to me. But…you must know it's time to end this thing. I trust you agree, and you should know I trust you completely. But…this isn't what my life is destined to be. You no doubt noticed I'm the only son, my parents are relying on me to produce an heir and—"

"But I thought you hated all that!" Edward blurted out, tears already stinging his eyes. He would have traded everything—not that he had much—to remain with Addison, who he loved with all of his heart.

Addison shrugged. "Doesn't matter what I think. I had a duty to my family, you know. And…you're amazing, it's true, but I don't want to live like that forever. Slinking around and hiding. I feel like it's time to get on with my adult life, and this can't be part of it. Same goes for you someday."

"But…I love you!" Edward cried. "You can't mean this!"

Addison turned a sad gaze on Edward. "I'm sorry," he said. "But I have no choice. You must understand. You know what happens to…people like us. Please, take care of yourself. And be careful, Edward. There may come a day when people would be very interested to know what you're up to. Don't let them hurt you. Please."

Edward nodded miserably as Addison gave him a hug.

After graduation, Addison departed for Cambridge, heading into the brilliant future his parents had designed for him. He left Edward behind, miserable and heartbroken for his remaining two years at Eton. There could never be any doubt now what he was, what God had made him, and he often thought of Addison's final words to him: "Don't let them hurt you."

CHAPTER 41
CAN THE KING BE A QUEEN?

London, 1986
The Sub-Committee reconvenes

AS THE CABINET RECONVENED ONCE AGAIN IN THE BASEMENT ROOM OF Parliament, Sir Markus looked down at the folder in his hand and felt he must have aged a century since this vetting process began. He had no doubt there had been harder successions—in the old days, successions often involved a sharp headsman's axe and a bloody fight for power—but in a way, this felt like a kind of death by a thousand cuts. When everyone was settled and watching him expectantly, he rose, cleared his throat, and announced, "The Committee will come to order. Lord Secretary, have we taken attendance and obtained a quorum?"

"Yes, Mr. Chairman," the Lord Secretary announced. "We are all accounted for and in attendance."

"Very well. I shall reveal our findings. After hours of exhaustive vetting, I present this report with respect to Edward Francis Stuart, also known as the Duke of Leicestershire." He opened the folder and withdrew a stack of papers, dreading what must come next. After a moment he looked up.

"There is no question the Duke Edward Stuart is next in line to the throne, should the Queen pass on. His claim is good both through bloodline and primogeniture. We have reviewed and confirmed documents, including birth certificates, church and police records, personal testimony made by living relatives, and government and religious officials. No disqualifying evidence could be found. His bloodline is pure and is directly traceable from King John VI, the Queen's deceased father. Edward Stuart is the eldest son of Prince Thomas, now deceased, who was King John's brother. The Duke is also the younger brother of Mary Louise Stuart and older half-brother to Richard Stuart. All records and documents have been attested to and confirmed. All appears to be in order and legitimate."

"So we have a rightful heir a future King?" a hopeful voice rang out, but Sir Markus couldn't see who it belonged to. He sighed, "Well, gentleman, it would seem so, yes—"

A lusty cheer rose in the cramped room. All of the Cabinet was tired and under pressure. Sir Markus waited for the cheer to die, then cleared his throat for silence and continued, "Unfortunately, though, it shan't be that simple. We have serious concerns with the Duke of Leicestershire's fitness to succeed our monarch."

"Concerns?" a Committee member said. "What bloody concerns now? You just said he's obviously the legitimate heir and there are no legal impediments to his assuming the throne should, or should I say when, our Queen passes!"

"Well, that is technically true. There is no question of legitimacy in his case. Rather, the problem is more of a personal nature. It seems that there are some rather provocative rumors concerning, shall we say, proclivities that have been loosely substantiated. Apparently it is an ill-kept secret in certain circles that Edward Francis Stuart, Duke of Leicestershire, leads a rather unconventional, but perfectly legal, lifestyle."

"Unconventional lifestyle? How does that translate? Get to the point, man."

"Unconventional with respect to proclivities towards, shall we say, members of the same sex."

"You mean he's queer?" barked out an aging member of Parliament who sat on the Cabinet. "Is that what you are saying?"

"Good God, man," interrupted another Cabinet member. "Can the King be a queen?"

Sir Markus desperately wished for a drink just then. "Well, I suppose one, if one wanted to be vulgar...one might say that. You see, in December of 1954, the criminal aspects of such behavior were abolished after the Wolfenden report recommended that the law be changed regarding imprisonment for homosexual acts among consenting adults. Therefore, Prince Edward's alleged, and I repeat alleged, behavior is lawful and...there is no legal obstacle to his ascension."

His last words dropped into the room like a stone cast into a hornet's nest. The Cabinet erupted in angry buzzing and members hopped to their feet and thumped on the table, shouting, "Never! Never!" and "This is an outrage!"

Sir Markus let them vent for several minutes, then banged the meeting back to order with his gavel. "I understand the gravity of your concerns. How could the legal head of the Church of England live in perpetual sin? How could the monarchy retain any support in this already perilous time if it was rumored the King was...is...indelicate. But—"

"How indeed!" interrupted another Cabinet member. "I daresay having a openly queer King would be the end of the English monarchy! It cannot be. It SHALL not be! Who else after Edward is next in line?"

The chairman took a deep, steadying breath. "To answer your question, the next in line is Richard Nigel Stuart, Duke of Gloucester and Edward's half-brother. However, he is not an option because Prince Edward is legitimately the successor."

Once again, the Cabinet erupted into shouts and angry buzzing, and once again Sir Markus gaveled them back to order.

"Gentlemen," he said, "let's not get ahead of ourselves. The Duke of Leicestershire's social choices and preferences are irrelevant given that the Act of Settlement does not deal with that issue whatsoever. By law, if exclusion for cause is not explicitly stated, the succession must stand. Therefore, there is no legal way to block the succession of Edward Francis Stuart or replace him with the next in line. Edward's succession would not only be legal, but mandated by law, and it is Parliament's responsibility to enforce that law."

He stared each of them down in turn, even as he was filled with doubt and dissatisfaction himself. Could he really live to be the man who put a suspected homosexual on the throne of Edward the Great or Queen Elizabeth? Yet he had no doubt of his role and duty, and eventually the Cabinet fell into angry muttering. A King they had, like it or not. The Cabinet adjourned for the day, giving the members time to contemplate this new reality until the next meeting.

CHAPTER 42
RICHARD THE NOT-SO-GREAT

Richard's Early Years

RICHARD NEGRIL STUART, DUKE OF GLOUCESTER AND YOUNGER HALF-brother to Edward, was everything his older half-brother was not. Where Edward had grown up starved for attention from his cold and aloof father, Richard had been spoiled from birth, allowed to run rampant over the help and even bully and banish his older half-brother. And where Edward had inherited his mother's looks, growing into an attractive adult, Richard more resembled his own mother: stout, unattractive, and pugnacious. And finally, where Edward had been well-liked by most people, even if they found him somewhat removed and even odd, Richard was almost universally loathed by all who knew him well—except his doting mother and, before his death, Prince Thomas.

He was, however, legally next in line to the throne of England.

Richard spent much of his early childhood discrediting and destroying Edward in his parents' estimation. He invented a number of outright lies, taking perverse pride in their success. His first truly successful lie involved an antique diamond and ruby broach belonging to their grandmother. When it went missing, Richard blamed Edward. He swore to his father that he saw Edward playing with it in his mother's bedroom. Edward, innocent of course, naturally denied the charge and claimed he had never even seen the piece. Richard, however, insisted that Edward had taken it and lost it. Richard, who actually had taken the broach away on his own, later planted it among Edward's things, where a housemaid found it. As punishment for Edward's "dishonest misbehavior" and Richard's "straightforwardness," Edward was made to relinquish his bedroom, which was larger and grander than Richard's. Richard gleefully moved into Edward's room, literally thumbing his nose at his half-brother.

Later, Richard raised the stakes. Two prize horses belonging to Edward's stepmother were badly injured when a gate was left open and the horses escaped. Each horse sustained serious injuries, and one had to be put down. Richard immediately insisted that he saw Edward taunting the horses and leaving the stable just prior to their escape. To make the story believable, Richard bullied one of the grooms into substantiating the story against Edward. Then, after the groom confirmed the story, Richard took the groom to the stable and forced him to remove his shirt after which he beat him thoroughly with a crop. Following the beating, Richard warned the groom that if he were ever to tell the truth about this matter, or of the beating, he would be killed. Although the groom, a boy himself, doubted he would actually be killed, he would not risk anything and remained forever silent.

Richard's campaign of deceit worked: eventually, Richard persuaded his parents to send Edward away to school. Once away at Eton, Richard hid Edward's letters home, helping to drive a permanent wedge between his hated half-brother and their parents.

As Richard approached advanced adolescence, his hormones reached a fever pitch. He began to chase women of all ages, taking advantage of his position and rank. Unfortunately, his rather homely appearance did not play well with the ladies. And as if his appearance wasn't enough, Richard's self-centeredness and arrogance sent every young damsel who came his way running for cover. Not even housemaids, fearing sexual harassment, would allow themselves to be alone in a room with this out-of-control youth.

After school, Richard married young. He chose a weak and somewhat unattractive mate with a royal pedigree and a handsome dowry. Predictably, he treated his wife with contempt and cheated on her regularly.

Using unprecedented influence, he managed to arrange his official appointment as director-general of the Secret Intelligence Service, MI5, Great Britain's leading spy agency. Ironically, it turned out that Richard was a natural for working with MI5. He had an almost God-given knack for deceit, although he wasn't above using his power to blackmail, threaten, and bully anyone who crossed his path.

As years went by, Richard gained weight and lost hair. He was a sort of human manifestation of the portrait of Dorian Gray. Behind his back, underlings called him "Richard the Not-So-Great," a play on the former King Richard the Great.

There was no question that Richard was keenly aware of the succession struggle going on in the Parliamentary Cabinet. He was in the business to know things, especially things that affected his own future. He watched closely as one candidate after another was disqualified, wondering if the throne was actually within his grasp—assuming, of course, he could somehow disqualify the hated Edward from the running.

But of course, he had no doubt he could do that.

CHAPTER 43
BARREN!

Annapolis, Maryland, 1986

Great Britain wasn't the only Western democracy with a crisis in leadership in those months: back in Washington, DC, President Lionel Keith's health continued to deteriorate, and the press swirled with rumors about Vice President William Carnegie's possible appointment as acting president and eventually president should Keith succumb to the cancer that was eating him from the inside out. In some of the seedier publications—certainly none of the national publications—there were even more far-fetched rumors: that Vice President Carnegie wasn't who he said he was at all, that he was possibly not even an American citizen and could be a Soviet spy.

It was against this backdrop that Speaker Jordan met Attorney General Carl Santos for a round of golf at the Congressional Gold Course in Bethesda, Maryland. Under most circumstances, it would be highly unusual for a Speaker of the House to golf with the Attorney General of an administration from the opposing party, but Jordan and Santos both came from Colorado and had traveled in the same circles for years before going to the capital.

It was an unseasonably warm day as the men met before their tee times, then headed to the famous Blue course, where innumerable congressmen, senators, power brokers, and even presidents had played golf and hammered out agreements. They were accompanied only by Jimmy, a caddy from the famous and imposing club, but there was no fear Jimmy would leak anything he heard. At a club like Congressional, even the caddies were extensively vetted. It was entirely possible that guys like Jimmy knew enough state secrets to bring down governments around the world. But they kept their lucrative jobs because they kept their mouths and eyes shut.

Jordan was first off the tees, and it was almost immediately apparent that he was the better golfer. By the fourth hole, Santos was gently ribbing Jordan that "it must be nice to have so much time to work on your short game," while Jordan was protesting that Santos must not be keeping score so well because he wasn't winning anyway. Santos just laughed.

"So," Jordan said as they approached the green for the eighteenth hole, walking alone in the middle of a broad field. "How do you see this thing with the president playing out? I hear his condition is bad."

Santos sighed and glanced sidelong at his golf partner. "Yeah, it's not looking good. The docs over at Walter Reed say they're doing everything they can. They brought in specialists from MD Anderson in Dallas."

"Sorry to hear it," Jordan said, sounding not sorry in the slightest. "I've read a bit about the vice president. You think he'll be up for the job if he's called to it?"

"Are you asking me personally or professionally?"

"Both." Jordan laughed.

"Personally there's no question," Santos said. "Carnegie is smart as they come and a real Boy Scout. I don't think I've ever heard the guy swear, and his idea of getting wild seems to be knocking off work early to go home to his wife. He's the real deal, no doubt about it."

"Okay," Jordan said, "then professionally."

"Well," Santos said, frowning slightly, "you've heard all these rumors, I'm sure. It's probably the worst kept secret in Washington now that the media is sniffing around his past. I don't know how it would be possible, because he was vetted when the president picked him, but the tabloids say he might not be an American citizen."

"You believe it?" Jordan said.

Santos laughed dryly. "No, not for a second. But…"

When he let it trail off, Jordan prompted, "But what? You don't sound convinced."

"Here's the thing. I don't believe it, but on the off chance, the very small off chance it's true, he would be impeachable. Clearly. I mean, the Constitution is clear on this point. The President of the United States must also be a natural-born citizen of the United States." He sighed. "It would be a disaster."

Jordan let that ride for a minute, then said, "Yeah, definitely. You know, I've got some connections. You want me to see if I can find anything out? At least with the rumors. I mean, it might be one of my guys planting them."

Santos looked over sharply. "Representative, I can't ask you to investigate the president!"

Jordan held his hands up. "No, no. Not investigate. Nothing like that. I'm just saying I can keep my ear to the ground. Let you know if I come up with something interesting. At the very least, you might be able to nip those rumors in the bud."

Santos was nodding slightly, but sounded reluctant. "Well, that would be nice. But…anything you tell me would be strictly off the record. You understand, I'm sure."

"Definitely," Jordan answered. "No question. Anyway, just in case, you know. You might want to run for office yourself someday, and it would be a shame to go down in flames because someone tricked you."

Santos kept nodding, no doubt thinking of his own home state of Washington and how nice it would be to get a bipartisan endorsement from a longtime politician like Luke Jordan...just in case he ever did decide to run for office on his own.

They finished out the eighteen holes, and Santos was genuinely surprised to find out he had beaten Jordan by seven. By his own informal count, he had been trailing rather badly.

"C'mon," Jordan said, "let's go celebrate with a drink. And don't worry...I probably won't turn anything up."

"Right," Santos said, truly hoping that Jordan was right.

***

After he returned to his office from the golf course, Speaker Jordan invited three familiar men into his office, led by Justin Tate. He thought of them as his "dirty tricks team," a little inside joke to himself, and he was all smiles as they gathered around a conference table and shut the door.

"Well?" he said when he was sure they were alone. "Tell me what you've got."

The men had traveled all over the world and the United States, digging into Vice President Carnegie's past—and Jordan could guess from the looks on their faces they had hit pay dirt.

Tate slid a manila folder across the table to Jordan. He opened it to find a sheaf of photographs showing an old medical record. He started to read even as they briefed him.

"This is Fiona Carnegie's primary school medical record," Tate said. "There's no question it's authentic. And look. At age sixteen, she had a total hysterectomy. It would have been physically impossible for her to give birth to William Carnegie twenty years later."

Jordan practically pinched himself to keep his composure, his heart starting to beat. He had hoped they'd find something good, but this was beyond his wildest expectations. "Amazing. So he's lying about his mother? What about his father? What are the alternative explanations?"

"Here's where it gets interesting," Tate said. "We can definitively disprove that his mother is his biological mother. That's a good start. But there are also no records of any kind of William's birth or legal adoption. Fact is, he seemed to basically materialize out of thin air. His entire legitimacy rests on a birth certificate issued by the U.S. Embassy."

"Right," Jordan said. Then it hit him. "Oh! But that's a fraud."

"Exactly. The birth certificate clearly lists Fiona Carnegie as his birth mother, as well as Ambassador Carnegie as his father. We can easily now prove his mother's role was fraudulent, and it's too convenient that his own father was the Ambassador who authorized the birth certificate."

Jordan picked up the thread. "So at the very least, we have evidence that William Carnegie's birth certificate was faked, that his father pulled strings to fake it, that his mother is not his birth mother...it's a short jump to questioning his father and therefore his American citizenship!"

"Yes, sir."

Jordan had to force himself to calm down and be rational. This was good—but he knew the stakes involved. He needed irrefutable evidence.

"At the least, this will be enough to set the press on a hunt...even better, on fire," he said. "And likely delay any official action on the part of the Cabinet until it's resolved. And you guys really did a great job here. But what we've done so far is prove who William is not. We still haven't proved who William *is*. That's what we need."

The team members nodded, and Jordan had a sudden image of them as a pack of hunting dogs that he was letting off the leash.

"Great job, guys," he said, rising to signal the meeting was over. "Now go finish the job."

They left one by one, to avoid attracting any attention.

***

Three days later, Jordan called Attorney General Santos, wondering if Santos would take his phone call. To his relief, Santos came to the phone immediately. Jordan knew he had him hooked, and it was a matter of time before he owned him.

"Morning," Jordan said. "You remember that I said I'd call if I turned anything up?"

"Yes?" Santos said warily.

"Well, I don't quite know what to do with this, but I figured I should tell you. Let you get ahead of it, because once the press gets ahold of this, all hell will break loose."

"Oh no," Santos said. "Go on."

Jordan quickly related the team's findings about the forged birth certificate and Fiona Carnegie, ending with speculation that Ambassador Carnegie himself might have engineered the fake certificate for some personal reason, possibly that William wasn't even his own son.

"But…this took place in the United Kingdom," Santos said. "If true, that would mean—"

"The vice president is not an American citizen," Jordan finished the sentence.

"Oh my God," Santos said hollowly. "Who else knows about this? Who is your source?"

"I don't know who knows about it," Jordan said. "I heard it from a junior staffer with family back in the UK. I'm not sure who's digging into it, but if I know about it…" He let it hang provocatively.

"Give me a minute to think."

Jordan listened to Santos breathing on the other end of the line. He could easily guess at the attorney general's thought process: if Carnegie wasn't a U.S. citizen, he couldn't be president; if the Cabinet named him president under a cloud of suspicion, any member of the House could launch impeachment proceedings that would result in a full investigation of these charges; any Cabinet member who supported Carnegie's elevation to the presidency despite knowing this information would be disgraced and possibly liable—including Santos himself.

"How sure are you this is true?"

Jordan forced himself to sound casual. "I don't know. I saw a Xerox of Fiona's medical records. They looked authentic, but you know…at this point, it's just a rumor. I suppose they could be faked."

"There are *Xeroxes* of her medical records floating around?" Santos sounded like a kid after someone told him there was no Santa Claus.

"Yes. At least what I saw."

"Oh God." He took another deep breath. "Thank you, Mr. Speaker. You've done me a great favor here."

"Of course. I thought you'd want to know, like I said." He paused a beat. "So what are you going to do?"

"Well, clearly we're going to have to look into this. I have a feeling we'll be booking some plane tickets to London this afternoon."

"Good luck," Jordan said. "And, I'm sorry to ask this, but could you keep my name out of it for now? I mean, we are on different sides of the aisle, after all, and it would look kinda fishy since Carnegie's loss could be my gain."

Santos uttered a hollow laugh. "Luke, if this blows up, there's no telling what could happen."

And it didn't take long to blow up. Within days, the existence of a forged birth certificate was covered in the seedy tabloids and the story quickly made the jump from the supermarket checkout line to the national media. It's true that reporters were quick to note that it was all "allegations" and "innuendo" at this point, that there was no proof, but Attorney General Santos was obligated to call a press conference and announce that his office was investigating his own president. Jordan watched the TV press conference with a glass of fifteen-year-old scotch, savoring every word of it and feeling almost sorry for Santos.

CHAPTER 44
Love in All the Wrong Places

London, 1984

After Eton, Edward Stuart finished the well-worn path of generations of aristocracy before him and became another "Oxcam" with degrees from Oxford and Cambridge. He studied fine art, design, and architecture, and after graduation spent some years working for a leading design firm in London, after which time he was appointed Minister of Fine Arts and Architecture. He had no illusions about his appointment: being the nephew of the King had its advantages. Still, he liked his work and was good at it, and he applied himself diligently to his new role.

As the years went by, Edward's personal life remained in a perpetual state of upheaval. With some maturity, he decided that Addison—his first true love—had been simply experimenting in school. This was much more common than most people admitted, but it wasn't true for him. Edward had no attraction to women. Instead, he was clearly and completely attracted only to men, an affliction that simultaneously filled him with the simple joy of meeting men he found interesting and attractive and self-loathing because he considered himself perverted and forced to live his private life behind closed doors for fear of discovery. Edward had no doubt what would happen if people knew he was homosexual. He could imagine it now: the "gay Duke." Especially with AIDS ravaging gay men throughout the world, there was even the possibility of violence directed at him.

So like so many other gay men his age, Edward lived a life of deceit and unsatisfying sexual relationships hastily conducted in often poorly lit clubs. His fear of discovery colored every part of his life: even the simple act of working out, which he did every day, was tinged with the worry that people would wonder why he kept himself in such perfect shape. Finally, Edward secured a flat in London where he could meet men privately, usually under an assumed name and always anonymously. He knew what effect this was having on him—he craved a real relationship with a man he could love and go out in public with, take to events and openings and share his life—but he was resigned to the fact that quick assignations were all he could afford.

On a cold January night, Edward hosted an open house at a recently restored national landmark. It was an ancient row house in Park Slope that had been saved from the wrecking ball.

After a few hours of shaking hands and making small talk, Edward needed to visit the men's loo. After finishing at the urinal, he headed to the basin to wash his hands and check himself in the mirror, but gasped out loud when he looked into the mirror. Over his shoulder, standing behind him at a urinal, he saw a face reflected in the mirror over the fixture. The image was repeated in the mirror over the sink. It was the man he dreamt about for years: Addison Sinclair.

Edward waited, his heart suddenly pounding, until Addison zipped up and approached the sink. Striving to strike a casual tone, before Addison recognized him, he said, "I say, is that really Addison Sinclair?"

"Why yes," Addison said. "And who..."

His voice trailed off as he recognized Edward.

"Oh my God," Addison said, at an obvious loss for words. "Edward."

Edward stood awkwardly for a second, then impulsively wrapped Addison in a hug. The spark was still there, and he wondered if Addison felt it. He doubted it; he had long ago feared that what happened between them was just an adolescent lark for Addison.

"I say, I can't believe it's really you. What are you doing here, anyway?" Edward asked.

"Well, I'm a guest of the Ministry of Arts. I'm in Parliament now, you know. So they invited me to come along."

"Fantastic," Edward said. "I always knew you'd do well. What say we, ah, go out and grab a drink, catch up?"

"Good idea. I don't think hanging out in a men's loo is suitable for an MP, much less a Duke."

Edward smiled thinly. He was no stranger to meetings in men's loos, but no sense in mentioning that to Addison.

The two men stepped out into the crowded main hall. It was too busy there to properly catch up, so they agreed to meet the next evening and exchanged cards. Alone later that night, Edward struggled to keep his expectations in check, telling himself over and over that this was simply a social call between old friends who had done some experimenting back in school.

They met at Edward's Chelsea Pied-à-terre, had drinks, and filled each other in on their lives since Eton. Addison had become everything his parents had planned for him. He was a member of Parliament and had married Elaine, the girl his parents had chosen for him. They had three children, two girls and a boy. His work was satisfying, he said, and he was wildly in love with his children, who were no doubt the greatest thing that had ever happened to him, and he and his wife got along famously. As he talked, Edward caught himself desperately watching for any sign that Addison still harbored some kind of feelings for him.

"What about you?" Addison said. "How are you getting on?"

Edward kept his bio rather short, but there was no getting around the fact that he'd had no serious relationships since Eton.

"I see," Addison said carefully. "I daresay. I'm not sure..." He trailed off and he looked pensively out the window at the lights of London. Then he turned back to Edward. "Are you happy, Edward?"

"I suppose so," Edward said, trying to smile and make light of it. But the smile slipped. "Or maybe I'd say rather not. You know...I...can't believe how awkward this is. But no, I suppose the truth is that I feel as if there is little place in England for a fellow like me. At least not in the open."

Addison nodded. "Yes, I know."

There was a moment of heavy, awkward silence, and Edward's heart leaped. Once again, he was receiving signals from Addison that confused and exhilarated him. It was just like in the dorm so many years ago. Maybe he had been wrong all this time—maybe he meant more to Addison than a simple experiment. With his heart pounding, he decided to take a chance. Edward leaned closer toward Addison and asked, almost verbatim, the question Addison asked him in his dingy little room at Eton decades ago: "Addison, don't take this wrong, but I think you and I have something to share. If I'm wrong, tell me so and that will be that. But if I'm not wrong, where do we go from here?"

Addison couldn't help but smile, but it was a sad smile. "Clever. Of course I remember. But...my life has changed. I've made no room for...that part of myself. I mean to say, it was only you. I don't think I—"

Edward held up his hand. "Of course," he said, and a strange part of him felt relieved while he was also heartbroken. "I understand. Your life is set. You're happy in it."

"I didn't say that," Addison said. "I mean, I am happy in it. But...oh, bother, I'm absolutely muddled with this..."

Edward put his hand on Addison's arm. "I understand. Let's not speak of it anymore."

"But what if that's not what I want?" Addison said with sadness. "Why else would I have come?" he asked, almost to himself.

And that was it. There they were, alone, in a Chelsea flat picking up exactly where they had left off as boys, but this time with the experience and pent-up ardor of men—and Edward realized that what had happened between them long ago wasn't just a lark for Addison. It had been real love on both sides.

After that evening, they met two or three times a month at Edward's flat. Addison remained conflicted about the infidelity—he had no desire to hurt his wife, a really "sweet girl"—but not his feelings for Edward. As for Edward, from that first night with Addison, he gave up his anonymous assignations in the night. He had lost his desire for anyone except Addison.

One rainy night, Addison and Edward were spending an evening in. Edward had dismissed his manservant for the evening so they could be alone for a few precious hours.

Without thinking about it, Edward said, "I wish you could stay forever, that every night could be like this."

Addison, who had been casually stroking Edward's hair, took his hand away.

Edward turned to look at him. "I'm sorry. Did I upset you? It was just an impulse."

Addison looked miserable. "No, no, I understand. And it's not to say I disagree. But…my life being such as it is. I just…I can't let myself think like that."

"I know. I'm sorry."

"Please stop apologizing."

Edward didn't know what to say and couldn't help the tears from springing into his eyes.

"God, Edward, why must this be so hard? To be honest, I don't want to leave either. I think of you all day. I…I think I've fallen in love with you. But the thought of hurting my family, my parents, of the public embarrassment and destruction of everything I've worked for. I just can't…but do you know what my secret hope is? That after my kids are grown, after I've finished with politics and no one much cares what happens to Addison Sinclair, after that, my wish is that we can be together."

"You mean that?" Edward said.

"Yes," he said fervently.

"Then promise me. Promise me that will happen."

"I promise."

Edward brushed tears away. "I feel the same about you and always will. You can be certain that I too will never betray your trust and affection. It will be timeless and endless. I would stake my life on it and, if necessary, die defending it. I will pay any price, forsake all others. I shall wait for as long as it takes until we can live our chosen destiny."

CHAPTER 45
The Proof Is in the Pudding

Washington, DC, 1986

William opened the door to Dr. Jeffreys' office, wondering if the next few hours would change his life. Dr. Jeffreys was carrying a satchel that contained the results of the DNA test he had commissioned comparing his DNA to Prince John's and his father's. Or at least the man he assumed for decades was his father, Ambassador Carnegie.

Dr. Jeffreys said a brief hello and barreled in as William led him to the drawing room, where they sat at a round table and Jeffreys spread his materials out.

"So how accurate is this?" William said, looking at the unfamiliar rows of squares and dashes.

"Well, you know this is new science of course, but we're confident it's typically between 99.5 percent and 99.9 percent accurate," the doctor answered. "The executive summary is at the back if you'd just like to skip to the results."

William flipped back and found a single sheet of typed paper. He read:

> *The three subject samples were analyzed and compared. Samples labeled A and B share the same DNA genetic code and indicate, with a certainty of 99.5-99.9 percent, that the donors of these two samples are either father and son or male siblings. Sample C shares no DNA genetic code that matches either samples A or B indicating, to a certainty of 99.5-99.9 percent, that there is absolutely no genetic relationship.*

William had been expecting this and carefully held his face still. Dr. Jeffreys had no idea who had supplied the samples, which meant he had no idea that William held conclusive proof, good enough for a court of law, that he was not related to Ambassador Harrington Carnegie by blood, but he was, in fact, related to Prince John, the Prince of Wales and recently disqualified King of England. A silly saying from his nanny occurred to him: the proof is in the pudding.

He smiled, aware that Dr. Jeffreys was watching him for some type of reaction to the report, perhaps waiting to explain more about DNA and for William to explain why he had commissioned DNA tests in the first place. But thoughts were racing through William's head too fast to control. He knew now that Fiona was not his mother, based on a note in his birth mother's own hand and substantiated personally by Rosemary, and that Ambassador Carnegie was not his father. From these reports, it was safe to assume that Queen Mary was actually his mother, just as Rosemary North had said.

Then an even more astonishing thought surfaced: if he was Prince John's older brother, it meant he was technically in line for the succession to the throne. Like the rest of the world, William had been following the tortured succession in the United Kingdom. His stomach seemed to float within him as he realized that, in fact, he had the world's most legitimate claim to the throne.

But no one would ever know that, because William was going to do everything in his power to stuff this news far down a hole and bury it. The stakes were simply too high. Keeping his face carefully neutral, he thanked the good doctor, and they chatted for a while about the miracle of DNA technology. Dr. Jeffreys was more than happy to advance his theory that DNA evidence would be the greatest investigatory tool ever discovered. "No more innocent people will be convicted," he said. "DNA evidence does not, cannot by its nature, lie. It's more accurate than fingerprints, and vastly more accurate than eyewitnesses."

Finally, the doctor left and William was alone to wander through the vice president's mansion, his mind reeling. It so happened that Liz and the kids were traveling, so he was alone to contemplate and consider. His first reaction had been to hide the news, push it away, but as the hours wore on, he realized how impossible that might be. Already, the press was rich with rumors about his birth certificate and his mother. No one had questioned his father at this point, but now he had absolute proof that the Ambassador was not his father, which led him to a series of terrible thoughts. The fact was, he was likely not a natural-born American citizen. He was actually born in England to English parents, probably Prince Anthony, and he had never been legally adopted by his American "parents." This meant William was legally not eligible to hold elected office in the United States. The Cabinet just then was debating naming him Acting President as President Keith's condition continued to deteriorate. It occurred to him like a punch to the gut that, with this knowledge, he could actually be held liable for knowingly breaking the law. The Constitution was clear on this point, that only "natural born citizens" could hold the presidency. It was a grim irony that the clause had been written specifically to prevent a naturalized citizen from Britain seizing the presidency and returning America to her colonial masters.

And there was the ethical component too. William's sense of integrity had always been a point of pride with him: he had never knowingly done the wrong thing. The closest he could think of was transferring money to Roan, despite misgivings about how some of it was being spent, and he had cut that off as soon as his misgivings grew serious. Otherwise, William had worked hard his whole life to do the right thing, to live within the laws of a country he loved dearly, and to uphold the family name he thought he had inherited. Assuming the presidency under these circumstances would make him one of the country's worst villains—a usurper—even if it wasn't directly due to his actions. He wasn't sure he could live with that and even if he could, his enemies would never allow it.

William needed help. As the night wore on, he considered who he could turn to. Telling anyone in politics was out of the question until he had formulated a plan. Liz would help, of course, but she couldn't help with the legal aspect of it. Then he had an idea: he could call Paul Whitman, a longtime family attorney who ran the trust, a personal friend of his father's, and a deeply ethical man who had advised his family through many rough spots. He placed the call immediately, telling Paul's wife it was an emergency. When he got Whitman on the phone, he said he needed to see him urgently. Whitman, ever the professional, agreed without hesitation or pressing questions. That could wait.

***

Paul Whitman looked every bit the elite lawyer he was. He was tall and rapier-thin, with distinguished silver hair and an immaculate pressed suit with Italian leather shoes. He carried a slim briefcase and shook William's hand as he entered the mansion first thing next morning. He was serious but maintained his respectful silence as they chatted and sat at a table in the corner of the room.

This time it was William who did the talking, spreading out the DNA report and the letter and laying all of his evidence on the table. Whitman took notes with a gold pen throughout, maintaining a careful silence that William began to find unsettling after a while. When he was finally done, he leaned back in his chair and said, "Well, Paul, tell me what you're thinking."

Paul set his pen down and took a moment to gather his thoughts. He had once served as general counsel to a president, so William knew that Paul would be considering every angle of the problem: the legal, the political, the personal.

"First," he said, "I am shocked beyond words to learn of this. I knew your grandfather and your father. We spent countless hours together, and I've advised your family for decades. No one has ever breathed a word of anything this remarkable. It's almost…beyond belief."

"I know. What can I do?"

Whitman took a deep breath and exhaled. "I'm afraid I can't give you much good advice, or at least advice you'll want to hear. William, I don't think there's any way you'll be able to keep this from getting out. Clearly you have enemies. Somebody is leaking those rumors to the press. Somebody is doing their own investigation."

"I know."

"So you have to assume this information will find its way into the public realm. You have to prepare for the idea that your legitimacy as vice president will be challenged by the same parties that are working against you now. You need to consider the effect this will have on the country, your family."

William nodded uneasily.

"And…" Whitman hesitated. "There is another matter I feel obligated to mention. You know how I feel about you and your family. You've always been a good man, William, and you've done your family proud. Your father…yes, your father in spirit if not by blood…was immensely proud of you. Please forgive me for saying that I, too, am proud of you. It has been my pleasure to watch you become the fine man you've become."

A nervous tingle went up William's spine. "Where are you going with this?" William said.

"You know I run your family trust, and you've never had much cause to get into the legal details of the trust, which is now valued at just under two billion dollars. The trust was set up by your grandfather in a different era, Andrew Blaine Carnegie. He was a remarkable man, but also a paranoid man. He forever worried that his family fortune would fall under the control of an outsider, that someone would marry into the family and manage to usurp the trust."

"Okay," William said.

"So he stipulated that the trust could only be controlled by blood relatives, unless there were no blood relatives and then it would revert to the control of the board, of which I am chairman."

"So what does that mean?"

"Well, there are certain members of the trust's board who would be all too happy to seize control of the Carnegie trust and exclude you. These members represent powerful charities and educational institutions that would stand to benefit a great deal if you were excluded from the trust. When this..."

"What are you saying?" William demanded. "That my inheritance is under question too?"

"Not to me," Whitman said. "I drew up your parents' wills. We had lengthy discussions, and their clear intention was that you would inherit everything that's personally theirs."

A nagging thought popped into Whitman's mind: how would a court of law view an inheritance to a legally nonexistent person named in a will? After all, William was not a natural-born son, nor was he legally adopted by the Carnegies. An argument could be made that William was persona non grata in the eyes of the law.

Whitman continued, "But, as I said, the board is not unanimous and the trust's assets did not belong to the Ambassador and Fiona. They were merely beneficiaries. I fear that, once this information gets out, you will find yourself challenged from the trust side as well."

A cold kind of fury seized William. "But...surely no one could force me out of the Carnegie trust. You...I..." He didn't know how to finish the sentence.

"William," Paul said gently, "I'm telling you as a friend and attorney that you must prepare for the worst here. Prepare for this news to get out, and unfortunately, because of your station in life and position, there is a great deal at stake. The presidency of the United States hangs in the balance. Billions of dollars. When the stakes are that high, people will do almost anything." He paused. "And, at least until this is settled, I would advise you to avoid anything connected with the Carnegie trust."

"Avoid anything connected with the trust?" William echoed. "Exactly what does that mean?"

"Well, as you know, the assets of the trust belong to the trust. This includes the various houses, club memberships, et cetera. But," he said hastily, "as long as you live here in the vice president's mansion and have access to the perks associated with your elected office, you should be fine while this gets sorted out."

"So what...you're telling me I can't go home? I have to avoid my own house?"

"I'm sorry, William, but it's not your house."

William sat for a moment, struggling to get his emotions under control. He had never thought, even for a second, that his inheritance was also in danger. He felt beset by enemies on all sides.

"And what about you?" William said, perhaps more harshly than he meant. "What side are you on?"

Whitman thought about it for much longer than William would have liked. "Like I said, William, I've always admired you. Always. But I also have a legal and fiduciary responsibility to the trust itself, which I helped design and have spent my career administering. Ultimately, I can be your friend, but I will have to do what's best for the trust in the long run."

"Is that a warning?" William asked.

Whitman shook his elegant head. "No, it is not. It's an acknowledgement, William, that you should realize the clock is running." He nodded at the papers on the table. "This will come out. And when it does, you'll be fighting for your life on every side. I wish I could help you more…I can give you the names of some friends who can help you plan and strategize. Because you'll need a plan, and you'll need it quick. But as for further legal help, I'm afraid it would be a conflict of interest for us to discuss this further."

William was shocked to hear Whitman's closing words, and once again, the enormity of this news hit him. "Fine, Paul," William said. "Then I guess you'd best go now."

Whitman stood up. "I can't tell how much this saddens me," he said. "Good luck, William. I'll do what I can for you."

CHAPTER 46
SAY CHEESE!

WILLIAM WASN'T THE ONLY ONE BUSY COMING UP WITH STRATEGY. BACK in London, Richard continued to scheme on the throne, looking for a way to finally and completely prevent Edward the Pervert, as he so often referred to him, from the succession.

Richard's first thought was to kill Edward, or at least have him killed. It would be easy enough: just find some young thug to put a few bullets in his head and say it was a lover's quarrel. Richard knew there were plenty of young men who could be bought for a task like this—he had enough money to buy virtually anything.

Yet…this was a dangerous course of action, perhaps too dangerous. Killing someone so close to the throne wouldn't be treated like a regular homicide, even a homosexual homicide. There would be tremendous scrutiny and Richard wouldn't be able to guarantee that his name wouldn't come up. After all, he had an excellent motive. Richard recalled another King Edward, Edward II, who was killed in 1327. Rumor had it they killed him by sodomizing him with a ram's horn and red-hot poker. For a fleeting moment, that sounded like a pretty good fate for Edward—but Richard would have to give up on his fantasies of killing Edward as too risky.

He needed something else. Fortunately, he had a backup plan.

It only took a few days of asking questions to discover everything he needed to know about Edward's current life. He easily discovered that Edward maintained a flat in Chelsea. His investigators reported that Edward kept only two in staff at the flat, including a day-help housekeeper, Maybelline, and a personal manservant, Thomas, who was sometimes used as a valet, footman, or occasionally as a driver. Richard first guessed those weren't the only roles Thomas served in—from the look of the photos his men took, he was a strikingly handsome 26-year-old, and Richard could easily see the older Edward lusting after his young manservant.

But based on what his snitches learned, that wasn't the case. Instead, it seemed that Thomas was a regular feature at certain bars, where he used his good looks and charm to entice men into going back to Edward's flat where they engaged in who knows what kind of perversions. It was rumored that Thomas himself engaged in some of these activities, warming up their guests for the main event. Better yet, they found out that Thomas had both a girlfriend and a youthful conviction on his record. It was perfect. Richard placed a call and had Thomas brought into the MI5 offices.

They sat him at a table and Richard had two men standing behind him, arms crossed and looking fearsome. He posed as the senior investigator of "vice," a title he made up on the spot. He had no worries Thomas would recognize him as related to Edward—they looked as different as night and day. Thomas was nervous, of course, because who wouldn't be nervous when called into an interrogation by Britain's secret service? But he didn't get really scared until the questions about Edward started.

"Why do you care?" he asked.

"Listen," Richard said, "you're not asking questions. You say that Edward had a steady stream of callers until recently, till this new man entered the picture. Who is he?"

Thomas shifted uncomfortably in his chair.

"I say, who is he?" Richard pressed.

"I have no idea," Thomas finally said. "I don't even know his name, just that he looks like an important bloke in a bespoke suit."

"Hmm," Richard said. "Here's what I want, then. I want pictures of him. And Edward. Together."

It took Thomas a moment to figure out the implications of what Richard wanted, and when he did his face drained. "Are you daft? You want me to get bloody pictures of the blokes doing the dirty? Do you want me to have them say 'cheese' too? No way! I don't care who you are."

"Listen, Thomas, you may be a *peacock* in Chelsea, but here you are a rodent. You are going to do exactly what I tell you to do."

"No bloody way," Thomas said.

"Would you rather we press charges? That your family and girlfriend find out you're a queer?"

"Queer?! I ain't no queer! You know *nothing*. Go screw yourself!"

"Listen, you little faggot, don't kid yourself," Richard sneered. "You are as queer as they come. We've been following you for a long time and I know you like it both ways. And when your girlfriend finds out about how you get extra pay from your *employer*, she'll be jumping in front of the first train out of Piccadilly underground. So don't bullshit me."

Thomas looked scared now. "You ain't got proof."

"I don't need proof; all I need is to have one of my associates have a little talk with your gal about your long nights at work. I can line up half a dozen or more fancy boys who would be glad to tell your little lady about where your privates have been. As I said, we've been following you for a long time.

You're the Pied Piper down there in Soho, and all the lads follow you right to Edward's Chelsea bedroom. And the way I hear it, you kind of like that pillow talk too!"

"You got it all wrong. I don't let any of 'em do anything to me. Maybe a peek or two, a quick feel, but nothing more than that."

"You think it'll matter?" Richard said. "Now shut up and listen to me." Handing Thomas a miniature camera, he said, "You get some titillating pictures of Edward and his gentleman friend doing the deed. Understand, you little piece of shit? I want them right away, too. And don't forget, I want pictures of their faces, not just their cocks."

"What kind of investigation is this?" Thomas asked weakly, but Richard didn't even bother to answer. He knew he'd already won.

***

Late on a Thursday evening, Addison arrived at Edward's flat. It was to be a private evening for just Addison and Edward—Thomas had been dismissed early.

Unbeknownst to Edward, however, Thomas had sequestered himself away in the butler's pantry with Richard's camera. The pantry door had slats on it that afforded him a perfect view of the foyer and living room beyond, where Edward had lit a large fire. He could hear everything perfectly as Addison said, "I'm so glad to be here. I had to lie about going to a meeting to get away from Elaine. I told her that I would stay at the club this evening. She believed the story completely, but I feel like such a hypocrite. She doesn't deserve this deceit."

"I know, hiding and lying is never easy, but for now we have no alternative."

The two men fell into an embrace, then came apart long enough to go into the living room and pour brandies, then sit on the couch in front of the fire. Thomas's view was ideal, and he was close enough to see every detail as they first talked, their hands resting lightly on each other in the way of lovers, and then as they embraced and began to kiss. It escalated rapidly, and hating himself every second for betraying a man he fundamentally respected, Thomas raised the camera and started taking silent pictures. It was easy to get good shots, and he had no doubt these were graphic enough to prove anything they wanted to prove.

Two days later, Thomas delivered the incriminating film to Richard. As he did, he couldn't help himself from saying, "I don't know what you're doing with this, but those blokes don't deserve it. They're in love, you know. True love."

"Charming," Richard said sarcastically. "For a couple of perverts. Who is the other man?"

"Don't know. I heard him mention a wife...woman named Elaine. But that's it."

"Good dog," Richard said. "You're dismissed now."

Richard could hardly contain his excitement while the pictures were developed in an MI5 darkroom that had seen too many pictures of this variety. The envelope was delivered to his office and he greedily tore it open, leafed through a few pictures, and shook his head in wonderment. These weren't just naughty pictures—they were downright pornographic. And best of all, it was easy to make out both men's faces.

Careful not to reveal the true nature of the photograph, Richard cut out a circle with Addison's face on it from one picture and gave it to a trusted man who specialized in photo identification. The results came back within the hour: the man was Sir Addison Sinclair, a member of Parliament and true blue-blood. His wife, Elaine, came from an equally prominent family. Together they had three children. Addison and Edward had gone to Eton together, where Richard had no doubt they had first started their illicit relationship.

Richard leaned back in his chair and grinned. He had built a near-perfect trap around his half-brother, who like a rat in a box was too stupid to realize his days were already numbered. All Richard had to do was threaten to release these pictures, which were damning enough to destroy both Edward and Addison, and the throne was his.

CHAPTER 47
FINIENDO VITAM REGALE
(ENDING THE LIFE OF A ROYAL)

HER ROYAL HIGHNESS, QUEEN MARY, LAY COMATOSE IN THE PRIVATE WING of King Edward VII Hospital. As he had for weeks, Cyril her husband sat at her bedside, watching Mary for any sign of improvement.

"Mary, dear, I don't know if you can hear me or not, but I'm here with you, my love," he whispered. "We all are. There are thousands of subjects right now outside the hospital, holding vigil. And they've piled flowers as high as a man at the gates of Buckingham. The whole of the country is praying for you, dear." He paused to hold back tears. "Don't be afraid. I will take care of you, as I always have. You are my life and I love you more than I could ever say."

Cyril had been struggling to remain hopeful as the world's best doctors came in from all over the world to see if there was anything to be done. Mary had experienced a severe spinal cord injury when her horse threw her, coupled with a traumatic brain injury. The doctors all looked at the records, then shook their heads. Spine injuries were devastating, they said, and even if she did awaken, she would likely be a quadriplegic, with no use of anything below her neck. Cyril had tried everything—he had offered to pay more, he had begged, he had yelled at doctors that how could they have devices that saw inside the human body and false hearts but be helpless against a spinal cord injury. Nothing had worked.

"Mary," he continued, "Our time together has been the best of my life. You have shown me the kind of love that, before you, was unknown to me. It started slowly, but over time I could see how you were able to give your heart to me as I had given mine to you. Love came to us late in life, and for you a second time. I loved you from the first time I saw you. There is so much I need to say to you, but so little time. I don't even know if you can hear me, but I pray that you can. My dearest, Mary, you are the love of my life, my beautiful Queen, and I am your devoted Prince. I cherish our life and the memories we have shared. You are forever in my heart and soul. I can hardly bear the idea of life without you. But if you must go, I pray to God and all the saints above that you will be with the angels and that our heavenly Father will look down upon me."

After a few more moments, Cyril rose from his bedside chair and went to the window. He saw an ocean of candles and flowers held by the mourners outside. It lifted his spirits.

There was a knock at the door and Prince John entered. He stood next to Cyril, looking down at his mother. The men didn't speak for a long time, until John said, "How long does she have?"

Cyril didn't move. "They can't say, or they won't. All they can say is there's nothing else to be done for her."

"Can she hear me?"

Cyril's eyes clouded with tears again and he quickly brushed them away. "They think so, yes. Somewhere. But she can't respond at all."

"So...what then? The machines are keeping her alive? Is that it?"

"Yes," Cyril said.

John looked over at his stepfather, horrified. "And how long can this go on for?"

Now Cyril couldn't stop the tears from leaking out. "They can't say, John. Perhaps a very long time. The doctors...they're saying we have a decision to make."

"To end her life, you mean?" John said. "To...unplug her?"

Cyril nodded miserably, now not even trying to hide the tears streaming down his face.

John looked back at his mother and fought against his own emotions. Then he approached her bedside, sat in the chair Cyril had spent countless hours in, and gingerly took Mary's hand. "Mama," he said. "I believe you can hear me. I...came to say goodbye. I wanted you to know that you've been a wonderful mother to me. And to the country. They love you as they haven't loved a Queen in ages. You should see them, Mama, lined up on the streets outside. You'd be so happy." He paused. "And I wanted to thank you, too, for teaching me the value of love. I wish you were here to counsel me, but I've had a terrible choice to make, Mama, and I chose love. I don't regret it, and I thank you for that. I will miss you and honor your memory always. God will bless you. You have been the kindest of mothers and the most noble of Queens."

He too was crying when he stood up, and Cyril laid a hand on John's arm as the son leaned forward to place a kiss on Mary's forehead. They walked out together and stood in the hallway.

"Have you told her?" John asked.

"About the succession?" Cyril said. "No. Why break her heart now? She wanted nothing more than to see you take the throne. If she can hear us, there's nothing she can do about it. And if she awakens, then perhaps she can set it right."

John sighed and looked down the hall. "So you think I did the right thing? In not telling her?"

"Yes, John," Cyril said. "You did the only thing."

John waited a long time before he spoke again. "What now?" he finally said. "What will happen?"

"I don't know," Cyril said. "The doctors want to meet with me soon. I'll wait to hear what they have to say. God willing, it will be a miracle."

"Yes. God willing."

But it wasn't. In two days' time, the Queen's medical team gathered with Cyril to discuss her situation. The medical consensus was that there was no hope for her. They had done imaging studies of her brain, and already it was starting to shrink and atrophy. The lead physician stressed that, for all practical purposes, the Mary they had all known was already gone and the body resting in the hospital room was but a mere shell of that woman. "There can be no hope of a recovery," he said. "We can keep her body alive for a long time yet, but as far as the Queen? She is already gone."

The grim machinery of a royal death set into motion. The Chief of Staff at King Edward VII Hospital contacted the Lord Chancellor, a member of the Cabinet. The Chancellor was the highest legal expert in the realm. In a formal written request, the head physician asked for legal guidance on the matter of terminating the life of the Sovereign, who was beyond recovery. The Chief of Staff needed assurance that what they were contemplating was not murder—after all, this type of life-extending technology was new, and they were all treading in new legal territory.

The Lord Chancellor looked at the physician's reports and came to the inescapable conclusion that the Queen could not be saved. He made plans to draw up a legally binding document that physicians could withdraw life-extending technologies from the Queen, and he notified Parliament that the matter would be brought to a simple vote expressing the will of Parliament and support for the extraordinary measure.

The Lord Chancellor was well aware of what this meant. The Cabinet had reached the inescapable conclusion that, with Prince John out of the running, Edward Francis Stuart, Duke of Leicestershire, was the rightful heir to the throne. The press had been having a field day with rumors regarding Duke Edward, and it would only get worse. But the law was the law, and the Lord Chancellor saw no other possibilities.

In an emergency session, Parliament passed a statement of support, and the Cabinet convened to consider the Finiendo Vitam Regale (Ending the Life of a Royal) directive. They could think of no precedent for what they were about to do, but they agreed unanimously that it was the right thing to do, both for the Queen herself and the country as a whole. After they had approved the directive, it was given to Mary's physician for implementation.

On a damp and gray London day, Cyril was beckoned to the royal suite at King Edward hospital. It was time for him to say goodbye.

Cyril again sat next to his beloved Mary and took her hand. The doctors had cleared out, giving the Prince Consort a moment alone with his wife. With tears streaming down his face, he prayed out loud, "Lord, you are taking my wife, my love and my Queen. I beseech you to receive her in your Kingdom with glory and brilliance and to save a place for me next to you both." He pressed a lone white rose into the dying Queen's hand.

There was a sound at the door and he turned to see the Archbishop of Canterbury entering, surrounded by acolytes and three other church officials.

"Your Highness," the Archbishop said, "with your permission, I'd like to administer Extreme Unction."

"Of course, Archbishop. May I pray along with you?"

"That would be wonderful." The Archbishop opened a small prayer book he carried and began to read, "In the name of the Father, Son and Holy Ghost. Oh heavenly Father, receive into your kingdom, your servant, Mary, who has served your church in an exemplary manner. Receive her in heaven as a redeemed soul who has cleansed her mind and body of all worldly goods and evils. Receive her to sit at the side of our Savior, Jesus Christ, Our Lord, in the name of the Father, the Son and the Holy Spirit."

They all knelt by her bedside as the Archbishop made the sign of the cross, then dipped his finger in holy oil, making the sign of the cross as he touched the Queen's brow. His voice filled the room, "May the blessing of the Lord be with you always. God bless you, may you rest in peace. God save the Queen."

With the small service done, the physician approached Cyril and whispered that it was time. Cyril and the others stepped out while the doctors removed the machinery that had been keeping Mary alive. When he entered again, the beeping and whooshing of machines was gone. The tubes were gone, and a clean sheet bearing the royal crest had been pulled up to her chin. She looked peaceful and quiet. The silence in the room was deafening without the chirping and whirring of the machines. Cyril gently picked her hand up from where it lay on the coverlet, and together with her doctors, her son Prince John, and the Archbishop of Canterbury, they watched in tearful silence as Mary gently and peacefully passed away.

The doctor held a stethoscope to her neck and watched his watch. After three minutes, he turned and said, "It is done. She's gone." Within minutes, the crowds surrounding the hospital learned of the passing of their Queen. They began chanting, "God receive the Queen, God save the Queen, may she rest in peace." The streets filled with the mournful sound of hundreds of people singing Britain's revered national anthem and the tolling of hundreds of bells across the city. Traffic stopped and everyone paused to mark the moment Britain lost her Queen.

After the official notification of the Queen's death, the Cabinet was compelled to announce that the throne had been passed to Edward Francis Stuart, Duke of Leicestershire. Just as the Lord Chancellor had expected, the press had a field day with it, with vicious headlines, including "*Welcome, Your Royal Highness, King Nancy*".

CHAPTER 48
Betrayal Is Not an Option

Things happened quickly after that. The Cabinet was forced to formally announce that Edward Francis Stuart was succeeding to the throne and had taken the name His Royal Highness King Edward IX. Plans were immediately put in place for his Coronation—and just as quickly, the nation was seized by ugly protests. Rumors regarding Edward's sexuality had been bouncing around in the seedier press for weeks, but once his succession was announced, they burst into the mainstream newspapers and the full public consciousness. Although the rumors were not immediately substantiated, for many people it was enough that the rumors were persistent and widespread.

While official Britain held its collective breath, the Catholic Church—still angry over the denial of Prince John's succession—issued a stinging rebuke from the Diocese in London, denouncing the "unprecedented and abhorrent" action of naming a monarch accused of "sinful, contemptible, and vile conduct." At the same time, Cardinal Mazzio was called back to Rome.

The Catholic proclamation seemed to open a floodgate of criticism from all corners of the political world. The anti-monarchists, known as the Republicans, poured into the streets to protest the final debasement of the monarchy and call for its immediate dissolution. Britain, they claimed, was turning into a nation of "perverts" and the people's tax dollars were wasted propping up a wicked tradition. Their allies in Parliament, without speaking out directly about the rumors of Edward's allegation, began to talk about introducing articles of dissolution into Parliament—and most worrisome of all, the vote counters watched the numbers in favor of abolishing the monarchy tick up in Parliament.

England, it seemed, was in danger of coming apart at the seams.

While the nation was embroiled in controversy, two men in the eye of the storm remained obscured. First was Edward himself, who made no public appearances and assiduously avoided the press. Deeply in turmoil, he had no idea how to defuse the terrible situation—and he lived in mortal fear that his and Addison's relationship would be discovered. He wasn't afraid for himself as much as Addison, who had a family and his position in Parliament to lose. It was true that Edward had a throne to lose, but what kept him up at night was the thought of his love for Addison causing his partner pain… or worse, destruction.

Unfortunately for Edward, this was exactly the outcome that the second man in the eye of the storm devoutly wished for; his half-brother Richard watched with immense satisfaction as his plans came to fruition. Like the soldiers in past ages, Richard forced himself to wait until the moment felt right before his attack. Finally, when the press was in a fever pitch and the anti-monarchists poised to strike and the streets filled with protesters every day, he sent a private message that he wished to meet with Edward over an urgent family matter. They met in an empty conference room in a building near Buckingham Palace that was known to only a privileged few.

Richard sat waiting for Edward, his hands resting on his enormous belly and a broad smile on his face. As Edward entered, looking tired but still thin and elegantly dressed, Richard noted with satisfaction the look of disgust that crossed his half-brother's face. He pointedly didn't rise to greet Edward or extend a hand as he looked forward to once and for all wiping that smug look off Edward's face.

"What do you want?" Edward said, refusing to sit. He glanced at the manila envelope on the table but no expression crossed his face.

"Is that any way to greet your family?" Richard said. "How about, 'Hello, brother' instead?"

"You're not my brother."

"Very well, then. I suppose we should simply get down to brass tacks, eh? Dispense with the formality, is that it?"

Edward waited in silence, contempt radiating from him.

"All right, then let me lay it out. I came here today to discuss your abdication."

That got his attention. Edward physically flinched as if he'd been stung and frowned. "My abdication? What on earth on you talking about? I have no intention of abdicating a throne that is rightfully mine!"

Richard waved a lazy hand. "Rightfully yours, my ass, *Your Majesty*," the words dripped with sarcasm and managed to come out as an insult. "You will never stay king, and you're not fit for the throne nor are you deserving of it! A pervert as the King of England. It shall not stand."

Edward's face drained and two high spots appeared on his cheeks. His lips compressed into a furious line. "How dare you speak to me like this?" he said. "Richard, I'm warning you, be careful what you say or you will force me to take drastic measures against you."

"Oh, posh, pervert," Richard said. "You haven't the *balls* to win against me. Fact is, dear brother, you've already lost and just don't know it."

"I'm leaving," Edward hissed, beginning to turn away. "And as soon as I do, I will begin the work to strip you of your titles and your position. You—"

"SHUT UP!" Richard bellowed, thoroughly enjoying himself as Edward froze on the spot. "Before you embarrass yourself further, I'd suggest you open that envelope on the table. And lest you get any ideas, you should know these are only copies."

"Copies?" Edward said, his voice faltering.

"Go ahead. Take your time."

Edward advanced two reluctant steps and took up the folder, opening it and withdrawing a stack of photos. His face drained of color, turning bone white as his hands shook slightly while he leafed through the pictures. "Good God," he said softly. "You're a monster."

"No, you are," Richard answered, leaning forward in his chair. "Unless I'm very much mistaken, that man with you…as much as it turns my stomach to contemplate your filth…is Member Addison Sinclair. Imagine the shock when the country and his family find out that a member of Parliament and the pervert King have been diddling each other."

Edward could do nothing but look at the photos, his heart sinking. Addison would be ruined.

"Not bad shots, eh?" Richard continued. "I especially like the ones where you can see faces. It's so much more interesting than the others, don't you think?"

Finally, Edward choked out the only question he could think of: "How did you get these?"

"Does it matter? Do you plan on denying that's you? Because I don't think that will hold water for long. Of course, we could let the court of public opinion sort it out. I'm sure people will be interested—"

"What do you want?" Edward said.

"What do I want?" Richard said. "I would say it's satisfaction enough to see the look on your face, but it's not. I want to be King, dear half-brother. I want you ruined. I am telling you that if you do not abdicate, I will make these pictures public, along with an army of young men who seem to be strangely acquainted with your little Chelsea love nest."

Edward let the pictures fall from his hands to the table, where they scattered. He stared at his half-brother and was seized with the purest bolt of hatred. But immediately, he knew that Richard had won. He knew in an instant he would give up the throne, because the thought of Addison's life being ruined—his lovely Addison, to whom he had pledged his heart and loyalty, his everlasting love—was more than he could bear. He would never be the instrument to hurt Addison. Ironically, he realized, this wouldn't be the first time a King named Edward relinquished his throne for the person he loved and could not live without.

"You are evil," he finally grated out. "The personification…"

"Oh, shut up," Richard said. "Tell me you will abdicate. Swear it."

"You know I have no choice," he said, looking Richard in the eye. "I will never betray Addison. Betrayal is not an option, something which I'm sure you'll never understand. I pray you rot in hell."

Richard laughed. "If I do, I'll save a place for you, next to all the other perverts! Now, get out of here, faggot. You're dismissed. And, Edward, if I ever have to see you again, as King I will strip you of all your titles and positions. You should thank me for my generosity."

Edward left without another word.

Within twenty-four hours, Edward directed his solicitor to prepare an Act of Abdication to be presented to both houses of Parliament. It read:

My Lords,

It is with great sadness and despair that I tender my abdication for personal reasons. It has become apparent that I will be unable to fulfill the sacred duties of my reign. For inexplicable reasons, I hereby supplicate

that I be released from all the obligations, responsibilities and privileges bestowed upon me as King of the British Empire, effective immediately.
King Edward IX Rex Imperator

An act passed within hours and Edward signed the Royal Assent to the Abdication. With the stroke of his pen, he was officially removed as the reigning monarch of the entire British Empire.

The chaos was nearly complete—but Richard moved quickly. He publicly called for the Cabinet to move on his succession, as he was legally the next in line to the throne. At the same time, he reached out to several influential members of the anti-monarchy movement—men who he had compromising information on—and suggested they temper their criticism of the crown now that Edward was gone. He let it be known that if they moved forward with their planned vote, there would be a string of revelations about powerful men in Britain: mistresses revealed, addictions made public, accusations and secrets unearthed. The anti-monarchy movement went quiet almost immediately.

Exhausted, and with little choice, the Cabinet met again and confirmed the ascension of Richard Negril Stuart, half-brother to the abdicated King Edward IX and head of MI5. It was a joyless vote—Richard was despised by those who knew him personally, and the rest feared him. But they followed the law and moved ahead, announcing Richard as next monarch and Keeper of the Realm.

Richard chose to rule under the name King Richard V.

CHAPTER 49
The Beginning of the End

Washington, DC, 1986

The U.S. press might have spent more time on the incredible English succession if it wasn't so consumed with the crisis unfolding in the White House. A steady stream of anonymous tips regarding William Carnegie found its way into the papers. There was talk that he wasn't a U.S. citizen at all, that his birth certificate had been forged, that his parents weren't really his parents and he was the world's most powerful imposter. As the pressure built, Speaker Jordan and others from his party began to fan the flames, calling for an investigation with a special prosecutor and some already muttering that articles of impeachment needed to be considered. The Cabinet was under tremendous pressure not to name William Carnegie acting president until the question of his birth could be resolved.

There wasn't much time, however. President Lionel Keith was fighting for his very life. He was almost never seen in public anymore, and when he was, he looked like a different man. He had aged seemingly decades in the past year, as the chemotherapy and radiation took an incredible toll on his body. The members of the Cabinet knew they would have to make a decision soon, but they feared a true Constitutional crisis.

Living at the heart of the storm, Vice President William Carnegie wrestled with an impossible task. He knew he must resign the vice presidency. While the jackals in the press speculated—and he knew by now that the source of these leaks was Luke Jordan—William alone knew the truth, and it was more incredible than anyone imagined. He alone knew that not only was he not the natural-born son of Ambassador and Fiona Carnegie—he was also the older brother to Prince John and direct son of Queen Mary and her first husband Anthony. Legally speaking, he was the heir to the British throne.

As the day he picked for his resignation drew closer, Liz and the children came home from London, and William was glad to have his family back. One night, as he had been working on his resignation letter, he found Liz sitting in the drawing room of the vice presidential mansion at the Naval Observatory. She was watching a fire in the fireplace, no book at hand and nothing but the flames to occupy her. William sat down on the couch and took her hand.

"How's it coming?" she asked, knowing what he was working on.

"Difficult."

She stroked his palm. "I'm sure."

"It's just…it's so unbelievable. I'm not sure whether to laugh because it's absurd or be furious with my parents. I just wish I knew what they were thinking."

"Sweetie, they were thinking about themselves, about Mary. She was in line for the throne, a teenager, the daughter of a sitting king. A child having a child and a scandal that would rock the Empire and even might put her husband in prison."

"I know," William said. "I know that, but…now we are here."

"Yes. Now we are here. But this is just a moment in our lives. When this is over, we will continue on as we have done before. I'm with you, William. No matter what they all say, I know who you really are. And you're the best man I know."

"Thank you. You know, it's funny…after this, I'm not even sure where we'll go. We don't even have a home anymore."

"We do," she said. "We'll make one. We don't need the Carnegie Trust to create a home, William. We'll be fine. Together. Like always." She leaned over and kissed his forehead.

William smiled. "I knew years ago while sitting by that beautiful swimming pool at Elmwood Bent that something special was coming into my life. I was nursing a broken heart and needed someone to push me away from my consuming self-pity. And there you were. You revived me. You took my broken heart and mended it with care and understanding and lots of laughter. And then you taught me how to love all over again, differently and even more passionately than ever before."

"I remember that day. It was the day I realized that there was more in life than my work and parties." She smiled. "I remember you walking out to the pool in that silly bathing suit and me thinking to myself, now that's a man for me. And you were, still are, and always will be the man for me."

He laughed despite himself. "Yeah, Liz. I remember that day too! I can still see you: a hot little tart in a two-piece bathing suit."

She playfully swatted him. "Hey! That's no way to talk to a lady!"

He wrapped his arms around her and pulled her close. "It's been a long time since I held you," he said into her hair. "At least that's one benefit. I won't be working so much."

She laughed. "See, there's always a bright side! Don't worry. This will be over soon. You can do this. I have no doubt in you whatsoever."

The next day, William prepared to meet the Cabinet privately.

CHAPTER 50
THE PARTY'S OVER

Washington, DC, the Cabinet Room

THE FULL CABINET WAS ASSEMBLED IN THE ROOM WHEN WILLIAM WALKED in. He didn't carry a briefcase or any of the normal stacks of paper associated with his job. Instead, he had only a slim white envelope. He nodded at the Cabinet members as he took his seat and poured himself a glass of water. He had known and served with some of these people since the beginning of the Keith administration. A few of them went further back, to his days at Harvard. He respected all of them and could see from the hopeful looks on their faces that they were looking forward to William squashing these rumors and making it possible for them to appoint him Acting President. He felt bad for the disappointment he knew he was about to mete out.

"Thank you for having me today," William said. "It's an unfortunate circumstance that brings us here together. I know how you all feel about President Keith, and I share those feelings. He's a great man, a great leader, and his loss will be the nation's loss." They all nodded. "It is extremely unfortunate that I have been thrust into this position. Trust me, no one was more surprised by the allegations currently in the media than myself. A year ago, I would have laughed them away with a wave of my hand. Today, however, that is not the case."

There was low muttering around the table. He opened the letter and took it out, spreading it on the table in front of him and taking a deep breath.

"It is my great disappointment to confirm to you that Ambassador Harding Carnegie and his wife Fiona were not my parents. The rumors are true. The birth certificate issued to me in London apparently is fraudulent." Various members started to speak all at once, but William held his hand up for silence. "I have pursued this matter myself, and the proof is irrefutable. I want to say, before I continue, that I was completely unaware of this myself until just this last week. My parents never gave any indication that I was anything other than their natural son."

"What does this mean?" asked the Secretary of the Treasury, a long-time colleague and friend.

"Well, to begin with, it means you cannot name me Acting President. It also means that I will be resigning the vice presidency immediately."

"You don't have to!" exclaimed the Secretary of Agriculture. "You can fight this!"

William shook his head. "Maybe. I might have a decent case. But the damage to the country would be immense. And, to be frank, I don't want to put my family or my party through it. In a few days' time, the Carnegie Trust will be announcing that, until this is resolved, my relationship with the Carnegie Trust is also severed. I'm afraid that, even if I was morally in the right, the legal and political case would be too draining."

"But—"

"I'm sorry," William said. "You'll understand in a moment. I don't know what their thinking was—my parents left no note—but it turns out they were protecting a secret. I'll tell you now, myself, because I suspect it will be discovered soon anyway. My birth mother was the recently deceased Queen Mary of England and her boyfriend at the time, Anthony, Prince of

Wales, who just prior to my birth became her husband. Apparently, they were covering the Queen's teenage mistake."

A hush filled the room, and then a burst of nervous laughter broke out. "You can't be serious," the Secretary of State said. "You're…Queen Mary's oldest son?"

"Yes," William said. "It's irrefutable."

"Do they know?" she asked. "The Brits. You know they're in the midst of this terrible succession mess. Wouldn't this mean you're the rightful heir?"

William shook his head. "They don't know. So far, aside from my wife, you are the only people in the world I've told. But…as I said, I believe this will all come out eventually if I don't get ahead of it myself. That's why I'm resigning today."

The Cabinet members looked at each other. No one in that room had any illusions about the upheaval this would cause, but it was the Secretary of State who stood up and said, "Mr. Vice President, if this is all true as you say, and I don't doubt you, then I'm very sorry. You would have made an excellent president."

William bowed his head but didn't say anything.

"As for what happens now, I think I speak for the others, we'll let you make your statement however you want," the Secretary said. "The timing is yours to choose. In the meantime, we'll consult with Attorney General Santos on what to do next. For now, President Keith is still in office and in charge, so God willing, we still have at least a little time to manage this."

"Thank you," William said, and most of them hugged him on their way out of the meeting, tears shining in their eyes.

Washington, DC, Speaker's Office

The succession for the Presidency is spelled out in the 25TH Amendment of the U.S. Constitution. With William planning to step down from office, the Cabinet had only one option. As noxious as it was, it was the Secretary of State who placed the call to Speaker Luke Jordan's office and asked him to attend an emergency meeting of the Cabinet. During the call, she briefed Jordan on the shocking twist in the story.

"Let me see if I understand exactly what you are saying," Jordan said. "Vice President Carnegie is resigning and claiming to be the heir to the British throne? Are you kidding me?!"

"No, Mr. Speaker," replied the Secretary. "That is *exactly* what he said."

It was everything Jordan could do not to laugh and to sound sincerely upset. "Well, either he has lost his grip, or this is the most incredible story in political history. For crying out loud, I thought I'd heard everything; and then something like this pops up. Can you imagine, King William? This is just too much!"

The Secretary didn't answer. Like the rest of the Cabinet, she loathed Jordan, both politically and personally.

"So," Jordan continued, "what does this mean, then? You're calling me because...?"

"Mr. Speaker, in February 1967, both houses of Congress passed the 25TH Amendment. It dealt with succession issues not clarified in the Constitution's Article II, Section 1 relating to the disability of the president and the appointment of an Acting President. Essentially the amendment called for the appointment of the vice president to the position of Acting President in the event the president becomes temporarily disabled. If the president should die, or become disabled long term, the Acting President would be named president. The amendment also provides for the appointment of a vice president to fill the vacancy created when a current VP becomes president.

"Go on."

"But in the situation we have here, things get complicated. You see, if the president chooses to declare himself disabled, there is no vice president to be named because Carnegie has already resigned. The 25TH Amendment does not spell out specifically who would be named Acting President in that situation. However, President Keith, prior to being deemed either voluntarily or involuntarily disabled, could conceivably appoint a vice president who would then have to be approved by Congress. But that would take time, something Keith may not have. If Congress approves Keith's choice for vice president, and when or if the president becomes disabled, the new VP would be named Acting President. Are you still with me, Mr. Speaker?"

"Yes, of course. Go on."

"The 25TH Amendment states that in the event the vice president cannot take the office of Acting President, Congress may, by law, provide for the Case of Removal of both the president and vice president. They would then choose the officer they see fit to act as president. Congress's choice would serve until the president is no longer disabled and resumes office, or a new president is elected in the next regular election. I believe that in the scenario I described, although not clearly mandated by law, Congress would more than likely choose you, the current Speaker of the House, as the officer to serve as Acting President. This would be the logical choice since the Speaker generally is next in line of succession after the vice president."

Jordan had to cover his mouth to keep from laughing out loud. Finally! After being cheated out of winning the presidency at the ballot box, he would win the presidency in Congress! He had to search for the right words; he didn't want to give away his joy at the perfect culmination of his plan. "Unbelievable. I'm sorry for the vice president. You say he just figured this out?"

"Yes. Apparently the vice president had no knowledge of this situation until now. To his credit, he has voluntarily come forward with the truth and has resigned."

"Very noble," Jordan said, allowing himself a small laugh. "I'd say it's almost royal."

The Secretary didn't answer but let dead air draw out.

"So what's next?" Jordan asked.

The Secretary took a deep breath. "The Cabinet will have to make some sort of declaration as soon as President Keith's latest medical evaluation has been reviewed. As it stands now, we have a legitimate president who is seriously ill and no vice president. Our main goal is to make sure government is not disrupted and the republic stays strong. There are some constitutional implications here since there isn't a clear precedent for anything like this. The Justice Department may have to be involved in this matter, and who or what else is anyone's guess. I hope I can count on your cooperation."

"Certainly. I will remain available at all times to assist in any way."

"And Mr. Speaker, if you don't mind, I asked the Secret Service to have some additional protection posted for you. Once this breaks…"

Jordan was smiling broadly now. "Of course. Do whatever you think is right. I trust you'll take all the right steps."

CHAPTER 51
HIS ROYAL HIGHNESS, KING NEXT

Hotel Park Lane, Central London, 1986

WILLIAM WAS BACK IN LONDON, STAYING WITH HIS FAMILY AT A SMALL estate Liz's parents maintained in the country. In a way, leaving the United States was like a weight lifting from his shoulders—he flew out of Washington and left the bitter residue of his downfall behind. Speaker Jordan was busy scheming his way into the presidency, and as much as William would have liked to prevent it, he recognized that his time in power was over. As far as politics in the United States went, William Carnegie was finished.

But he wasn't completely done yet. He and Liz had talked at great length about their next move. They considered all of the options—from buying a little place on a deserted island and disappearing to hiring the best lawyers in the world to take on the Carnegie trust and Jordan. Eventually, and with a growing sense of surprise, William realized what he most wanted was to discover and claim his own heritage. He had always identified himself as a Carnegie, and he had spent his life striving to uphold the Carnegie name. But now, with this incredible turn of events and the betrayal from his own parents, he wasn't so sure any more. Now he wanted to know who he really was and, if necessary, claim what was rightfully his to replace that which had been taken from him.

It was this decision that led him to a hotel room in central London, waiting on Owen Hasting Crawly. From what he had heard, Crawly was the consummate English solicitor: dignified, graying, impeccably turned out, and wickedly smart. He was a senior partner in his firm and they said he rarely lost a case.

A knock sounded at the door and William rose to let Owen in. Just as advertised, Owen was an impressive figure, every inch of him polished and turned out in the finest clothes and jewelry. "Thank you for meeting me," William said. "I truly appreciate it."

"Of course," Owen said. "I've been following the news, old man. It looks like a fine kettle of fish you've got yourself into over there in America."

"You can imagine," William said, leading them back to a small round table where he had spread out a series of folders and envelopes. "But of course, that's not why I called you here. That business is behind me."

"Yes," Owen said, his voice more than a little skeptical. "You mentioned a rather extraordinary circumstance. You say you might be the firstborn son of our departed Queen Mary? Seems rather fantastic, William, if I do say. Yet my friends tell me you're a serious man of impeccable integrity and someone to be taken most seriously. So, tell me the story."

William launched into the whole story, beginning with the discovery of his mother's safe and moving through to the present day. Along the way, he presented Owen his evidence, unveiling each piece as if he were arguing the case in court. He presented the letter his mother had written, the scrapbook pictures from Rosemary Firth along with her firsthand story, the DNA evidence, his birthparents' real marriage certificate, and finally the signet ring itself.

When he was finished, Owen rocked back in his chair and uttered a low, very unrefined four-letter word. "I say, old man, this doesn't happen often, but I must admit that I'm speechless. Even worse, thunderstruck."

"So?" William said. "Do you believe me?"

Owen slowly shook his head. "I feel like I might be crazy for thinking it, but yes, I do. I'm familiar with the emerging science of DNA evidence. It's virtually incontrovertible. And the letter...the signet ring...a personal statement from the Queen's own girlhood friend...the letter in your own mother's hand. I say, if this was a court case, I'm convinced I'd win it!" He paused. "Which brings me to the question, sir. Let's assume all this is true, what do you hope to do with it? What's your plan?"

William leaned back himself and steepled his fingers, sighing. "As you can imagine, I've thought a great deal about that. Trust me when I say that it's occurred to me I could simply vanish and take this with me to the grave. But..." he paused, suddenly nervous to put into words thoughts he had only shared with Liz. "You understand, I've lost everything. My inheritance. My sense of who I am. My career is in ruins. I've wracked my brain trying to think if I've done something to cause my own ruin. Did I bring this on myself somehow? Did I earn it? It's a valid question, right? And no, Owen, my answer is no. I've done nothing to deserve this. I didn't ask to be born a teenage princess. I didn't ask for my parents to lie to me for my entire life. And I certainly didn't ask to pay for the mistakes of all these people decades ago. But here I am, paying and paying and paying. And I realized that I'm through paying for it. I believe this is true, not only because of the evidence but because it feels true. I've studied their pictures, my birth mother's and father's, and I have their look. You ask what my plan is? My plan is to claim what is rightfully mine after losing what never should have been mine."

Owen slowly applauded as William concluded his speech. "Bravo! Yes, I don't blame you a bit," he said. "I think any man would do the same, given your background and this situation. But you must know, you may be a Brit by birth, but you're an American through and through. You will need to win over the British people. How would you do that?"

William nodded. "I've thought about that, and I've been reading about the British monarchs feverishly. Here's what I've learned. The first way to win the people is to win the throne."

Owen burst out laughing. "Well said! Well said! Perhaps you understand us better than I thought."

"So," William said. "Will you help me? Will you represent me before the Cabinet?"

"You mean will I help you take the throne?" Owen said, a gleam in his eye. "Are you asking if I'll take the case of the century, no, the case of a millennium, and restore the rightful heir to the English throne?"

"Yes."

"You're bloody right I will!" Owen exclaimed. "Your Majesty, it would be my honor!"

With their agreement in place, they fell to planning an assault to win the Crown. Owen planned to first petition the Cabinet with a request for a full review of William's claim. Simultaneously, he would talk to some of his friends in Parliament to launch a review of King Richard's ascension in light of this new development. Lastly, he told William that, "From this moment forward, you're an Englishman. You understand? I don't mean putting on some dreadful accent like you Americans love to do. I mean you'll need to read up on English history, English law, English customs. You'll live on tea and biscuits and breathe nothing but sweet English air. You'll immediately get rid of those very American clothes and get yourself to Savile Row and have a tailor outfit you properly. And you'll call this firm immediately." He produced a card as if by magic and slid it across to William. "This is perhaps the best public relations firm in the United Kingdom. If anybody can turn a Yank into a king, it's them."

William smiled.

"Now, to work," Owen said. "We have a crown to claim."

CHAPTER 52
BACKDOOR BRIBES

RICHARD WAITED IN HIS OFFICE, ENJOYING SPENDING A FEW MINUTES absorbing the impact of this place. It was literally a room fit for a King. The large gilded furniture and millwork dated back centuries. The royal crest hung high over the desk occupied by the monarch. Flags and other medieval regalia were placed throughout the room. Portraits of past monarchs dating back centuries adorned the walls. The room reeked of royal authority, and Richard enjoyed wondering how many historic decisions had been made here.

There was a knock at the door and Richard's secretary opened it to allow entry to Sir Melvin Batton, a senior member of the Cabinet. Sir Melvin walked in warily. Richard couldn't help but notice with satisfaction when Sir Melvin's eyes flickered over the trappings of royal power and there was a faint gleam of…fear?

Sir Melvin bowed deeply. "Your Majesty, I am honored to be received by you. May I be among the first to offer my congratulations at your succession, and I give you my full and complete allegiance. You will be a Sovereign we will always respect and admire."

Richard would have preferred "respect and fear," but he figured that part was coming soon enough. He patted his stomach as he leaned back in his chair, pointedly not inviting Sir Melvin to sit down.

"Sir Melvin, so gracious of you to accept my invitation," Richard said. "I am pleased to have your pledge of allegiance and expect nothing less. I have some bidding that needs to be done."

"Of course, Your Highness. How can I be of service?"

Richard knew that this wouldn't be the first time Sir Melvin had been called into service. Sir Melvin had been bought and sold by Richard years ago when he was the object of an MI5 investigation. Having saved Sir Melvin from disgrace and ruin from a number of notable missteps, Richard kept this Cabinet member as a mole within Parliament, calling upon him at his pleasure to provide inside information and to further his influence.

"As you must be aware, there are some ridiculous notions going around attacking the legitimacy of my reign. The eminent Cabinet that you serve on is currently evaluating those notions. I need to be assured that you, as my confidant and trusted friend, will do everything in your power to influence a favorable outcome for this reign."

Sir Melvin made a sour face. Richard—who had long counted on Sir Melvin to handle political issues for MI5—raised his eyebrows.

"Your Highness," Sir Melvin said, "that could be difficult given the nature of the challenge. Although the Committee has not had the opportunity to review and vet the evidence, it seems there could be something to what the American is saying."

"That's tosh. I don't care if he is the love child of my dear departed aunt. I want the matter dismissed."

"I understand, Your Majesty, but I'm saying that I'm not sure that will be possible. The Cabinet wants to get to the bottom of these claims."

"You don't seem to understand, Sir Melvin. I am not *asking* you to make this situation go away; I'm *commanding* that you do. Failure to do so could be disastrous…to you personally."

Sir Melvin swallowed nervously and looked desperate.

"Do you understand?" Richard asked. "Am I making myself clear?"

"Eminently clear, Your Majesty. I will do what I can."

"Very well, now bugger off. And don't even contemplate letting me down."

After Sir Melvin scuttled out of the room, the King next summoned an old colleague from M15. This meeting was much easier: the faithful spy promised to deliver a complete account of William Carnegie's time in England from his childhood until now in the next two days, leaving no stone unturned.

CHAPTER 53
BODY OF EVIDENCE

WILLIAM'S SURPRISE CLAIM TO THE THRONE THREW THE COUNTRY INTO immediate turmoil. Having suffered through months of a tortured succession, the Britons were exhausted already, and this new twist seemed to be the straw that broke the camel's back. Anti-royalist sentiment flared up immediately and quickly became personified in the form of MP Thomas Cunningham, a dedicated Republican who had spent his time in Parliament for years fruitlessly railing against the monarchy. Now, however, he channeled the growing rage and disgust of the British people and quickly installed himself as the head of a powerful new movement to abolish the monarchy. Sir Melvin fought him every step of the way, and their passionate arguments were covered extensively in the press, but it seemed nothing could stop the tide of anti-royal sentiment sweeping the country.

For his part, William did his best to ignore the more acrimonious elements of the debate. Instead, he spent his time holed up in a hotel room with Owen Crawly, working on arguments to defend his claim to the throne.

When William did go out, it was always carefully scripted by the new public relations firm, Smyth, Whiting, and Atwhisle, that Crawly had contracted for him. Based on their advice, William even adopted a new name: William Carnegie Bolin-Stuart. By adopting his birth mother and father's surnames, William hoped to bolster his legitimacy and name recognition with the Cabinet who would be considering his claim and the English people. Crawly had every confidence that William would prevail. "Your case, as they say, is unassailable."

When the day finally came for Crawly and William to attend their first meeting, they were prepared. They carried three attaché cases of briefs and papers, the result of investigative work that spanned the globe. Researchers had traveled everywhere from Gibraltar to Canada, putting together an incontrovertible brief proving that William was the rightful monarch.

They arrived at the House of Parliament to find the building mobbed by press and protestors. William and Crawly exchanged a glance.

"Someone tipped them off," Crawly observed mildly.

"Looks like it."

"No matter."

William watched the people outside as they realized he was in the car. It looked like a mix of press, anti-royalists holding signs and chanting, angry women's libbers who were still upset over Mary Louise, and Catholics protesting the age-old Act of Settlement. Some even pelted the car with eggs. The press started yelling questions and surging toward the car. "At least half of them are American," he observed.

"More's the pity too," Crawly said. "The American press corps only serves to remind people that you're American. But nothing to be done about it. Let them write what they want for now."

William smiled bitterly. "They probably think we're the story of the century."

Crawly looked over as the car passed through the gates. "Don't sell yourself short, William," he said. "This is the story of the millennium."

William's smile grew slightly.

"Now," Crawly said, as the car stopped. "Let's go grab that throne."

They stepped out of the car together as the other lawyers following behind also parked. They entered the Parliament building in a group, leaving the raucous demonstrations on the street behind as they stepped into the hushed halls. A uniformed guard escorted them to an oval theater-style chamber with tiered seating rising up the walls and a raised dais on the floor. The walls were covered with portraits of Prime Ministers from years, even centuries, gone by—William found himself staring at a portrait and into the eyes of Queen Mary, his birth mother, as his group settled around a table and spread out their files and papers. Above them, members of the Cabinet and Parliament filtered in and took their seats. William recognized Sir Melvin and Thomas Cunningham from their published pictures. He had been following their debates in Parliament and knew that neither was his friend. One denied his right to be King, and the other denied the right of anyone to be King. The members of the Cabinet who would be judging today's proceedings began to gather at an elevated table on the dais.

A gavel sounded as Lord Markus Butler, chairman of the Cabinet committee, called the meeting to order, then introduced Owen Crawly to the assemblage and asked for an opening statement.

Owen, well trained in courtroom theatrics, swaggered up to the podium and took a moment to carefully open his notes and then look piercingly at the members of the Cabinet assembled before him. Then he began speaking in his rich, smooth baritone.

"It is with great humility and honor that I have this opportunity to address this august gathering." He stopped to bow his head in the direction of Queen Mary's portrait. "Let me start by first paying respects and admiration to the late great Queen, former ruler of our great empire and mother to my client, William Carnegie Bolin-Stuart." He waited for the meaning and significance of his words to sink in, then continued: "Today, I am in a position to present facts, sustainable and irrefutable facts, as well as supporting evidence that will conclusively prove beyond any doubt that my client, William Carnegie Bolin-Stuart, is not only the first legitimate son of our beloved late Queen Mary, but the rightful heir to her throne. His claim will supersede the legitimacy of the current reigning monarch, King Richard XI. This is clearly called for in the Act of Settlement, which reads: 'Whereas the eldest legitimate heir in the bloodline is the lawful successor to the deceased Monarch.' Further, I am here to request that King Richard, the current reigning monarch who was erroneously allowed to succeed, be removed from the throne immediately and be replaced by the proper and lawful heir, William Carnegie Bolin-Stuart."

His remarks were met by a kind of echoing, stunned silence, followed by pandemonium as the members all rose at once and began speaking.

"My Lords, order please!" Chairman Markus barked, pounding his gavel. "Order! Mr. Crawly, I can't stress enough how important it is that you dare not come here today to waste the time of our Cabinet and to further inflame what has a tremendous series of succession nightmares. For if that is the case, you and your client Mr. William Carnegie Bolin-Stuart will be held in contempt of Parliament and face the most severe of consequences."

Crawly didn't seem disturbed by this threat in the slightest. "My Lord," he said, "I can assure you that at the end of these proceedings, this eminent body will be completely convinced that our indisputable evidence can lead to but one conclusion: my client is the true and only rightful heir to the throne of his beloved mother, Queen Mary, may she rest in peace."

"You may proceed, Mr. Crawly," Sir Markus growled. "But I warn you, sir, be *very*, *very* careful."

Owen began by establishing that Mary was the only child and rightful heir of King John and the Queen Consort Martha. This was a matter of record as well as historical fact and received no opposition. When he was satisfied his point had been made, he went on, "So, my Lords, we clearly have established that the late Queen was the rightful heir. I now would like to place before you two marriage certificates both inscribed with the names of Mary Stuart and Anthony Bolin. You will note that both of these certificates document that the marriages were performed in the Church of England. However, one certificate predates the other by five years, thus establishing that the royal couple was lawfully married at the time of William Carnegie Bolin's birth, 31 August 1936. The second marriage was merely ceremonial."

"This is ridiculous," Sir Melvin interrupted, rising to his feet to speak. "First of all, how do we know that the earlier marriage certificate is true and legitimate? And secondly, you can't marry the same person twice, can you?"

Owen smiled at this question. He had been hoping someone else would ask it so he could present the irrefutable evidence of Mary and Anthony's marriage. A member of his firm's investigation team had traveled to Gibraltar and found the little church where the ceremony had been conducted. Although the vicar who performed the marriage was no longer living, the church records clearly showed that Mary and Anthony had been married on the date in question. Both of them had signed the church registry as well, attesting that they had received the Sacrament of Marriage in the Church of England.

With respect to the legality of marrying the same person twice, Owen had researched both British common law as well as the laws of the Church of England. Nowhere could there be found any prohibition of a second marriage ceremony, and common law held that the date of the first marriage takes precedence.

As Owen circulated copies of the first marriage certificate, he also announced, "Sir Melvin, my Lords, I present a sworn statement from Sir Miles Betancourt, Britain's foremost authority on handwriting. In this statement, Sir Miles has authenticated that both the Queen's and Prince's signatures on this marriage license are genuine."

Sir Melvin, however, would not be convinced so easily. He hardly glanced at the paper in his hand before retorting, "Even if this is true, it does not provide that William is their child at all, only that they were married."

"Quite right," Crawly said. "I'll be getting there. As you know, the Act of Settlement says the throne can only be passed to a direct blood descendent of a monarch who was legally married. These documents prove that Mary and Anthony were legally married in the Church of England before William was born. So now I shall turn my attention to proving William's parentage." He produced another sheet of paper. "I hold in my hands a note written on September 2, 1936, by the late Queen Mary. It is written in her own handwriting, which Sir Miles has authenticated. Further, the stationary the note is written upon bears the heading *Summerset*. This was the name of the yacht on which Mary spent several months during her pregnancy and before delivering her son William at the English possession of Gibraltar. Aboard the yacht, other than a small Portuguese crew, were two other guests: Lady Fiona Firth Carnegie and Rosemary Firth, the Princess's schoolmate, best friend, and younger sister to Fiona. I have taken the liberty of tracing the origins of the stationary on which this note has been written. The engraved stationary was produced by the Social Department at Harrods Department Store. It was commissioned in 1932 by Martin Landon, a member of Ambassador Carnegie's personal staff. Ambassador Carnegie was the registered owner of the vessel *Summerset*. Although *Summerset* is long gone, Harrods maintains the copper plate and the billing information linking multiple stationary orders from 1932 to 1942 to the Ambassador's office."

He paused again to let this sink in. "So, my Lords, to reiterate, Sir Miles has clearly established the authenticity of the handwritten note as the product of Queen Mary's own hand, and Harrods verifies the origins of the stationary on which it was written. I shall read the note to you now."

As he read the note aloud, heads within the chamber began to shake in wonder. Before he could finish, however, Sir Melvin once again jumped up and interrupted. "Mr. Chairman, sir, I appeal to you to halt these proceedings immediately. This is preposterous, insane, fabricated, simply impossible, and patently false. Old letters and stationary, a teenager's marriage certificate that could easily be fabricated. There is no mention of a birth certificate, no record of a hospital. Nothing. Sir, we mustn't fall for this pretender's tricks. His Majesty King Richard is the only lawful successor and that is that. I demand that this entire matter be dismissed immediately."

"My Lord, the reason there is no birth certificate presented to this committee is that there never was one," Crawly said. "However, I would think this committee would take the written testimony of their beloved Queen as proof positive that the child she bore and gave away is, in fact, her natural-born issue, William Carnegie Bolin-Stuart."

Before Sir Markus could respond, Thomas Cunningham leapt to his feet and shouted down the gavel. "Lords! Of course this is ridiculous! We are the leaders of a modern democracy. The idea that we should sit here and debate the idea that God has granted a certain child with the right to be king, with no other qualifications, no support from the people, is an insult to our country and ideals! I say the time has come to abolish the monarchy! No more divine right!"

Sir Markus was red in the face by the time Cunningham was done. "Sit down, sir!" he barked. "This isn't a Parliamentary debate!" After Cunningham slowly returned to his chair, Sir Markus turned to Crawly. "Please, sir, do you have anything else we need to consider? Is this it?"

"No, m'Lord. There is more."

"Go on then."

"Mr. Chairman, my Lords, I would like to—"

He stopped speaking abruptly as the back of the room erupted in chaos. The doors slammed open and dozens of police poured into the chamber, setting up a perimeter around the room with grim faces.

"I say!" Sir Markus yelled. "What is the meaning of this?"

"Gentlemen," said a lieutenant in a voice that almost sounded apologetic. "We've received word there has a been a security breach and there are an unknown number of potential threats within the building. We do not know if they are armed or carrying explosives. Please prepare to exit the chamber immediately."

As if one, the members jumped up and began filing quickly from the room as Sir Markus gaveled the chaotic session to a close with little resolved.

CHAPTER 54
Skeletons in the Closet

King Richard received the long-awaited report in his royal office. He had grown very fond of the office and taken to conducting most of his business in the august room. He especially loved to watch the faces of his visitors as they entered. The monarchy was like a suffocating blanket that sucked the oxygen from the room, overwhelming his visitors. Many of them were virtually speechless by the time they reached his desk. Sometimes, Richard thought, it was good to be King.

"So?" Richard said, looking distastefully at the thick file the spy had lain on his desk. "You don't expect me to read this, do you?" He lifted it up and let it drop dramatically—it hit the desktop with a solid thud. The report was more than 200 pages long.

"Uh, no, Your Majesty," the spy stammered.

"And yet you stand there like a fool. Out with it, man. What does this say?"

The spy cleared his throat and permitted himself a small smile. Richard's heart leapt. The smile could only mean one thing: they had hit pay dirt.

"Well, Your Highness, there is in fact something significant. In searching all records for anything containing the Carnegie name, a military attaché found an obscure report filed in 1977. Apparently there was an apprehension of two IRA militants. One Roan Kelly and one Shaun McCabe. It seems that during a routine military operation these two leaders were found, arrested, and interrogated. Kelly, apparently a leader in the IRA, died during interrogation before he could provide any valuable information. However, McCabe was much more helpful. Before he escaped custody, Mr. McCabe provided some key information regarding the whereabouts of a number of high-ranking IRA militants, as well as various locations of arms and ammunition. He also disclosed a key source of funds being provided to the IRA. According to McCabe's oral statement, documented in writing by a Major Horace Stanly, a great deal of money was filtered through a Belfast bank to the IRA. A disclosure order was filed and the bank was ordered to reveal the originator of the wires. Apparently the money came from an American bank in New York, via wire transfer. The account sending the funds belonged to the Carnegie Family Trust. It was further documented that the trust listed William Carnegie among its beneficiaries. These transfers started while Mr. Carnegie was working at the American Embassy, but they continued for a short while after he left the country and returned to the United States."

"Good God, man," the King said. "You're telling me that William Carnegie was helping fund the IRA? Why on earth would he be so stupid?"

"Your Majesty, it seems that Carnegie was romantically involved with Miss Regina Kelly. Roan Kelly's sister and a member of the IRA herself. She was killed during an interaction with the military."

Richard started at the spy in ecstatic disbelief.

"There's more, Your Majesty. We've been able to link the money Carnegie provided with certain purchases of weapons and munitions. Some of these armaments were used in the attempted assassination of the then-Princess

Royal, Mary and her husband, Prince Anthony in a roadside ambush. As you well know, the Princess survived the attack but the Prince and others in his party were killed."

Richard couldn't help it: he began to laugh. "This is almost too good! William's money helped fund the assassination of the man he would later claim is his father!"

"Yes, Your Majesty. That is almost assuredly the case. At that time, William was by far the largest donor to the IRA."

"Amazing!" Richard marveled, feeling in a better mood than he had in weeks. "So tell me, what type of proof do we have? How solid is it?"

"Your Majesty, Shaun McCabe is still alive and in custody. He is currently serving a 40-year term at the HM Prison Dartmoor at Princetown, in the county of Devon."

"Will he cooperate?" Richard asked.

"Your Majesty, he will have no choice."

"Excellent! Arrange for his transfer immediately. I want him here. And tell Sir Melvin what you've found. As soon as possible, I want this bloke McCabe shined up like a new penny and ready to tell his story."

"Yes, of course, Your Majesty. It will be arranged immediately."

CHAPTER 55
FOR THE GREATER GOOD

THE CABINET RECONVENED AFTER A TWO-DAY HIATUS. IN THE MEANTIME, the building had been searched from end to end. No explosives were found. Nevertheless, when the session was called to order again, it was done under heavy guard. Nothing was being left to chance.

"My Lords, we are in session," Sir Markus said after gaveling them to order. "Mr. Crawly, the stand is yours."

Once again, Owen rose to the podium, looking calm and ready, as if nothing had intervened. "My Lord," he began, "when we last finished, we had established that Mary was the true heir to King John and that she and Anthony Bolin had legally wedded. We will now establish beyond the shadow of a doubt that William Carnegie Bolin-Stuart is their natural issue and firstborn son, thereby making him the legal heir to the throne, as opposed to the newly and erroneously installed King Richard."

With great aplomb, Owen picked up a velvet pouch from the podium and removed a glittering ring.

"My Lords, I will present unassailable evidence. But first, there is this. No doubt none of you will recognize this ring, although you will certainly recognize the coat of arms of the Princess of Wales. This ring was a gift from King John to his sixteen-year-old daughter Mary on her birthday. She later passed it to Fiona Carnegie upon the occasion of handing over baby William to be raised as the Carnegies' own child. If one were to carefully examine the ring, they would find a small inscription which reads: 'HRH Mary, Princess of Wales.' There is also a hallmark from Garrard, the royal jeweler. I have in my possession an affidavit from Garrard's stating that this very ring was crafted by their London workshop in 1935."

Sir Melvin began to jump up, but Crawly held up his hand. "Now wait, My Lord. I understand, of course, that a ring and a letter, however compelling they might be, however unimpeachable their authenticity, are not enough to depose a sitting King of England. Of course. My purpose here is to build a supporting wall of evidence, to show that it isn't just one or two pieces of evidence suggesting the truth of William's claims, but in fact it is the accumulation of both circumstantial and scientific evidence that leaves no other possible conclusion."

Sir Melvin, still half out of his chair, had no choice but to sit back down.

Crawly continued as if he'd never been interrupted, "My Lord, what type of evidence could be so unassailable, so beyond a doubt? Certainly we would agree that eyewitness testimony would fall into that category, to hear from a person who was actually present during Mary's pregnancy, who held the baby William seconds after he was delivered, and who witnessed his passing into the Carnegie household. As a matter of record, there are only five people who would qualify as eyewitnesses. The first three—the late Queen, her husband Anthony, and Fiona Carnegie—are all deceased. And of course, there is William himself, who was an infant at the time and obviously could add nothing in the way of testimony. That leaves but one living eyewitness: Rosemary Firth North, sister of Fiona Carnegie and lifelong friend and confidant of our late Queen Mary. So, my Lords, I ask you to give your kind and full attention to Rosemary Firth North, who has so graciously agreed to testify on behalf of my client."

A murmur ran through the gallery as Rosemary appeared and was escorted along the aisle, toward a small witness box near the podium. Even William was surprised by her appearance—Crawly had played his cards close, and no one knew that Rosemary would be present. This became instantly obvious from the outraged reactions among certain members of the gallery. William noted who they were, mentally marking out his enemies. Loudest among them was Sir Melvin, a man William had never spoken to before but who was turning out to be an implacable foe of his ascension.

Rosemary's progress toward the witness box was slow, as she had trouble walking and was slightly stooped from osteoporosis. When she passed by William, however, she winked at him, and he could see that her eyes were bright and sharp as ever.

"My Lords, may I present Rosemary Firth North," Crawly said as she settled into the seat facing him. "I hold here her official identification in the form of a Canadian passport and a naturalized Canadian citizen verification form."

Sir Markus nodded his assent and Crawly turned to face the witness.

"Please rise as the clerk will swear you in."

Following the formality, Sir Markus said in a kindly voice, "Madam, could you please give us your name and residence?"

"I am Rosemary Firth North and I currently live in the Village of Saint-Benoit-du-Lac located in the Commonwealth of Canada," she said in a clear voice.

"Thank you, Mrs. North," Crawly said. "And thank you for agreeing to make this long trip to talk to us today. First then, for the purposes of this proceeding, I'd like to hear how you came to know William Carnegie Bolin-Stuart."

Rosemary glanced at William and smiled. "Well, sir, I first met William when he was less than one minute old."

"Less than one minute old, you say? How was it that happened?"

"I was present at his birth," she said simply. "I was the one who fetched the towels to wrap the child seconds after he was delivered."

"Seconds after his delivery? And when exactly was that?"

"It was August 31, 1936, in the little village of Catalan, Gibraltar, at the villa owned by the Carnegies."

"And I assume you can identify his mother?"

"I certainly can. She was my best friend, my schoolmate, and later the Queen."

"Just to confirm, you know you've given an oath here. To perjure yourself could have serious consequences."

"Pish posh!" the old lady said. "Perjure myself! I stood in the room next to Mary as she gave birth. Unless my own eyes are lying, you can be assured that's the truth!"

A titter ran through the room, and William couldn't help but notice that Sir Melvin had gone white as a sheet.

Crawly continued, "Mrs. North, what else happened in the Village of Catalan, Gibraltar prior to William Carnegie Bolin-Stuart's birth?"

"Well, Mary and Anthony got married in the local church. I was the maid of honor. She insisted upon it, before the baby was born."

"I see. And, madam, could you specify your relationship to Fiona Carnegie and her husband, Ambassador Carnegie?"

"Fiona Carnegie was my older half-sister by more than twenty-three years. Ambassador Carnegie was her husband."

"Would it be fair to say that you have close personal knowledge of Queen Mary, Fiona, and Ambassador Carnegie?"

"Of course," Rosemary said. "I lived with my sister growing up. Some years later, I lived with Mary and Anthony in the palace as a lady-in-waiting. As for the Ambassador, he was my brother-in-law and part of the family."

"Excellent! Now, perhaps in your own words, could you relate exactly what happened over the course of those fateful months so long ago? It's terribly important that we get the full picture."

Rosemary took a deep breath and began talking, her words clear and strong. She talked about her days at Highwood School, the meeting of Mary and Anthony, and the unplanned pregnancy. She related how she and her sister, Fiona, concocted the story that the baby would be Fiona's and how Fiona faked her own pregnancy. Rosemary verified that the ring that Owen had shown the Committee was indeed Mary's, given to her while at Highwood by the King. She further testified that the Ambassador was oblivious to the fact that Mary was William's birth mother.

"Excuse me," Crawly interrupted, "but are you testifying that the Ambassador thought that William was your baby, not Mary's?"

"Yes, that is correct."

"Why would that be?"

"My sister Fiona and I knew that if the Ambassador thought the baby was really Mary's, a future Queen, it would be far more complicated for him politically if something should go wrong," Rosemary said. "He might not even agree to take the baby. It was much safer for all concerned if I admitted maternity. And naturally, taking the child of one's own sister-in-law was much more acceptable than taking in an heir to the throne."

"Didn't the Ambassador notice that you weren't expecting a baby?"

"These were difficult times. There was the pending war in Europe, a faltering economy, and diplomatic chaos and upheaval in the world. The

Ambassador worked tirelessly at the embassy and rarely saw anyone. He spent little time at home. He believed what he was told, which was that I got in 'trouble' and was having a baby. I was to be whisked away, out of the public's sight."

"I see. Please continue with your recount."

Rosemary started to tell the story of the simple wedding, when Crawly interrupted again.

"I'm sorry, Mrs. North, you say you attended a wedding. Exactly whose wedding was it and where did it take place?"

"As I told you, the wedding was that of Mary and Anthony. The only people in attendance were Mary, Anthony, myself, Fiona, and the vicar. It took place at a charming Anglican church in the village of Catalan in Gibraltar." Rosemary smiled at the scene in her memory. "Mary looked so beautiful and young and innocent, even though her belly extended well beyond her dress! She was a lovely bride, indeed. I remember the vicar commenting that the wedding was none too soon!"

"Do you happen to remember the exact date of the wedding?"

"August 29, 1936."

"And how do you know that date is correct?"

"Obviously, young man, you aren't listening. I told you before, I kept the wedding certificate so of course I know the exact date. And I certainly don't need a *piece of paper* to remember such a monumental event!"

Owen smiled. Rosemary was a perfect witness as he next asked her to identify the signet ring and the wedding certificate. Finally, when he was satisfied that she had told everything she could, he asked, "Now, about the baby, when he was born exactly?"

Rosemary: "It was two days after the marriage. Mary went into labor and delivered the most gorgeous baby boy. Like I said, August 31, 1936."

"Then what happened?"

Rosemary explained that several days later, the baby was taken back to England with Fiona and Ambassador Carnegie, where they claimed William as their own. She recounted in exact detail how the Ambassador took measures to ensure William had dual citizenship in both the United States and Great Britain and had a birth certificate issued by the embassy. Then she went on to say that her and Fiona fell out of close touch over the years, but she got the occasional note with news of William's growing up and his career.

"So you rarely saw your sister, Fiona, and William?"

"That's true. But we did write. In the beginning, once in a while Fiona would send a snap of William and I would show it to Mary. But that was too painful for Mary so I stopped showing her the pictures. After a while, Fiona and I communicated less and less. Years later, I moved to Switzerland and later to Canada."

Finally, Crawly produced his last piece of evidence: a lock of hair. He presented it to Rosemary.

"Do you recognize this hair?"

"Yes. Of course I do. I kept it with me for decades."

"Is this William's hair?"

"No, it belongs to William's brother. It's Prince John's hair. We kept it after he got his first haircut and it was among the things I took when I left the palace."

"Are you absolutely certain of that?"

"Absolutely! I cut the hair off John's head *myself.* I tied it with that bow, put the date on the ribbon, and kept it for years in an album of snaps and memorabilia. I brought it with me when I moved to Canada and just recently gave it to William."

"Before giving it to William, did the lock of hair ever leave your possession?"

"Never!" she exclaimed.

"Thank you. I have no further questions. Would you like to add anything to your testimony?"

Rosemary, with tears brimming in her eyes, talked of William, then spoke of how hard it was for Mary to give William up, but that she felt she had no choice. She told of how Mary was melancholy for years, how Rosemary and Fiona had sworn a vow of silence. Now openly weeping, Rosemary ended her testimony by saying, "I feel that now I can tell the world the truth because I realize that it can no longer harm my treasured friend. With my testimony, once and for all, William's destiny as rightful heir will be fulfilled. I believe Mary would have liked that very much." Pointedly looking at William, she said, "May God bless you, William, Mary's beloved son and our rightful King. You can never know how much your parents loved you."

Her testimony had an electric effect on the gathered Lords and legislators. Many of them could be seen discreetly dabbing at the eyes, as if to wipe away tears.

Crawly let the moment draw out. "Thank you for your testimony. It was very helpful." He gallantly helped Rosemary from the witness box as the members looked on. Rosemary carefully walked away and then abruptly turned and looked directly into William's kind and admiring eyes. To the amazement of the entire room, she said, "Your Majesty," and gave a deep and reverent curtsy. The crowd gasped.

When she had walked away, Owen returned to the witness table and opened a file folder. "My Lord," he said, "you've now heard the story from Mary's best friend, an eyewitness who was in the room when William was born to Mary and a thoroughly credible source. I have but one more piece of evidence to show you." He removed a simple sheet of paper and approached the dais, handing it to Sir Markus, then returning to his table.

"Mr. Chairman, what you are holding is the results of what is called a *DNA* test," Crawly said. "You may be aware that DNA is a *new* science that is able to determine paternity and relationships among humans from samples of hair, saliva, and other bodily fluids, using the genetic code that is unique to each human being and that is inherited from your birth parents. The results are generally 99.9 percent accurate. In this case, we compared three samples to determine their relationships. The first two samples came from John, the Prince of Wales, and William. The third sample belonged to Ambassador Harrington Carnegie. As you can see from the sheet of paper, the DNA determined that John and William share the same DNA, which makes them siblings. The third sample, that of the Ambassador, contained DNA that did not match either of the other two samples, which proves that the Ambassador was not related to William. This test conclusively and scientifically proves that William is John's brother and, by extension, the son of his mother, Mary." Again Crawly let a dramatic pause sink in. "Further, because John was born after William, he is the younger son of the Queen. Gentlemen, there can be no other conclusion than William Carnegie Bolin-Stuart is the natural-born eldest son of Queen Mary and Prince Anthony and therefore the legitimate successor to the throne."

Sir Melvin rose again to speak, but was gaveled into silence. Then Sir Markus set the gavel down wearily and rubbed his eyes. "Thank you, Mr. Crawly. The Cabinet will now take this matter under consideration. We are adjourned."

As the members filed out of the chamber, Owen turned back to William and smiled. Already, he could hear the chant in his head: "Long live William, long live the King!"

CHAPTER 56
ONCE A SNITCH, ALWAYS A SNITCH

HM Dartmoor Prison at Princetown, County of Devon

SHAUN McCABE GAZED INTO THE SMALL DIRTY MIRROR IN HIS CELL. THE man he saw staring back at him was unrecognizable from the boyish and handsome reflection he had long known. His skin was sallow and grey, pouched and baggy. He had fresh scars on his face, and his teeth were brown and deteriorated. But the worst were his eyes: frightened, darting, and watery. He set the mirror down and stared at the wall, preparing himself for another day of waiting and endless emptiness. If he was lucky, he would make it through the day without attracting the attention of the guards or some of the worst of his fellow inmates. He had been branded a traitor to the IRA from the beginning of his sentence and had suffered extravagantly ever since. He had no allies in here. The other Irish prisoners were only too pleased to beat him—and his guards could be far, far worse.

His dark thoughts were interrupted by the rattle of a key in the lock and his cell door was flung open. Instant terror filled Shaun and he cowered back against the wall as Officer Joe Sick entered, casually swinging his truncheon from its leather strap.

"On your feet, boy," Joe snarled. "Today's your lucky day."

Shaun knew better than to ask any questions or respond in any way. He climbed to his feet, desperately trying to hide the shaking in his legs and his eyes glued to the floor. Joe Sick wasn't this man's real name—Shaun had no idea what that might be. No, Joe Sick was the name he had earned.

"C'mon," Joe said, grabbing Shaun's arm and making him flinch. "Out you go."

Shaun was shoved into the hallway, where two more guards waited. He was still too afraid to ask where they were taking him. Any questions would likely earn him a clubbing in the kidney or a quick trip to one of the dark "interrogation rooms."

Instead, they took him to the showers and made him strip, then brought out a high-pressure hose and hosed him down. They threw a bar of soap at him like he was an animal and watched as he soaped himself, then they hosed him down again. When he was done, they gave him clean clothes and watched as he shaved with an electric razor. It felt good to be clean, but Shaun would have preferred to remain alone in his cell rather than confront whatever devilry he was sure was waiting for him. It wasn't until they were walking again, heading toward the front of the prison, that Joe Sick snarled, "You've got yourself a visitor today, boyo. Looks like they're not done with you yet."

Shaun was handcuffed and led into a small meeting room with a two-way mirror along one wall. The room was bare with the exception of two chairs and an oblong steel table. At the table sat a well-dressed and distinguished-looking man. As the prisoner and guards entered the room, the gentleman rose. Shaun was pushed down into an empty chair and shackled to the table.

The visitor sat and opened a file folder on the table in front of him. He leafed through the pages of documents and pulled out a large eight-by-ten black and white photograph. Holding it up high, he compared the image to Shaun. "Let me introduce myself to you. I am Sir Melvin Batton." He waited while Shaun nodded, then continued, "I am led to believe that you may be of some help in a situation we are facing. You are Shaun McCabe, are you not?"

"Yes." The word felt strange in Shaun's throat, like he had to force it out. He was struggling against the fear.

"Excellent," Sir Melvin said. "I have a few questions for you about a man known as William Carnegie. I have it on good information that you knew him."

Shaun mumbled something.

"I'm sorry," Sir Melvin said. "Speak up. I can't understand you."

"I never heard of him."

Sir Melvin steepled his fingers. "Hmm. I find it hard to believe you, Mr. McCabe. You must understand how important this is. You will cooperate with me and tell me the truth. The only question is how hard on yourself you choose to make it."

Shaun shifted his eyes around the room, as if he was looking for a way out. "What if I did know him? So what?"

"How exactly did you know him?"

"He used to go out with the sister of a friend of mine."

"Yes, Regina. We are aware of that. Very good. Now tell me about the money. He gave you money, yes? For your operations?"

A cold finger of fear slid down Shaun's spine. The Carnegie money had never come up before. "I don't know anything about any money," he mumbled with downcast eyes.

"Hmm. You're quite sure about that? He never transferred money to the IRA?"

Shaun shook his head. "No. I swear it."

Sir Melvin shook his head. "I'm sorry to hear you say that. Because I know you're lying. I'll tell you what, since you apparently don't think this is important enough to tell the truth, I'm going to leave for a while and come back this evening. Perhaps between now and then you'll have a change of mind."

Sir Melvin rose and left a terrified Shaun at the table. He stepped outside the door and Shaun heard low voices, then the three guards burst into the room, their clubs drawn. One of them hit Shaun on the shoulders a few times while the others roughly unshackled him, then they dragged him down the hall, down a flight a stairs, and into a small, dank, windowless room. Shaun was shaking and gasping for air as they shackled him facedown across a table, bent at the waist and left standing. "No! No!" Shaun yelled, only to be silenced with an excruciating blow to his kidney. Then they left and he was alone, until he heard a dreaded voice behind him.

"Well, well," Officer Joe Sick said. "I was hoping we'd meet again here."

Shaun didn't answer, and his silence seemed to infuriate Joe Sick. A series of painful blows rained down on Shaun's legs and back. He held his cries as long as he could, but after only a few minutes, he burst out screaming.

"You're going to tell Sir Melvin what he wants to know," Joe Sick said, suddenly yanking Shaun's new, clean pants down around his ankles so Shaun was exposed. "Right? Tell me you'll tell him whatever he wants."

Shaun was too terrified, too traumatized to speak as Joe Sick dipped his truncheon into a bucket of liquid soap on a nearby shelf. He slid it between Shaun's legs from behind. "You remember my friend here," Joe said, breathing heavily. "He's missed you."

Joe Sick began to violate Shaun as he applied pressure to the club.

Shaun suddenly found his voice. "Stop! I'll tell him! I swear! Please, no more! No more!"

The pressure stopped and Joe's voice came again near his ear. "Okay, then. That's a good boy. I didn't want to send you up there bow-legged anyway. But remember, boyo, one false move and you and me and him," he jabbed the club again and Shaun screamed, "will have a long, long time to go over your mistakes."

Joe Sick left the room without pulling up Shaun's clothing. Shaun was shaking so bad it hurt and he realized he had urinated on the table. The two guards came back and muttered in disgust as they unshackled Shaun and told him to yank his pants up. Shaun knew this story would circulate among the prison population—which was precisely why Joe Sick had left him naked and strapped to a table with soap dripping down his legs.

The guards watched him get dressed again. When his pants were pulled back up, one of them suddenly struck Shaun a tremendous blow on his leg. Shaun collapsed and let them drag him out into the hall by his arms. They took him back to the same visiting room, shackled him to the table again, and left him there. The hours slowly ticked by until finally Sir Melvin came in again, looking fresh and well-fed. He gave Shaun a look that settled somewhere between pity and revulsion.

"Well?" he said. "How is your memory?"

Without hesitation, for the second time in his life, Shaun told everything he knew. Throughout, Sir Melvin took careful notes and asked dozens of pointed questions, mostly about William Carnegie. When they were done, Sir Melvin had built the whole story in his notes. He stood up and brushed his suit off, as if to remove the grime of the prison, and called for the guards. He instructed them to move Shaun to a secure facility outside London, away from Dartmoor, and keep him in isolation until such time as he was called to testify.

CHAPTER 57
LONG LIVE THE KING

ALL THE PLAYERS WERE ASSEMBLED ONCE AGAIN IN THE THEATER. WILLIAM and Owen Crawly sat at their table with a cadre of lawyers surrounding them. The Cabinet sat at their table up on the dais. And the gallery was packed with interested parties and members of Parliament. Today was the day the Cabinet would render its judgment, and everyone in the room knew that the eyes of the world were upon them.

Sir Markus gaveled the meeting to order and made a few general remarks, then got down to business.

"My Lords, the members of the Cabinet have examined two propositions currently before them. First was the resolution from Mr. Cunningham and company calling for the Parliamentary dissolution of the hereditary system, abolishing the monarchy, and replacing it with a Republican form of government."

He continued: "We have seriously considered Mr. Cunningham's proffer and have concluded that consideration of such a proposal is inappropriate and does not reflect the opinion of the vast majority of the membership of this august body. And for that matter, the British people in general. In addition, such a measure may well be far beyond our lawful authority, and even if it were not, it would take years to resolve such a matter. Therefore, the request has been denied and resolution to move forward has been rejected."

There was muted reaction to this news—no one, probably not even Cunningham himself, expected them to abolish the monarchy.

"The second matter under consideration is that of Mr. William Carnegie's claim to be the heir of Queen Mary. We have examined and re-examined the physical evidence and read and re-read the transcript of Rosemary Firth North's eyewitness testimony. We have had independent scientific experts confirm the authenticity and reliability of this new DNA science. The Cabinet has also completely reviewed the applicable articles in the Act of Settlement, which is the prevailing law covering succession. Further, the Cabinet requested and received from the Solicitor General for England and Wales his legal opinion relative to our interpretation of the evidence and our collective findings. In his detailed brief, the Solicitor General has overwhelmingly supported our conclusions. Therefore, in an almost unanimous vote with just two members dissenting, Sir Melvin and Mr. Cunningham, we have declared the following: the man known previously as William H. Carnegie has conclusively proven, beyond the shadow of a doubt, that he is the first and true son of the late Queen Mary and the Prince Consort Anthony Bolin. Because of this fact, his rightful name would be William H. Bolin-Stuart. It is also avowed that being the first son of the late monarch, and under the provisions of the Act of Settlement, he is hereby declared rightful heir to the throne and King of the Empire. The laws of succession dictate that once a successor is proclaimed, he is immediately considered the monarch."

Sir Markus paused to let this historic news sink in. Then he continued, "Furthermore, the Cabinet forthwith has issued an Order of Nullification which calls for the removal of King Richard VX as the reigning monarch."

There was a long pause of total and complete silence. Every breath in the room was held, no one shuffled papers. Then, one by one at first as a whisper and eventually reaching a crescendo, the legislators in the room rose and added their voices to the traditional cry: "Long live the King!"

William and Owen shook hands but there was no fist-pumping, no hugging, because William almost instinctively knew it would have been totally inappropriate for a King to act in that manner. What William knew in his heart was that this new life would not be easy. He had to win the hearts and minds of the English people, many of whom were opposed to this "Yankee" becoming their King.

And yet…he had the words. He was King!

He felt a gentle pressure on his elbow and realized that Crawly was steering him from the room, into the hall, and out in the bright sunshine outside the Parliament building. The news had already traveled to the throngs on the street, and William stepped into the light to the roar of the crowd. He heard them yelling "Long live the King!" but also voices shouting in protest, again reminding William of the long road ahead of him.

"We did it, old boy," Crawly whispered in his ear as they neared the car. "We did it."

"It'll take a bit to sink in, I'm afraid," William said.

They were almost to the car when they became distracted by the sound of more shouting and voices approaching them rapidly. For a second, William was scared it was another possible threat, then he saw a phalanx of blue-suited bobbies and regular army infantry closing in on them. It was the police.

"Wait!" a man commanded from the front of the crowd. "Pardon!" This man was a detective of some sort, showing a badge but wearing a nice suit and expensive shoes.

William and the group stopped as the men approached him.

"Sir," the detective said, "I regretfully inform you that I am here to serve you with a warrant for your arrest. You are being charged with High Treason, murder and high crimes against the Crown. You will please come with me." Five enlisted men surrounded William and began moving him toward a military vehicle parked in front of William's awaiting ride.

"What the hell is this about?" William shouted over his shoulder to Crawly. "Owen! What's going on?"

CHAPTER 58
The Death of Honor

WILLIAM WAS TAKEN INTO CUSTODY AND DELIVERED TO A MILITARY holding facility. His treatment was respectful, for he was the King after all. Later he was moved to a comfortable but secure suite of rooms adjacent to the holding facility. They were attractive and fully secure rooms maintained by the facility for the confinement of high-level prisoners while awaiting trial or sentencing. William was stunned and bewildered. As King, he was allowed many special conditions while in confinement, but he was still a prisoner in the truest sense of the word.

Month after month passed, and William remained confined. Owen and he met tirelessly, preparing for what was going to be a trial that could change history. They meticulously combed the charges and strategized a defense. Unfortunately, the facts left little room for argument, and William knew it. He had, in fact, transferred large sums of money to a shadowy Irish bank account and he had no doubt that his money had found its way into the IRA coffers. At his worst moments, he cursed himself for being so stupid and trusting, for not listening to his own instincts about what Roan was doing with the money. He had only viewed the money as a way to stay connected to Regina, without truly thinking of the consequences of his own actions. Now, accused of providing the money that financed the terrorist operation that killed his own father, William was consumed with guilt.

The appointed court day finally arrived. Crawly glumly informed William that the former King Richard, who was eager to see William convicted and his crown restored, had instructed the Crown's personal counsel to appoint the best and most accomplished solicitor to prosecute the case.

When the trial started, it was under heavy security and scrutiny. Headlines had been anticipating the event for days—"King versus King!" and "King for a Day?"—and the streets were mobbed with the morbid and fascinated. Only two monarchs had been convicted of treason before, the most recent in the 17TH century.

After the court was called into session, the Crown Solicitor gave his remarks. "We are here today to prosecute His Majestic King William V for high treason, patricide and other murders, as well as high crimes against the Crown. Under governing law, the Treason Act 1351, His Majesty, King William V has been charged with numerous commissions and infractions. First, being party to plotting the murder of the Sovereign's eldest daughter and heir to the throne. Next, egregiously aiding and abetting the Sovereign's enemies, giving them aid and comfort and attempting to undermine the lawfully established line of succession. His Majesty is further charged under other prevailing laws for the commission of patricide, the killing of one's father: in this case, Prince Anthony Bolin, husband to the late Queen Mary. Finally he is charged with illegally transferring funds to a bank in Ireland, intended for using to violate the United Kingdom's rule of law and in conflict with the United Kingdom's prevailing Commerce and Trade regulations."

Next it was Crawly's turn to deliver a statement, one they had carefully crafted but that William knew was weak.

"Thank you, My Lord," Crawly began. "Today I am here to defend the King of this great land. He is a stranger in a strange land. His reputation is not that of being a King or a royal, but one of being a good person, a devoted family man, and an honorable public servant. The acts his Majesty has been accused of are horrendous and barbaric in nature and completely abhorrent to him. He was never a willing participant in or had direct knowledge of these or any crimes. What my client knew was what he was told. Told to him by an innocent bystander herself, a woman he intended to marry and one who dedicated her life to helping children. She too was deceived by her brutal outlaw brother. His Majesty had no reason or motive to commit these crimes and therefore should be found innocent on all counts."

William watched the members of the court throughout this statement. He noted they didn't look impressed. Things got worse when they began to call witnesses and Shaun McCabe made his way to the stand. He looked like a broken man to William, nothing like the cocky, handsome, and idealistic youth he had met in a London pub with Roan so many years before. Shaun took the witness stand and, with every question he answered, William's hopes sunk a little more. Shaun readily identified William and related that he had personal knowledge of William's transfers, that he had been witness to one such time William agreed to send money. He said they had even discussed the operations it would be used for. Crawly objected to this, but he was quickly overruled.

"So he knew then?" the prosecutor asked. "You sat and heard with your own ears William Carnegie's admission that he was fully aware what the money would be used for?"

"Yes," Shaun answered. "Of course he knew. William was like Roan's brother; they ate together, drank together, and William was even sleep'n with his sister."

"Mr. McCabe, do you have any knowledge as to how much money was deposited in the Belfast account?"

"I don't know, probably a lot since we were able to get plenty of weapons and make plenty of bombs."

The Solicitor General produced bank wire transfer records and said, "Apparently, it looks like more than 500,000 American dollars, dating back to 1958. Does that sound right to you?"

Shaun shrugged. "I suppose."

"Are you aware if any of the money that Mr. Carnegie provided purchased the ordinance used in the murder of Anthony, the Prince Consort and the late husband of Queen Mary?"

"Of course. Almost all of the money we had come from Carnegie, especially for big stuff like that. Do you think the pennies we collected from the blokes in Ireland were very much? That money wasn't enough to buy the box we put the bombs in. So I say, sure, it had to be his money because there wasn't anybody else's!"

"Thank you, Mr. McCabe. Lastly, has anyone promised you anything in exchange for your testimony here today?"

Shaun shook his head vehemently. "No! I swear it! Nobody's promised me *anything…ever*! I'm just tell'n the God's honest truth, just like my Mum taught me to. I swear to you as God is my witness, may he strike me dead if I am lying."

"Mr. McCabe, thank you for your testimony and truthful account of the entire matter. I have no further questions. Your witness."

Crawly glanced at the jury on his way to the witness box. They looked engaged, interested. Was this a good sign? Did it mean they believed Shaun's testimony? It was now up to Owen to discredit him and save the King.

"Mr. McCabe, you said you knew Regina Kelly, did you not?" Crawly began.

"Yeah, I knew her. She was Roan's sister."

"What was her relationship with the defendant?"

"Regina was his main squeeze. They lived together. I think they were going to get married."

"Did you know that Regina was a major player in helping to relocate orphans from Belfast to London so they could be saved and out of harm's way?"

"Yeah, she helped lots of kids, mostly orphans, it was her thing, you know?"

"And was the defendant involved in helping Regina with those orphans?"

"He was in love with her so I think he would do anything she asked."

"Like giving her money to transport, feed and house orphans?"

"I guess so."

"To your knowledge, did Regina Kelly have inside knowledge as to how the money freely given by the defendant was being used?"

Shaun shrugged. "She must have. Roan was always there asking her to persuade Carnegie to send more money."

"Send more money to who? Militants or orphans? Is it possible that Regina hid that information from the defendant?" Crawly asked.

"Like I said, I don't know what she told him, but I heard him talking about it with Roan. And there's no way he could have believed all that money was going to orphans even if she was hiding it. I mean, every orphan in Ireland would be living in a mansion for that much money!"

"Why do you think it isn't possible that the defendant trusted and believed his fiancée and his best friend when he was told that the money was going only to the orphans?"

Shaun fidgeted. "I don't know. It just seems they were all so cozy and that having secrets would have been tough."

Looking at the notes he made during his endless talks with William, Owen moved on. "And when you last had contact with the defendant, what was your relationship?"

"I don't remember."

"You don't remember that he and Roan had a horrible argument because his money was unaccounted for and possibly being spent inappropriately?"

"Like I said, I don't remember."

Owen, holding a finger to his temple, walked toward the jurors: "Let me see if I got this right. You seem to clearly remember everything else but this, do you not?" He paused. "You know, a famous man once said if you tell the truth, you won't have to remember anything." Owen took a breath and changed tactics. "Mr. McCabe, you are currently an inmate at HM Prison Dartmoor, are you not?"

"Yes, sir, I am."

"And how are your living conditions there?"

"I'd hardly call it living."

"And your sentence is for how long and for what?"

"It's a 40-year sentence, for treason."

"Treason, I see. But Mr. McCabe, treason is usually punishable by death, is it not?"

"Well, yes, I was given the death penalty, but we plea-bargained for a lighter stretch."

With an exaggerated and incredulous voice, Owen said, "You plea-bargained?"

"Yeah, that's right. So what?"

"Well, I'll tell you, Mr. McCabe, why 'so what' doesn't work for me. You see, if you were willing to take a plea bargain then, how do we know you aren't taking something now for your testimony today?"

"I ain't! And I already told that other guy, I ain't getting *nothing*, *nothing* out of this."

"Really? Are you certain, Mr. McCabe?"

For the first time a look of doubt crossed the jurors' faces. Was it possible that this witness was lying? Had he been given something for his testimony? It seemed very plausible.

"Your Honor, I object to this badgering of the witness," the Solicitor General put in.

"Objection overruled," the judge intoned. "This questioning does not constitute badgering, but I warn you, Mr. Crawly, not to lead the witness and to keep to the facts."

As Owen pressed on, more uncertainty about the witness's truthfulness was planted in the jurors' minds.

Owen finished his examination and sat back at the table, beside his very worried client.

Shaun was escorted out of the witness box by an armed guard. However, instead of being removed to a cell, he was taken down a long corridor to a small room with a window in it, looking down twelve feet or so onto a sidewalk and a narrow lane. Shaun was terrified at first, afraid the British had cooked up some new kind of torture for him and half expecting Joe Sick to appear in his room at any moment. As paranoid as he was, he almost pissed himself when he heard the first pebble hit the window. Too afraid to look for himself, he cowered on his bed until he heard a third and then fourth pebble hit the window.

"Psst! Shaun!" a voice called to him.

Finally, his legs shaking, he climbed off the bed and went to the window. Below in the street, almost impossibly, he saw a shock of red hair and a distinctly Irish face. He didn't recognize the man himself, but he recognized the style of his coat and the way he moved: IRA. He shrank back in fear again.

"Open the window!" the man hissed. "It's unlocked."

Shaun made no move toward the window, certain that if he approached it, he would be gunned down.

"C'mon!" the man said. "I'm here to help you!"

Shaun, without thinking hard about it, got up and crossed the room. His legs began to shake as he looked out the window to see a man on the street

He gingerly tried the window, and to his amazement, it slid up silently, as if it had been greased.

"Good!" the man below said. "Now jump and let's be off!"

"Who are you?" Shaun said. "What do you want with me?"

"Want with you?" the man answered. "Look, we know everything you've done. Everything you are. I'm here to give you a chance, man, a chance to make right by your country and your people. You've got some friends in pretty high places, mate."

"What are you talking about?"

"C'mon now!" the man said. "We've only a few minutes before they'll be around again. Jump down and I'll tell you everything. Quickly! There isn't time!"

Without thinking about it further, Shaun slid his legs over the window sash and let himself fall out of the window and to an uncertain future.

***

While Shaun was running down the road, the inner chamber filled again as the Cabinet convened to hear the final testimony regarding William's crown. The prosecutor's closing statement was simple and powerful: "We have proved with both financial records and eyewitness testimony that William Carnegie provided the funds to a known terrorist organization, knew what those funds would be used for, and was complicit in the murder of his own father, Prince Anthony Bolin. These facts are not seriously in dispute. Your only job as the jury is to render the justice you have sworn to uphold."

Crawly kept his summation simple too, trying to raise as many damaging questions about Shaun McCabe's credibility as he could.

"After all," he bellowed at the end, "it all boils down to whom you believe: a traitor and convicted felon or your country's King, even though he may have arrived on the throne in the most curious of ways?" Crawly moved closer to the jury box. "Which will it be? A man who kills Englishmen or the defendant, a good Samaritan who was obviously swindled by a pair of manipulative anarchists?" Walking right up to the foreman's face, Crawly concluded in *sotto voce*, "It's for you to choose. It's up to you, and God forbid you choose wrong."

Owen Crawly stood beside William as the jurors left their seats, their faces unreadable. Everyone knew a guilty verdict would once again put the monarchy into chaos and uncertainty. Reluctant to say it out loud, in his heart of hearts Owen thought his client's chances for acquittal were at best slim. William quietly figured as much.

Forty hours later, the verdict was in. As the room filled and the court convened, the presiding judge asked William to stand: "Your Majesty, please rise." Dutifully, William stood and faced the jury as the judge asked the foreman: "Have you reached a verdict?"

"Yes, your Grace, we have."

"Then proceed, what say you?"

Owen and William held their breath as they watched the stone-faced foreman's lips annunciate the verdict as if in slow motion.

"Your Grace, we the jury find the defendant, William Carnegie Bolin-Stuart…not guilty!"

The room erupted. Many spectators were stunned by the verdict and others were jubilant, but none more than William and Owen.

For a second time, William and Owen triumphantly walked out into a crowed courtyard filled with reporters, their clicking cameras and shouts: "Your Majesty, Your Majesty, how do you feel about the verdict?"

The crowd pushed and security encircled William and Owen as they walked toward a waiting motorcade, pushing through a raucous crowd. As they approached the running Daimler limousine, William could see his beautiful Liz sitting in the back. She beamed from ear to ear and held a huge bouquet of brilliant red roses fit for a King.

Even as his face broke into a huge smile, a single figure pushed through the crowd, creating a disturbance as people yelled and fell away from him. William and Owen looked up and saw a man coming toward them, hurling people out of his way as he pushed through. The man's arm was raised and he appeared to be waving as he threw an egg at them. It was a familiar face, but William couldn't place it for several long seconds. At the exact moment they put a name to the face, the man hurled the egg in his hand, which revealed itself in the air to be a hand grenade.

Owen dove into the car, pushing Liz to the floor as he screamed, "Shaun, it's Shaun."

The scene erupted into a huge fireball, with body parts and blood spraying the crowd even as armed guards turned on Shaun and shot him through the heart.

When the smoke cleared, people lay moaning in the street, and in the gutter, amid the blood and burned shrapnel, lay a critically wounded King.

CHAPTER 59
THE RESURRECTION

Washington, DC

JUST AS BRITAIN WAS GRIPPED IN ITS MOST CONTROVERSIAL SUCCESSION IN at least a century, the United States was consumed by political crisis. Before his resignation, Vice President William Carnegie had been an immensely popular figure. With him gone, there was a vacuum at the top. President Lionel Keith started a new regimen of chemotherapy that left him weak and unable to appear in public. Finally, when he could no longer put it off, President Keith signed a document stating that he was temporarily unable to discharge the powers and duties of his office.

With President Keith stepping back, the Cabinet met and decided it would be appropriate to appoint the next in line of succession as Acting President. This meant naming Luke Jordan, Speaker of the House, as Acting President, even though he was a member of the opposing party. Party leaders on both sides agreed that party affiliation was less important than a continuation of the world's strongest democracy. A vote was held and the die was cast. The Speaker was sworn in and assumed the office of Acting President within hours of his confirmation. Acting President Jordan was appropriately sorrowful as he was sworn in, but if you looked close enough, the victory was clear on his face. He had finally vanquished his mortal political enemies and was only a heartbeat away from achieving his lifelong dream.

Jordan quickly appointed a temporary cabinet and named a long-time confidant, Charlie Romano, as his chief of staff. The two met every day in the Oval Office, sometimes literally measuring the drapes and other times discussing ways to rescind the Keith policies they didn't like with executive orders. It was a long list.

"I want everything ready for the day Keith dies, and that won't come too soon as far as I'm concerned," Jordan was fond of saying. "We'll clean house and show those contrary bastards in Congress how to run a country."

Six weeks later

The weeks passed in a welter of activity in the West Wing. Jordan and his team had drawn up a raft of executive orders he would issue on the day that Keith died. His only issue was Keith's dogged perseverance—by all accounts, the old man should have been dead by now. Nobody survived lung cancer.

Very early one morning, one of the two phones by his bed rang. He glanced at the clock and saw it was 5:45 a.m. His heart quickened. Was this the news? He knew he would only be awakened for the most dire of circumstances. He noted with relief that it wasn't the red phone, which could only mean one thing.

"Yes, who is it?" he said, eager for good news. "What is it?"

But instead of grinning, Jordan's face slipped into a scowl that deepened into a frown. "What?" he said, sitting up. "How can that be? Charlie, you better get your ass over here in ten minutes and tell me this is a joke."

Minutes later, Jordan met his Chief of Staff in the Oval Office and heard the unbelievable news.

"Luke," Charlie said, "it's true. I've confirmed with the new Speaker and the President Pro Tempore of the Senate. They both received a letter of intent last night. The chemotherapy is working. President Keith is fit to serve again."

"That cannot be! He was almost dead! Isn't there some doctor who can declare him incompetent?"

"No, sir. In fact, it was the doctors who declared him competent. Fact is, he's not cured. But his chemo worked and his cancer has officially gone into remission. I heard from a staff member that his hair is actually growing back. It's like a resurrection, sir."

Jordan was so angry he wanted to punch Romero. It took an act of will to hold back. "So what now?" he grated.

"Well, sir, if Congress agrees, and no doubt they will, President Keith will be back behind the desk in a week."

It was too much. Jordan grabbed a glass container of jelly beans from the desk and threw it against a wall, where it shattered in a Technicolor explosion. "Shit!"

CHAPTER 60
THE CROWNING GLORY (PART II)

London, 1986

OUTSIDE THE BROADCAST STUDIO, THE CROWDS WERE STILL YELLING IN A chaotic outpouring of joy, confusion, and even protest. Inside the booth, Matt Christian was listening to an exhausted-looking Sir Markus Butler explain how the Coronation would work and how England got to this point. Everybody agreed it was baffling.

"Matt!" Joy chirped in his headset. "The crowning is starting!"

The camera cut away from the studio to show Westminster Abbey, where at that moment the Archbishop of Canterbury was setting the ancient ceremonial crown upon the bowed head of the new monarch. It is indeed the Crowning Glory.

After a moment, Matt turned back to Sir Markus. "So, Sir Markus, they say the new King has chosen King William VI as his choice. What do you think of that? It's almost provocative."

Sir Markus shrugged. "The name William is an ancient one, dating back centuries. But the choice in this situation reflects a rather significant symbolism since it was also a family name."

On the monitor, the camera zoomed in on the face of the newly crowned monarch, wearing his crown for the first time.

"Look at him!" Joy exclaimed. "He is so handsome and young, and he looks so frightened."

Onscreen, the picture showed Tyler Harrington Carnegie Bolin-Stuart, the 20-year-old son of William and now the rightful King of the British Empire. He smiled a little shyly, perhaps himself still confused by the turn of events that had plucked him from obscurity and landed him in the most powerful throne in the world. With the medieval crown of St. Edward firmly on his head, a tear rolled down Tyler's handsome face, one that remarkably resembled not just his father's but that of a beloved Queen.

The world, he reflected, could be a very strange place. Very strange indeed!

Nearby in a darkened hospital room

An attending nurse sat by a mortally wounded William. He was no longer King. He was gravely injured and most likely dying, so the Cabinet had moved quickly to present him abdication papers to sign, allowing his son to take the throne rather than plunge the country into another succession nightmare. Still, his mental state was stable enough that he knew what was happening at Westminster Abbey not too far away. He turned to his nurse and said, "Sister, can you write a note for me?"

"Of course, sir."

Fetching a pad and pen, the dutiful nurse sat by William's bedside and listened.

"Thank you, Sister," William said, then he began to dictate:

> *My dearest son,*
>
> *Destiny has played me its last card. Soon I will no longer be with you and our family, which breaks my heart. I have tried to lead an*

honorable life, but through happenstance, misguided loyalty and naiveté, I was led astray. For this I am most remorseful. But now it is time for your destiny to be delivered. I pray that it will treat you more kindly than mine has. My legacy will be mixed, but my heart will be filled with the knowledge that I tried to always do the right thing. So, my dear son, go forward into your new and strange world. Be vigilant of those around you and be true to your God and country. God bless you my son. Long live the King!

Your loving father

The nurse finished the note and asked William if he would like to sign it. Struggling to hold the pen, William was barely able to scroll a semblance of his signature at the bottom.

Within the hour, as William lay in his hospital bed staring at the ceiling, his facial expression seemed to change. His nurse noticed it right away: William was smiling. He looked intensely into what he perceived as a bright light that shone down from above. In the light he could see a woman, a beautiful and regal one with outstretched hands. She looked like someone he had seen before. It was the face of the woman he had seen in a portrait that hung in the chambers where he was first declared King. He knew who it was.

William closed his eyes and quietly slipped away and found eternal peace. The nearby and ever-vigilant nurse looked at William's still body and whispered to herself, "God save the King."

The End

EPILOGUE

SEVEN YEARS AFTER KING EDWARD FRANCIS STUART ABDICATED HIS throne, Addison Sinclair divorced his wife, Elaine, and moved to France, where he and the former King purchased a remote country estate. They remained committed partners until they both died in an automobile accident three years later while touring in their new sports car along the Amalfi Coast.

King Richard Negril Stuart, after being deposed from the throne, sired two children with his wife Anne, who later left him when she learned he had been diagnosed with AIDS. Prior to his death from the disease, he fathered three other children, all illegitimate.

After President Keith's remarkable recovery, he returned to office. Under the 25TH Amendment, he appointed a new vice president. Upon completion of President Keith's term, he lived for another three years. In the next election, the vice president he chose handsomely defeated his opponent former Acting President Luke Jordan.

Twenty-six years after William VI was crowned King, he died childless and his brother George succeeded to the throne at the age of forty-three. George fathered four children, all male and in line for the next succession.

On October 28, 2011, twenty-five years after the unprecedented succession debacle, David Cameron, prime minister of the United Kingdom, announced at the Commonwealth Heads of Government meeting in Perth that they had unanimously agreed to abolish the gender-preference rule. They also agreed that future monarchs should no longer be prohibited from marrying a Catholic, a law that dated from the Act of Settlement 1701. However, since the monarch was also the Supreme Governor of the Church of England, the law that prohibited a Roman Catholic from ascending to the throne would remain. It was reconfirmed that only individuals who are Protestants may inherit the Crown.

Made in United States
Orlando, FL
02 August 2024